Seven Summits:
The Magical Talent

Sidney G. McPhail

Deep Sea Publishing

Deep Sea Publishing ISBN: 0983427631

Deep Sea Publishing ISBN-13: 978-0983427636

Deep Sea Publishing E-Book ISBN-13: 978-0983427650

***

www.deepseapublishing.com

***

Printed in the United States of America
eBook created in the United States of America

DEDICATION

This book is dedicated to my friends back in eighth grade, when the very first draft was written. We called ourselves the Seven Dorks, and were proud to. The Summits are not fashioned from them, but I placed parts of their amazing personalities within my characters. Rachel, Kira, Elizabeth, Josie, Olivia, and Katie, I wouldn't have ever tried to publish without your never-ending support.

Another one of my closest friends I've known since first grade. She's put up with me and my one-in-the-morning text messages for years now. Love you like a sister, Jen.

My mom was my first-ever editor and I appreciate her and love her for helping me take this opportunity. And Dad, your determination and drive is something I'll always look up to.

And last but far from least, Granny, thank you so much for your love and support in everything I've ever done.

Table of Contents

Dear Reader,

To tell you the truth, I don't really know what I want to accomplish by telling you my story. I guess I have these crazy ideas that if I did then you would be able to learn something from it all, know our existence, and of course if you have any sense join us in our seemingly never ending battle to forever rid our Universes of **It**. Please don't ask me why you guys have gotten out of this ordeal nearly scot-free up until now, because I honestly don't know. But for your information, **It** would be the someone who's been out to destroy us all, even you, for hundreds of years. Before his first attack, my world was one of six completely separate Universes. Now, only two of them are left. And thank you for your concern, but the others did not all get destroyed. Only one of them. Anyway, four of the remaining five were forced to join together for survival--now one Universe split into four dimensions. This, dear friend, is my world--the one I'm responsible for--the one that totally and completely depends on me. Not like there's any sort of pressure or anything intended in that. Alright all you math people, listen up. If one got destroyed and four combined then one must be left, right? Yep, that one is your world; your Universe, and the one I'm desperately trying to reach. So if you're reading this, I must have succeeded. Now, before I start telling you about my poor, sad, little home that woefully lacks your IPods and microwavable popcorn--you need to know that I'm not sitting here, spending my time writing, to entertain you. I'm giving you this information as a warning. If all falls apart in my Universe, **It** *will* come after you next. Maybe when you receive my message you'll do everything in your limited power to contact me and join forces before time runs out. Or maybe you won't believe me. Maybe you'll think I'm just some random person trying to prank you and we don't even exist. Whatever you do with my story is up to you, but if particularly dark and ominous clouds cross your skies, don't say I didn't tell you so.

-Lealight

Prologue—The Grand Summit

Chapter 1 – 100th Day of the 203rd Year

The world would be surprised at how hard it is to hide from something that's devastatingly evil, ten times more powerful than you, and wants you dead. The situation was simple: Veronica needed to defeat Hyvecuous--a ruthless man who would murder countless innocent people all for nothing but this idea of power. He was also particularly callous when it came to disposing of those who stood in his way. And as her luck and Universe would have it, one of those few was Veronica. Needlessly stated if she failed, her entire world would literally come crashing down on top of her.

Just four days before, Veronica and the others were at home in the Citadel when dank, and unusually dark, clouds rolled in, leaving the first dimension in nearly total blackness. Assuming that they meant nothing more than a bad, incoming storm, no one paid them any heed and went about their daily lives. That was until twenty four hours later when thirty people suddenly disappeared and everyone, though they would never admit to it, began to suspect them to mean something more. Of course Veronica had her own theory as to what was going on, but she dared not bring it up to the six people she'd grown up with and considered her family, much less the remaining eight hundred in the Village. It would cause nothing but complete panic. But, as everyone found out later, she was right in her guess. Hyvecuous was back and he was not leaving without doing what he came to do--kill the Summits and destroy their Universe.

Veronica was in the third dimension when she and the others were ambushed. Thankfully, the place was nothing more than a huge, open piece of nearly flat land that was designated as a safe zone for the Summits to practice on many years before her. This thought was her only positive one, as no ordinary people who could be hurt were around. But regardless of skill level, willing of the Talents takes plenty of energy and focus so after many hours of them trying to defend their Universe, they were fading fast. It was only the seven of them versus an army, which was becoming increasingly powerful the longer they fought. Truth be told, it was a miracle they had lasted this long.

Although the Seven Summits are the only people in the Universe who could use the six Talents to their full potential, Hyvecuous had strength in numbers. His Shadows, as they were called, had never been viewed as a danger by anyone, much less the seven, until this moment when everyone's lives were on the line. Shadows, like their master, were to be feared despite what they at first appeared to be. Maybe, thought Veronica, the phrase "everything is not what it seems", had some truth to it. And now that they were attacking by the hundreds and she and her family were becoming less able to fight, she felt like nothing but a fool. Shadows were not the first thing in the past several days she'd misjudged, and they couldn't afford to make mistakes anymore.

Two hundred years he'd had to plan this out, two hundred years to ensure it happened exactly the way he intended it to. So long to hone his power to ensure it could easily defeat anything she could possibly do to him. Two hundred years, yet Veronica was barely twenty one and had been realized no more than five years ago. It unnerved her even more to see that the Shadows seemed to anticipate everything they did before they did it, as if they had been watching and studying their every movement since they were all children. *Perhaps they have been*, she thought. She wouldn't put anything past them. And if they could only just handle the Shadows, how were they to last five minutes when Hyvecuous came? Veronica was the Grand Summit, yet even she only knew of his infamous past through stories she had heard when she was younger. If there was an ounce of truth in any of them, the disappearance of thirty people would look like nothing compared to what he would do to her. Veronica had not asked for this job, she was born already marked for it. However she knew Hyvecuous would not see it this way. The Grand Summit existed, therefore, they must die. Veronica had no doubt in her mind he would not give a second thought if the cloak was draped on the shoulders of a twelve year old. Their cries would be meaningless, their tears hold no purpose. She momentarily wondered if he would even give her last words.

Veronica shivered and held her cloak tightly. She knew that the presence of Hyvecuous could send a vile, frigid feeling deep into your bones if you got too close to him, and sometimes even his Shadows. For this was not the first time she had encountered either of them. Trying to ignore the chill, she began to run back in the direction of the battle to help the other Summits. No more than two minutes earlier, she had been forced to teleport out of it after becoming surrounded by fifteen or so of the Shadows. She was now alone about a quarter mile away from where the others continued to fend off as many of their attackers as possible. However, they were not having much success considering how little effect even the most powerful of Talent practices had on the Shadows. And then there was the fact that no matter how many of them they took out, they simply kept coming on... and on... and on....

Veronica pushed this thought from her mind and continued running towards the others. She had just caught sight of Nathaniel frantically throwing lightning in all directions, and decided to go help him when Hyvecuous materialized less than ten feet away from her. With a simple flick of his wrist, he set the ground all around Veronica ablaze. Trying to hide her absolute horror, she managed to collect herself and locked eyes with him. But Hyvecuous clearly saw right through her act, and he laughed at her. Coldly, without emotion. His cackle cut through the air, and made Veronica shiver.

Impatient to finally finish off the leader of the very few people who prevented him from laying waste to this Universe, Hyvecuous stepped forward and Veronica in turn stepped back. Her breathing was shallow, her shivering had become an incessant tremble. She was at first oblivious to the dense fog slowly rising from the ground directly in front of her. When she came to her senses and saw the terrifying display, Veronica's eyes grew wide and she barely kept herself from screaming. She knew that even she couldn't withstand that fog if it surrounded her.

Meanwhile Cerria, the Water Talent Summit, had just trapped a group of the Shadows within four giant slabs of ice and was about to go help the others. That was until she saw Veronica standing in the midst of Hyvecuous'ss fog off in the distance. Knowing what that could mean for her, she took off in her direction while shouting "*Guys*! Come on, Veronica's in trouble!"

After hearing Cerria scream, the five other Talent Summits followed her gaze and looked in horrified disbelief at Veronica, frozen with fear and almost completely encircled by the thick, black clouds.

"No! *Veronica!*" they yelled in unison as Connan, the Air Talent Summit, shot upward and flew toward her.

Unaware of the others desperately trying to break through the Shadows to save her, Veronica couldn't think of anything besides her failure to defeat Hyvecuous. She had been fighting for hours, yet it took him less than three minutes to find her, to corner her. Perhaps it would take four for him to kill her. Even after everything they'd been through, the seven of them were going to be killed. All of their people who depended on them would soon follow. But that still wasn't the worst part in her mind. The most unbearable thing for Veronica was that it was all her fault. As the

Grand Summit, it was her job to protect her Universe. She was sworn to preserve it, to keep it alive and to see it prosper. Allowing herself to be murdered so easily, she thought, would render her existence useless, and everything she had accomplished up to that point meaningless. That was completely unacceptable. Failure simply was not an option.

"Snap out of it, Veronica!" a voice interrupted her thoughts from over twenty feet above the ground.

Hyvecuous regarded the Air Talent Summit as if he were nothing more than a pesky mosquito and raised his arm skyward, sending a section of the fog shooting out at Connan. Almost immediately after it had come within a few yards of him, he dropped like a stone and narrowly caught himself in time to become completely surrounded along with the rapidly approaching Cerria. Their panic-ridden faces were the final straw for Veronica, and she now shook with rage as she balled up her fists.

Hyvecuous at first seemed amused by the fact that she was still trying to use Talents even after being encased in the fog. But his expression quickly changed when a faint golden haze rose around her. It immediately lashed out at him, creating a piercing sound similar to that of thunder. The impact alone sent Hyvecuous somersaulting backward until he smacked against a tree. He then fell to the ground motionless.

Without any direction from Hyvecuous, the fog lifted. Veronica rushed out, about to deliver a death blow, only to remember that her Universe's nemesis didn't have a true form. He simply inhabited an existing body permanently. So if she killed the person who lay before her, Hyvecuous would just escape and find another to possess.

Veronica paused and wondered what she was supposed to do then as the fog and the Shadows evaporated. In their places, were the thirty missing people. They stood huddled together, and with absolutely no idea what had happened to them. After trying to no avail to assure the large group everything was going to be fine, the others led them over to where Cerria, Connan, and Veronica stood. The Talent Summits shared her uncertainty as she wildly searched for some indication of what to do. But then Veronica abruptly smiled. She had an idea.

Veronica focused harder than she had ever in her life and a section of the water from the river in front of her stopped flowing. Instead, it rose about ten feet in the air. It was a little higher than Veronica had expected, but she continued. With the same gaze, she sent it rushing over the unmoving form of Hyvecuous and then froze the water, encasing him in the ice.

The others finally caught on to what she was doing, and Cerria and Connan stepped up to help her. Standing side by side, the three rose the ice block upward with their gazes. It shone brightly as Connan and Veronica took over and made the air around it cave inward, casting it off to the fourth dimension. The Summits had finally won.

The others, including the recently recovered people, were elated, but Veronica simply painted a smile on her face. She knew this was only temporary. Hyvecuous would definitely find some way to escape and return, and when he did, he would be unspeakably strong.

About an hour later, when she'd managed to return the freed people to the Village and announce that Hyvecuous had been defeated, everyone was overjoyed. As soon as they returned home, Veronica snuck away to the Grand Summit's Library, where scrolls upon scrolls on all Talents, Charms, dimensions, and various other things were kept--along with a very rare and powerful book, which she kept hidden in a location known only by her.

The octagonal shaped room was dimly lit by twenty-four candles that were mounted three per wall. Over thirty huge shelves of scrolls were set in rows to the left, columns to the right, and a few just mixed in between where they could be fit. The walls were entirely made of stone, and the floor used to be before old, splintered wood was set on top of it. Against the eighth wall, were two large, dirt-colored chairs and a small oak table.

Veronica walked over to a shelf resting against the seventh wall and reached under it to pull out a small, ancient-looking chest. She unlatched it to reveal a little silver disk in the lid and the purple cloth that lined the inside, which was Charmed to keep things completely safe for many years.

Knowing that, Veronica reached up and took a gray, bumpy rock from the table and set it hesitantly inside the chest. She searched for and found a fountain pen with an old piece of torn scroll paper and wrote out a message that she could only hope would be discovered by the right person. Two hours later, she folded it up, and placed it inside the chest along with the rock.

Veronica snapped her fingers and wondered if anything would happen considering she'd never read a page in any of the books and only knew of the Charm from a supposed legend. But the box then began to glow so brightly she had to shield her eyes as it floated in front of her. When the light finally subsided, the chest closed itself and shot across the room--maneuvering its way between the shelves of scrolls. It eventually nestled itself in the fourth corner of the Library and turned almost completely invisible

Satisfied, Veronica stood up and made her way toward the stairs. She returned to the Summit's Citadel, but never stopped thinking about the box she had left in the dark nook, where it would remain for the next four hundred years.

Part 1—One Catastrophic, Apocalypse-Related Event at a Time, Please

Chapter 2 – 100th Day of the 603rd Year

Some people wake up to little songbirds chirping a tune; others, to the warm sunlight leaking through the curtains. But me? No, I heard a small clanking noise in the dark corner of my room. Anyone else would have ignored the sound, but being the paranoid person I am, I jolted upright and saw a dark silhouette of a person about six feet tall pace across the area. It seemed oblivious to the fact that I was watching it through half-closed eyes. I kept rubbing them to make sure I was indeed seeing things.

Unfortunately, the being didn't fade away like I'd expected, and I knew I wasn't hallucinating. Just *spectacular*. And that early in the morning, too. Usually the catastrophes waited until at least after six.

I made a fist, extended my arm toward the form, and bent my little finger. Light soon shone from the palm of my hand, illuminating the room just enough so I could make out the figure.

But it wasn't a person at all. In fact, it looked like a Shadow: dark, mindless beings that are human-shaped, but completely featureless. The only purpose they serve is to operate under direct orders from It. Unless they were completely destroyed, they would do anything to accomplish the mission they were sent to do. And this time, the thing was holding a small, wooden chest

I'd never seen before. But regardless of what it was after, a Shadow's presence never meant anything good and I jumped out of bed to face it. The thing still took no notice of me as I gathered a ball of air in my arms and launched it in his direction. Of course the Shadow conveniently picked that time to become aware of its surroundings. To my surprise, it ducked and ran out into the hallway with the chest in what I guessed was the equivalent of a hand.

I quickly shook off the shock from a Shadow actually responding to my attack and sprinted after it. For some reason, I felt as if I should recognize the box from somewhere and just *knew* that if It ever got his hands on its contents, it would spell D.O.O.M.S.D.A.Y. for everyone.

As we ran, I launched various rocks, balls of air, ice, and even lightning, which nearly destroyed the hall but had no effect on him. And just as I started to wonder how the others could possibly be sleeping through all the noise, I noticed what else was wrong. We hadn't reached the bottom of the staircase leading to the roof at the end of the hallway yet. Honestly, this thing was going on and on and on to the point where I thought we would never reach it.

But aside from that issue, the Shadow didn't seem to get winded at all. I, on the other hand, was getting slower and slower until I eventually stopped all together.

"Alright, that's it," I said to myself under my breath.

I resumed my run, threw myself into the air, and flew after it. The others might call me crazy for actually being able to laugh in that situation, but I did as I slowly caught up to the Shadow. I was practically on top of it when I noticed a dead end finally appearing. I dropped to the ground, and the two of us just stood there--him holding the chest, and me prepared to blow it to smithereens to get it.

I took a step forward. The Shadow and the box promptly disappeared, leaving me standing alone in an empty hallway.

***

Down in the Library, I jumped out of a large, brown chair in a cold sweat. I buried my face in my hands and yelled out in frustration. Thank goodness I was at least thirty feet underground so no one heard.

You'd figure that I would be used to dreams like this by then. But in my defense they can be pretty nerve wracking and creepy... considering I never know what they mean and, if they go on long enough, they almost always result in a quite vivid obliteration of my Universe. Because as mentioned before I tend to be paranoid even though It hadn't personally showed up to try to destroy everyone since Veronica Calodie, the Grand Summit over four hundred years ago, apparently got weak knees during battle and decided to banish him to the fourth dimension instead of just ridding us of his threat forever. But we do know he eventually escaped, only because when he left the Universe, the Clouds, huge blankets of darkness that "only appear if It is near", finally cleared. And leave it to humanity to come up with a rhyme about impending death and destruction on that one.

Of course he is presumed dead by most people, or too tragically weak to ever attack again, or even afraid come back. So naturally, the past couple sets of Summits had a pretty boring and purposeless job without having anyone to actually protect the Universe from.

But back to reality, last night I was digging through and organizing some of the few and ancient scrolls that hadn't been replaced by my predecessors with just regular books in my Library--a collection of all knowledge on Talents, Charms, dimensions, and other things in a list that goes on endlessly. One of my many jobs is to keep the place updated. And since the single most important task of protecting and running the Universe generally took care of itself, nearly every waking minute I didn't spend with the others I spent down there.

I surveyed the area. Though nothing seemed abnormal, I still felt shaken from my dream. That night wasn't the first time the chest had appeared in them and, not to sound all "ancient sage" or anything, but I was sure it meant something. And to torture me further, I knew I was supposed to recognize it, but I had no clue where from. See what I mean? The crises start almost immediately after the day does.

But anyway, I figured I didn't really have time to uncover anything on the topic or the others would start to worry where I was. So I gladly started making my way across the Library towards the stairs. *You* spend the night underground and we'll see how claustrophobic *you* feel afterwards. Of course half way across the room, a particularly heavy book fell from one of the taller cases and I narrowly saw it coming in time to stop myself. It hit the floor with a piercing "*thump*" right at my feet. Rolling my eyes, I picked it up and brushed some dust from its cover. There was nothing written on it. It had a faded brown, leather cover like most of the others. I figured that while I had it, I'd use it to my advantage and said aloud "The sundial". The leathery cover disappeared to reveal a picture of the one in the Citadel's yard. The front covers of all the books in my Library can show simple, unmoving images of anything you need to see... more or less. There're several loopholes in the word "anything". The biggest one is that when you ask *any* of them to show you It, you will get a simple image of darkness. Figures, doesn't it?

But they're not completely useless. They did come in handy for some things, and I knew for a fact the one I was holding could show me the time from all the instances I'd used it in before. Of course nothing ever went perfectly with those things and the image was blurry. It took me a while to make out the way the shadow was cast on the sundial. It looked like about six-thirty or so, and I knew I needed to get out of there before the others started wondering where I was. So I placed the book back on a random shelf and walked briskly toward the stairwell. As I went by, I grabbed my cloak which had been handed down from Grand Summit to Grand Summit for hundreds of years. I draped it around myself. If you ask me, the whole idea that I have to wear it in the first place makes me look stuck-up and conceited. But the last thing I needed to do was confuse people by leaving it here, or get caught without it by Litheney. Yeah, more information on her and our delightful history later. Besides, at this point the thing is so ancient and well known that it's practically sacred. And no one ever asked me. It was not by choice but by expectation that I wore it.

Anyway, I ran up the seemingly endless flight of stairs to the top where an antique, wooden door with a large silver ring in its center rested on sturdy hinges. The disc automatically recognized me by my Magic, opened, and shut with an echoing "*thud*" when I stepped into the empty hallway.

Chapter 3

Remember in my explicit dream where that Shadow and I were playing a friendly game of tag over a hunk of wood while running down the magical endless corridor? As you probably assumed, the thing being that long was just a figment of the dream. Nevertheless that same hallway sits in a semi-circle about three quarters of the way up our home in the Citadel, where the Summits have lived over the years. And let me tell you, it looks incredibly daunting from the outside--almost cylindrical, some eighty feet high, and made entirely of stones all different sizes and colors. You take maybe a grand total of six shallow steps up to the wooden front door and walk into this abnormally shaped room that looks similar to a plump peach with a giant bite taken out of a side. That chunk is a small kitchen we have containing not much more than a brick oven that we light every time we use it, a dark-wooden cupboard, a rickety table, and ten straight back chairs. Just to the right of the front door is the first set of the many stairs throughout the place. They wrap around the building like a very wide spiral staircase for five stories, which you're saddled to walk, or fly, or teleport, or do something to get to the top of. Anyway, you'll then find a large, rectangular room with one ceramic table in the center, three massive windows that look out onto the grassy, yet equally rocky, yard and the surrounding woods, and the doors to the Summits' rooms. By walking straight ahead, you will see that previously mentioned hallway to your left that has an additional seven (though only three of them were occupied) rooms on the right side. These are the ones that belong to the Charges, and you'll also pass the door to my Library on the opposite wall before reaching yet another staircase. Said staircase goes onto the roof, from which, you can see almost everything over the trees from the top half of the school to the very edges of the field. It's just a few miles of barren hills near the outskirts where everyone goes to "practice" (a.k.a. mess around) with their Talents. It's restricted, of course. I have to make sure no one can accidentally drop a flame around two little kids playing with a ball of light.

Speaking of which, this might be a good time to tell you about the six Talents, Air, Earth, Fire, Light, Water, and Woodland. A normal person is born with one, and they can only get but so good at it. So simply stated, the powers are limited. A regular Earth Talent might be able to lift a large rock about three feet in the air for a couple seconds before they run out of energy and drop it.

Talent Summits are also born with one, but they can become masters at them very quickly and relatively easily once they are realized. For example, an Air Talent Summit would be able to teleport himself anywhere in the Universe by bending the air around him. Seeing the difference?

All children over the age of seven go to the Talented School. In their first year, they learn very basic things to do with their Talent that's discovered shortly after birth. Yeah, we do stuff like arithmetic and history too, but we stick to the things kids are actually going to need to know in their lives. Anyway, and then every year after that, they practice until they finish at the age of nineteen. The Grand Summit, however, is not born with one of the Talents. I clearly remember when I was seven years old and everyone else had them except me. Instead, I had to go to my first day of school and tell them I didn't have a Talent. And if after your first year of life you don't have yours, it is highly unlikely you will ever get one. Basically being a No Talent is viewed as the equivalent of mentally disabled. The teachers then set you aside in a class where you learn simple, and increasingly boring, trades and other subjects until you graduate to choose from a pretty limited selection of things you want to do with your life. It's pretty depressing to think that your friends will go on to do these really cool (or at least they were cool to me at the time) things. Talented kids will have options as to what they want to do, but a No Talent's future is almost totally predetermined. Unless, of course, while you're in school the Test rolls around.

It only takes place when the Summits retire usually around the ages of seventy or eighty, and it's time to appoint new ones. You see, the amount of power and capability a Summit has changes as they get older. They're in what people call their "Peak of Power" from age one-year-after-realization to sixty or so. From that time on, it slowly goes south until the point where they're no different from anyone else. At some point they have to decide that they can no longer provide the Universe with the protection it would need in case of an attack, and announce that they've chosen it's time to realize the next set of Summits. And last time the Village heard that speech, my class of the eight disappointments without Talents were center-stage in the gossip world because everyone knew that one of us was the next Grand Summit. Even though no one paid any attention because everybody thought it just *couldn't* be them, it seemed like a big step to go from being a failure to being the only person in the Universe with the Magical Talent--which enabled its beholder to master Air, Earth, Fire, Light, Water, Woodland, and then some.

But anyway, Testing was very short. If you were aged seven to nineteen you were eligible. The Teller, the person that delivers the Test and is also the dean of the school, is a towering woman with long, blonde hair, probably in her early thirties by now. She pushed kids through like cattle, clearly wanting to get it over with. When it was my turn, she took out this two ton textbook that naturally made my eleven-year-old brain groan, made me read a passage, asked one question that I don't even remember, and that was it. I walked out of there thinking "What just happened?", as did everyone else in my class.

Ninety days later, on the 100th day of the 600th year, the Talented School's teachers, retiring Summits, and the Teller called the entire Village together. They separated all of the students into the usual groups: first group: Air Talent, second group: Earth Talent, third group: Fire, then Light, Water, Woodland, and last my group, the "No Talents". For once, the other children didn't make fun of us as we made our way to the place at the end of the line.

The Teller stepped forward, and gave some insincere speech about how proud she was of everyone's hard work, and proceeded to announce the next Seven Summits. She read all of the names for the Talent Summits as a mixture of gasps and total silence came from the crowd. Each time, a petrified-looking kid walked to the front of the groups to stand next to her. Finally, she reached the name at the bottom of the list, the next Grand Summit. She took her sweet time reading it too--not as if she was trying to create suspense, more like she still couldn't believe the name written on the paper. I could've sworn I saw her shoot our predecessors, who were standing off to the side the entire time, a "*We are in trouble now*" glance. Some boy next to me actually yelled "Come on!" before the Teller finally, and almost reluctantly, called my name. And in absolutely no way, was I prepared for that. The field fell completely silent, and all eyes darted my direction. I felt like I was going to jump out of my skin. I hated it when people stared at me even back then. As much as I wanted to take off running in the other direction, my feet started walking toward her.

When I reached the front of the field, the Teller said a few more words that I didn't catch in my panic state, and motioned to the seven of us. I managed a half-smile as everyone simply stared. We were allowed to say good bye to our family and friends for five minutes before moving (if you can call it "moving," we couldn't take anything with us) into our new home. And that, everyone, is part of my relatively depressing childhood. Though it has been several years, that day never seems to fade into my memory.

Now, while I've been boring you with my life story, the hallway had remained unchanged and surprisingly silent--which is rare and in my case thoroughly nerve wracking. Everyone is usually up and walking around at five, ready to leave at seven. Why do we get up that early you ask? Well, it's not because we're morning people, I'll tell you that. If we want any time to go to the third dimension together, it has to be either too early in the morning or very late at night because we're usually kept pretty busy during the day. Even if we're not, we have to hang around the Citadel just in case something happens. Apparently, the entire Universe's population shares my paranoia.

Ten minutes went by, nothing. Fifteen, twenty, twenty-five, and not a soul showed up. I decided I should head down and see if they were in the yard. As I started walking toward the stairs, I heard a faint voice, and I thought they were trying to do one of their surprise attacks again.

We do that to each other all the time, partly as a way to make sure we all stay on our feet, partly because it's hilarious. Deciding to play along, I sauntered down the staircase and acted as if I was completely oblivious to my surroundings. At the bottom, I expected to see a giant boulder heading seventy miles an hour in my direction, but no one was there either.

I was on the verge of just yelling for them to cut it out, when I saw the back of someone with dark auburn, shoulder-length hair wearing the unmistakable red tunic, tan-colored slacks, and brown moccasins through in front window. It was Katrina, Amiselle's Charge.

Originally, the purpose of Charges was just to have extra hands in case of an attack. In return for them promising to stick with the Summits, they got to study their Talent from the seven masters. It was a pretty good win-win situation, and for the most part still is. Of course, we haven't been attacked in four hundred years, so that part has been sort of unofficially cut out. But still, she, Dillon, and Jarmony were all genuinely nice, and I liked having them around.

I opened the door, hoping she knew where everyone was. She turned around and because of her broken focus, the water that she was practicing with dropped to the ground with a loud *splash*.

"Hey Katrina," I said "have you seen the others? I can't find them anywhere."

She looked very surprised and confused to see me.

"Yeah, they left hours ago. At seven like you guys always do."

Just perfect.

"Thanks for letting me know, I guess I better go meet them then."

"I think Aaron left you oatmeal or something on the stove from break-"

"No time, see you later," I interrupted while heading back inside. I heard her begin to say a goodbye before the door closed behind me.

Why was I suddenly in such a panicked hurry? Well apparently when the book showed the sundial, it must have shown it at an angle. It wasn't six thirty, it was past eleven. Well, that's my luck for you.

I immediately started taking the stairs two at a time. I paced through the great room and hallway, and up the next flight all in under a minute in my haste to get to the roof. Once I reached it, I was pretty much out of breath. Well, yeah, I could have teleported out from right behind the front door, but I really did like being up there and taking in the entire dimension as a whole.

The extensive view made it possible to see almost everything. It truly was beautiful. Besides, the wind is always ten times stronger up eighty feet, and it seemed to help me focus better for some reason.

The Citadel is entirely made of stone, so the roof is simply a flat surface, about forty or fifty feet across. I walked to the center and looked out over the dimension as I always did. As usual, the sixty-mile-an-hour winds stung my eyes and blew my nearly elbow-length hair in my face. Of course I wasn't complaining-- those are the perfect teleporting conditions. Just to clarify, that would be the powerful wind part, not the burning eyes and mouthful-of-hair part.

Teleporting isn't that hard, it just takes tons of focus. You need to close your eyes, and picture your destination and your destination only. Otherwise, you might accidentally send yourself somewhere else... like the fourth dimension. By the way, that would be an inescapable, pitch-black labyrinth that keeps anyone unfortunate enough to be there lost in its soul-sucking darkness forever.

So yeah, that's bad.

Anyway, then you gather a ball of air around yourself--never stopping the mental image of your target. The transportation takes care of itself. When I opened my eyes, sure enough, I was in the third dimension, a plain field with few trees that stretched to the horizon and beyond.

Only Summits were allowed (and could get) here for the same reason as the whole "Fire ball" vs. "playful sphere of light" situation but on a *much* larger scale. I smiled at the rare occurrence of showing up somewhere to peace and quiet for a moment before looking around in search of the others. It didn't take very long, and I quickly saw the faint outlines of six people about a half a mile away. I didn't waste any time with running all the way there. Instead, I shortly kicked off the ground--flying toward the six figures.

Chapter 4

Apparently the others saw me coming because they met me about halfway. Instead of a warm welcome, I was greeted with a fast, powerful lightning bolt I deflected just inches away from my nose--compliments of Harmon, our all things Light Talent. I guessed I got my surprise attack.

"Hey, you're a bit late!" Illydia called as I landed next to her and the others.

She's our Woodland Talent, which means she specializes in all things growing in nature. Aaron, Macalynn, Illydia, Merrhet, Harmon, Amiselle, and I made up the Summits. We all wear the traditional beige, long-sleeved tunic with a red sash across the middle, charcoal-colored slacks, and brown boots. Only my previously mentioned cloak differs from the others. It singles me out as the Grand Summit and, as you may have noticed from earlier chapters, I don't particularly like being pin pointed, but I also don't have a choice.

Anyway, as far as our age differences went, we were lucky. There wasn't much of one. Merrhet was the oldest at seventeen. He was followed by Aaron and Harmon; both of them sixteen. Illydia was fifteen with me and Amiselle close behind at fourteen. And then little thirteen year old Macalynn is the youngest. Aaron, Macalynn, and I all have ranging shades of blue eyes. Amiselle, Merrhet, and Harmon have relatively light green ones, Illydia's are a chocolate color. Aaron and Merrhet have straight brown hair. Harmon's, Amiselle's, and mine is curly and very dark. Illydia and Macalynn are both dirty-blondes that we only can tell apart from behind because Illydia's is shoulder length and wavy while Macalynn's is long and straight as a pin. I could go on with this massive info dump but I'm sure you can live with the horrible disappointment of me deciding not to. After all, the point of me writing my life story down for you is so you know about your neighboring Universe--not so I can drone on and on about little things like this that no one cares about.

"Did you think you could get out of coming this morning just because it's your birthday?" Illydia continued with a smirk.

Well, I knew I was forgetting something. It's not that hard to overlook or be too busy for things as small as that when you're in our positions. But carry the one and that would make me fifteen.

"Wait, it's her birthday?" Harmon chimed in. "Why didn't I know that?"

"Because apparently you weren't listening when I told everyone maybe ten minutes ago, 'Hey, don't forget Lealight's birthday today'," Illydia's eyes narrowed and everyone started snickering.

Deciding to interrupt their conversation, I smiled back at her.

"Mhmm, thanks for caring, Harmon. And no, I read the sundial upside-down, so it looked like six thirty, not nearly noon."

"Wait, you have a sundial in your Library?" Merrhet, our Water Talent, asked.

I was about to answer that extremely rational question when Aaron spoke up.

"Yes, Merrhet," he said in the same voice you might use if you were speaking to a person hospitalized in an asylum. "Lealight has a *sun*dial in her *underground* Library. That just makes perfect sense."

Aaron moved his thumb inward, promptly sending a small rock into the air that thumped Merrhet on the side of his head. Even under his glare, we all laughed. Though our jobs were technically supposed to be the most serious and important in the entire Universe, we were all really close and had grown to love and hate each other like brothers and sisters. And if you wanted stern and irritating sticks in the mud for Summits, you shouldn't have picked a couple of kids.

Besides, nothing major ever happened. Just a few ancient Shadows left over from hundreds of years ago wandering around and freaking people out every once in a while, and maybe a dispute in the Village. Other than that, absolutely nothing.

"She saw the sundial in the yard on the cover of a book, genius," said Macalynn as she messed around blowing blades of grass everywhere with small air blasts she emitted from her fingertips. "Not that we'd expect you to know that, you yourself said you were always off in your own little world during class."

We all laughed again.

"So this book showed you the sundial upside-down?" Amiselle said. "Well, that's craftsmanship for you."

I shot her one of my famous death stares, and she just smirked and went back to practicing her own version of what we, to her sheer annoyance, referred to as a "Fiery-Death-Trap". And of course, more laughing came from the Summit Peanut Gallery.

"And before I forget," I continued. "Thank you, Harmon, for your generous birthday gift of almost killing me with one of your lightning bolts, *again*. Now, if I'm flying toward you at seventy miles an hour, you probably shouldn't launch one at me at a hundred miles an hour. Do you know how close that thing was to my face?"

He just smiled at me.

"How was I supposed to know that you were you?" he said in an as-a-matter-of-fact tone.

"I don't know, maybe that only Macalynn and Lealight can get in here alone… and Macalynn's sitting right there," Illydia said with a sly grin.

"What?" Macalynn came back to reality at the mention of her name and the six of us kept snickering.

"Moving on, so what have you guys been doing for the past four and a half hours?" I asked.

"Just random goofing off," said Aaron. "Not much to do without someone here to boss us around."

That comment just begged for a snarky response, but we needed to do something productive, and I decided that actions speak louder than words. I raised one of my arms up to my chin causing a large stream of water to shoot out of the river and loom above his head. Aaron's eyes grew wide.

"You wouldn't," he said along with his best glare.

"I think we all know I would. And maybe you do need me here to give constant instructions," I told him mockingly. "Lesson one: *nobody* outdoes *my* death stare."

With that, I broke my gaze and the water dropped, soaking him. Everyone burst out laughing--even Aaron was chuckling between coughs.

"You're *dead*," he threatened, yet somehow hearing that from someone who's laughing while choking doesn't make you feel that intimidated.

"Chill out, Aaron," said Merrhet as he reached out, as if to grab the air, and the water obediently evaporated.

"Though it did serve you right," Amiselle added.

I looked up toward the sun.

"Come on guys, we only have another thirty minutes before we need to get going, so let's stop messing around and do something halfway constructive," I said, particularly eyeballing Harmon for his lightning target practice.

"Correction," Illydia spoke. "We have about thirty *seconds* until we have to go because today marks the third year since the seven of us became the Summits."

Oh yeah, that. Okay, I was definitely off that day. I mean, first the sundial, my birthday, and then the whole "the day we were realized" thing... which everyone knew I enjoyed *so* much. And I guess my usual enthusiasm for the occasion was noted, because they all started laughing again.

The 100th day of every year marks the day we stepped up to become the Summits--not that we had a choice or anything. But it's supposed to be this big ordeal where we visit the Village and go to the school to teach the children cool things to do with their Talent that they wouldn't learn otherwise. The others had fond memories of the previous Summits coming to show them new stuff, but I always hated it. They never bothered to talk to the No Talents. While everyone else in school got to learn more things about their abilities, we watched from the window. And every time they passed by us they averted their eyes. Back then I thought they were just being stuck-up jerks, but now that I'm in their shoes it's easy to see why we were ignored.

The other Summits don't truly understand it the way I do (they don't know what's it's like to not have a Talent), but the past two times we'd visited I'd been trying to avoid the gazes of those who are in my former class. Not because I think any less of them, but because it's painful to know there's nothing I can do to help them. No one can give them a Talent. So they're basically stuck there being yelled at all day by the teacher like I would be right now if someone else had turned up in my position.

"Alright then, in that case let's get out of here," I told her.

The seven of us formed the usual circle and joined hands. Macalynn and I, being the only ones who could teleport, needed to create a very large chamber to fit everyone, lift it, and focus it on the top of the Citadel. It would be completely impossible for a regular person, but pretty much elementary for the two of us.

When we appeared on the roof, Harmon and Illydia started complaining about air travel again. Our journey down all the stairs to the yard of the Citadel was filled with remarks of how it lurches everyone forward and makes them feel sick. Finally, Macalynn turned around and snapped.

"Well, your alternative is being left behind in the third dimension so you don't have a choice. If you ever find a way to teleport by sunshine and flowers I'm sure we'd all be just glad to hear it!"

Amongst all of our snickering, they were obviously taken aback-- especially Illydia, who was very sensitive about her Talent. She insisted that she couldn't do anything with trees and shrubs that another one of us couldn't do with one of the other five. I've been trying to tell her for the past two years that the Woodland Talent has great advantages (I'll let you know when I think of some), but you might as well tell it to a brick as stubborn as she is.

Anyway, we ran into the Charges around the back of the Citadel.

"What are you guys still doing here?" Jarmony asked us. "We thought you'd be on your way by now."

He always worries when things weren't going perfectly according to a relatively nonexistent schedule. Heaven help us if he ever saw Clouds.

"Relax, we're leaving now," Aaron answered.

Dillon and Katrina didn't look too comfortable either. None of the Charges liked being left alone in the Citadel. No matter how many times I told them nothing was going to happen, they always felt uneasy.

"While we're gone, why don't you guys practice something in those books Lealight let you borrow?" Harmon suggested.

When Dillon, Katrina, and Jarmony first came only a couple months or so after we were realized, I had never seen anyone so incredibly shy in my life. They got very embarrassed if one of us saw them practicing. Which was a lot: ten people, one tower.

I felt bad for them so I started bringing up books on their Talents, Fire, Earth, and Water, from the Library for them to work on. The books showed basic stuff that you would probably find in a regular library in the Village at first. Then I started lending them more complex studies. I still don't let them read anything past a certain level because they wouldn't be able to do it regardless. But they've definitely advanced more than a regular person could ever dream about. Yet still, they acted as though they couldn't take on a Shadow walking merrily down the hall.

"That's a good idea, and make sure you don't forget to meet us here in the yard after we're finished at the school," Aaron added.

They nodded uncertainly and turned toward the front door.

This dimension, which by the way is the first of four, encompasses the Citadel in a large woods that cuts the seven of us off from the Village. But still allows us to get there when needed. In other words, it allows us to get there almost every day. The dimension itself is almost a perfect circle--the circumference lined with both looming mountains and rolling hills which were, at that time of year, capped with snow that didn't seem to melt until the middle of spring. And aside from a long and relatively narrow strip of land in the shape of a crescent where all the food is grown in the southeast, starting at the base of the inclines and stretching out for several miles inward are the more densely packed trees that eventually meet the Village. But don't be fooled by its name, the Village is nowhere near small. Since it nearly takes up the entire dimension, the Village is also almost a perfect circle except for the lopsided slant in the northwest created by the two mile thick woods that surrounds the Citadel.

It used to be that all of the Summits would have to split up, each going to a separate school on a different Talent. But during Veronica Calodie's time, she made it so there was one large school for all of them. Something about how aside from learning more about your own, you also must learn how to work together with others of different Talents. Of course none of the teachers honored her notion anymore, and the classes with different Talents almost never saw each other.

We made our way down the path in silence. The woods to the others were similar to the Library to me: the only peaceful place in the Universe. But the quiet was eventually broken by Amiselle.

"So... how are we going to do it this year?"

"Do what?" Harmon asked with a tone of annoyance in his reply.

"You know, everything we have to do on the 100th day."

"Today's not that much different from any other day, Amiselle" I answered. "The only thing is we have to go to the school. And you know what to do there--you take thirty five Fire Talents, Aaron takes thirty five Earth Talents, Illydia takes thirty five Woodland Talents, so forth and so on, and I take whoever's left. We keep it basic, but interesting and original, then we can go home for a while until we come back later in the evening and do our regular rounds like we do almost every day."

After I finished the half-hearted sounding outline, the silence continued with a slight awkwardness about it until the woods opened up to reveal the hexagonal shaped, stone building that was the Talented School.

Chapter 5

Once we were noticed, all of the students who were talking to friends and goofing off silenced.

"Great, it sounds just like it did around this time three years ago," I said under my breath.

Merrhet apparently caught it, and whispered something that sounded like it was meant to be encouraging, but I couldn't make out the actual words. The seven of us and the two hundred of them just stared at each other for a few seconds before Aaron bravely stepped forward and motioned for his group to go with him.

The first thirty five Earth Talents walked out of the crowd and followed him to the left side of the field. Then Illydia, Macalynn, Amiselle, Harmon, and Merrhet each led their groups to an open section of the land. Those who were left over, two Air Talents, four Earth Talents, a Fire Talent, three Lights, four Water, and five Woodlands joined me in the center.

Honestly, I had no idea what to do with them. I couldn't get into anything advanced, because they wouldn't be able to do it. But I needed to find something better than what they usually did. Also, I wasn't really the best person to ask about that kind of stuff. Another thing I was clueless about was what these kids did in class all day. I know all we did was copy from books and daydream while the teacher, who was constantly irritable that she had to "waste her ability to teach the Talented kids on us", paid absolutely no attention.

"So, is there anything specific you guys want to learn?" I asked the group.

They could obviously tell I had no idea what to do and were surprised and possibly annoyed by that. Well, they'd have to get over it because I was there for the next three hours showing them how to do *amazing* things. Like freeze a *whole drop* of water and levitate rocks *three inches* off the ground.

"I want to know how to make flowers bloom," said a shy Woodland Talent girl who looked about nine years old.

Wow, an actual, reasonable request. For the past two years I'd had Air Talent kids saying they want to teleport and others wanting to strike things with lightning. I would have to tell them very slowly that I couldn't risk them getting stuck in the fourth dimension... or killing someone.

Another Woodland, a boy, probably about eleven, groaned.

"We already know how to do that. Isetha is just slow."

The girl looked like she was going to cry.

Here we go again, I thought to myself. I cannot stand it when kids act like they're better than other kids because of their Talents. I would know. The six years I spent at school were filled with ridicule about me not having one. But we're not going down that road right now.

"Look," I told him "I am well aware of your... various skill levels and I am here today to help each of you do something new. And if Isetha wants to make flowers bloom, I will help her make flowers bloom, understand?"

My voice was a little louder at the end than I had anticipated, but he nodded. I really wish that every time I looked angry these kids wouldn't act like I was going light them on fire at any second.

"While we are working, I want you guys to each pick something *reasonable* for me to show you," I continued.

They agreed with uncertainty and started talking amongst themselves as Isetha and I sat down across from each other a few feet away. She put her hand on the ground and moved it gingerly across the grass. A small stem started rising slowly upward, but when it reached its maximum height, the flower bud would not open.

"And this is where I'm stuck," Isetha said with a sigh.

I examined the stem, but it was completely flawless.

"Okay, what are you picturing when you're trying to get the flower to bloom?" I asked her.

"Exactly what Ms. Dosibe told us to do," she replied. "She said to imagine the actual flower opening up."

Well, she was dead wrong. And yes, to those of you who are wondering, things as simple as growing flowers are indeed *this complicated*.

"That's not right. Think about it this way, what do flowers need in order to bloom?"

"Um, sunshine… and water," said Isetha.

"Exactly, so picture them and try again," I told her encouragingly.

She smiled and closed her eyes to focus again. Almost immediately, the flower's bud opened up to reveal a pink daffodil.

Isetha squealed with delight and called everyone over to see what she did. The others gathered around her, but looked somewhat disappointed at what they saw.

"Oh, it's... very pretty, Isetha," one of the older ones finally said, and the little girl smiled triumphantly.

"Can we move on now?" the same kid that almost made her cry earlier asked impatiently.

"Alright," I told him "What have you guys got?"

All things considered, the things they wanted to know weren't that bad. I showed the rest of the Woodland Talents how to grow small, fruit-bearing bushes, the Lights how to work in large groups to deflect the sun's rays, and etcetera, etcetera.

During the time we were at the school, tons of people gathered around the area and just watched the seven of us helping the kids. Personally, it makes me feel like an animal in a zoo being gawked at by total strangers. On the up side, everyone pulled through with no accidental torching, freezing, electrocuting, burying, squashing, blinding, or blowing anyone else into oblivion--so I called that visit a modest success. But honestly, don't those people have jobs or something?

And except for that one brat, the kids in my group were all pretty good natured. I was sad to have to leave them in the hands of the teachers, many of whom are some of the most unpleasant people around. Man, I would have loved to see the face of the Woodland Talent instructor when Isetha told her that I, the Grand Summit, personally said she was wrong.

Toward the end of our time at three, it had warmed up a little but we could all still see our breath. The others were just finishing up with their groups when the teachers began coming out of the building to call everyone inside.

After saying goodbye, we started toward the gate and down the path that led home. We had been walking through the peaceful serenity of the woods for a while before I could have sworn I heard someone screaming.

I debated whether or not to act on it because as I mentioned before, I tend to be a relatively paranoid person. I turned to ask the others, and they were looking around with the same expression I had. They heard it too.

Wordlessly, the seven of us headed back toward the Village, at first in a brisk trot, then breaking into a run. Screaming is something none of us take lightly. I checked the sky. There were no Clouds. Yet, the closer we got to the Village, the larger the feeling of dread was in the pit of my stomach. We were turning around the last corner before the Talented School when I collided into another kid who was also in a full sprint. The impact made me fall backwards, and I hit my head on a giant rock jutting out of the ground.

First off, wow that *hurt*. Taking Illydia's outstretched hand, I stood up slowly and rubbed the back of my head.

"Oh, I'm so sorry, I didn't mean…" the boy stammered.

"It's fine," I interrupted, sounding snappier than I had meant.

"What's wrong?" Aaron asked him.

The boy was about to answer when Katrina appeared from around the bend.

"*EVERYONE…*" she screamed "the Citadel is on *fire!*"

Chapter 6

"WHAT?!" We all shouted simultaneously as Katrina ran up to us, wheezing.

"I tried to put it out... I really did. But it's *huge*... the entire building is engulfed... in flames."

The seven of us and Katrina took off toward the Citadel with the boy trailing curiously behind us. As we neared it, the smoke grew thicker, making us cough heavily and our eyes water. When the trees parted to show the tower, it was burning freely in an array of yellows, reds, and oranges.

The rest of the group skidded to a halt at the edge of the woods, but Merrhet, Katrina, Amiselle, and I darted onward toward our home to join Dillon and Jarmony.

"What happened?!" Amiselle yelled over the crackle of the flames at the two Charges.

Dillon, who was desperately trying to put out sections of the fire to absolutely no avail, seemed not to hear. Jarmony stood behind him shouting something I couldn't make out. He totally ignored her.

"Forget that!" shouted Merrhet "Just put it out!"

He and Katrina stepped up to the tower, and together, they lifted huge amounts of water onto the building with their gazes. Amiselle ran around the base of the Citadel, snuffing out large parts of the fire as she went along. I flew up to the top of the tower and did a frantic mixture of the two approaches on the roof.

If you've bothered to read this far in my story, you're probably wondering why seven masters can't handle something as simple as a burning tower. Why can't we just snap our fingers, and the entire thing vanishes? Well, quit dreaming--it doesn't work like that.

One person, even a Summit, can only handle so much at a time. I mean, I might've been able to kill the horror show singlehandedly, but only if I flew up the Citadel taking the entire fire with me as I went. Once I was up there, I'd not only have no way of getting rid of it, but the move would also drain my energy completely and I would drop like a rock... and as fun as it may sound, free falling from eighty feet up without any way to stop yourself *never* ends well.

As soon as the flames had died down just enough to reveal the staircase, I swooped down into the Citadel. If you've ever been caught in the middle of a fire, you know what I mean when I tell you how terrible it smells. I had to hold my cloak over my nose just to keep breathing as I walked down the hallway, narrowly missing falling stones, trying to put out as many flames as possible with my remaining water.

After completely drenching what was left of the Charges' rooms, I was out. Let me tell you--there is nothing worse than being stuck inside a burning building with no water. On top of that, I was hacking so hard it hurt. Normally, I would have taken some water out of the air, but couldn't because it was too polluted with smoke. And I just wasn't able to fight my panic long enough to focus that hard.

I could hear the beating against the tower from the middle of the great room. It was almost as if our home was not burning down, but being power-washed. Yeah right, that's it. The good news: Merrhet, Amiselle, Katrina, and Dillon had extinguished the fire around the outside. The bad news: the door was definitely barricaded from all the fallen debris. So it was up to me to finish the job in front of the last staircase.

Without any water, all I could do was snuff out the actual fire, which isn't the best approach because it leaves the unbearable heat of the ashes and smoke, and includes the possibility of it reigniting. Lacking alternatives, I dropped my cloak and slowly flicked my wrist. The flames compliantly smothered themselves from left to right, leaving nothing but ash in its place.

I was relieved the fire had finally been put out, but afraid of choking to death with the overwhelming smoke drifting everywhere. Yet somehow, I needed to get down the last flight, and clear the remains of the ceiling away from the door.

As I struggled to get around the piles of cinder, I realized that not only was it becoming impossible to move around without narrowly being crushed, but also I was going to black out before I was even halfway down the stairs. So I decided to use one quick burst of energy and fly straight to the bottom.

Probably not my best decision.

After almost being flattened once more by a huge falling stone near the end of the stairs, another coughing fit overtook me and I was forced to drop down clumsily, almost twisting my ankle. If there wasn't enough clean (as in--not smoke-infested) air to control, you couldn't at all. No Air Talent translates into no flying. Wasn't that the perfect time for it to get picky?

The loud banging noises of someone trying to get inside then came from the other side of the door--along with voices all sounding worried.

"Where's Lealight?"

"I don't know. I haven't seen her since she flew up to the roof."

"I did. She went inside."

"She did *what*?! She'll get herself killed!"

"*Guys!*" I yelled weakly.

"Is that you, Lealight? Are you okay?" Harmon's voice called back.

Well, I'm trapped on the inside of a tower flooded with smoke, coughing to the point where I can't breathe, and I have absolutely no way out. So with that being said, yes Harmon, I'm doing just fine.

"I'm alright, but the door is barricaded with fallen stones."

"Well, can you open..." his question was interrupted with my pathetic hacking.

I really hate smoke.

"You're the Earth Talent, you move the stones."

"They're on the opposite side of the door; you can't control things you can't see."

"Okay then, Illydia, the door is made of wood. Can't you... crumble it or something?"

"You know just as well as I do that it has to come straight out of nature, and this thing has been here since the Citadel was built. Its connection is long gone."

A short-lived silence set in.

"Then look through the window and move the stupid stones from there!"

"The window is blocked with the same kind of wood."

"Alright what do you suppose we do, make a giant hole in the wall?!"

And on that note, all talking stopped.

"We don't have many options here, Aaron. You have to blow an opening in the side."

"You can't exactly do that to the foundation of an ancient, eighty-foot-tall tower. The entire thing might collapse!"

I finally doubled over and started painfully coughing again.

"We don't have a choice, just do it!" Amiselle's desperate yell sounded through the small cracks in the stone.

"But Lealight will be crushed!"

Oh, well wasn't that a pretty picture? On one hand I could choke and die in the smoking remains of the Citadel. On the other, the ceiling could come crashing down on top of me.

It was official. That day totally *sucked*.

"Well, Lealight will *suffocate* if we don't do something! And if you make sure the hole is just big enough for you and Illydia to squeeze through, clear the debris, and open the door the place won't give way."

Everyone was once again mute for what seemed like endless moments.

"Stand back," he finally answered.

Ten seconds later, a hole appeared in the side of the tower, spraying stones all around as if they were mere droplets of water. I then heard two sets of footsteps moving quickly across the floor, one heading in the direction of the door, and the other coming toward me.

Unwilling to let the others see me, the supposed strong, invincible Lealight, looking so incredibly weak, I gathered my remaining strength and stood up.

"I'm okay," I choked as Illydia put an arm around me and starting walking towards the door.

She didn't respond. Even though my vision was blurred from the smoke, I could see the expression on her face that obviously meant she didn't believe me as we neared the exit only to find that the stones had been thrown into two tall piles on either side of the door.

"There we are," said Aaron.

The three of us rushed out of the Citadel and the doorframe promptly collapsed behind us. Ignoring it, I took in huge, deep breaths of the significantly less smoky air. I had all of two seconds to decide I would never take oxygen for granted ever again before Macalynn ran up and hugged me.

"Don't you ever scare us like that again."

"Guys, I'm fine... really," I said from over her shoulder--noticing the nine pairs of worried eyes staring at me.

But my response was once again not bought as Macalynn let me go. I wasn't exactly helping my case by hacking so hard. Fortunately, I was saved by an abrupt change of subject.

"*What happened*?" Amiselle asked for the second time.

Dillon seemed to have a sudden fascination in his shoes.

"Dillon, Jarmony, Katrina did you hear Amiselle? She asked you *what happened,*" Merrhet repeated vehemently.

"Jarmony and I were in the woods." Katrina finally spoke up. "We were practicing the stuff in the books when I noticed something...

abnormal floating above the trees. So I told him I'd be right back, and went to check it out. When I got to the Citadel, I saw this huge fire burning in the doorway. I tried to put it out, but I couldn't extinguish it fast enough and... well, it spread."

"And I heard her scream, so I ran back here as fast as I could," Jarmony added. "By the time I got to the edge of the yard, she was gone, and the fire had almost engulfed the entire tower. At first I thought Dillon was still inside and probably stuck there because he... couldn't put it out fast enough. When I started running toward the path to get you guys, I saw him on the other side of the place. I went over to ask what happened and what I could do to help just as you showed up."

Jarmony looked both upset and guilty. It was very clear that he felt like he was pinning the weight on Dillon, who hadn't looked up once.

"Dillon, do you have any idea what actually caused the fire?" Harmon asked after a few seconds, trying to sound nice and forgiving, but failing.

"There was an... um... accident," he finally replied, now in total awe of the grass.

An "accident". A freaking *"accident"*.

"How in this Universe do you light the Citadel on fire because of *an accident*?!" Macalynn, who was definitely on the verge of screaming, demanded.

"I was... uh... practicing in my room, and I kind of did something wrong, and the wall caught on fire. It grew too quickly for me to snuff it out, so I ran outside."

Speechless, all of us stared at him in disbelief.

"Okay," I said calmly, finally getting my hacking under control. "Is there any particular reason you were practicing with fire inside? Or why you didn't go and get Katrina when the fire first started?"

We all listened intently for a response for the next two minutes, but one never came. I was about to speak up again when Dillon at last said, "I guess I just... panicked. I was worried you guys would be really mad at me, and I... I'm really sorry."

I sighed. I had no idea what to say to that. No one did. So we all just stood there and stared at the smoke pouring out the windows of our ancient home. It looked almost the same from where we were (you know, besides the gaping hole Aaron had blown in), but we knew the inside would be another story. There was also no telling what any of our rooms looked like, or the Library for that matter, and then there was the fact that all the debris scattered throughout the place had to have come from somewhere....

"Was there something wrong in the Village that you came to tell us about when we ran into you in the woods?" Amiselle asked the kid who still stood there, breaking yet another silence that day.

He shook his head.

"Oh, um... someone at the school said they saw the smoke above the trees, so I was sent to tell you that the Citadel was on fire."

Really? You don't *say.*

"Alright then, please go back and tell them the fire is out, and everything is fine. Also, that we are running behind schedule and will be coming later tonight so we have some time to... fix this."

He nodded, and we watched him eagerly take off and disappear between the trees.

Chapter 7

"The first order of business is to clear out the Citadel," I told the others. "All the ash and debris can be dumped here on the yard until we figure out what to do with it."

Everybody agreed, so we walked up and into the Citadel and got to work.

Of course the second everyone stepped through the hole (since the door was no longer existent), we found out where all the wreckage had come from. The ceiling had several breaks, some big, some small, in it. Stones were still falling. Everyone simultaneously groaned. The support beams for the roof just had to be the only things made of wood in the entire tower, didn't they?

Macalynn and I looked at each other in dread. But we knew it had to be done. She came over and took my hand as if to combine our energy and together we placed a widespread air dome just under the disaster. We hoped it would prevent us from being hit in the head with giant rocks as we cleared the lingering smoke from what was left of the building. Afterward, it was pretty easy for the place to rid itself of the smell because of the many new... skylights, and the ten of us spent the next two hours cleaning out the cinder and wreckage--though it was a bit harder after the first staircase almost completely fell apart from second story down. For the most part Aaron, Jarmony, and Harmon were in charge of collecting all of the stones together. Macalynn and I were once again needed to carry all of the useless junk down from the second floor (flying: a blessing and a curse), and everyone else either used other Talents to help clear the building, or had some fun doing manual labor. Merrhet never said one word to his Charge and Dillon never said one word at all.

By the time we decided to leave for the Village again, the only thing left to do structurally was to replace the base of the stairs and of course fill the holes in the ceiling. Then there was the actual interior to worry about later, but I thought that was pretty okay progress for ten kids. Besides, baby steps are good when you're reconstructing a giant tower.

When everyone was outside in the debris-ridden yard, Macalynn and I finally dropped the air we'd held in place and breathed a sigh of relief. We'd never kept up something that long before and even though it should have been something simple for us, we, believe it or not, were a little out of practice when it came to the "Keep-A-Shield-Up-For-Two-Hours-To-Protect-Everybody-Trying-To-Rebuild-Our-Home-Just-In-Case-The-Charges-Light-It-On-Fire" drills.

"Normally we'd tell you to work on something, but given the circumstances, let's stay away from those books for a while," Harmon said to the Charges after everyone had finished their hearty dinner of an apple from the tree Illydia had grown (because our little kitchen was reduced to rubble) as the seven of us stood up to head back to the Village.

"Seriously, the last thing we need is a flood tearing through the woods or an earthquake dividing the dimension in half," Amiselle added.

We all nervously smiled at that.

"Not going to happen," Katrina said hastily. "I think we're just going to see what we can salvage from the rooms and-"

"That's fine. Just be careful about the stones," I interrupted her once again that day, knowing that we needed to leave right then unless we wanted to walk through the woods in the dark.

They took my hint and waved us off. I don't know if I've mentioned this to you yet, but walking through the woods at night is especially creepy. Even the seven of us, who are very used to it by now, tread very carefully. Maybe it's the eerie glow of the moonlight, or the rustle of the dark leaves in the wind. Or maybe it's the fact that back several hundred years ago in the time when Clouds were a regular thing, three Summits and countless other people disappeared there and were never seen again.

As if to avoid the same fate, we rushed through them as quickly and quietly as we could manage. When we rounded the corner to the school, we came face-to-face with Litheney Hallsmen (remember the name from Chapter One?), who I swear had loathed me even more than she loathed the rest of the Universe for the past three years.

You're late," she snarled and her expression quickly changed from anger to distaste. "And you all look like wrecks."

Well, excuse us. We spent all day clearing out and rebuilding parts of an *eighty foot tall* tower.

Holding back, I calmly said, "You didn't get the message? Well, what happened was...."

"I know what happened," she snapped. "And that was a most vivid display of carelessness on your part, Summit Lealight. You, of all people, should know better than to leave the Citadel in the hands of a bunch of irresponsible trainees."

It took all of my strength not to tell her that those "irresponsible trainees" could take her head off, so she didn't even want to know what we could do.

"Litheney, there's no need to get so upset. It really wasn't anyone's fault," said Macalynn with a nervous smile.

As mentioned earlier, she was only thirteen so she still might've been able to pull off a sweet, innocent girl act... just not on her.

"I wish to be referred to only as Teller Hallsmen, if it's not too much trouble for you."

Wow, touchy.

"Anyway, people have been waiting for hours, so I expect there is some explaining to be done," she continued.

I knew she was right, but how I was going to tell everyone that the Seven Summits just burned down their own home was beyond me.

"Well, go on!" the Teller yelled at us, pointing at the path as if we didn't see it.

We shuffled past her, and she walked closely behind us like a teacher trying to control mischievous children.

"I don't know what's scarier," Aaron said under his breath, "that we'll probably have to walk through these woods at night or the fact that she's allowed around kids."

We all stifled a laugh at that, but it's pretty sad that he was absolutely right.

When we came upon the school, the sun had just set. I guessed we wouldn't be getting back before dark.

"Everyone is up ahead in the square. I'd hurry if I were you." Litheney Hallsmen continued, "I'll come by later to make sure you didn't ruin everything again."

I was about to ask her why everyone was there, because no one actually "gathered" for the 100th day. In fact, the only time that happened at *any* point during the year was if there was some very important, and usually catastrophic, news to be told. But Litheney turned around and headed toward the school before I could speak. While we are on the subject of the good Teller, you're probably wondering right now why I let her speak to us that way. Even though we're the ones in charge, we agreed on that day exactly three years ago that we wouldn't let being the Summits change us. In fact, everyone *used* to call us by just our first names, until Litheney chewed them out for it. And only she insisted on the formality of titles.

"Gee, thanks for your wonderful words of encouragement and wisdom," said Merrhet.

My thoughts exactly.

"Ignore her," I told the others. "Let's just get this over with."

The square is only about a quarter mile away from the front of the school, so everyone saw us approaching beneath the moonlight. We visit about five times a week, and my previously mentioned "regular rounds" are nothing more than a way to make sure all is well, blah, blah, blah, and to help out with small things that the people can't handle on their own. The most extreme that's ever gotten is when some little kids wandered into the woods surrounding the Citadel and got lost. Of course Macalynn and I found them within ten minutes of our aerial search, playing in a tree about thirty feet away from the yard.

At any rate, the seven of us were basically walking up to face an endless sea of at least four hundred people--all wanting to know what exactly had happened earlier that day. The good news was that we could probably get away with only staying for ten minutes or so because of the dark--even though that time would indeed be spent trying to offer an explanation for the day.

When we approached the square, people started whispering, no doubt about the fire. I knew I had to clean the whole mess up before it turned from an accident to something much bigger. You'd figure having a bunch of teenagers in charge would worry them anyway, but it's relatively normal. Yet another old custom: Summits are appointed between the ages of seven and nineteen. It's that way to make sure that the only people who stand between It and our Universe are able to fight, and those in their eighties aren't exactly agile enough. And if you're selected to be a Summit, you don't have a choice because you're the only person alive with the ability to master the Talent. Or in my case, the only one who has Magic.

Anyway, when we stepped into the square, the people immediately started asking questions.

"Calm down, everyone," I said. "As you may have heard, there was a... small incident at the Citadel."

The few people that dared to laugh at the fact I just called a giant fire a "small incident" were immediately silenced by others glaring at them.

"But it's out now, and we should be done rebuilding it within a few days."

"Was the entire tower destroyed?" someone in the crowd asked. "And what about the Library?"

I hadn't even bothered to check it since the fire.

"No, not completely," Harmon began. "The only major problem left is the holes in the roof. Since the support beams were made of wood they burned easily. But it shouldn't take that long to come up with a temporary solution of some kind, and then we'll have to look into something permanent later."

"And the Library's door is fireproof, so I don't see how it could have been affected," I continued, hoping it truly was and guessing I'd find out when we got back.

"How did it even start?" someone else in the square asked. "Your Charges weren't inside, were they?"

"We don't know. Katrina, Dillon, and Jarmony were all in the woods." Illydia lied.

Amiselle frowned at her disapprovingly, but I agreed with her choice to lie about Dillon. If we told the truth, they would demand he be kicked out for being so incredibly careless. I was considering it on the way, but decided not to bring it up. I was afraid that if I did, Merrhet would be very angry with me for even suggesting that his Charge be expelled. And arguing was the last thing we needed to be doing.

The seven of us stood there for a couple seconds before I finally said, "We're very sorry this fire worried everyone and interfered with us coming today. We can assure you that everything's going to be fine as far as that goes. But it's getting late, and we need to try to make some final repairs before it gets too dark. So we'll have to bid you all a good night."

Everyone just stared at me for a while until I shot a glance at the others reading "*help me*".

"But we'll be back within the next three days," Aaron added.

Everybody still looked pretty confused, but nodded respectfully. The adults grabbed their small children's hands, and they all made their way out of the square to their homes.

Once everyone had cleared out, we headed back toward the woods. I had to ignore my instinct to avoid them at night by flying over it, and I could tell Macalynn was fighting the same temptation as we were swallowed by the trees.

We walked very quickly and in complete silence through the two miles of unchanging landscape (dense, dark trees) and howling wind. Once the Citadel came into view, everyone let out a sigh of relief. Leaving the woods behind, we approached the tower. The front door had been replaced, and all the ash and debris we had dumped on the yard not that long ago had vanished. I was immediately apprehensive about our lessened workload and my concern quickly doubled when we stepped inside and the place looked like it had before the fire.

Katrina and Jarmony met us at the bottom of the fully repaired stairs.

"I... I think we fixed the door okay but as for the rest of the place..." Katrina began before her voice trailed off in both astonishment and confusion.

"This is impossible," Amiselle said squarely after a few seconds of silence. "How did you finish so quickly?"

"I might not be a master, but I can still place stones one on top of the other," Jarmony replied slightly hurt.

"No, she didn't mean it like that," Harmon cut in. "Amiselle's talking about the interior. I mean, it looks like it was never on fire. The burnt rugs I could've sworn we threw out are in their places completely untouched, the staircase's railing is back, the candles are mounted again.... How did-"

"We really don't know," Katrina interrupted. "We were trying to adjust the front door from the outside. When we'd fixed it and came back in, everything looked back to normal."

"And that doesn't seem the slightest bit strange to you?" I asked her.

"Of course it does! We've been looking for what might have caused it for the past half hour!" Jarmony snapped, though he quickly realized his tone, and looked sheepishly at the floor.

"Lealight, you need to go see if your Library is still intact. If it is, it might have some information on how the Citadel rebuilt itself," Macalynn said with a look of guilt and concern, as if she knew something we didn't.

I looked at her suspiciously, but nodded, and started walking upstairs. Though I gave up about halfway there. How the others could stand walking up and down and up and down all the time was yet another thing that was beyond me. So I decided to simply teleport to the top of the steps. I closed my eyes to picture the great room. But several seconds later, I hadn't moved yet. Assuming that it meant nothing more than I was tired from the day's work, I shook it off and had no choice but to continue upstairs on foot.

When I reached the top, I noticed that, once again, the place looked just like it had twenty-four hours earlier. The table was dead center of the rectangular room, and three windows looked out onto the now miraculously cleared yard.

They say never to refuse or question a gift, but I was becoming increasingly nervous the more I saw of the suddenly structurally-sound building. Just to prove my suspicions, I quietly floated toward the ceiling. Noting the replaced wooden support beams, I gave them as good a kick as you can while airborne. Absolute stability--not even as much as a vibration.

At that point, I was freaking out so much I was practically shivering as I lowered myself awkwardly in front of the Library door. When I was directly in front of it, I felt for sure I was being followed. That was confirmed when I heard footsteps coming toward me.

Someone then gently shook my shoulder, and I jumped about a foot in air before turning around.

"Sorry, I didn't mean to startle you," Macalynn said.

"It's okay," I answered trying to sound calm--but she could definitely hear the unease in my voice.

"You're going to think I've gone completely insane, but I want you to walk down the stairs very quietly and be careful in there."

I wanted to ask what the heck she was talking about when she abruptly reached out and hugged me like she would never see me again. She then disappeared around the corner.

I groaned in exasperation. Now on top of my nervousness, I had to go find her and figure out what she meant after I found the fate of my Library. My nervousness began churning around when I faced the door again. Ever heard the phrase "butterflies in your stomach"? Yeah, it was more like I had a hive of killer bees in mine.

Of course after I'd worked up the nerve to go in, the Library door wouldn't open for me. That didn't make any sense at all. It always knew who I was. The silver ring even recognized my voice sometimes as well as my Magic and unlocked automatically at that point.

I put a hand on the disc, and nothing. As a last resort, I stood there for several minutes, focusing very hard on the door. When it finally, and almost regretfully, creaked open. I was absolutely exhausted, as if I was going to collapse walking down the dizzying amount of steps. And yes, I agree with those of you that think needing to go upstairs only to go back down once behind the door is pretty weird. It only adds another five stories of steps going to ground level again before the three more that actually lead under the earth. But hey, I didn't build the place and we're all pretty sure that whoever did wasn't the sharpest tool in the shed.

Of course I was relieved when I reached the bottom and saw my Library untouched by any damage. But for some reason, I still felt very on-edge. Assuming it was Macalynn's weird advice, I walked around the bookshelves checking and accounting for everything until I heard a loud "*thud*" near the fourth wall. And voices.

I quietly ducked behind a nearby bookshelf, and peered around it. What I saw shocked me so greatly, I almost fell over.

All I could think of was how I was going to tell the others. There just weren't many logical, positive, explanations as to why Merrhet was there, in *my* Library.

Chapter 8

You know that feeling when part of a situation makes perfect sense and the other half is about as clear as mud? I hate that so much, and yet, it *always* finds a way to... come up. On one hand, I hadn't seen Merrhet since Teller Hallsmen left us standing by the school. He could have easily snuck through the woods and come back to the Citadel. But on the other, the Library's door only opens when it senses my Magic, so how did *he* get in?

"Did you find it?" Merrhet's irritated voice called from across the room.

Dillon appeared from behind another shelf. Terrific, he was there too?

"No, and did you really expect you would? If something's been missing for hundreds of years, chances are it's pretty well hidden," he replied.

"Of course I expect to find it!" Merrhet yelled at his Charge. "And we can't leave this place until we do!"

"But what if she comes back?"

"I'm not worried about Lealight or her dumb Library, you idiot!" he screamed. Regaining his composure, Merrhet continued, "You know what will happen if we aren't back with it in time."

"Why does he need, or even want this thing?" Dillon complained. "Why does it have to be something that Veronica person hid, like, forever ago?"

"Quit whining and just find it," he answered. "We didn't spend three years looked for this thing so we could drain Lealight Roverdee's Magic and search the Library to return empty handed."

They had been doing what?!

I tried to assure myself that was completely impossible. The only way they could is if they had a jewel so incredibly rare and powerful that could attract my magic and trap it deep within the natural facets of the stones. The only two in existence had been locked away and secured by a Grand Summit who lived well over a hundred years ago. But of course five seconds later, Merrhet produced a triangular, white colored gem from his pocket that was no bigger than half the size of a tennis ball.

Oh come on, really?

Dillon stared at it for a while, as if afraid of it. Then he nodded and continued searching.

Well, that was just spectacular. Merrhet and Dillon had drained enough of my Magic into that gem so now even the Library door believed that they were me. Plus, I had absolutely no idea how I was going to get it back. All I could do at that point was watch in dismay as the two searched my Library, and it was only a matter of time before I was discovered.

"You know if we find this thing, he said we could finally get out of here. When he comes back and finally destroys this place, we will be at his side," Merrhet's voice broke the quiet.

"Hmph" Dillon sounded in disbelief, and walked over to another shelf.

"Don't be like that! We're lucky you didn't get yourself expelled when you nearly blew our cover by *destroying* the Citadel. I told you to burn down enough to keep the others occupied so we could sneak down here--not set the whole place ablaze. So thanks to you, we had to waste some of the Magic in here to reconstruct the entire building and you know it automatically went back to Lealight afterwards. So now she has maybe one ounce left in her as opposed to the none it *would have* been" an annoyed Merrhet replied before going back to his monologue. "And then even the Summits won't be able to stop us. Once they're out of the way, everything will go according to plan, finally."

Dillon rolled his eyes and walked over to search another section of the room, but stopped abruptly.

"Um, Merrhet," he called.

"Not now," was his answer.

"Uh, *Merrhet*" Dillon urgently yelled.

"I told you not now!"

"*MERRHET*!"

"What *is* it, can't you see I'm-"

"Yeah, but I think this is something more important!" Dillon cut in.

"Uh, Lealight is here."

I stopped breathing.

"What do you mean she's here?" Merrhet asked "How would you know if everyone's back from the Village or not?"

"No, I mean she's right there," he said, pointing in my direction. "Right next to that bookcase."

Thank you, Dillon.

Suddenly, the shelf I was hiding behind caught fire. Even though I quickly jumped out of the way and drenched the flame with a shaky pool of water, I still felt pain sear through my right side. I swallowed a scream of pain.

Merrhet smiled victoriously upon seeing me struggle to do something as simple as putting out a three foot tall fire. He knew it was because I was missing almost all my Magic.

"Okay Merrhet," I threatened. "Give me that gem, and I won't have to hurt you."

He just laughed.

"You honestly think you could beat us without this?" He tauntingly shook the white jewel. Even though I was furious, I knew he was right.

"Now, let's try it the other way around," he continued. "You give us the chest and *we* won't have to hurt *you*."

I had no idea what he was talking about.

"What chest?"

Merrhet's face turned a scarlet red, and he yelled, "Lealight, I'm going to give you *one* chance. Don't be stupid; we are getting it regardless. So either you show us where it is now, or else."

Stillness lingered until Merrhet finally lost his patience, and lightning bolts started appearing out of nowhere. My eyes grew wide. Now *that* was impossible. Merrhet was a Water Talent. So now he wasn't only a traitor, he wasn't who we thought he was, either.

The lightning flashed and made faint humming sounds as it grew in between us.

"Still refusing to speak up?"

"Still don't know what you're talking about," I told him.

"Well, that's too bad. You could have been a useful addition."

On that note, one of his lightning bolts shot out and wrapped itself in a circle around me, only a couple feet away.

"Any last words?" he said mockingly, clearly enjoying every second of my terror.

Without my Magic, there was nothing I could do to prevent Merrhet's swirling lightning bolt from getting smaller and smaller until it hovered only about a foot away. I was trying to keep on a menacing face and think clearly to find some way out. But my horror was continuing to grow until I was reduced to screaming for help even though I knew there was no way the others could hear me. Definitely not one of my finer moments.

Merrhet smiled with a disturbing kind of happiness when the lightning was only six inches away from me. But then, his expression changed from twisted delight to shock. He abruptly fell over and landed face down on the floor.

When the lightning vanished, I ran as fast as I could toward him. And you know that saying "only if you pry it from my cold, dead hands"? I was really hoping that wasn't the case here.

I cautiously reached down to take the gem. Somewhat to my relief and somewhat to my disappointment, he was still breathing. Being afraid of him jumping up at any second, I snatched the jewel away. Once I had it, a feeling that I imagined might be similar to electricity ran through my veins. I watched the pure white gem slowly turn an ebony color as I slipped it into the pocket on the inside of my cloak. I had my Magic back.

"Get *away* from him, Lealight!" Amiselle's voice echoed throughout the room. I glanced up just in time to be grabbed from behind. I was pulled away so quickly I lost my footing and found myself being dragged more than walking. I impulsively screamed once again before I realized it was Aaron and Harmon.

"What are you guys doing here?" I hissed under my breath.

"Shhh," Aaron told me as they stopped several yards away from Merrhet. I'd barely regained my balance for three seconds before being nearly knocked over again by Illydia, Amiselle, and Macalynn, all of them taking me into their arms as if they expected me to start sobbing on the spot.

"Lealight, I'm so sorry I didn't say anything to you," Macalynn was the one who was teary eyed. "I should've told you guys the second I heard, but I was just too afraid of what you'd think and how you'd react."

"What are you talking about, Macalynn?" I tried to sound gentle, but my voice was shaky.

"I've suspected Merrhet of not being who we thought he was for a while now. I overheard him and Dillon talking secretively a couple weeks ago. I couldn't hear much--only something about a gem and draining Magic. Then I noticed he wasn't with us on the way back, and I thought that maybe... but I never dreamed he was planning something like *this*."

"Are you okay, Lealight? Did he hurt you?" Amiselle cut in before I could respond.

I nodded.

"Yes, you're okay or yes he hurt you?"

"I think I got burned a little. But other than that I'm fine," I answered. "How did you guys get in here in the first place?"

"The door didn't close behind you, and we knew something was up just from that," Harmon began. "And then Macalynn told us what she'd overheard and we decided better to be safe than sorry. Thank goodness we did. I just... I can't believe Merrhet would betray us like this."

"I think he's more than a traitor, Harmon," Illydia whispered as she and the others let go of me. "How do you think he did that? He can't be a Light Talent *and* a Water Talent."

"Lealight is," Amiselle pointed out.

"No, this is something... different," I spoke up. "I'm not a Talent of any sort, Amiselle. I never have been. I have Magic instead. That's why once he had it trapped inside the gem, I couldn't do anything."

I paused, and considered a possibility I'd been trying to prove wrong since the moment I saw Merrhet down there. But I decided the others deserved to know no matter how disturbing it was.

"Not to alarm you or anything, but I think he was sent by It," I said as if I was afraid of the devil himself hearing me.

"*What*?" was everyone's unanimous response.

"I'm not saying that I know this for sure, but I think Merrhet is one of his... followers. And as you know, Summits are born Summits. So I think if he never was one, then our true Water Talent was never discovered."

I waited to let what I just said sink in.

"I think you're right," Aaron finally said. "So, then who is Merrhet? A Shadow?"

"I am most certainly not a Shadow!" Merrhet snarled while trying to stand up, only to fall back over with a yelp of pain.

Harmon stepped in front of the rest of us protectively.

"You act like you've never seen lightning before, Merrhet. You know, if that's your real name."

"Of course it's my real name!" he yelled. "And let me just say one thing, *your highnesses*, you all are *toast*." Merrhet then stared directly at me and said, "And *you*, we will get that chest! And when we do, not even you will be able to stop us!"

I didn't realize how violently I was trembling until Illydia slipped her hand into mine and squeezed it reassuringly.

"How *could* you Merrhet?!" Amiselle choked.

I had been thinking the same thing. Exactly three years ago, when Litheney practically dumped us off here and left, he was the first one to speak. The first time Macalynn and I tried to get everyone to the third dimension and back, and we basically went everywhere but, he was the one who made us keep trying until we finally got there two hours later. He was like a big brother to all of us and had been for a long time. But now? The real Merrhet laughed at the sight of her being so hurt.

"How could I? I'll tell you how. I never was a stupid Water Talent in your little group, and I cannot believe you all fell for that for three years. When people finally wise up and realize that you six aren't even capable of protecting yourselves, much less a Universe, they'll lose all faith in their *precious little Summits*. They won't even be surprised when you fail at stopping It's return!"

His last words were ringing in my ears. *It's return. It hasn't shown up for four hundred years*. In fact, most people thought he was *dead*.

We all just stood there for what seemed like an eternity.

"Now, I'd love to stick around and show you people what a *real* master looks like, but I have an appointment elsewhere."

Macalynn suddenly tore from our huddle and flung her arm in the direction of the ceiling. Merrhet promptly hurdled upward. Every time he struggled, she slammed him hard against it. We learned our dear friend had a very colorful vocabulary.

"Macalynn, wait," Aaron said as he walked up next to her.

"This is no time to get compassionate, Aaron. You saw what he tried to do and you know if we let him go, he'll surely come back to kill us later!"

I fully agreed, but didn't speak up. A couple seconds later, Aaron nodded hesitantly.

"Lealight, come help me. We have to get this right the first time," Macalynn continued as Merrhet yelled out in frustration.

I stepped up and we stood side by side, communicating our next move without one word. The fourth dimension was going to have a new resident, besides Shadows, for the first time in over four hundred years. As we stared up at Merrhet, the air around him turned translucent and began swirling around. Within the next few seconds, Merrhet gave a final yell for revenge, and he disappeared like water vapor into thin air.

Chapter 9

During our little production of Summit Terminator, Dillon had been standing in the middle of the floor with a shocked look on his face. Apparently, the encounter between Merrhet and I didn't go as he expected. Hey, didn't particularly go my way, either.

Now it was the six of us and him, each waiting for the other to make the first move.

Though after about three minutes, the whole "suspense" thing gets old.

When I started heading across the room, he balled up his fists and launched slow, weak flames toward me. I put them out in mid air before they had even traveled three feet.

He quickly changed his approach to the situation, and put his arms over his face to try to protect himself from whatever he thought I was going to do.

At that moment, my feeling toward him went from anger to pity. I had no idea what motivated him to do this, or if and what they threatened him with.

Hoping I wasn't making a huge mistake, I sighed and said simply, "Get out."

He slowly lowered his arms. "What?"

"Look, I don't want an explanation for why you did what you did. Just don't make me regret my decision to let you go. Get out of here and go back to the Village. If anyone asks, you got expelled because we found out you started the fire. And if I find out you take one step out of line, you will be joining Merrhet faster than you can *blink*. Understand?"

He was practically frozen with fear, but gradually started walking.

"Aaron, Harmon, please show him out," I continued.

They actually listened to me for once and followed closely behind Dillon as he climbed the stairs. After the sound of their footsteps above us faded, I caught sight of the shelf that was burned. It looked like nothing more than blackened wood mixed in with some ash.

Macalynn, Illydia, and Amiselle followed my gaze and knelt down to help me dig through the remains. We only found a few books that were too charred to read.

"This place is amazing, by the way," said Illydia as we gave up on the idea of finding anything in the pile. "Was there anything important on that shelf?"

"I have no idea. But probably nothing I can't replace within a few weeks," I answered. "And you guys know you have to pretend you never saw it right?"

They smiled.

"Aw man, I was hoping to discuss it with Litheney, I mean, Teller Hallsmen," Amiselle smirked.

"Oh, she'd enjoy that. I can see it now," Macalynn chimed in. "How could you go into the Library? How could you be oblivious to your own Magic being drained? How could-"

"Stop it. It's creepy how much you sound like her," Illydia interrupted.

I couldn't help but grin at that.

"Not to put a damper on things, but what are we supposed to do now?" Amiselle asked grimly.

"As much as I hate to say it, I think we need to go tell Litheney," I answered.

Three groans followed my response.

"Come on guys, if she brings any of that up then maybe we could come up with one of our own accusations… like, how could *you* pick the wrong Water Talent Summit?"

We all started laughing.

"That would be a satisfying turn of events," Illydia said, smiling at the thought.

"Sorry to interrupt your slumber party, girls," Aaron's snarky voice came from the bottom of the stairs.

"Oh, shut up! Or we'll have Macalynn and Lealight send you for a play date with Merrhet!" Amiselle snapped.

"Sounds like fun, but we actually came down to tell you that it might be a good idea to let Jarmony and Katrina know about our interesting situation," Harmon added.

As much as I wanted to avoid giving more bad news that night, I knew they needed to be told what happened.

"Okay, let's get out of here."

The six of us walked up into the hallway in a single file, only to find it empty and dim.

"Well it didn't look like this when we were up here two min-" Harmon began under his breath before Amiselle, who obviously didn't hear, cut him off.

"I guess we assumed too quickly that they'd be up this late... But heart breaking news can wait until a bright, new morning, don't you think?"

Even in the blackness, I could see Macalynn roll her eyes.

"I think what Amiselle means is that there's no point in waking them up for this. Let's just wait until tomorrow."

A small, flickering light then appeared in Harmon's hands, illuminating the place just enough for us to find our rooms.

After I closed my door behind me, I slumped onto the floor against the wall and hugged my knees. The others had no idea how much it took out of me when Macalynn and I sent Merrhet to the fourth dimension. The only way I could convince myself to go through with it was to remember that he was really going to *kill* me, and I wondered how someone who acted like everyone's big brother for three years could actually work with It the entire time. It was all pretty depressing.

I stayed there for at least half an hour, and must have eventually dozed off because when I opened my eyes, the sun was poking out over the trees.

My bones complained like I hadn't moved in days as I stood up, smoothed down my hair, and pulled my cloak over my shoulders. When I opened the door, I saw Katrina, Amiselle, Aaron, and Jarmony all talking on the other side of the room in front of the windows.

As I got closer, it became visible that Jarmony was choking up and Katrina was crying.

"I just can't believe Merrhet would do something like that. I mean, *kill* Lealight? He tried to kill another Summit?" I heard Jarmony say to Aaron, and he nodded solemnly.

"Yeah, he did. We went down there, and he already had lightning swirling around her. She couldn't do anything to defend herself without her Magic. Harmon had to strike him down. Besides, he was never really one of us. He is… or I guess was working with It. Probably sent to kill us in the first place."

"What happened to Dillon?" Katrina cut in.

"Lealight decided to expel him," Amiselle answered very unenthusiastically.

"But why didn't he get sent to the fourth dimension with Merrhet?"

"I don't know why she did what she did. That's something you could ask her."

The four took notice of me when I joined them by the window. "I let him go because we don't know what they may or may not have done to force him into it. Now I'm not defending his choice to betray us in any way, shape, or form, but who knows what his motives were… or if he had any other choice if he wanted to live."

We all looked out the window and over the treetops watching the sun rise higher into the sky.

"Okay, so what's going to happen when people start asking questions like why he got expelled? You can't tell them the truth," Katrina reasoned out loud.

"I told him to tell everyone it was because he caused the fire."

There was another long silence until everyone else started coming out. Pretty soon, all eight of us were standing in a semi circle just staring off into space.

"I'm going to go see Teller Hallsmen today," I spoke up.

"*Why*?" everyone asked simultaneously.

"Look, I'm no more of a fan of her than you all are, but she needs to know what happened so we can find out who our real Water Talent is. Besides, if Merrhet and Dillon were working for **It**, then who knows who else might be? And if anything ever happens we will need all seven Summits."

Everyone looked at the ground, and I knew it was time for me to step up.

"Guys, we can't do anything to change Merrhet and Dillon. They are who they are. We need to let them go and move forward; find out who the seventh Summit has been all along."

No one looked up and I was already nearing the end of my rope for what I could say to them.

"Yesterday... also made me realize how much we all need each other. And the eight of us, or soon to be the nine of us, need look after one another--no matter what happens."

After my first inspirational sentence (because I'm not gifted enough to come up with a few dozen inspirational speeches) almost everyone had tears in their eyes. But then I felt compelled to end with something that sounded a little more like me, and I continued to say: "So if there are any more fake Summits or Charges please speak now, or forever scheme in peace."

Everyone starting laughing, somewhat nervously, but anything was an improvement on the uncomfortable silence. "I'll be back as soon as I can," I said slowly heading toward the stairs.

"Wait," Illydia called. "Why don't you eat something with us before you go?"

"I think this is more important. Maybe when I get ba-"

"Let me rephrase it, then," Harmon interrupted squarely. "What Illydia means is that we're not letting you go until after you eat because it can't be any warmer than thirty degrees out there not even considering the wind and you won't make it halfway through the woods without something hot in you. I don't mind making breakfast, but only if you stay for it."

I paused a few seconds before nodding.

"Alright. I'm sure we're all starving, anyway. Yesterday was an increasingly long day to go without any food."

"Well, I grew the apple tree," Illydia pointed out, and everyone simply looked at her.

"Yesterday was an increasingly long day to go without any food," Amiselle repeated in agreement as she followed Harmon down the stairs. "I'll light the fire."

The rest of us trailed behind the two and when we were about halfway down, Macalynn came up next to me.

"If you absolutely have to go talk to Litheney, then do us all a favor and for once don't let her get away with talking about us like you know she does."

I smiled back.

"Don't worry, I won't. And if all else fails lightning never seems to."

Chapter 10

The warmth from the hot milk I drank with breakfast was annihilated the moment I encountered the biting wind outside of the Citadel. As much as I would've liked to just fly over the trees toward the school, I didn't want to raise any more of a commotion than I was already going to just by being there. So I sucked it up, pulled my cloak tighter around my shoulders, and headed toward the woods. After walking the weaving path to the school, I noticed that the yard was empty.

Good, I thought. *Maybe I can walk through unnoticed.*

Of course the second I closed the gate behind me, I saw the kids walking through the halls stop to look out the window. I kept my gaze focused on the door as more and more perplexed faces watched me walk across the yard towards it. Before I even knocked, a little boy with bright red hair answered. I smiled kindly.

"Hi there, do you think you could go get..."

One of the Air Talent teachers came up behind him. His angry expression from class being interrupted changed when he saw it was me.

"Oh... we weren't expecting you to come today, Summit Lealight," he said.

"I'm sorry to disturb everybody, but I came to see Teller Hallsmen," I told him in the sweetest voice I could manage. He looked surprised. Everyone, and I do mean *everyone*, knew that we didn't get along with her and she downright couldn't stand us. "It's very important," I continued.

He started walking down the hallway. "Okay, I'll go see if she's available right now."

"No," I answered.

He turned back around, now obviously more annoyed than anything else.

"I must speak with her privately."

The teacher sighed, "If you insist. Her office is down this first hall and the second door to the right." I thanked him even though I clearly remembered from my many, many days at the school and everyone moved out of the way as I stepped inside.

When I reached the nearly eight foot tall door that led inside Litheney's office, I tapped gently and waited for a response. But after about sixty seconds no one had come and I thought that maybe they had tiny peepholes or something, so she already knew she wasn't going to like who she saw once she opened it. I knocked on the door again, a little more forcefully. It was promptly yanked open. Litheney stood there with a hand on her hip.

"What do you want?" she blinked a couple times when she saw it was me.

Scratch that peephole theory, everyone.

"Why are you here?" she asked a little less unpleasantly than I had expected.

"I need to talk to you, Li- I mean, Teller Hallsmen," I told her.

Even though the teachers were still busy trying to herd the kids back into class, they stopped and looked our way; probably waiting to see if she would let me in or not. Everyone knew that I could demand she did, but on the flip side, they also knew I wouldn't if she refused.

"I don't know if I-"

"It's very important," I cut in.

She paused as if to consider what I said, and at last answered, "Very well."

She waved me inside, and yelled something to the people in the hallway about getting back to class. Her office wasn't much bigger than my room, about twelve by ten feet. The place had a wooden desk and a few chairs that faced it, along with several bookshelves against the walls and a circular, red rug on the floor.

Litheney paced across the room, closed an open book on the desk before pushing it aside, and sat down at it. She then motioned to a chair in front. I hesitantly joined her, having absolutely no idea where to start or how she would react.

"So?" she finally asked after several seconds of silence.

"There's just a small... problem and I think you need to know about it."

Teller Hallsmen chuckled.

"I figure it's a rather large problem considering you willingly came to see me about it."

Well, she wasn't wrong.

"I don't really know how to put to this," I stammered "but-"

"Do spit it out," she interrupted irritably.

Now *that* sounded more like the Teller we knew and thoroughly hated.

"Okay, well I found out that Merrhet and Dillon weren't who we thought they were when I caught them in my Library last night."

Her eyes grew wide.

"How did they get in?"

I was about to answer, but we ended up saying, "The gem", at the same time.

She shook her head in both disappointment and disbelief.

"That stupid thing. People have *told* them over and over it needed to be destroyed before it fell into the wrong hands, and sure enough it did."

She sighed deeply and looked out a window.

"I'm going to go ahead and assume that you got your Magic back and the fourth dimension has some new residents?"

"Well, one," I answered.

Litheney's eyes darted back to me.

"How did Merrhet get away?"

"He didn't," I replied. "He's somewhere in the fourth dimension now. It's Dillon. I let him go."

She looked pretty ticked.

"*Why*?"

"I didn't-"

"Compassion and pity are *weaknesses* when it comes to situations like this, Lealight. You cannot give them the opportunity to come back."

I don't know what shocked me more: the fact that she just gave me some advice that seemed at least somewhat sincere, or that she just called me by my first name without putting "Summit" in front of it.

We sat quietly for a few minutes before I continued.

"Anyway, I'm positive Merrhet was never our Water Talent and-"

"How do you know?" Teller Hallsmen asked, offended.

"My major hint was when he almost killed me with lightning," I answered her.

She looked a little more than surprised.

"Alright then... what are you suggesting? We go tell everyone about what happened and have another test?"

"We can't do that," I said.

She thought about it for a few moments and then sighed again.

"I agree. So how do you want to find this person?"

I wasn't about to tell her this, but that's the reason I was there. I, once again, had no idea.

"Well, I can slowly pull kids from the Water Talent classes that are around your age and track down the ones who just graduated. But in order to cover it up, I'd need at least a week," Litheney suggested. I thought it sounded like our only option that wouldn't result in disaster.

"Okay... Do you want me to come back next-"

"Probably not. You and I are both going to get millions of questions as to why you were here in the first place. No need to add to it. I'll come to you."

I nodded and stood up to head home. When I was halfway out of the room, I paused. I had been debating whether or not to tell her about that chest Merrhet had mentioned several times. For some reason, I had thought she would know what it was. Ten seconds later, I found myself blurting out, "Um, when Merrhet was holding the lightning he kept saying over and over that I better give him a chest. And something about how we won't be able to protect ourselves, and once we're gone, It's going to… come back. You wouldn't have any idea what chest he's talking about, would you?"

She at first looked shocked, then horrified, but caught herself quickly, and calmly said, "I've never heard of any chest" And get this--she actually looked *concerned* when she continued. "And you all have nothing to worry about. He must be bluffing. Disregard what he told you."

How's that for someone who obviously knows more than they're letting on but thinks I'm stupid enough to let it go?

"Okay then" I answered apprehensively. "I'll see you next week."

With that, I closed the door behind me and walked briskly out of the school.

Chapter 11

To my relief, no one was outside. So I was instead greeted with the same bone chilling wind that I had encountered earlier. Dreading the long trudge back to the Citadel, I decided to wait until I'd been walking through the woods for about two minutes before just floating upward and weaving my way through the branches airborne. Some might call it lazy, and those some are probably right. Of course, I did have the excuse that I promised everyone else I'd be back as soon as possible, so I went with that. No more than a couple minutes later, I was hovering over the roof of the Citadel. After landing in front of the staircase, I headed back inside, where there was nothing but quiet.

Really? They ditched me *again*?

I walked down the hallway and into the great room--no one.

"*Hello*?" I yelled.

"Good, you're back!" Amiselle stood up. "You need to come see this."

"What is it?" I asked her, not being able to imagine things getting any more... exciting than they had already become since yesterday.

"Just come on," she answered as she opened the door to Merrhet's room.

I stopped in my tracks. We never went in each other's rooms. Even though he wasn't there anymore, it just seemed wrong.

Now I know what you're thinking. I was worried about invading the privacy of someone who recently tried to *kill* me. Well, I think I won the award of Biggest Goody Two Shoes *Ever*.

"Guys, Lealight's back," Amiselle said into the room, and Illydia and Harmon appeared in the doorway.

"You won't believe what we found!" said Harmon as they waved for me to come in.

I was about to start giving a lecture about how this wasn't right, blah, blah, blah, and what did they hope to gain from this, yadda, yadda, yadda, when something caught my eye.

All of our rooms were the same: stone walls and floors with a wooden nightstand and four poster bed. But there was definitely something different in there.

My curiosity eventually got the better of me, and I joined everyone inside--immediately realizing what was wrong. On the entire left side of the room, scrolls were shoved pretty much everywhere from being neatly stacked on bookshelves to lying in random piles on the floor.

"What the--where did all these come from?" I asked.

"Don't look at us--we didn't think they existed anymore except in your Library," Macalynn answered as she stopped rummaging through the shelves and moved to stare out the window.

"Well, yeah... but I only have maybe one case of these things. You saw when you were down there. They were all replaced with books a long time ago just like they were in the Village."

"For goodness' sake, Lealight," Aaron rolled his eyes. "First, this is a lot more than one case. Second, how could you not notice *every single* scroll down there disappearing?"

"But none of them were missing yesterday. Before I saw Merrhet last night, I checked the shelf to make sure everything was there because of the fire."

No one answered for several seconds.

"Well if they're not from your Library," Jarmony chimed in "then the only other explanation is Merrhet wrote them himself, or they belong to... It. And if that's the case, maybe this is how he knew where that gem was."

I took down a random one, undid the ties, and unrolled it to find a map of what looked like nothing more than the first dimension. But when I inspected it closer, I saw many series of winding and interlocking lines drawn as tunnels leading all throughout the Village that seemed to connect the Citadel to the school.

"What's that?" Macalynn asked and only then did I notice she had come back over and was standing right beside me.

"I... don't know," I began as everyone else moved toward us to see what she was talking about. "I've never seen anything like it before, which means that Jarmony's probably right. I don't see who else it could've come from besides It. And the way it's been handled... how it seems like it's been rolled and unrolled a hundred times... and the way some ink looks to be as old as the Universe itself and some like it was just added yesterday... it makes me nervous about what Merrhet was doing all this time when we weren't watching."

Aaron sighed and put his arm around my shoulders. "You have nothing to be worried about. We'll get rid of these. Take them all out somewhere and burn them so no one will ever find them again."

I shook my head. "We can't do that. There might be something in here about how Merrhet ever sabotaged Litheney's Test in the first place or where he got a hold of that gem... Or maybe even where It is right now."

The others looked at me apprehensively.

"Do we *want* to know that?" asked Katrina.

I looked to the floor.

"Look, Merrhet is pretty much concrete proof that It is still out there somewhere, right?"

They nodded.

"And so if he sent him then that must mean he's closer than anyone thought he could ever get again. I know it's not something we want to think about, but the fact of the matter is that it's our job to be ready if it happens. I'm not saying it will, though. Just because he's still around doesn't mean he's *definitely* coming back or that he's strong enough to. But still... we need to be safe and keep them somewhere we'd know automatically if they were missing. And even if we reduce them to ashes I'd never be one hundred percent sure that no one can ever see them again. We don't know what It is capable of after all this time."

Seven pairs of unsure and pretty freaked out eyes stared at me for several seconds before Illydia answered.

"Yeah, she's right. We need to keep them somewhere safe for now."

"Library?" Harmon asked.

"I guess so," was all I managed.

Chapter 12

By midafternoon, I had all forty five of them back in my Library stuffed in a formally abandoned corner where I honestly hoped I'd never have to touch them again. After I climbed back up the stairs, I saw everyone either standing around looking out the windows or sitting against the wall and staring off into space. I joined them. No one seemed to want to go to the third dimension or to the Village, and since Merrhet and Dillon had kindly reconstructed the Citadel for us, there wasn't much that needed to be accomplished.

"So, what do we do now?" Macalynn finally asked.

"Beats me," Harmon answered her.

"This is truly sad," Amiselle groaned. "We're the Seven, I mean, um, six *freaking* Summits. We are supposed to be these people born with amazing Talent and ability and we're supposed to run this entire Universe and keep it safe. And here we are, sitting around doing nothing."

"Well, I think we have a pretty decent excuse!" Aaron snapped. "We found out one of our members never actually was one of us when he tried to *kill* Magic-less Lealight!"

I couldn't help but take that personally. When Harmon came up behind Merrhet and struck him with lightning to save me, I was too focused on getting that gem and thinking of a way out to realize how weak and helpless the whole thing made me look. And I *don't* do weak and helpless.

My blood started boiling. If Merrhet was going to try to kill me, he could have at least done the honorable thing and let us have a fair fight so I could *rip his traitorous head off*. But no, he had to go find some stupid Magic draining gem instead! So he was not only going to electrocute me, but also make me look pathetic in front of everyone while I fried. And that was *not* okay.

"Don't try to put the blame on anyone, Aaron. None of us could have possibly known what was going on," Illydia said in a calm voice that sounded strained.

"I'm not trying to blame her!" he insisted unconvincingly and I knew it was time for me to say something before stuff started to, literally, fly.

"Guys, just cut it out. We're not going to accomplish anything by sitting here accusing each other. Now, no one had any reason to suspect what Merrhet was doing, and that's why he got away with it for so long. But he's gone now and we have got to accept that he *never* was one of us, and that Teller Hallsmen is going to secretly conduct another Test and we're going to have our results by next week."

My last words hung in the air as everyone took them in.

"So basically our real Water Talent is going to be here... probably within the next seven days?" Macalynn asked.

"Pretty much. And we can't be talking about Merrhet when he or she comes. Keep in mind this person is already coming in at a disadvantage because they didn't know who they were as soon as we did. They're going to need a little help getting used to all of it," I answered her. "In other words, don't go right to the mastering stuff, okay?"

Macalynn then started laughing. "Remember what happened with your last thing in Air, Lealight? That was hilarious!" I rolled my eyes. Whenever she hears anything even remotely related to when we were all still trying to master our Talents, she always had to giggle about that.

"Really? Hilarious? I was about to kill you after what you did!"

"What'd she do?" Aaron asked.

"You guys seriously don't remember the whole flying ordeal?"

"I'm sure they do, but we never told them about this story," Macalynn answered before anyone else could.

"And by the look on your face, trust me, we would've remembered if you'd ever said anything to us to about it," Harmon added.

I glared at him before I gave in and began with, "Fine. Okay, so you all do remember how terrified I was of flying. And how Macalynn kept *bugging me* about it every day until I made the huge mistake of agreeing to go out on the roof with her... like, two years ago."

They nodded and Macalynn continued the story.

"Of course when we were up there, she started to back down *again*, so I decided to give her a little nudge in the right direct-"

"Oh, you gave me '*little nudge*' all right," I interrupted. "Right off the edge of the roof!"

Everyone started cracking up.

"In my defense, I had six Talents to master and you guys already knew the basics of yours," I said above their laughter.

"Point taken," Amiselle answered. "But it's still pretty funny. Oh, I would have loved to have seen your face!"

"Well, you learn pretty quickly when you're free falling from eighty feet up" I told her. "And of course you want to torch the person standing back on the roof laughing her head off, *Macalynn*."

She smiled innocently and the others started chuckling again before Aaron thankfully changed the subject.

"Remember when I trapped Harmon underground?"

"Come on! Don't tell that story," he groaned.

"Please, everyone has to be embarrassed sometimes," Illydia pointed out in an as-a-matter-of-fact tone with a smirk, mimicking him.

"Anyway," Aaron continued. "I was out on the yard with Jarmony when he opened the front door and apparently decided to play a prank on me or something."

"Yep, I came over and shocked him when he wasn't paying attention. He was so startled, he accidentally flipped the ground from underneath me, and I fell at least eight feet down," Harmon continued--doing air quotes around the word "*accidentally.*"

"And no matter what we did Jarmony and I couldn't get it to flip back over, so we went to find Lealight. But of course, she wasn't around."

"I was in my Library most of the time back then, genius," I retorted. "But when I ran into you guys in the hallway, you were freaking out that you had accidentally trapped him underground and it had been..."

"Half an *hour*," Harmon finished my sentence.

"And after the three of us finally got you out, you looked like you were going to hit Aaron and me with lightning," Jarmony finished.

"I would've!" Amiselle and Illydia said at the exact same time.

We all laughed again, and for the next several hours continued to tell stories. Some of the most popular ones being the time Katrina froze Macalynn solid and when Illydia grew flowers all over Jarmony--most of them a deep pink. It was actually pretty sad how many mishaps we could think of.

By the time we retold at least six embarrassing moments of each person in the room, the last of the sun's rays was disappearing below the mountains.

"I think that just about covers everything funny that's happened during the past three years" I said as we watched it disappear from the floor of the great room.

Everyone sat in silence by the glow of the candlelight for a while before Harmon spoke up.

"Not that this isn't fun or anything, but I believe we're right back at asking ourselves what do we do now?"

I shrugged and looked out the window.

"There's not much to do until Litheney finds the real Water Talent Summit. I mean, it's a little late to go to the Village, so…"

I stopped dead and felt my eyes widen in disbelief.

"Lealight?" Katrina asked after a few seconds.

I didn't respond.

"*Lealight?*" Amiselle persisted. I heard her and the others shuffling over in my direction. They weren't paying any attention to what I was looking at. "You feeling okay? Are you sick or something?"

I shook my head, but when I tried to speak nothing came out.

"Well, then what's wrong?" Aaron kept on. "You're paler than a ghost."

"If you'd quit *gawking* at me and look out the stupid window, you'd see *exactly* what's wrong!" I finally snapped. The others looked taken aback before glancing over their shoulders to see what was freaking me out so much that I'd lash out at them like that.

They figured it out pretty quickly. Macalynn screamed and sank onto the floor next to me. Everyone else was too shocked and mortified to do anything. Don't get me wrong, I wanted to say something reassuring, and I wanted to step up and tell everyone what we needed to do next. But I still couldn't find my voice and felt too scared to move--much less lead. Why is this, you may ask?

Well, let me sum it up for you. Huge blankets of darkness were slowly covering the sky--coming from all directions over the trees and gathering above the Citadel.

Clouds, the sign of It's return, were rolling in.

Chapter 13

Well, everyone, there you have it. It was not only alive, but was apparently there. In *my* Universe. For the first time in over *four hundred years*. Great, thanks a lot Veronica.

The eight of us stayed there completely horrified for what seemed like hours watching the Clouds appear everywhere, covering everything and leaving us in total darkness.

"Oh my g--how on--Lealight, what do we do?" Amiselle asked in a shaky voice--sending seven pairs of terrified eyes toward me.

I sat there racking my brain for an answer that wouldn't throw everyone into an even worse panic. Fortunately, I was jolted by yelling coming from the edge of the woods. There were so many people coming toward the Citadel from the path at one time it was impossible at make out what they were saying. Then the unmistakable yelling of Teller Hallsmen silenced the crowd. "Everyone stop it! Go back!"

"Are you totally *blind*?" someone's voice rose up. "There are *Clouds* in the sky! That means It is here! He's going to-"

"You think they don't know that?" Litheney interrupted.

"Of course they know that!" another person snapped. "The question is if they know what to do about it!"

That was enough for me. I spoke in the most confident voice I could manage at the time.

"Everyone out, now. Meet up at the head of the group, get their attention, and then follow my lead."

Seven consecutive nods followed my instructions before Aaron and Jarmony jumped out of a window and skated down the tower. Okay, in retrospect, I guessed I should have added "once we're on the ground" to my "get their attention". But with no time to turn back, I stood up, grabbed the shocked Macalynn by the arm, and ran up to the roof as everyone else took the easy way by heading down the stairs.

When we reached the top, I threw her off first (sweet revenge) and then followed closely behind as people started to notice us, the guys sliding down the Citadel, and the rest running out the front door. How ironic. I hated being pinpointed and singled out, but there I was falling from the top of an eighty foot tall tower.

Macalynn quickly got her bearings, and started to gather air around herself as I landed next to Litheney and the others joined us.

"Everyone, listen up!" I yelled as loudly as I could.

No one did of course. They were too busy screaming.

"Everyone, *LISTEN*!" I said again, still to no avail.

I then decided just talking to them wasn't going to work; especially since they were under the whole "we're all gonna die" impression.

So I shined a blinding light into the crowd and shouted once more, "*EVERYONE, STOP PANICKING AND LISTEN TO US*!"

The people finally stopped yelling and shielded their eyes from the only light visible under the Clouded sky.

"Now, everyone needs to go home--lock the shutters and doors. Don't leave unless absolutely necessary. That means school is canceled for the time being."

Teller Hallsmen shot me a look that read "You-can't-make-that-decision-without-consulting-me" but I really couldn't have cared less about offending her right then and there.

"But you do need to have people that can come through the woods and tell us if there's an emergency. Have at least one person on twenty-four/seven and we will also be coming everyday from now on unless I personally come and tell you otherwise." I chose to leave out the option "Or you know, we get killed by It" because it seemed like it just might stir up panic again.

"What will we do if-"

"We'll deal with that when it happens," Illydia interrupted the woman who'd begun to ask the question we were all dreading-- referring to when It himself attacked.

And his most famous battle strategy? Freaking out the entire Universe by capturing anywhere from one to one hundred people before gracing the Summits with his presence.

"Where is Summit Merrhet?" another person asked.

I figured since It had suddenly showed up, I couldn't keep the fact that we didn't have a Water Talent from them anymore.

"We found out Merrhet was a... was a fake. He was never the Summit's Water Talent, never a Talent, period. He was working with It this entire time as a spy of some kind, and we sent him to the fourth dimension."

There was a mixture of murmurs and gasps after I finished. And of all people, Litheney backed me up.

"So needless to say, the true Water Talent Summit was never realized and I'm going to begin the Testing tomorrow morning at the school. All Water Talents between the ages of eleven and nineteen need to be there no later than six."

After the whispering died down, we all stood there in the dark stillness before she finally continued to yell, "And you all heard her, go on!"

At her command, the entire crowd turned and practically ran down the path. I guess Teller Hallsmen just has that effect on people.

After the sound of footsteps from everyone ceased, I expected her chew me out for something (that's just what she does when she's ticked off). Instead, she said simply, "Since everyone knows about Merrhet, I should be able to Test everyone tomorrow and give you the results by evening."

The others looked relatively surprised that she didn't start complaining about incompetence or obliviousness or any other oversized, ill-meaning word that ends with an –s sound. I guessed since I went and saw her that morning she had seemed slightly less bitter toward us. Hey, maybe next year we could exchange Holiday cards.

"Good. The sooner they come, the better," Amiselle replied. "We need all seven of us here now more than ever."

She nodded and hastily said, "Agreed then. Have a good night."

She turned to follow the crowd.

"Figures how the Clouds had to roll in to make her more pleasant than usual," Harmon pointed out when we were back inside.

First, only he would try to be funny at the start of a full scale apocalypse. Second, no one even smiled at his attempt to make us laugh. We stood at the bottom of the staircase for a while when Aaron suddenly burst out saying everything we were all thinking.

"Fantastic, just freaking *fantastic*. Now not only do we have almost a thousand people relying on us to lead and keep them from getting, oh I don't know, *abducted*, we have to avoid being killed ourselves! Who knows how powerful he's gotten? Who knows what he's capable of? How do we know if he's not in this tower right now?"

Thank you so much for getting us to picture that lovely scenario, Aaron.

"That's the thing, we don't know," I answered. "But freaking out is going to get us nowhere, so the best thing we can do now is to wait until tomorrow and get the results of the Test. We'll help whoever that person is catch up, and go from there. It's all we can do, really."

The others nodded in agreement and, after wordlessly agreeing no one felt like dinner, we all went to face the stairs.

Two minutes later, everyone else had gone into their rooms and I was just standing outside my door. I didn't think I could sleep after what happened that day, so I decided to go back to the Library... which of course looked like a twister had come through with all of the extra scrolls just lying around in that corner and some, having already found their way out of the stack, rolling around in the middle of the floor. I wanted to just pick them up, plunk them back on top of the pile, and forget about it. But I knew the whole purpose of not torching them in the first place was to see if there were any with useful information, and that required sorting through them. So I reluctantly spent the next several hours unrolling each and every one. Almost all of them made little to no sense or were too faded to read anymore. They stayed in the corner. Of course there was that map which continued to unnerve me. I decided to keep that one around until I figured out what it was. But carrying a foot long scroll everywhere isn't realistic. So I gently tore around the edges of the drawing until it came out. I folded it up, and slid it in my pocket along with the gem. After I finally finished the long and disappointing process by placing the last one on top of the stack, I counted to make sure I had them all.

But only forty four of the forty five were there. I started panicking and turned around to see if it was spinning on the floor like some of the others had been. Finding nothing, I took several steps away from the corner. I located it within ten seconds of hitting my head on the edge of a bookcase after stumbling over the thing that was indeed rolling along the floorboards. Almost positive I'd just given myself a bruise that would be pretty impossible to explain to the others with one ounce of dignity, I picked up the scroll and untied the string around it. I saw the first two words of the title and I immediately stopped before rolling it back up. It'd read _The Gem_. I had already seen three others beginning exactly that way that turned out to be a waste of time. And I'd changed my mind and decided I wanted nothing to do with any information Merrhet might have used when he tried to kill us, regardless of what it was. So I tossed it with the others and started making my way out of the Library.

Once the door had slammed shut behind me; I lit all of the candles in the nearly pitch black great room and looked out the window. Stupidly hoping the sky would look different than it had a few hours earlier, I was shocked for a moment at the sight of Clouds overhead that completely blocked the moon and stars I could usually see early in the morning. I decided there'd be no point in doing anything productive (not that there was much) without any of the others, so I just stayed there and stared out into the unchanging blackness for the next two hours.

Chapter 14

"Hey, what's up?" someone asked from the other side of the room.

After staring into space for so long, the sound of another person's voice quickly snapped me back into reality.

I spun around ready to squash someone with a giant rock only to find Illydia, Amiselle, and Aaron walking over.

"Clouds," I answered. "Still Clouds."

They joined me over by the window.

"Really, you don't say," Aaron said sarcastically, for which, Illydia punched him hard on the shoulder and gave him her signature "What-The-Heck-Is-*Wrong*-With-You?!" glare.

We all stared out the window lost in our own thoughts for a while before Amiselle asked me, "You okay?"

Well, a horrible monster who disappeared over four hundred years ago just popped up out of nowhere, and you want to know who he's gonna go after first? Us. How could I be okay?

"I think we all know that none of us are," I began. "I mean, there's no use lying to each other. If **It** attacked us, right here, right now, then we'd be done for."

Everyone else was starting to come out and was gathering around as I spoke.

"Not because we aren't powerful enough, not because we don't have enough practice with teamwork, none of that. It's because we've let Merrhet accomplish his mission, or at least part of it, which was to make us not trust each other anymore."

The others all looked at their shoes. I really hoped these early morning inspirational speeches didn't become a regular thing.

"I know I said this yesterday, but then, I was talking about us getting over the situation for the sake of our real Water Talent. Now, I'm talking about us moving on for the sake of every single person in the Universe. I've read stuff about It in some of the books in the Library. It's not very specific, but it does say that last time he attacked the Summits first, and they were alone. He probably assumed he'd get rid of the seven people who stood in his way and then move on to destroy everything. And this time, he's going to be smarter, stronger, and more powerful than all of us combined. In order to get out of this alive, there're some are things that need to change. Any ideas?"

Everybody was silent for a few moments.

"Let Merrhet and Dillon go. Remember they were never really... who we thought they were." Katrina finally said--not looking up.

"Good--no more dwelling on the past. Anything else you guys can come up with?"

"When our real Water Talent comes in, they are most likely going to be twice as scared as we are. It's our job to work with them to make sure they can get adjusted here, quickly," Harmon added.

I nodded at his response.

"Mhmm, There's more."

Wow, I was really starting to get the whole "leadership" thing.

"On that note, we can't be freaking out. It does no good, and when people see us like that, they'll be like that. We can't count ourselves out of this battle," Illydia answered confidently.

"Excellent. And the last one I'm going to cover," I responded, slinging my arms around Amiselle on my left and Aaron on my right. Everybody caught on quickly, and we soon stood with all our arms around each other in a huddle.

"All traces of distrust, regrets, doubt, and everything related must go now. From here on out, we're all each other has got and no one gets left behind or given up on, no matter the circumstances. We cannot lie to each other, and we will need to watch each other's backs. And until that sky is bright blue again, we will never, ever stop fighting. Agreed?"

I watched as one by one everyone's frowns turned to determined smirks.

"Agreed," they all said at the same time.

We separated, turned back toward the window, and looked at the Clouds, which had imposed horror and confusion less than five minutes ago. Now, I don't know you all, but I was only thinking one thing. Tragedy, betrayal, plus annoying yet touching monologues equals a very overdone soap opera. And that's what my life had turned into over the past two days. It's incredibly spooky when you come to a realization like that, everyone.

"So now that we've established that, what are we supposed to do today?" Amiselle asked.

"We wait until Teller Hallsmen comes by with the results of the Test," Illydia answered her.

"I still don't get how it works," said Aaron "I mean, it's just a piece of paper she asks you to read."

"I don't think we're supposed to get it," Macalynn shrugged. "It's just the way-"

Her sentence was cut off by knocking on the door, after which, everyone tensed up.

"I'm going to go see who it is," I said after a few seconds of silence. "Be prepared to leave now if we have to."

The others nodded, so I paced toward the stairs.

When I turned around the bend, I took the steps two or three at a time--thinking that there were no ends as to what could happen now that It was there. At the bottom of the stairs, I yanked the door open expecting to find maybe a ten year old kid there crying and telling us to come down immediately. Instead, I found myself looking up at Litheney Hallsmen.

"Good morning," she said. "May I come in? I have news for the six of you."

I nodded and moved aside for her.

"We thought you'd still be Testing," I began. "I know the Clouds cover the sun so you can't really tell the exact time... but it's still pretty early."

"All thirty two children showed up at six this morning and it's close to nine now," she looked around absently. "I told you all I'd be coming this evening because I thought I'd need time to decipher the answers, but something... unexpected happened."

Well, something "unexpected" can go either way.

"Where is everyone else? You all need to hear this," she continued.

"Upstairs, follow me," I answered.

Since Teller Hallsmen didn't have a Talent, I couldn't exactly fly or teleport up to get the others. So I was saddled with having to walk with her in silence for the five stories. When we reached the top, everyone looked puzzled, and frankly so was I.

"I thought you were Testing everyone today," Harmon said as we walked over.

"Yes, I did. And I finished about half an hour ago. I have your results," Litheney replied.

Everyone raised an eyebrow.

"How did you get to everyone so quickly?" Amiselle asked skeptically.

"Like I just told Lealight, all thirty two children showed up at six this morning and I finished in only three hours because something unexpected happened," she replied irritably.

"And that would be..."

"I could eliminate very quickly, and now, I can assure you all that the Water Talent Summit does not attend school or live in the Village."

Well, that bites.

"How do you know?" Macalynn asked.

Litheney paused as if she was coming up with a response.

"I cannot speak of anything related to how the Test is given," she finally said. "But I can tell you that this person doesn't exist among all thirty two Water Talents who attend or just graduated from school. I'll let you fit the pieces together."

We were all silent.

If all of the Water Talented kids at the Village weren't it, then the only other Water Talent who could even possibly be one of us was-

"I know who it is," I said, promptly sending all eyes in my direction.

"I figured you might," Litheney said--actually smiling.

"The only eligible Water Talented person who didn't show up this morning is Katrina," I turned toward her. "You must be the Summit's Water Talent."

She looked horrified. Gee, thanks.

"What? No I'm not!" she practically yelled.

"Do not count yourself out, Katrina" Teller Hallsmen said while pulling a thick, black textbook out of her bag. "Let's find out for sure."

Chapter 15

The thing ended up being so heavy that Katrina sat back against the windowsill. She stared at the pages opened to her blankly before looking up at Amiselle.

"It's alright, Katrina," she smiled unconvincingly. "Just read it so we can clear this mess up."

Amiselle then moved to stand beside her but Litheney abruptly said, "You all have to stand back."

"Why? Is your book going to explode or something?" Harmon glowered at her.

"That is just how it's done."

Litheney soon wore a glare that was admittedly more frightening than Harmon's.

"And I didn't invent this, I simply have to carry it out. If you just step back this could go a lot faster and I would be much obliged."

We looked around at each other before hesitantly backing away, leaving Katrina and Litheney standing alone. Everyone was silent for a while before she spoke up.

"Whenever you are ready, Katrina."

She looked at us nervously before averting her gaze down at the book in her lap and beginning to read the page. The eight of us stood in an awkward silence waiting for her to look back up. She stared at Litheney as if to say "Okay… and?"

"Oh, did you finish it?" Litheney seemed strangely detached as she took the book back from Katrina. We all simply looked at her and marveled at her seemingly utter disregard of how much it must have weighed. "And surely you remember the question you are supposed to answer."

She nodded.

"Uh... yeah, it's about some box. A small, ancient chest that's been lost for over four hundred years. It's also really important to a particular-"

"Exactly right," Litheney abruptly, and very nervously, cut in.

My eyes grew wide in disbelief as she immediately shoved the cinderblock of a book back into her bag. Litheney Hallsmen must have thought I was a total idiot. She said the day before she knew nothing about the chest Merrhet was snooping around for and now here she was trying to pass off a paragraph about it as the Test. And I didn't exactly think there was some other ancient box lost for hundreds of years lying around the dimension.

"Who?" Aaron asked only to be silenced when Harmon elbowed him hard in the ribs.

"What the heck was that supposed to be?" he demanded.

"I do not know what you are talking about."

"That was *not* the Test."

"Of course it was!" she snapped. "You dare call me a liar? Like I just told you all, I did not invent this, I just have to give it, alright?"

We were silent.

"Anyway, there you have it," Litheney hastily continued. "the real Water Talent Summit. You all might want to go down to the

Village later today to tell everyone. And now if you'll excuse me, I must be go-"

"I'll show you out," I interrupted irritably, much to the Teller's very clear distress.

Everyone looked my way, obviously not surprised. We all knew something wasn't right with her. She made it pretty blatant, too. It wouldn't take a genius to figure out someone acting so flighty and frantic was hiding something. And no one spoke up as the two of us headed toward the stairs. Once I was sure the others couldn't hear, I snapped.

"Honestly, how stupid do you think I am?"

She looked shocked by my tone. I had never talked to her in the way she spoke to us before.

"Did you think I couldn't figure it out? That I would just let it go? You have *a lot* of explaining to do, Litheney. First, you and I both know that Harmon is right. That little story you gave Katrina about the chest I mentioned to you yesterday that you said you knew absolutely *nothing of* was not the normal Test. You are trying to hide something important from us, and I will not stand for it. And aside from that issue, you are also not telling me the truth about the chest itself. Cutting off Katrina right before she said who the thing was important to was clearly intentional. So Litheney, explain yourself."

It took everything I had to hold back from slapping her when she started laughing.

"I never thought of you as stupid, Lealight. In fact, I believe you're owed an apology. It was actually thought you wouldn't catch on soon enough. Of course I knew you would, but my opinion doesn't matter all that much, I suppose."

What the heck was she talking about?

"Anyway, you all are correct. That was not the normal Test, but I am not lying to you. Katrina truly is the Water Talent Summit. And I know that chest like the back of my hand. I'll tell you everything there is to know about it when you bring me what's inside. Then I will be happy to *explain myself* to you. Now are we done here?"

I wanted to demand she tell me what she knew immediately, but something about her expression and tone said she was telling me the truth. This was something she couldn't elaborate on even if she wanted to. So when we reached the bottom of the stairs, I nodded and she left without another word. Note to self: find the suddenly un-imaginary chest and track down Teller Cuckoo later.

"Hey, what happened?" Illydia asked from around the corner.

Great, had she heard that?

"Nothing," I answered. "It's just-"

"You said, and I quote, 'we cannot lie to each other' about ten minutes ago," she interrupted with her hands on her hips. "Are you going to make me call you a hypocrite?"

I sighed in exasperation. Illydia had a tendency to use things *I* say against *me*.

"No."

She smiled triumphantly.

"Well then, let's go back upstairs and you can explain to everyone."

She was also like the annoying older sister I never had sometimes.

"Did they hear?" I asked her.

"No, but I did. And I just want to say that woman is a self-absorbed, no good *liar*."

I couldn't help but smile at that.

Everyone was waiting at the top of the stairs, including Katrina, who still looked thoroughly terrified. Well, I guess I'd be too if the Universe's doomsday was suddenly my problem and I wasn't expecting it. Oh wait, I *wasn't*.

"So?" Macalynn asked. "We know you didn't offer to spend a couple extra minutes with *her* because you felt like being nice."

I looked at the floor.

"It's... kind of a long story depending on how much you guys heard two nights ago when Merrhet was in my Library."

"We've got time," said Harmon.

And so I told them everything. From when Merrhet insisted upon the chest up until right then when Teller Hallsmen said that in order to get an explanation, I'd need to bring what's inside of it to her.

"And as if our lives aren't complicated enough," Aaron began. "Now Litheney's practically demanding some random box and we don't know what it looks like or have any idea where it is or-"

"Enough with the "we don't knows". They're not helping" Amiselle interrupted.

"Well," Katrina spoke for the first time since she found out who she was. "Since Teller Hallsmen only told Lealight, then my guess is it's in her Library somewhere."

I was pretty embarrassed that someone who was so incredibly horrified a few minutes ago came up with the first reasonable theory instead of me.

"It's a good place to start," I answered. "And that book you've been reading I can probably take back, Katrina. It's going to get very below you, very quickly now that you know who you are."

She frowned.

"I guess. But how am I supposed to know how to-"

"Don't worry, you already know beyond the basics so everything else is going to come really easily with practice. You'll see," Harmon tried to assure her.

Katrina still looked unconvinced, but I didn't have the energy to give another inspirational speech right then. But because I'm a gutless jellyfish, I continued with: "Of course if it makes you more comfortable, then you can come down with me and I can show you some of the stuff you're working with now."

Everyone just looked at me for a few seconds. I tried to ignore them.

"I thought only you were allowed inside the Library," said Katrina.

"I guess that's how it's always been just because of how the door is. But technically, it belongs to me and I can let any of you guys in if I choose to. And everyone else saw it when Merrhet was down there because the door didn't close behind me, anyway."

"Mhmm. We decided we ought to go inside when we heard screaming," Aaron added.

Nice critical thinking, everyone. Very impressive.

"Well, are you okay with me coming with you?" Katrina asked.

"Or forever scheme in peace, remember?" I answered. "And if anyone comes or if something happens or *whatever*, break down the door if you have to."

Aaron and Harmon looked a little too okay with the idea. Alright, I probably shouldn't have said that.

"I meant that as a last resort. Please knock on it before breaking and entering," I clarified.

"I know that! Why would you think-" Harmon tried to defend himself, only to be interrupted by Amiselle, Illydia, and Jarmony all speaking simultaneously.

"Because it sounds like something you and Aaron would do."

We all laughed at that, but their glares silenced us.

"On that note," said Macalynn. "You guys should go now before something does happen."

Really hoping she didn't just jinx the situation, I went over to the door with Katrina tagging behind me. When it flew open, she leaped back in surprise.

"Yeah, it opens out. Watch out for that," I warned her.

She stared at me as if to say "Thank you for that slightly late tidbit of information", but let it go as we walked downstairs.

Chapter 16

"I can't understand any of this, Lealight," Katrina complained for the thousandth time in twenty minutes.

"Hold on a second," I answered her for the thousandth time in twenty minutes.

I had been ransacking every shelf, looking under every rug, and even floating upward to feel around the ceiling for some secret compartment. Yeah, I was getting pretty desperate at that point. But I only found pieces of wood and one spider, which shortly became a green spot of guts on the floor. For all I knew this thing could be hidden under the ancient floorboards... or invisible.

I groaned and slumped into a chair.

"Oh, um, I'm sorry. Am I distracting you?"

"No, Katrina. You're fine. It's not your fault. It's just that I've been in this place almost every day for the past three years, and I've never seen any chest"

"But we'll find it eventually," Katrina said encouragingly from the other side of the Library.

"That's the problem," I responded. "We don't know if eventually will be soon enough."

She paused. "Well, everything usually works itself out in the end."

I don't know about you, but perkiness in a situation like *that* made me want to claw someone's eyes out.

Noticing my irritation, she quickly changed the subject.

"This whole day feels weird, you know? Like it's nothing but a dream," she looked at the floor. "I can't even read this stuff, how am I supposed to catch up with you guys?"

I sighed. It looked like I might as well be giving those lengthy and annoying inspirational speeches every hour on the hour.

"The idea certainly takes a while to get used to. But you will, and if there's one thing I figured out from all the hours studying this stuff--it's never as hard as it looks. You learn a lot more a lot faster by doing anyway. But... what do you mean you can't read it?"

I stood up and walked over to where Katrina was leaning against the wall with one of the books in her lap. Shortly after sitting down next to her and seeing the first sentence of the page, I started laughing.

"What?" she asked.

"Well, no wonder you can't read it. This book's not written in English, Katrina."

She stared at me blankly.

"They must've missed it when everything was translated some couple hundred years ago. It's in one of those ancient languages. Like here, the first line on this page is talking about traveling between the dimensions."

"Wow... Lealight, you can actually speak this?" Katrina asked in disbelief.

"You're joking right? No, I only remember a few phrases and letters from this code you can use to translate in some other book down here. If I found it again, I could tell you what the rest says but without it I can't read anything past that line any better than you can."

"Oh," was her response. "Well, if it's not in English I guess I better find something that is."

"That would be helpful," I answered and she smiled weakly before faint knocking came from the door. We stayed there just staring at each other for a few seconds before standing up, putting the book back, and pacing towards the staircase. The closer we got, the more nervous I became. Even though I'd been expecting we'd need to leave at some point, I didn't think it would be so soon.

"We have a visitor," said Macalynn when the door opened.

Reading my mind, Katrina groaned.

"What does Teller Hallsmen want *now*?"

Macalynn shook her head.

"It's not Litheney. I don't know who it is. They're asking for Summit Lealight."

My eyebrows rose, but she just shrugged and motioned for us to go with her.

As the three of us moved through the great room, I started to hear muffled voices and sobbing drifting up from the front door. That sent me walking slightly ahead of Katrina and Macalynn down the stairs as fast as I could.

"Calm down, you're safe here," I heard Illydia say as we reached the bottom.

"Look, here they are," Harmon added, motioning toward Macalynn, Katrina, and I as we joined everyone standing around the front door.

"What's going o-," I began only to stop myself when I saw who was there.

Four of the kids from our groups back at the Talented School were on our yard. Two boys and two girls, all with horrible, scared expressions. I only recognized one of them by her light brown, tousled curls and now solemn green eyes.

"What happened, Isetha?"

She immediately burst into tears and the older girl I remembered seeing in Amiselle's group knelt down to comfort her.

"Our families are... gone," one of the boys answered for her.

"What do you mean *gone*?" Aaron asked dumbfounded.

"Our parents, brothers, and sisters--all of them just vanished last night," said the older girl who was still trying to console Isetha. "They disappeared right after the Clouds rolled in, and we haven't seen them since."

Excuse me for being insensitive, but all I was thinking of at the time was if **It** could already abduct, he was a lot stronger than I had thought. And everyone knew the last time people started disappearing, he attacked no more than a day or two later. Now, please excuse me for being a pessimist by thinking, *we're all screwed.*

"Why didn't you go to the school and tell Lith-Teller Hallsmen?" Jarmony asked only to be glared at by the seven of us for saying what we were all thinking out loud. I know I must sound like a hypocrite right now, but honestly, he wasn't supposed to say that *in front of them.*

"We did, she sent us here. And she also said for us to give this to Summit Lealight."

Mhmm, well Summit Lealight was fuming. I knew--no, we *all* knew that Litheney was a cruel, thoughtless, irritable, crabby, impatient, coldhearted, demanding she-devil... but she would never turn away four orphaned and homeless children and send them here like messengers, would she? Survey said she would when one of the boys pulled an envelope from his green, nearly knee-length jacket and handed it to me.

I thanked him, but tossed it on the windowsill without opening or even looking at it. Anything she wanted to tell me she could tell me in person, not send some kids, particularly kids who just lost their families, to do her bidding.

I made a quick, and probably irrational, decision.

"Well, you are all welcome here," I said, which caused the others to stare at me as if I had lost my mind. I ignored them, and waved the children inside. They rushed in, almost trampling Amiselle and stood at the base of the stairs.

Now that they were in the light, I got a decent look at them. Isetha, who had finally stopped crying, stood behind another girl with light blonde hair that hung in a single braid down her back, and the two boys were as unmoving and silent as ever. All of them looked really wiped out.

"What are your names?" Harmon asked. "How old are you and who in your family disappeared?"

None of the kids responded immediately.

"I'm Asteria," the older girl finally said. "I'm twelve and I lost my father and older brother. And that's Tarron," she continued-- pointing to the smallest boy with strawberry blonde hair and huge, blue eyes. "He's seven and lost his mom, dad, and older brother and sister. He hasn't spoken since."

Asteria paused and the other boy cut in.

"My name's Greo. I'm eleven and my twin sister, mom, and dad have disappeared."

I nodded at him and there was an uncomfortable silence as Isetha stared at the floor.

After about a minute, she still hadn't said anything and looked on the verge of crying again. Feeling a pang of guilt for just standing there expecting some little girl to talk about her missing family, I knelt down, took both her hands in mine, and smiled warmly. This, as the others could tell you, can mean one of two things.

One: I'm trying to be encouraging and friendly. Two: You are *so* dead.

Fortunately, Isetha interpreted it as option number one, so she quietly answered, "My mom and dad are missing. I'm nine."

I smiled at her again.

"Well like I said, you all are welcome and very safe here. And don't worry, we'll get everyone back. I promise."

I really hoped I sounded more confident than I felt, but the four of them beamed at me--so I figured I had.

"We have five empty Charge rooms... so there's just enough space for each of you to get your own," I continued. "It'll be tight while you guys are here, but it's all we can do at this point, okay?"

They nodded and I realized how much I was starting to act like a leader.

Now *that* is something you should be *petrified* of.

Chapter 17

After leading the four up the stairs and telling them to go get some rest, Jarmony abruptly said he was going to head out to the river and left the seven of us standing alone in the great room.

"Not that we're not glad you invited them here and promised we'd get their parents back or anything," Harmon began, "but how exactly are we going to do that?"

I paused because I, once again, had no freaking clue where to start looking for people who were abducted by It. Maybe in his gingerbread house?

"I don't know," I told them. "But we can't turn them away... I'm furious that they weren't allowed to stay at the school with the other orphans. And not only that, they were sent here with a *letter*. Like... like little *messengers*. I'm finding it hard to believe that even Litheney would be that heartless."

They all raised an eyebrow as if to say, "Wanna bet?"

"Right. Teller Hallsmen would never be that cruel based off what we've seen her say and do," said Katrina. "But anyway, they're here now. What are we supposed to do until we can get everyone back?"

I shrugged.

"I guess they'll just have to understand that we're trying the best we can and wait it out."

"That's easier said than done for a bunch of young kids," Amiselle added.

There was a long silence.

"What did that envelope say? What did she want this time?" Illydia finally spoke.

"I don't know," I answered. "I stuck it on the windowsill. Anything she needs to tell us she can come tell us herself."

"You need to get it and see what it is," Macalynn told me, catching us all off guard.

"Why?" Aaron asked. "What could possibly be so important that she'd have homeless children bring it over?"

We all paused.

Something, I thought, *that better be pretty dang important.*

Wordlessly, I headed towards the stairs and ran down as fast as I dared to go with the kids asleep. At the bottom, I grabbed the letter and immediately started back up. Whatever that thing said, I wanted the others to read it with me.

Once I had joined them by the window again, I was out of breath. In retrospect, I probably could've just flown down with no noise-- but the thought just didn't cross my mind. How convenient.

"Relax," Harmon said with a reassuring smile. "What's the worst it could say?"

Well, I could think of a whole lot of awful things that I'd rather not get into here, but I nodded anyway and unsealed it. I stood with my back to the window and the others looking over my shoulders as I unfolded the paper.

"**Lealight**," it read. "**Make sure you are alone when you read this--for the sake of yourself and the others**."

Katrina started to move away, but Amiselle grabbed her arm. "Lesson one," she said strictly. "We don't take orders from Litheney anymore, especially when what she's trying to do could hurt a member of our family." Her former Charge nodded, and we continued reading silently to ourselves.

"**I felt guilty about leaving you to go on a wild goose chase for some chest you knew nothing about**."

What do you know? It has feelings.

"**So here's what I can tell you. First off, I'm afraid I was misleading when I said I know that chest like the back of my hand. I do know everything there is to know about what's inside and what it does, but I, too, have no idea what it looks like. All I know about the location is that it's in your Library. I'm sorry I can't be more of a help as far as that goes**

Misleading? I was going for flat out lying.

"**I also don't think you realize the importance of finding the chest as quickly as possible. I can assure you and the other Summits that *It* wants this chest badly, and if he finds it before you, he wins. It's as plain and simple as that. But if you find it, we might stand a chance. And I did not send the children to the Citadel because I was refusing to keep them here. I told them to go find you because they need your** protection. I don't know much on this matter, but I can say that these children's parents and siblings weren't randomly picked up by followers of *It*. He wanted them specifically for a reason unknown at this point. I figured that if he wanted their parents and siblings that much, then he probably wants them just as much. You mustn't let that happen."

Great, more pressure.

"I also want you to know that I, despite what you think, am not deliberately trying to lie to you. I honestly cannot speak of what you want to know without the chest because of the task I was assigned the day I became the Teller. Or it is simply not in my place to. Surely you understand that. And as you know there is much to be found and recovered, but allow me to keep this brief. *It* himself is tirelessly searching and he's dangerously close it getting what he wants. And according to what I've uncovered, I'm sorry Lealight, but without the information inside the chest I can almost guarantee your immediate death the moment he sets foot on our ground."

Oh, so that's the worst it can be.

Having recently faced being choked, crushed, burned, and electrocuted, I'd daresay I've been closer to death more times in the past two days than I'd been in my entire life. But it was the last sentence of the letter that made my blood run cold through my veins. My face must've turned a ghastly pale as I dropped the letter to the floor. The others were at loss for words. I didn't feel like I could face them, and I let my eyes dart from the wall to the table to my boots for an extra-long moment of silence.

But I soon felt someone's hand on my shoulder and heard a familiar voice.

"No. No, that's not going to happen. We won't let it." Illydia spoke with no uncertainty.

I turned around and looked at six confident and reassuring faces that frowned when they saw the horror in my eyes. Almost as if they had communicated their next move telepathically, the others reached out and enveloped me in a giant group hug. I felt like I was the lunchmeat in a Summit sandwich. And yet, I found myself on the verge of tears just before everyone pulled away.

"Illydia's right," said Harmon. "There's no way we'd let that happen. We've got each other's backs, remember?"

Nothing snaps you back into reality better than someone bringing up one of your pathetic speeches you've been trying to forget about.

"We'd like to help you look for the chest," Amiselle added "with your okay, of course."

I didn't trust myself to speak without sounding shaky, and only nodded at their offer. The seven of us then headed toward the Library's door.

Chapter 18

Leaving the kids upstairs alone to wake up thinking the worst had happened to us was most likely a bad idea. So, Aaron and Illydia volunteered to hang around the great room to wait for them while Macalynn, Amiselle, Katrina, Harmon and I headed onward.

We immediately split up to look.

"At least we've narrowed it down to this place," Katrina said after half an hour with no results.

"Mhmm. But you do realize that it could be anywhere in this one room. Like, anywhere from behind a bookcase to behind the wall." I answered.

"Well," Harmon began using his dreadful as-a-matter-of-fact tone. "We're underground, so isn't ground behind the walls?"

I rolled my eyes.

"Valid point. But we're talking about *Magic* here, Harmon. Common sense and reasoning don't apply."

He shrugged and continued digging around under a shelf just as Macalynn, who had been floating around to check the tops of the very tall bookcases, slumped onto the floor.

"Lealight, we're not going to find this thing just by searching for hours," she told me. "It's like you said. We're dealing with Magic. So this place practically has a mind of its own. How do we know that whoever hid this thing didn't Charm it or something? Wasn't that around the time when that's what the Magic Talent was for? Charming things?"

I then remembered something I had overheard Merrhet and Dillon talking about.

"Veronica hid it."

"What?" the others asked simultaneously.

"Four hundred years ago, Veronica Calodie, my predecessor, hid it. I heard Merrhet say it himself. Since he's so closely associated with It, he must know more about it than anyone."

They just stared at me.

"Okay," Amiselle spoke. "So, how do we know this Veronica person didn't Charm it?"

I glared at her. "Don't look at me like that. It's just something we know about it, okay? And Macalynn, you're confusing Grand Summits with Charmers. They were the ones who did that kind of stuff. Come to think of it, I'm pretty sure the last one was in her time. Maybe she got help from him. I mean, she was probably fully capable of doing Charms; she just needed to see someone about it. She probably wanted to make sure it couldn't be found easily if it's really this important. You would want to make sure your Charm wouldn't wear off and leave something like that out in the open for every Shadow in existence to see."

Macalynn's expressionless face suddenly lit up.

"Wait!" she exclaimed. "I think I know what we need to do."

As we all gathered around, I looked at the others' faces. It was somewhat comforting to see that I was not the only apprehensive one.

Undeterred by our expressions, Macalynn continued. "When we cleared out Merrhet's room, I remember seeing a couple scrolls on all these old Charms. One of them is bound to have something on the Charm she used. More importantly, we may find out how to undo it."

A couple seconds went by before Amiselle spoke up.

"Well, it's a place to start. Where are all of Merrhet's scrolls?"

"Sorry guys," I answered. "They're over in that corner, but I sorted through all of them last night. They're senseless. Either written in one of the ancient languages or too faded to even see the words."

They groaned and we stood quietly mulling over our situation for another minute or so.

"But... I have some stuff down here on old Charms. Some of the scrolls over there might say something about it, and I know there're several books."

They looked at each other doubtfully.

"And we don't have any other choice," I continued, "besides certain death, that is. So, you coming or not?"

Katrina, Macalynn, and Amiselle all sighed and Harmon stared at me as if to say "You just *had* to bring that up, didn't you?" But we still wasted no time and headed towards the other side of the Library.

One thing about searching for a *single* Charm in *hundreds*: it gets really frustrating, really fast. By book lucky number thirteen, page lucky number hundred and something, I was about to pull my hair out. At least three hours later, every one of the books and scrolls had been opened and read. There was absolutely nothing on invisibility anywhere.

"I can't believe this. I just can't believe this!" Amiselle shouted, rattling the ceiling. "I found Charms on everything from making glass to changing colors, but *nothing* on invisibility? This is so *messed up*!"

I put my hand on her shoulder and nodded, but quickly pulled away when she lit herself on fire.

Word to the wise: don't get near a ticked off Fire Talent. Especially Amiselle, who will feel no guilt at all for giving you a nasty burn.

Of course, being on fire didn't hurt her. She just sat there in the middle of my Library burning off her anger until the rug under her began to ignite. Katrina then stepped in with a huge pool of water.

You can guess what happened after that.

Soaked, Amiselle marched over to her.

"What was *that* for?!" she yelled.

"You were burning the rug, genius!" Katrina snapped back.

"I had everything under control, Katrina. In case you forgot, I mastered my Talent *two years* ago!"

"Well, the giant charcoal spot on the floor says otherwise!"

After that, all I heard was senseless squabbling as the two screamed at each other.

"Enough!" Harmon shouted over their voices.

Of course they took no notice of him and continued. Fed up, Macalynn stepped in the middle and balled up her fists, promptly sending Amiselle and Katrina hurdling through the air in opposite directions.

"Knock it off--both of you!" she said sternly as Amiselle smacked against the floor somewhere towards the stairs, and Katrina fell on top of a bookcase against the fourth wall--knocking it over.

Who would've guessed that having four of the most skilled and professional people in the Universe in my Library would result in mass destruction?

Yeah right. Skilled? Definitely. Professional? Not by a long shot.

"You're forgetting the reason we're here. To find that chest. So Amiselle, quit treating Katrina like she's still your Charge, and Katrina stop picking fights!"

Wow, harsh.

But before either of them could say "*I am not*", Macalynn raised an eyebrow and they both shut up pretty quickly.

"Sorry about your bookcase," Katrina changed the subject while setting it upright.

I just shook my head and started to pick up the books.

"You're not talking much," Harmon said sounding concerned.

Yep, getting a letter that says you'll die most likely within the next three days unless you find some box that had seemingly vanished off the face of the Universe strangely seems to make you less of a conversationalist. I shrugged and continued gathering the rest of the fallen books as an uncomfortable silence once again set in.

At least five minutes after we finished setting the bookcase back up, Katrina broke it.

"You know, just because Litheney says something that doesn't make it true" she said gently as if she expected me to burst into tears.

"And what could she possibly have to gain by lying about something like that?" I asked. "Litheney wouldn't bother to tell me if she didn't truly believe it. And as long as this chest is hidden, I'm..." I stopped myself to avoid choking up.

The others sighed sympathetically, and I found it impossible to meet their gaze for the second time in one day. That was until Amiselle, making squishing sounds in her sopping wet boots, appeared from around another bookshelf. She was beaming like a little kid in a candy shop.

"I think I found it," she looked up at us. I noticed she was holding the scroll I had tripped over. She clutched it as if the thing was life itself--which it just might have been for me at that point.

I reached out, just as Merrhet had done to Aaron, and the water immediately evaporated before everyone else crowded around her.

"I found this on top of Merrhet's pile over in that corner that Lealight said was of no use to us," she said while unrolling it. "But look at it."

The title read *The Gem and Charms That Were Lost*.

Chapter 19

"Okay, in English?" Harmon looked at the shriveled up scroll blankly.

"Lost is some old term that means something was either wrong with it, it was proven too dangerous, or it was used by someone to help It. Basically, it can be any reason that made people think it should never be used or known about, " I answered. "It would be up to the Summits and, if there were any, the Charmers, to get rid of every trace of the thing until there was no record of it anymore."

Now that I thought about it, it would make sense that Veronica would execute the Charm and then erase all evidence it ever existed if she didn't want anyone to find what she hid.

"Well, what are you waiting for? Let's see it!" Macalynn said eagerly.

First off, that scroll was *long*. We went through at least three feet of paper before we got to anything that looked promising. And the chapter was very, very small--with the same micro-print as everything before it.

"Did you see anything?" Katrina asked after about two minutes.

"It's not there," Harmon shook his head grimly. "There's nothing even remotely close."

I felt my heart sink into my stomach.

We still had *nothing*. At *all*. After *three hours*.

I groaned and rubbed my temples.

"Wait. Move your hand," Macalynn said to Amiselle.

My attention focused back on the scroll as she did as she was told and I saw what Macalynn was talking about.

In even more tiny and almost illegible handwriting, on a faded slip of paper that looked like it'd been torn out of something else and pressed into this scroll we were now looking at, was one last entry. Many tears cut into the writing and I could barely read it. All I could gather from it were the words:

> **"Created... Unknown; ... Lost... Grand Summit Veronica Calodie-The Charm... specific person... future... If done correctly... the chest... permanently undoing it."**

And the ending part was missing. Well that's constructive now, isn't it?

"Okay then," said Harmon. "So this is helpful how?"

I sighed. "I don't really know. But don't you see the edges?" I traced them with my finger. "It looks like it was torn out of something and stuck in here. If we find the other part, we might find some answers... Maybe there's another copy so we can fill in all these blanks where we can't read the words."

They looked unconvinced.

"I guess it's progress," Amiselle eventually mumbled.

"And it seems we need all the information we can get on this thing if we're ever going to find it," Katrina added. "On that note, I think we should head back upstairs to see how everything's going. I mean leaving Illydia and Aaron to babysit much longer would be pretty cruel, don't you think?"

I stifled a laugh and nodded in agreement. Them trying to handle four kids was like a Fire Talent trying to make it rain. Long story short: be glad Illydia's a Woodland and has no lightning up her sleeve.

"Yeah, let's get out of here," I answered.

When the five of us walked into the great room, Aaron, Illydia, and the four children were sitting around waiting for us.

"Did you find anything?" Illydia asked us hopefully.

I knew I needed to select my words very carefully with the kids right there.

"We didn't find the chest, but we found some interesting information that is definitely helpful," I replied, hoping the four wouldn't ask any questions.

Fortunately, they were all too interested in watching Aaron and Greo pass a small rock back and forth in the air to hear. Illydia also wore the "we'll talk about it later" expression on her face.

"What have you guys been doing?" asked Macalynn as she joined the children on the floor.

"Exactly this," Aaron answered just as Greo dropped the stone.

The kids all groaned out of boredom. *Well sorry, but this wasn't a vacation.* We weren't really in the entertaining mood considering we had spent hours reconstructing a giant tower, Merrhet and Dillon had betrayed us, the Clouds rolled in, and I had received a letter telling me I'm dead in seventy two hours all in two short days.

"Did you guys get something to eat while we were d-"

"Wait," Katrina interrupted frantically as the color drained from her face. "Where's Jarmony?"

Chapter 20

I had totally forgotten about him.

"Oh no, Jarmony!" Aaron choked and scrambled to stand up. "He hasn't come back yet!"

The children were now alert and looked frightened.

"We have to go find him," Katrina continued in a sheer panic. "What if he was-"

"Calm down," I interrupted. "We'll-"

"*Calm down*?! My Charge is probably lost and alone in the woods *at night*--not that you can tell with the *Cloud coverage*-- and you're telling us to *calm down*?!" Aaron practically yelled.

"You didn't let me finish," I huffed angrily. "Calm down--we'll go and find him right now."

I turned toward the four kids and asked them, "Talent?"

Asteria responded quickly.

"I'm Fire, Tarron's Light, Greo's Earth, and Isetha is Woodland."

"Okay," I thought about how I was going to organize this for a second. "Asteria; you, Greo, and Isetha will stay here with Katrina and Amiselle," I paused, remembering the incident in my Library. "And you two--try not to kill each other. Everyone else is coming. Tarron, I'm going to have to ask you to go with Illydia... for light. I trust you can do that?"

He responded by making a small, brightly glowing sphere to prove he could help.

"Good. Harmon, Aaron, you two need to go together. Macalynn, you come with me and we'll start on the ground and if all else fails do an aerial search. Everyone got it?"

The others looked pretty surprised that I seemed to have gotten over the vast selection of issues from earlier that evening. They nodded before the six of us headed down the stairs and out into the yard.

I'm asking you to imagine what your sky looks like at midnight. Now, picture it again without a moon or stars. Almost pitch black, right? Just add a frigid wind to it, and you have what that night was like.

"You ready?" Macalynn asked once Tarron and Illydia had set off towards the river and Harmon and Aaron in the direction of the field.

I smiled back through the darkness as my answer, though I don't think she saw it. We headed onward into the trees that we knew would eventually open up at the school.

"Oh, and don't think just because I was in shock means I don't remember you pushing me off the roof yesterday," Macalynn said after about five minutes of walking.

"Well, that makes us even," I answered. Even under the blackness of Clouds in the dead of the night, I could still see her stick her tongue out at me.

We quietly continued walking until we reached the outskirts of the Village. As the two of us turned to check elsewhere, someone, the only someone out actually, apparently saw us and started pacing in our direction. The figure was waving and appeared to be asking us to wait. In that situation, I normally would have just ignored whoever and kept going... but I couldn't do that to someone after all that'd happened. Besides, they knew I had seen them because of my hesitation.

Macalynn had already started rising into the air before she noticed I was hanging back.

"What's wrong?" she asked.

"Someone's out there. They want us to wait." I answered, which was followed by a groan.

"You keep going, and I'll catch up when I take care of whatever this is" I continued. "And if something goes wrong, I'll meet you back at the Citadel."

She rolled her eyes and said something about me being more trouble than I'm worth sometimes, but nodded and flew off. Meanwhile, I started heading in the direction of the approaching person before they started yelling and woke up half the Village.

"Can I help you?" I asked shortly after coming within ten feet of them. I was still unable to make out who it was until several seconds later when my eyes adjusted to put a name with the dark silhouette. I felt my face literally twist in disgust. "What do you *want*, Litheney?"

She looked unaffected by my tone and continued to say, "I wanted to make sure you got my message."

"Well, that's real courteous of you!" I tried to keep my voice quiet. "And here's a tip: if you're going to tell people they're as good as *dead*, the least you can do is tell it to their face. Next time don't send a bunch of orphaned *children* to deliver the notice!"

Someone must've heard me because candles were being lit in the window of a house close to us.

"You are not as good as dead, Lealight. I was only warning you what would happen if you don't find that chest," she said calmly.

"Mhmm. And are you aware that the thing's most likely *invisible*?" I asked.

She stifled a laugh.

"What makes you think that?" she asked--clearly amused by how insane I sounded. Who knew? Maybe I had gone crazy.

"It's common sense this thing is Charmed. And we found half a note taped to the end of a scroll from Merrhet's room. We think it says exactly what the Charm is, but we won't know for sure until we find out where it came from along with that map with all the underground tunnels-"

At the mention of "underground tunnels", her face went pale.

"How do *you* know about that?" she demanded just as Amiselle burst through the trees.

"What are you doing here?" I asked her as she ran up to us. "I thought you were going to stay with the kids."

"I *was* with the kids, but I thought you might want these. She handed me the *Charms That Were Lost* and Teller Hallsmen's letter.

"Well, how did you know I was here?" I continued.

"Because I know you that well," her eyes narrowed at me. "Macalynn stopped by and said you had most likely run into Litheney because she heard you yelling at someone. So I figured you might want them. And before you ask, she gave me a lift via teleportation and I took them as we left your Library. I meant to give them to you, but this whole thing came up so I didn't get the chance."

"Sorry to interrupt, but what "thing", exactly?" Litheney cut in.

Amiselle scowled.

"If you must know, Jarmony went out into the woods and never came back. But we figured you wouldn't care what happens to any of us considering the little letter you sent. And for the record, adding "I'm sorry" before continuing to tell someone they're screwed does *not* make it okay!"

I have such awesome friends.

"You showed them? I specifically told you not to!" Litheney exclaimed, fuming.

"She didn't have to. We read it with her," Amiselle answered for me.

Teller Hallsmen sighed.

"Honestly Lealight, I thought you were smarter than this. If I tell you to do something, chances are I have a good reason for it. You've got to trust me."

I couldn't believe what I was hearing.

"Okay," I responded. "First off--trust you? Trust *you*? You've been nothing but horrible to us for the past three years and particularly during the past couple days. Starting with "vivid display of carelessness" and ending with "your immediate death"! So naturally, I'm having trouble finding one good reason why I *should* trust you!"

Teller Hallsmen's expression looked hurt, but she stood her ground.

"Look Lealight, I'm telling you this for your own good. Everything I've ever told any of you has been for your own good. You've got to believe that or we'll never accomplish anything even if, on the off chance, you do find that chest. I know for a fact I've said this multiple times, and I also understand you are all under a lot of pressure, but your main focus has got to be on getting it. After that, we stand a fighting chance. And I keep my promises--so once you bring it to me, I will answer your questions to the best of my ability. But until then, there is nothing I can do to help you."

Amiselle and I stood there without responding for at least two minutes before she continued.

"And I'm sorry to hear about Aaron's Charge. I hope you find him. However, I believe I asked you how you heard of the tunnels."

I rolled my eyes. Teller Hallsmen is so sincere, isn't she? I gave the scroll and envelope back to Amiselle, who promptly stuffed them into a small, leather bag I didn't know she was carrying or even owned.

"His name is Jarmony, and thanks--we appreciate that. And no offense intended, but since you've decided not to tell me anything until after I find the chest, I will wait until after you answer my questions until I answer yours. Don't worry--I keep my promises, too."

She looked annoyed. Mission accomplished.

"Very well, then. Good luck with your search," she answered before walking off down the darkened path and disappearing around the corner.

Chapter 21

"I swear she gives me the biggest headache since-" Amiselle began after she had gone.

"Knock it off, Amiselle. She's just being her usual self and I really don't want to talk about it right now," I interrupted. "Let's just go."

"Go where? Home or are we still searching?" she asked.

"I guess we'll keep looking for Jarmony until he turns up. Are you gonna head back to the Citadel to help Katrina with the kids or do you want to tag along?"

"I'll go with you," she answered quickly.

I raised an eyebrow.

"You're upset about something."

"What makes you think that?" she asked, but I stared her down until she sighed. "Is it that obvious?"

"No." I answered. "I just know you that well."

She smiled.

"So seriously, what's up?" I persisted even though I was pretty sure I already knew.

Amiselle shrugged and she turned toward the woods--her thick, black braid swishing behind her.

"Oh come on. We both know you weren't really that ticked off only because Katrina put you out," I called as I chased after her.

She abruptly stopped and glared at me.

"Excuse me, could you say that a little louder? I don't think they heard you *in our neighboring Universe!*"

Well, at least I got her to talk.

"You're upset because Katrina turned out to be a Summit, aren't you?" I continued.

She looked away.

"I was caught off guard, alright? My Charge suddenly turned out to be the unrealized Water Talent Summit."

"So what exactly are you upset about?" I asked. "Just because she's not your Charge anymore doesn't mean you guys aren't still close. I mean, look at how the seven of us were before we found out Merrhet was... who he was. I have a feeling the new seven of us will be just as close if not closer after all this is over."

She turned back and looked at me.

"Do you really think all this will be over one day? And we'll be alive at the end of it?"

Um, well I, uh....

"Of course I do."

We continued walking around in silence until Amiselle continued to say, "But I mean it. If she *ever* extinguishes me again, she'll be a pile of ash on the floor."

I couldn't decide whether I should laugh or scream. So I did neither and the quiet continued. That was until loud rustling and slow stomping noises hit us. It was obvious these weren't coming from the usual wind.

"Lealight, what was that?" Amiselle asked nervously--clenching my wrist with quite impressive strength for someone as thin as she was.

"First off, I'm losing feeling," I answered. She loosened her grip, but didn't let go. "And I don't know. Maybe we should head back."

A dark figure then appeared out of nowhere and blocked our path. Amiselle screamed and grasped my wrist again so violently I was afraid my entire hand would fall off. Yet I had enough built up anger from the past couple days to focus hard enough to gather some lightning around us. I was about to fire when the light emitting off of a single bolt helped me make out the terrified face of our "attacker". After seeing him, I immediately dropped the lightning and smiled, but this time, it was unquestionably option number two.

"*JARMONY!*" Amiselle dropped my wrist and I shook it to try to get some feeling again.

"Jarmony!" she yelled, half relieved, half furious. "You just about scared me to death! You know how we are about the woods at night, and you just jumped out of the middle of nowhere in the darkness!"

"Sorry," he answered. "I heard someone coming and I came to see who it was. But why are you guys out here in the first place?"

"Looking for you," I replied. "You just disappeared and we thought something horrible happened! And here you are, merrily taking a stroll? Do you have any idea how long you were gone?"

"I didn't think four hours was that long."

"It is under *Cloud coverage!*" Amiselle crossed her arms and glowered at him.

"Anyway," he ignored her stare. "I'm glad I ran into you guys. I need your help figuring out what to do with this."

"Do with what?" I asked as he motioned for us to follow him.

Amiselle and I followed behind as Jarmony weaved through the endless trees, shrubs, and rocks. Just as I was starting to wonder how the heck he knew where he was going, Jarmony slowed down. Even though I couldn't see anything, I could hear what he was talking about. At first it sounded like gibberish. Then I could tell they were human voices, then completely terrified human voices.

"Calm down everybody," Jarmony spoke as if addressing a large group. "I found someone who can help."

He moved aside so they could see me. No matter how hard I squinted, I couldn't make out anything in the darkness. After giving up on the possibility of night vision, I clasped my hands together and moved them slowly apart to create a brightly glowing ball of light. I quickly saw the situation. Several people, men, women, and children alike, were standing there looking as petrified as I'd ever seen anyone look. There were at least eight of them.

"How did you all get out here?" I asked.

No one said anything. It was as if they were frozen.

"W-we don't know," one man finally answered.

"Okay, well everyone follow us. We'll go back to the Citadel and get into the light" I sighed deeply--knowing the place had already gone way beyond its maximum occupancy.

Shaking the thought, I made my light brighter to illuminate a path.

"Jarmony, would you lead the way back?" I asked, taking him by surprise.

"What?"

"I asked if you'd lead the way back. We rarely go off the path and you seem to know these woods inside out. So could you walk ahead?"

He nodded and moved to the front, followed by me, the line of people, and Amiselle last. As we started walking, those toward the back of the line were tripping over roots and small rocks due to the lack of light. So Amiselle decided to follow my lead. She created a tiny flame in her hands to provide more--making all the people jump. I guessed the sight of sudden fire less than a couple feet away would make me on-edge, too.

We continued to walk through the woods for at least five more minutes before I could see the roof of the Citadel from the bottom of the cliff.

What? Did you think when I said "cliff" earlier it meant bottomless abyss or something? It's only twice as tall as I am--so about eleven feet or so. Still, getting eight people plus the three of us over was proving to be a challenge. It seemed as if all of them were either Light or Water. And while lightning has served us well, it can't get you over an anthill much less an overhang. At the end of my rope, I stomped the ground. It obediently sank.

Great, wrong direction. Just goes to show what a lack of energy will do--even for us when we go more than a day without eating anything. Besides, earth is so stubborn and uncontrollable and I still figure it's just to make our lives more difficult. So after making myself look like an idiot, I stomped the ground again and it shot up twice as fast as it should have, almost knocking off a couple people who were standing along the edges. But at least we were all on the yard in one piece.

The first thing I noticed was Katrina, Asteria, Isetha, Greo, and everyone else who I'd sent out earlier waiting for us. I tried to ignore the others' stares that, even in darkness, obviously read "you brought *more* people?!"

"You found Jarmony!" Harmon noticed as we walked up to them.

"And other people... lots of other people" I heard Katrina say under her breath and everyone was quiet for a while.

"Wait, is that..." one of the boys in the group began only to be cut off by the "We don't know" guy.

"Asteria!" he yelled as he ran past the boy toward her. She turned in his direction, surprised by the familiar voice.

"Dad?" she half asked and half exclaimed as not only the father but also the boy (who I assumed to be her previously mentioned older brother) joined together in the family huddle. Slowly, the people in the group realized that their lost children were standing in right in front of them.

Lots of "Oh thank goodnesses" and hugs followed. Frankly, standing there watching made me feel like I was intruding on their reunion.

After everyone had calmed down, Tarron's father approached me.

"Thank you so much for taking care of our children while we were gone," he said while shaking my hand so hard I thought my arm could pop out of its socket.

"No problem. It was only a couple hours," I answered. "I hope you don't mind my asking, but where exactly were you all?"

Their smiles immediately vanished.

"All I remember is we were at home when at least a dozen Shadows sprang up out of absolutely nowhere... and then we were in the woods next thing I knew" said Greo's sister.

"Wait, *what*?" Macalynn asked with an edge of panic in her voice that worried the group.

Shadows didn't surprise or scare us in any way, but them *ganging up on* and *kidnapping* people was something no one had ever seen before. But then again, I had a feeling the next couple days would include a lot of... unpleasantly new things.

"Okay," I continued. "I don't think they'll bother you again, but you know where to find us if anything happens. And you, your neighbors, and everyone else in the Village have nothing to worry about. We're handling..." my voice trailed off when I noticed what was wrong.

Asteria, Tarron (who still refused to speak), and Greo stood with their returned families. But Isetha wasn't around.

"Where's..." I began, only to see her alone against the side of the Citadel.

"Isetha?" I asked. She shook her bowed head and kept her eyes fixated on the ground. There had been no reunion in this group for her.

I turned my attention back to the group. "You all had better head home before too long. And if you run into Litheney, I'd expect to be questioned."

Fortunately, they were smart people and could take a hint. The eight of us received several "thank you's" before they all turned and headed down the path. Everyone, that is, except Isetha.

Chapter 22

"Where *were* you?!" Aaron demanded back in the great room after we had agreed to let Isetha be alone on the roof for a few minutes. "You nearly gave us all a *freaking heart attack*!"

"It was only four hours" Jarmony answered for the second time.

"Those four hours were from around eleven to three--that means you were in the woods at night" said Macalynn.

"You guys are *way* too paranoid about the woods. I've been down there a lot of times at night and nothing bad has ever happened" he retorted.

"That's beside the point, Jarmony. Now that It is here, *anything* could have happened to you!" Katrina spoke up.

Jarmony's face flushed with anger and he shouted, "Well, look at you! A Charge *yesterday* and now you're already acting like-" he stopped himself. But it was too late.

"Like what?" Katrina asked a little louder than normally "*What am I acting like*?"

"Forget it" he responded.

"Oh no, I'm interested to hear what you think we act like, Jarmony" Harmon cut in.

Jarmony looked to the floor as he spoke.

"I don't know. I mean, before all this mess came up, you guys were really close and the three of us were really close... and while we were all friends, we were still worlds apart. So Dillon betrayed, Katrina turned out to be the unrealized Water Talent Summit, and so where does that leave me?"

Did this conversation sound familiar, or was it just me? Had these people learned *nothing* from my speeches?

"You're not alone, Jarmony" Katrina answered. "The eight of us are... like a team. We all watch out for each other."

"No" he still wouldn't look at us. "The seven of you are a team. The Seven Summits are always a team. I'm like a sidekick. And I was okay with that before today, but now, I'm the only one."

"That's where you're wrong" I began. "We never considered you guys *sidekicks*--and I don't know where you got that idea from. If I had meant only the seven of us are a team, I would have said "the *seven* of us will need to look out for each other", not "the eight, or soon to be nine of us". Whether you realize it or not, you are important. We *all* need one another, including you. As far as this whole night goes, what we mean is that the days where one or more of us could be gone for five or six hours and no one would worry are over. Now, I'm not saying that if someone decides they want to be alone for a while, leaves during the day, and stays an hour or two that we're going to freak out. But when it's even more pitch black than it usually is and you're that deep in the woods... with It here? No one would hear you scream, Jarmony. And I really don't think that after everything that's happened these past few days we could deal with losing someone else."

The others nodded in agreement and Jarmony wore an embarrassed half-smile.

"Okay, I'm sorry I scared you guys by being out there that long at night. Did I miss anything important?"

He had no idea--and I really didn't want to go over the details of Litheney's friendly letter and our failure to find the chest. Fortunately, the others knew me well enough to know when I didn't feel like discussing something, so Amiselle took out the envelope and handed it to Jarmony. As he read, his eyes grew wide.

"Well, that's real nice of her" he handed it back to Amiselle.

She held it out for me to take, but I shook my head and she shoved it back into her satchel--which I had finally remembered used to be her schoolbag and so she had it with her on the day we were realized.

"I'm going to assume by the looks on your faces that you didn't find it yet" Jarmony continued.

"No, but we did find this" Amiselle answered while giving him the "*Charms That Were Lost.*"

"What does this have to do with finding a chest?" Jarmony asked as he skimmed the extensively long first section.

"Oh that? Nothing. It's the second part at the very bottom" replied Katrina. "We know for a fact that this thing is Charmed to be invisible."

Jarmony looked at her the same way Litheney had looked at me earlier, but continued on to finish the chapter.

"I don't see anything on invisibility Charms" he said dismally after reaching the end.

"We didn't notice it at first, either" said Macalynn. "But do you see the very last part? You can't really read it, but it looks like it was torn out of something. So we're thinking if we can find a lead as to what that something is then we're one step closer."

There was a long silence.

"Wow, that's... really weird" Illydia finally spoke up--at lost for words. "Who tears just *half* of something out of a book and seals it in a scroll? It doesn't make any sense."

"It's Magic, Illydia. Common sense and reasoning don't apply" Harmon interrupted--mimicking my voice jokingly.

I shot him a glare, but nodded. Common sense and reasoning didn't apply to a lot of things.

"So let me get this straight" Aaron began. "You have to find this thing before **It** comes otherwise... bad, but it's invisible? No offense Lealight, but I'm really starting to hate this Magic stuff."

Amiselle rolled the scroll back up and we sat in silence for a while before I answered.

"I'm not a huge fan either at this point. But I've got to find this box if we're ever going to make it out of this. So I'm going to go talk to Isetha and then I'm heading back down, okay?"

Everyone nodded and looked at me sympathetically, as if they had already given up on the idea that I would make it out alive.

Gee, thanks guys.

Chapter 23

Isetha sat on the edge of the roof with her legs dangling over the side, her face streaked with tears, and her eyes staring off into the distance. She twisted around when she heard my footsteps, but quickly went back to looking out over the trees and whispered something as I sat down next to her.

"What did you say?"

"They're dead, aren't they?" she responded a little louder, her voice shaky as it was caught by the strong winds.

I sighed. What are you supposed to tell a little girl when her family's purposefully kidnapped by a wicked, murderous, and insanely powerful monster? A normal teenager (yes, even one here in my Universe) doesn't have to deal with this kind of stuff. Do I? *Of course.*

"There's no way of knowing, Isetha," I began while handing her a bowl filled to the brim with hot porridge and then taking the other one I brought up for myself. "But you do know I'll do everything I can to get them back, right?"

She nodded solemnly.

"I know. Thank you for doing this... you didn't have to. I can't even imagine what it's like to be one of you guys right now... with the Clouds and whatnot. Especially you. I mean, everyone knows Teller Hallsmen is grumpy a lot, but I didn't know she'd send a letter like that to *anyone.*"

"*What?*" I demanded.

Her face flushed. She quickly took a heaping spoonful of the porridge and stuffed it in her mouth.

"I kind of overheard you guys talking about that letter we brought over from Teller Hallsmen and I sort of followed you and Summit Macalynn out when the others weren't paying attention. I heard your conversation with Teller Hallsmen in the Village." She took another bite of porridge before continuing, "But I almost got caught by Summit Amiselle when I started following the path back to the Citadel. So I hid behind a tree for a couple minutes. I just made it back as everyone was coming out onto the yard. I guess they assumed I'd been there the entire time because they said nothing about it."

"*Isetha!*"

"I'm so sorry. I didn't mean any harm. I was just curious. But... are you really going to die and there's nothing we can do about it?"

I sighed and looked down at my own food that I had yet to touch even though I was starving. How the heck was I going to answer *that*?

"No, of course not," I told her. "Nothing's going to happen to me, or you, or any of us just because she says so. And you really shouldn't eavesdrop and follow people around. It'll only get you into trouble."

She stared at her black boots sheepishly, and I was reminded of myself when I was her age--before any of us were the Summits. I used to get in huge trouble for not doing homework, goofing around, and, despite my good intentions, meddling. My dad used to say it was because I had an "overactive sense of curiosity for things outside of school--the things that mattered" when I was seven or eight to try to take my mind off not having a Talent.

But just before my ninth birthday, our house burned down and, being a Woodland and an Earth, both my parents were trapped inside. They, well, they were killed. So, from the time I was nine to the time of the Test, I stayed in the school with about a dozen other orphans who had no other family they could live with. Don't feel sorry for me, it wasn't all bad. I had one friend who I met back before they died, and she let me go over to her house almost every other day so I didn't have to be at the school all the time. The two of us basically stuck to each other like glue until the 100th day of the 600th year at eleven in the morning. Let's put it this way: it was a miserable five minutes that we were allowed to say goodbye to our friends and families... and I haven't seen her since.

Remember when I told you about how we were all constantly made fun of and that was part of my relatively depressing childhood? Well everyone, this is the other part. And I never talk about it--at all. In fact, the only reason the other Summits eventually weaseled a fraction of the story out of me was because we were talking about our families one day before Dillon, Jarmony, or Katrina showed up. They hammered down on me until I finally told them that I hadn't seen my mom or dad for a while. After which, all they said was "Oh" or "I'm sorry" before dropping the subject. So I consider the fact I'm writing it down here progress.

"Are you *crying*?" Isetha's concerned, but equally as shocked, voice broke through my flashbacks.

I quickly snapped back into reality and realized, to my annoyance, that I was.

"No," I answered hastily while wiping my face on my sleeve. I couldn't believe that even after all these years I still couldn't think of my parents without choking up.

Isetha obviously knew I was lying, but dropped it. Great, had I really stooped so low that I couldn't even convince a nine year old I wasn't breaking down?

"And I know you didn't mean any harm. But please don't do that again. You never know who or what you'll run into if you follow us around."

"You mean **It**?" she asked.

No, I meant Litheney, but he works too.

"Yeah--**It**."

We finished eating in silence. When both of us had practically scraped the bowls clean, Isetha swung herself back onto the roof and stood up.

"Come on," she said insistently while tugging at my cloak.

"What is it?" I asked.

"You're going to go find that chest," she answered as strictly as a little girl can. "I mean, it can't be that hard. It's just a box. And not to be disrespectful or anything Summit Lealight, but if it's that important and we don't have long to get it then let's stop wasting time and go find it right now."

Had to admit the kid had a point. Then again, it was probably just the cute little determination in her voice that made me believe we had any hope at all. I stood up next to her.

"Please, just plain Lealight is fine. And agreed. Thank you, Isetha."

She beamed up at me and the two of us went back inside.

Chapter 24

If you were the Grand Summit in the 203rd year and had been tasked with hiding a chest containing something vital to defeat **It** when he returned, where would you hide it? Because I had *nothing*. Not like that's a first, but I didn't even know how long I'd been in the Library. Every so often I'd simply pass out in the middle of the floor, but never long enough to actually rest. I knew the others were probably asleep in bed and had been for a while. I was tempted to give up for the night and follow their example. But no, there I was, again, desperately trying to find this box that if you ask me also had an "elude-someone-whose-life-depends-on-finding-you" Charm as well as the invisibility thingy. But my mind was made up.

I was not leaving until I found it--period.

And as the past few hours had proved, that just might be by my fiftieth birthday. But I had days to figure this whole thing out--not years. So I kept searching, and searching, and searching until I was so done in it literally hurt. After leaning against the wall hugging my knees for what seemed like eternity, I decided to go flip through some of the books again to hopefully either find something in them, or get hit with some great idea. But who was I kidding? It'd be more likely I'd get sucked into the fourth dimension on the spot the moment I opened one.

Willing to take the risk, I did pretty much the exact opposite of spring to life, and headed over to a random shelf. But if you take how much the last couple days had sucked, pour in the level of exhaustion I was feeling, and add a pinch of my luck, you get *nothing*, even something as simple as walking across a room, that ever turns out in your favor. Pretty soon, I face-planted on the floor after tripping over something. Well, actually "face-planting" and "tripping" are understatements. It was more like I walked into some mini-explosive that went off the second I neared it. Whatever the thing was, it tossed me back several feet. A perfect ending to a not so perfect day, right? Now doubly as infuriated as I had been ten seconds ago, I stood up to put back whatever book or scroll I'd "tripped" over--but saw nothing.

Oh, joy. *More* invisible/nonexistent junk.

I took a few steps forward, only to accidentally kick something that felt similar to just hauling off and booting a solid brick wall. And for those of you that are slow--that means *ouch*.

Yet, I still saw nothing. It was almost like there was a little force field around something in the middle of the floor that--

Wow I was stupid, duh.

Feeling a small sliver of hope for the first time since Litheney's letter, I cautiously reached out only to feel a spherical, smooth surface that promptly shocked my hand. I groaned in exasperation. Somewhere, Veronica really didn't want me to get this thing. Not caring, I started looking for a book on how I could undo this brand new problem. As I rummaged, I heard a little clanking sound. Merrhet's Magic-draining gem fell out of my pocket and spun around on the floor. I knelt down to pick it up, but of course it rolled straight into the force field that was so kindly set up for me, and slowed to a halt inside.

Just as I was about to start pulling my hair out in frustration, a golden glow shone, and a loud sizzling sound echoed around the bookshelves. The gem, which had apparently just drained the force field, clearly sat resting against whatever was inside. And although I thought I knew what it was, I couldn't eliminate the fact that this could be some ancient scroll gone wrong or another lost Charm, so I tried to keep my anticipation under control.

And when that didn't work, I stuck the gem back in my pocket and ran my finger along the edge of the invisible thing next to it.

Less than five seconds later, a dark, wooden chest with a bronze lock appeared.

Part 2--Magic Causes Nothing But Extensively Long Headaches--Trust Me On That

Chapter 25

"Guys!" I shouted as the Library door slammed shut behind me. I ran into the great room. "*Guys!*"

Everybody was already out and waiting for me.

"What's wrong?" Illydia asked as she ended her apparent conversation with Amiselle and stood up. Her face was riddled with concern. "Are you okay..." her voice trailed off when she noticed I was carrying something and genuinely smiling for the first time in several days.

I skidded to a halt at the table and plunked the chest on top. Everyone simply stared at it for a while.

"You... found it" said Isetha--practically jumping up and down with excitement. "You actually found it!"

"Well, where was it?" Jarmony asked.

"In the middle of the floor and-"

"The middle of the floor?" Amiselle interrupted. "How the heck did it get into the middle of the floor?"

"It couldn't have been there originally," I thought aloud. "I think it was next to the bookcase that Macalynn blew Katrina into, the one against the fourth wall. When the bookcase fell, it knocked the chest out into the open."

The others paused as if to consider my theory like a bunch of philosophers, even though I thought we'd already established no reasoning/common sense was necessary with Magic multiple times.

"I don't see why it couldn't have," Harmon eventually spoke. "but here's the real question: what are you supposed to do with it now that you have it?"

"Now that I have it," I replied "I go get some answers because Teller Hallsmen always keeps her promises, remember?"

They smiled and chuckled to themselves at the thought.

"Do you want us to go with you?" Aaron asked.

"It's probably not a good idea for all of us to show up unannounced at the school. It'll make people think something's wrong more than they already do. Besides, you know Litheney. She's already annoyed that you guys know about her letter. There's no need to make her even angrier. I'll go alone."

The others nodded uncertainly, and I suddenly felt horrible for shutting them out like that.

"We get it, Lealight," Katrina said--noticing my wavering. "This is something between you and Litheney. And that's okay. There are no hard feelings just because you want to go by yourself."

I smiled and realized once again how lucky I was to have such understanding and supportive people for a family, and how creepy it was they knew me that well. So with a wave, I set off toward the stairs with the chest in hand.

Guess what? More freezing wind howled outside. Still, I convinced myself that nothing was going to keep me from finally figuring things out and I trudged on through all two miles of the woods to hopefully run into as few people as possible. And since flying or teleporting is pretty much a dead giveaway that you're coming, my only other viable choice is by foot.

Since I had closed school, the place seemed similar to a ghost town. The only things missing were the tumbleweeds and obnoxious harmonica music.

"They're here!" a voice called from the other side of the schoolyard.

So close to getting there unnoticed--and yet so far.

I sighed and stopped to face whoever decided to ruin my moment of finally finding the chest. "It's just me this time," I answered as some kid headed in my direction.

"We were actually going to the Citadel now," he began. "You guys didn't come yesterday and people were worried that something bad might have happened."

Well, I knew we were forgetting something.

"I'm sorry about that. Things have been a little... hectic. But it seems like everything's okay here."

"Everyone's holding out alright. But... where are the other Summits?" he asked.

"At the Citadel. I actually came to see Teller Hallsmen" I held the chest underneath my cloak--hoping he wouldn't notice it.

The boy stared at me weird, obviously surprised. Told you *everyone* knew.

"Okay, well I won't hold you up," he said while walking away.

"Wait, could you do me a huge favor?" I called after him.

"I can try," he answered uncertainly.

"Could you spread the word that the Water Talent Summit has been found?"

"Who is it?" he looked suddenly interested.

"Katrina Denisal."

"I thought she was a Charge."

"She was. But as it turns out, she's been a Summit this entire time," I continued--talking quickly to hopefully push the conversation along.

Understanding my tone, he responded as he headed onward.

"Alright, I'll ask my friends to help me deliver the message around."

"Thank you!" I yelled after him as he met up with another kid at the edge of the yard that I could have sworn I knew from somewhere.

After quickly shaking the thought and deciding I had more important things to do, I continued up to the door. Teller Hallsmen promptly yanked it opened. Okay, she really needed to quit acting like she knew everything that was going to happen before it happened. It was really starting to creep me out.

"Well, it's a surprise to see you here after what happened last night," she said. "I figured that-" Litheney stopped when I pulled the chest out.

"That was fast," was all she was able to manage. "But nevertheless, have you seen what's inside yet?"

"No," I answered. "You said you'd answer my questions after I found the chest. Here it is. Let's get on with this."

Chapter 26

"So let me see if I'm understanding you correctly," Litheney began. "You found this chest, the single most important thing in defeating It, just lying in the middle of the floor?"

The two of us had been standing in her office for about ten minutes, all of which I'd spent trying to explain when and where I'd found the chest and dancing delicately around the fact that I had let the others into my Library. Oh, and by the way Teller Hallsmen was overjoyed to hear Jarmony was fine. She said, and I quote, "That's very nice. I'm glad to hear Aaron's Charge is safe. Now, did you just say this chest had a *force field* around it?" Even when she wasn't insulting or yelling at us, she was still Litheney.

"It wasn't there to begin with," I answered for at least the third time. "It was against the fourth wall and then a bookshelf... fell over and the chest was knocked out into the center of the room."

"How did-"

"Not to be rude, but if this thing is that important then are we going to open it or not?" I cut her off, knowing I couldn't answer anymore questions without just blatantly lying.

"Alright, do you have a key of some sort for it?" she asked.

Um, *no*.

"You said you knew what to do from here on out."

"I said I knew what is inside and what it does. I never said anything about knowing how to get it open."

And there we were at another dead end.

I sighed and took the chest from her desk.

"I highly doubt if this thing had a Charmed repelling aura around it and eluded It for four hundred years that you can just pick the lock," said Litheney dismally.

"I'm not trying to pick the lock."

"You're not seriously thinking about breaking it, are you?" her voice rose slightly at the end.

"Of course not! I'm looking for a-" I was interrupted by a soft "*click*" and a golden glow shining from inside the chest as it slowly and reluctantly creaked open.

"One of those. I was looking for one of those," I continued, pointing to a silver ring on the inside of the lid that was identical to the one on the Library's door.

"How did you know there was one in there?" Litheney asked.

"I didn't. It was just a guess. But it's a nice touch--putting the disc on the inside where no one would even think about it."

She rolled her eyes.

"That was probably the idea. But apparently, your tendency to think of the most random and irrational solutions to problems is helpful sometimes."

"I beg your *pardon*?"

"That was according to your old teacher."

Oh yeah, her. If it was possible, I had even less fond memories of Miss Cyerson than I did Teller Hallsmen.

"Anyway," Litheney continued "Whenever you are ready."

Unable to wait any longer, I sat the chest back down and saw what most would think to be in a four hundred year old, life saving box--at least an inch of dust.

Well, the only thing I could think of regarding dust's usefulness to our situation was it gave us the ability to make **It** sneeze to death. Of course as I looked closer, I faintly saw purple cloth underneath. Now as much as I would have loved to dig through the filth, Litheney then impatiently flipped the chest onto its side and everything poured out.

"I believe these belong to you," Teller Hallsmen said while pushing the purple packet across the table in my direction with a pen as though the dust it was covered in was really toxic waste.

"I thought you said I needed to bring it to you."

"No, they are yours. I just needed to make sure you had them."

I quickly took the cloth and unfolded it.

Inside was a gray, bumpy rock and a crumpled piece of paper. Not exactly what I had expected my life to depend on, or to be stuff **It** would want.

"You must take those back with you," said Litheney. "It's fine if you want to show the others the rock, but please read the message when you're by yourself. I mean it Lealight, *alone*. This doesn't concern the other Summits, Aaron's Charge, or that little girl, understand?"

"Speaking of that little girl," I began. "My first question is if you believe that the children's siblings and parents were all kidnapped for a particular reason then why did we find Asteria, Tarron, and Greo's families lost in the woods but not Isetha's?"

"Yes, I ran into them on their way home. The only explanation I can offer is that whoever was in their houses at the time was taken. After he had them, perhaps It discovered that he only wanted Isetha's parents. So he dumped everyone else off with no memory of being kidnapped. I do not know what he plans on using them for," Litheney answered.

I swallowed. That would be difficult to explain to Isetha.

"What did you mean by you couldn't tell me the truth because of the task you were assigned the day you became the Teller? Someone *told* you to lie to us?"

"Not directly. But in a sense, yes, I suppose they did. You all aren't supposed to know anything about what I do. So, I've acted this way during the past three years so you would come around as seldom as possible and therefore have no reason to be apprehensive because you would never stay long enough to see anything."

"And that ties into my next question about what exactly it is that you do? I mean I know you're the head of the school and gave the Test when it was time... but you seem to know certain things are going to happen before they happen and have some sort of... I don't know, secret."

Teller Hallsmen sighed and reached under her desk. She brought out a giant book bound with black leather that looked very similar to the ones I had in my Library. It took me a few seconds to realize it was the same one she used to give the Test... and the one she brought with her to try and fake it with Katrina. After plunking it on the desk, spraying the dust straight into my face in the process, she flipped to a seemingly random page and said, "The first part of your answer. This book offers random and fragmented glimpses of almost anything it can come up with... often it is possible futures. This is how I know who the Summits are, how I knew you needed to find the chest, and how I realized that the Citadel would catch on fire shortly before it did so I could send that child to tell you all. And just so you know, I'm never supposed to show this to *anyone* so you should understand that if I'm telling you all anything about what I've seen--then it's very, very important."

"Wait," I couldn't keep the accusing tone out of my voice. "This book is how you know who the Summits are? Then what's the purpose of the Test?"

She looked to the floor.

"The Test is fake."

Litheney flipped to the inside of the back cover. Engraved into it, were all our names.

"**It** himself did something to this book... I do not know what or how. But he did, and so when Merrhet Drotter was born, it showed his name. But shortly after you came and told me about his betrayal, Katrina's came up instead. So I knew it was she who is the Water Talent Summit. But the Test is formality; people truly believe that is how it works. But it isn't."

I simply stared at her for several seconds of uncomfortable silence.

"You said that was the first part of my answer. What is the rest?"

Litheney bit her lip.

"I... I can't tell you that. Right now, anyway. Believe me, you will find out soon enough."

I raised an eyebrow suspiciously and, to my surprise, Teller Hallsmen genuinely looked sorry. I dropped the topic.

"Do you have any idea what I am supposed to do with this rock?"

"That is something you'll have to figure out on your own," she answered.

Of course it is, silly me for thinking something might be easy.

"Thank you," I began as I took the map from my pocket, unfolded it, and placed it on the desk in front of her. "And I found this chart of the underground written on a scroll we found in Merrhet's room. Some of the ink looks ancient and some of it looks brand new so my guess is he might've been down there adding to it all this time."

Teller Hallsmen was quiet as she looked at the paper.

"Well," she finally said. "I really don't know where Merrhet could've obtained something like this. So I suggest you keep it hidden in your Library until you find where it came from."

I nodded and stuffed the rock and both papers in my now full and heavy pocket, but once again hesitated at the door.

"Is something wrong?" Litheney asked.

I took out the gem, which had gone from an ebony color to a murky gray because of the Magical force field it had drained, and twisted it around in my fingers.

"As long as you're keeping the actual chest, could you hold onto this for me?" I asked while walking back over and placing it on the edge of the desk.

Litheney looked shocked.

"Why?"

"Because I think it's safer here. I mean, if I carry it everywhere then it could easily fall out or get stolen. If I leave it in the Citadel then **It** could easily send Shadows to get it. But I don't think he would look for a Magic-draining gem here. Plus I'd always know where it is and who has had access to it. Are you okay with me leaving it with you to keep in the chest?"

"If you would like to, it's fine," she answered. "I'll keep it on the table if for some reason you need it."

I thanked her again and left with one less thing to worry about.

Now, what inside of me said I should trust Teller Hallsmen with something like that?

I had no idea.

Chapter 27

The wind slammed the Citadel's door behind me and Macalynn, who was at the bottom of the stairs, smiled sympathetically.

"That bad, huh?" she asked.

"Not really. The wind slammed the door. It was okay, I guess," I shrugged. "Here it is."

I took the rock from my pocket as I sat down next to her.

"That was inside the chest?" her mouth dropped open slightly. "A *rock*? We went through all this to get a *rock*?! What's so special about it?"

Funny, I was wondering the exact same thing.

"It's just a rock as far as I know. And Litheney said that I'd have to figure out what it does."

Macalynn rolled her eyes and groaned.

"Of *course* she did. Did she even answer the questions like she promised?"

I nodded.

"And?" Illydia's voice said from behind us as everyone else came down. We all crowded at the bottom of the stairs.

"Turns out the Test was never real. The whole thing's a complete sham. She has this book that she says shows her who the Summits are. It somehow rigged it and so that's why Merrhet was picked. But shortly after we sent him to the fourth dimension, Katrina's name came up. That's how she knew."

They stared at me blankly.

"Oh, and Litheney also mentioned the thing can show certain things in the future. That's how she knew about the chest and the fire. But then she said that all this was half my answer and refused to tell me anything else."

"Figures," Harmon rubbed his forehead in exasperation. "But about the book... do you believe her? It sounds a little farfetched."

"Yeah... I mean, come on. I know Litheney can be annoying and crabby but do you really think she'd do anything to deliberately hurt us?"

"Let's see," Amiselle began. "She apparently lied to everyone for years about the Test, yells at us almost every time we see her, and I'm sure you haven't forgotten the letter. Lealight, it almost sounds like you're defending her."

"I am *not*," I insisted, feeling as if I was being put in the spotlight for an answer I didn't have. "I'm just saying that I don't think Litheney's lying this time, alright? And she seemed to think we'd find out about the rest soon, anyway. Maybe she thinks we can figure it out better if we do it ourselves rather than just being told."

My words hung in the air for a while before anyone continued.

"Do you have any idea at all as to what that rock does?" Aaron changed the subject. "Or is this another life or death goose chase?"

Having failed to even consider the idea of more hide 'n' seeks turning into find 'or' dies, his question caught me completely off guard.

"Not really, but..."

Everyone groaned and shook their heads in disappointment. I couldn't tell whether it was in our situation or in me.

"*But,*" I continued. "She didn't stress this thing as much as she did the chest. I've never heard of Litheney being reluctant to tell us depressing news, so I think it shouldn't be that hard."

They looked dubious.

"Mhmm--'It shouldn't be that hard' will be your famous last words if you keep it up," Katrina, the perky one, said dismally.

"If I keep what up?" I snapped. "Because it's obviously *my* fault It suddenly showed up after four hundred years, and *my* fault that we couldn't get out of this alive without some stupid box, which only had a little rock in it that we don't even know what to use for after all of it!"

Katrina looked taken aback and I felt another pang of guilt.

"I'm so sorry. I'm just, this whole thing..." I decided I ought to shut up before I said something, or should I say something else, I'd regret.

"I... shouldn't have said that," Katrina finally answered. "It's not your fault we keep running into dead end after dead end after-"

"Thank you, Miss Dejection," Illydia interrupted. Katrina looked sheepishly to the floor. "But I think what she means is, we get it. We're all under a lot of pressure right now, but it's like you're caught in the center of it all with the letter, then the chest, and now this rock thing. And we're probably not helping by being skeptical about your choices. Like you said, we're all in this together. But if this particular thing is something between you and Teller Hallsmen, then we'll help you in any way we can, right guys?"

"Right," everyone chorused and we all started cracking up for no apparent reason other than how pathetically cliché we sounded.

But almost as if simply laughing with my family for more than twenty seconds was illegal for me, I noticed something was wrong.

"Where's Isetha?" I asked the others.

"She went out into the woods for a while," Aaron answered nonchalantly, for which, I was about to rip his head off.

"You let a little girl go out into the *woods* with *It* here?!" I demanded.

"Relax, it's the middle of the day and Isetha said she knows her way around. She'll be fine"

"Even if she does, you forgot the *"If he wanted their parents and siblings that much--then he probably wants them just as much"* from Teller Hallsmen's letter. I asked her about that and she said that the other kids' families were dumped off in the woods because It decided he only needed Isetha's parents, and so he's probably waiting for the right time to pick her up, too!"

The others looked at me as if to say "You can actually recite that?" until Aaron said, "Oh."

"Yeah, *oh,*" I retorted. "I'm going to go find her."

Before the others had a chance to volunteer to come with me, I was on my way up the first flight of stairs.

Chapter 28

I decided on the roof that flying wasn't a good idea considering I still wanted to avoid being seen and answering questions. So from there I dropped down and continued walking, searching every branch and Isetha-sized nook in the woods. Not worried about getting lost, (because by floating straight up above the trees you figure out where you are pretty quickly) I barely followed the usual path and went every which way until I was almost positive I'd seen a particular rock at least a dozen times.

Groaning, I leaned against a tree, took the paper out of my pocket, and twisted it around mindlessly. You'd figure something that had been locked away for over four hundred years would be brittle and I'd be afraid of simply having it out in the open. But it was in surprisingly good condition for its age. I decided to take a break from looking around for Isetha and unfolded the paper. If there was going to be that annoying "suspense" music, there'd be no better time.

"*Dear–*" it read in very old fashioned and barely legible handwriting.

But either Veronica still didn't want me to read her words or because the Universe just *hates* me for some reason, a strong gust of wind came through and tore the note from my hand. If I was *smart*, I would've halted it and that would have been that. But I wasn't thinking, and I ran after it like a regular person. I guess part of me will always think I'm still a No Talent kid chasing after my homework that I actually did for once after it was swept up by the ceaseless wind.

The note seemed to deliberately taunt me by always keeping less than a foot out of my grasp. I continued to do a mixture of speed walking and running through the trees until *another* impressively strong gust came through and the letter was blown higher and higher before it landed on a branch just shy of the treetops.

"Great," I said aloud. "Just *great*. I finally get a hold of that *stupid* chest and then the wind just *happens* to pass through and the letter is-" I stopped, feeling like the biggest idiot ever to walk the woods.

Oh, right. I can fly. *Duh*.

And so, I did. Parallel to the tree's thick trunk until I reached the branch I'd seen it land on--only to find it resting safely in the hands of Isetha.

"Hi, Lealight," she said cheerfully from behind a sea of multicolored leaves that had blown in front of her. "This is yours, right? What is it?"

"I don't know. I haven't read it yet" I half-lied.

"It was in the chest, wasn't it?" she asked, already knowing the answer.

I sighed and hesitantly said "Yes, and Teller Hallsmen needs me to start reading it now so I can figure it out soon."

Isetha frowned, but nodded and gave the paper back to me.

Tired of just floating there, I settled down into a branch slightly below and only a couple feet away from hers.

"How did you get all the way up here?" I asked--noticing the first twig on the tree was at least five feet high. Nothing else looked like it could hold someone even Isetha's size for several more.

"I climbed" she replied--avoiding my gaze.

"Really?" I began. "Because the first branch that looks like it could support a person is well over eight feet off the ground.... Thoughts?"

"I *did* climb," she insisted. "By making branches up the trunk that I could step on. But once I got up here, I made them go away so no one would bother me."

I don't know about you, but I was reluctant to believe that a little girl who wanted me to help her make flowers bloom four days earlier was suddenly climbing sixty or so feet up a tree by creating her own branches. But on second thought, I probably wouldn't have recognized myself right then from only ninety six hours before. Reading my expression, she quickly added, "Not that you're bothering me. I meant those annoying kids that used to bug me all the time. They come through the woods a lot. If there's one thing I don't miss it's them... and Ms. Dosibe."

I laughed.

"I hated my teacher, too. Don't know one kid who didn't. The only thing I was excited about on the day the seven of us left was that I got out of several more years with her, and I'm almost positive she felt the same way."

Isetha smiled.

"I never said I *hated* Ms. Dosibe. And by the way, she was really mad that you said she was wrong about blooming flowers. She said you had no right to tell her how to do her job."

"Please, anyone can tell her how to do her job if she's wrong. And you may not have said you hated her, but you were obviously thinking it."

She suppressed another laugh and nodded. The two of us sat there in silence looking over the dimension while the wind blew leaves around carelessly before I remembered the note.

I slowly unfolded it again--holding it by the corners tightly so that when the next wind came it billowed out like a sail, but didn't blow away.

Dear a Grand Summit some couple hundred years from now,

I guess I should probably start by explaining exactly what happened to the seven of us within the past couple days. First, I found this rock that you have before you behind a shelf against the fourth wall. I thought it was useless, set it on the table, and forgot about it for several hours before I left the Library to find the six other Summits and our four Charges gathered at the window. They were all looking out over the woods completely ashen. I joined them and quickly saw what they were staring at. These massive and nearly pitch black clouds were rolling in from all directions and leaving the entire first dimension in a state of darkness. Nathaniel seemed to think it was nothing more than a very, very bad storm, but Cerria quickly told everyone what I'd been thinking. Storm clouds are dark, but they are not black. We stayed there throwing out ideas for the next several hours as to what these things meant before we heard knocking at the door. A crying child was there and she told us that a lot of people had just disappeared. I thought she meant a large family. I could not have been more wrong. We followed her back to the Village, and I quickly heard the number--thirty. Thirty people gone just like that. I then knew what was happening. And no more than five minutes later when everyone was asking us if we knew what was going on... I could not bring myself to tell them the truth. First, it would cause nothing but complete panic; second it would make all those whom had lost family despair. Even I believed their chances were not spectacular. So I lied to them all. I said I did not know. When we returned home, I immediately went back into the Library, convinced that the reason Hyvecuous had suddenly appeared had something to do with the rock I had found. The stone's grooves and edges lead me to believe it came from something bigger, and things are rarely what they seem to be. I puzzled over what it was and what I was supposed to do with it for hours before, frustrated, I threw it against the wall. As it fell, it managed to find its way into a hole I had never seen before. It seemed a perfect fit, emitting a golden color that I recognized only from the execution of Charms. The wall then came out and slid aside to reveal some sort of passageway. This was truly one of the most bizarre things I'd ever seen. And I had no idea what I was supposed to do, again.

Yeah, welcome to my world.

But I eventually decided I needed to find out what was there, for the sake of the others. I won't go into the details, you will find out soon enough on your own. What is most important here is that everyone in your time needs to know that Hyvecuous is not dead. This may or may not be news to you depending on if the same clouds I described have come again. What I've done *on this day is merely a delay for him. He will come back, and be twice as strong and powerful as he was earlier this evening. I'm going to Charm the chest to only appear to the Grand Summit during the time when he returns. I'm assuming that's you.*

Unfortunately, and I figured that Veronica was referring to It by his real name when I read "Hyvecuous". And one that was pretty stupid if you ask me. The name sounded like a disease, and I guess in some way It actually was.

I did this because you and the other Summits must defeat Hyvecuous this time. Not expel him to the fourth dimension like I have done, but rid us of his threat forever.

What a nice way of saying "kill". Lo and behold, Veronica was a bigger hypocrite than me. Who was she to say I needed to murder someone when she had the opportunity to do so only hours before?

You are probably wondering why I didn't when I had the chance, and the answer is simply this--Hyvecuous doesn't have a form of his own. He just takes over people permanently. So if you kill whoever Hyvecuous possesses, then you basically set him free. He'll then jump into another person. Maybe even you, since you'd be standing right there. And I'm sure you're smart enough to figure out that someone like him having the Grand Summit's Magic plus his own is something no one could stand up to. In order to get rid of Hyvecuous forever, you'll have to drain his power. Without it, he literally becomes nothingness. The only way to do that is by using, well, Magic. But I am not referring to the Talents that you're used to. I mean real, pure Magic--something no Grand Summit has ever done or even attempted before. No one even knows how to go about it. But do not be misled. If you think you can win without Magic or if you think you know what Hyvecuous is capable of, you are going to get a rude awakening. I thought I could defeat him, and I didn't even try to figure out Magic when it was right there in front of me. It seemed too farfetched, something impossible. But because of my ignorance, we very nearly lost today and have only succeeded in securing your future in this battle. Basically, the lesson here is never underestimate Hyvecuous, or yourself. And before I forget about it, I want at least one person in the future to know that today was my second encounter with him. I know everything and everyone in your time will say Hyvecuous came only once during these years that I am the Grand Summit, but there is no record of the first time because he didn't launch a full scale attack. I still believe it was just to scare us since there were none of those clouds and he just showed up one day while we were in the third dimension. He didn't stay for even ten minutes because after at least five of the seven of us standing there completely mortified, I pulled some lightning and it went right through him--no damage done at all. After that, he laughed at us and disappeared. The other Summits have managed to convince themselves it was nothing but a premonition. However, I will always know that was just as real as the attack today. We only survived because of an excerpt I happened to find in one of the books only days a few days ago. So honestly, our "victory" had very little to do with me and the Charm was lost in the process. But I'm not writing this just to tell you what happened to us. The more important purpose is to convince you right now that you must learn Magic in order to drain Hyvecuous for good. If he escapes again, I don't think there could be any hope for future sets of Summits. Besides, would you really want them to inherit this? Something that I should have stopped but instead I've passed on to you?

I sighed. I wouldn't wish anything we had been forced to do on Merrhet--much less a new set of Summits.

I highly doubt you would, but trust me. You really don't want to suffer the guilt I feel right now knowing that you will have to face him. You're probably very confused and have lots of questions. I wish more than anything I could be there right now to help you, but obviously that is not possible. It is all up to you and the Talent Summits now. So whether you're eleven or thirty years old, you've got some huge decisions to make that are going to affect not only everyone alive currently, but every single person that is born from here on out. I'm not saying this to add to the pressure you are under, but to help you realize the situation. So as the last thing I'm going to tell you in this note, please learn from my story so no one ever has to go through what we have had to ever again. Rid this Universe of Hyvecuous once and for all. Don't let anyone convince you that there is another way. I know you're hesitant to search for and then master another Talent, especially one that's never been attempted before, but I know you understand just as well as I do that the sooner you begin this, the sooner everyone in the Universe will be safe again. I wish you the absolute best. Never stop fighting.

By the way, I teleported another note behind the wall for you to find. I hope it will explain things a little better.

Chapter 29

Was it me, or was the ending of the letter becoming the story of my life? I mean, find something, and everything will be okay. That is until that something you found makes you have to find *another* something. I guess that's what Litheney meant when she said "there is much to be found and recovered," but a bit redundant, perhaps.

"Are you okay?" Isetha's concerned voice once again broke into my thoughts.

I had to think about her question. Well, I knew what I had to do and why I was doing it. This was a first in the past couple days. The others had made it clear that they were going to stick with me no matter what kind of muck I dragged us through, and I didn't feel as if I needed to pretend to be fine when I wanted to scream for once. I'd say it was probably the best mood I'd been in for a while.

"Yeah" I answered as I pulled my wildly blowing hair out of my face. Isetha seemed shocked by my smile that, for the first time in what felt like forever, wasn't fake or forced. "But I have tons of work to do."

"Well, let's go back right now," she began to inch her way down the tree.

"Isetha, we don't have to go back now if you don't want to," I began. "Besides-"

"I do want to. You've got everyone on board with this whole box thing, but don't you think that just because you found it means we're going to stop bugging you," she cut me off again with a sly grin. "Cause by now, you've got all our help whether you want it or not."

I laughed. "Of course I want it."

"Then come on, Lealight!" she called from already ten feet below.

I pushed myself off the branch and caught the air, hovering next to her. Isetha rolled her eyes and murmured "showoff" under her breath. I shrugged as she jumped to the ground giggling manically.

"Hey, look it's Flower Girl!" a voice echoed from not that far away. I almost whacked my head against another tree as I shot back upward out of sight.

Isetha stood below and stared the mess of branches and leaves she knew I was hiding behind, but then nodded in understanding and turned to face the owner of the voice.

"Where you been, Flower Girl?" the voice continued. "No one's seen you around for days."

A group of three boys appeared from around the bend. One of them I recognized as the brat from my group back at the school. He had another, smaller, and obviously freaked out kid trailing behind him. The owner of the voice was the oldest and apparently the ring leader. Little sunlight came from temporary gaps in between Clouds--it filtered through the dense trees, making the scene look almost as if we were in the middle of the night. And the whole situation ten times creepier even though they were just kids.

"I don't have to explain anything to you, Verron," Isetha said angrily. "Just go away."

"We can do what we want. You don't own the woods," the brat chimed in. "And seriously, what happened to you? Did you run away from home or something?"

Even from behind a shield of leaves and branches, I could tell Isetha was choking up at the mention of her home.

In a shaky voice, she answered, "No, I didn't run away. My parents..." Her voice trailed off and I dug my nails into the bark to keep myself from jumping down and yelling at the three. I was not about to sit there and let Isetha face a bunch of bullies, who obviously weren't going to leave without making her talk, alone.

My compromise was to get down off the other side of the tree. When I landed, it sounded like nothing more than leaves rustling in the wind. And so the boys took no notice of me as I walked up behind them with my arms crossed and in my best stern, authoritative voice demanded, "Just what do you think you're *doing* back here?"

The boys all looked like they were about to jump out of their skin and stood as if glued to the spot shortly after they turned and saw it was me. Particularly me sounding very annoyed.

"Oh, um, we were, uh..." the smallest one stammered before being cut off by the one Isetha called Verron.

"Just walking. We were just walking," he answered.

"*Really*? It didn't sound like you were just walking to me. Anything Isetha can help you with I'm sure I can as well. Now what was that you were doing, again?"

They didn't answer, but looked surprised that I knew Isetha by her name--and even more so when I walked over next to her, took her hand, and repeated, "You three haven't answered my question. I asked what you were doing."

"We were looking for...." The oldest one, whom I'd taken a particular disliking to, began before I interrupted with an alternate end for his sentence.

"Trouble. You all were looking for trouble. And that's something you don't want to do anywhere--especially in these woods. It's a very dangerous place right here where we're standing, and if I were you, I'd get out now."

The smaller boy and the suddenly (*thank you*) mute brat started to eagerly trot down the path, but were stopped by Verron again.

"If this place is so dangerous then why are you in it? I think you're threatening us."

Wow, that kid had nerve. But don't worry, I fixed that when, to the horror of the group, I started laughing.

"Don't be ridiculous. I would never threaten you. I'm just saying that with Hy-:...*It* here, you ought to avoid this place as much as you can. And I think the seven of us can manage just fine, thanks for your concern."

"Then what is *she* doing here? You don't seem to care the she's alone in the woods."

Isetha shrank back, and I squeezed her hand reassuringly before answering.

"Isetha is not alone. She's with me. But you all, on the other hand, have five seconds to leave before I *personally* go and tell your parents that you were not only lollygagging around in here, but you were also picking on a little girl. One..."

"Wait, how do you know our parents?" the youngest one asked nervously before the brat finally decided to speak up.

"She doesn't."

"Yeah, she's bluffing" the other added.

I was usually laid back with the whole "Grand Summit" thing, but I was still used to a little more respect than that.

"That's right. I don't know your parents. But I have my own ways of figuring things out. Two... three... *four....*"

The still wide eyed group regretfully turned and ran down the path as though I'd fry them on "five". They disappeared around the same bend they had come from.

Chapter 30

"Thank you," Isetha spoke up again two minutes into our walk along the path to the Citadel.

"No problem. I'm always happy to make jerks feel like wimps" I answered--making her smile. "Who are they, anyway?"

"Some morons from school. They're just a bunch of annoying bullies who love to pick on everyone else smaller than them. They call pretty much every female Woodland Talent "Flower girl". But I don't think they'll bother me again."

"Do me a favor. The next time you see those guys, tell them I said I'll turn them into human hash browns if I ever catch any of them bugging you again. And if they really say that about Woodland Talent girls, we better make sure Illydia never hears... she'll strangle them all."

Isetha laughed, but suddenly got a serious look on her face and asked, "Who's Hy?"

"What?"

"When you were talking... you said Hy, but then stopped yourself and said **It** instead."

I rubbed my forehead. This kid was surprisingly observant and critical for a nine year old. "Well, Teller Hallsmen says she thinks I shouldn't talk about the letter until I can figure some of this stuff out," I began. "The others don't even know it exists yet. They only know about a rock that was also in the chest."

"A rock?" Isetha now sounded surprisingly like Macalynn. "All that for a *rock*?"

"It's not just some random stone, Isetha. And the letter practically spelled out what I was supposed to do. For once something made easy. Or easier, anyway."

She frowned. "Can you at least tell me who Hy is?"

Seeing no harm in her just knowing that It had a name, and a quite lengthy and hard to pronounce one at that, I told her.

"Apparently, It has an actual name that was found out during Veronica's time... it must have been lost or something over the four hundred years he's disappeared. His name's Hyvecuous. And that's what I began to say before I realized they'd have no idea what I was talking about."

She just looked at me. "That letter is from Veronica? As in, Veronica *Calodie*? I thought she was the Grand Summit in, like, the early two-hundred's. How did-"

"Some lost Charm," I interrupted.

She nodded in understanding. "And did you say It's real name is Hive-a-cious?"

I stifled a laugh. "No, Hyvecuous. Hy-vecu-ous."

She smiled. "Oookay. That's a really weird name."

"Weirder than Hiveacious? And he's got to be well over six hundred years old, so who knows and who really cares about his past? He's out to destroy us now. So our main focus is making sure he not only doesn't succeed this time, but that he can never come back again."

She stared up at me earnestly and asked, "How are you gonna do that?"

"That's what I'm going to find out" I answered after deciding that I didn't want Isetha to learn a clearer definition of "murder" at her early age. Speaking of which...

"And Isetha," I continued with a tone of dead seriousness that halted our progress at the door of the Citadel. "You can't go wandering off like that anymore."

"But the woods is the only place I can be alone!" she protested. "I know my way around just fine, and I don't think those guys are going to bother me anymore."

"Calm down and listen to me carefully, Isetha." I felt horrible that I had to bring this up. "You've got to stay close to me or at least to one of the others until this all blows over, alright? It's not because I don't think you can handle yourself or that I'm punishing you. It's because you're in danger. Real danger, Isetha. When Hyvecuous kidnapped you and the other children's parents, he wanted them for a specific reason and you're very lucky you four were out of your houses when he came for you. He dropped off Greo's, Tarron's, and Asteria's families in the woods with no memory of what had happened because he found out that he only needed yours for whatever he's doing."

Isetha's face drained of color as she took in what I was saying.

"If Hyvecuous wanted your parents that badly, then he might want you just as much. He might be waiting for the right time to pick you up with no one around to try and stop him. I'd never forgive myself if something happened to you, Isetha. So you've got to trust me and stay close by for a while."

She looked up at me with those giant green eyes. Nothing short of horror filled them--she looked ready to cry. I was already kicking myself telling her this. How did I think a little girl was going to react to hearing her parents were a part of It's master plan to destroy us all? But Isetha just swallowed and nodded.

"I do trust you, Lealight. And I know that you'll beat Hive-Hyvecousus, or um, Hyvec...uous and that everyone will be safe again. I--we all really do. You know that, right?"

I couldn't help but grin as I pushed open the door.

"I know that now."

Chapter 31

Ten feet away. Ten feet away was the wall that had my answers behind it. After Isetha and I had walked through the front door, we heard everyone else in the kitchen. Turned out Harmon had made one of his stews that we all loved so much. We just sat and enjoyed each other's company over dinner for a while. Though after about an hour had passed, I somewhat reluctantly told everyone I thought I had an idea (which caused skeptical stares and broad smiles alike). I told them that I'd be gone for one, two hours max, and came into the Library thinking that all I'd have to do was look for some kind of hole about half the size of my fist. But as usual, nothing is ever as easy as it seems.

Not only were there colossal bookcases in front of *all eight* walls of the room, but I had to check behind every single one. That means I took all of the books off, slowly lowered the shelf onto the floor, and closely examined the wall behind it. When I found nothing, I replaced the shelf and the books to their rightful places before moving on to the next case. And as luck would have it, the very last one I looked behind had a hole in the wall the perfect size for a rock. It was smack dab in the center of the fifth wall (I somehow skipped over it in my haste and it cost me a good hour or so). So there I stood, staring blankly at the hole as if I expected it to disappear any second.

But it didn't.

I reached into my pocket for the rock that had seemed like nothing more than useless junk not too long ago. Of course I was now about to use it to unlock a room that contained the information we needed to get out of this alive. However, I abruptly stopped when a horrible shiver went down my spine. It was by far the most freezing thing I'd ever felt before. I pulled my cloak tightly around myself, but the cold didn't go away. It, in fact, got much worse as the seconds ticked by.

"Stupid wind," I said under my breath shakily before I remembered.

Wait, I'm inside. And not only that, I'm underground.

"Chilly? I'd figured you'd be used to it by now, Veronica," said a voice that was, as cliché as this sounds, much colder than I felt.

I turned and saw a man towering over me. He had short charcoal hair that was dusted with gray. His skin was olive colored, and his eyes bloodshot. Whoever this was must have really loved black because that's the only color he wore from an inky cloak to scuffed, dark boots. His teeth had a yellowish tint to them that made his already malevolent, twisted smile even more disturbing. Once he saw my face, it faded slightly.

"You're definitely not Veronica, are you? You appear shorter, but you certainly look like your predecessor. Excuse me for forgetting people and things change over four hundred years. They say the memory is the first thing to go. Anyway, I was hoping I would get back in time to finish her off, but I guess you will have to do, won't you Lealight?"

I stood shivering--not from the cold that was still seeping into my veins, but from the total mortification of standing face to face with Hyvecuous. I was quite sure he didn't come to meet my acquaintance.

"Although if you would be so kind as to answer my questions, then I shall make death less painful for you. So Lealight, have you stumbled across a particular chest I was informed my dear, deceased friend hid for you some couple hundred years ago?"

I said nothing.

"Are you hard of hearing? I asked…"

He suddenly vanished with no trace at all. I slowly took a couple steps forward, but not too soon, a bare hand shot out from behind me, wrapped itself around my throat, and I was lifted off the ground.

If you have seen a chest--wooden, with a bronze lock, I believe," Hyvecuous finished.

I kicked, punched, screamed, and of course I launched every single thing I had at my disposal. And as a master of six Talents--that's a lot. But the blasts of air, rock, vines, lightning, ice, and fire I had made all went right through Hyvecuous as if he were nothing but a vacuous spirit. However, the tight grip he had around my throat was anything but ghostlike. The more I struggled, the harder and more inescapable it became. By my third bolt of lightning, I was almost positive I'd black out if he squeezed any harder. So I had no choice but to stop and hang there like a dead fish.

"Are you done now? I must admit, I'm quite impressed with your ability to do so much with so little at your age, but obviously you've just realized you won't get anywhere with Talents. Smart child--I was about to choke you without an answer. Which, by the way, you have two minutes to give before I change my mind. And to be fair, I should warn you that I *will* know if you lie to me."

I glared menacingly into his eyes, all the while searching for some sign of reluctance to kill a fifteen year old girl for a box. Absolutely nothing was there. Deciding I'd play the next couple minutes to buy some time, I answered slowly and under my breath, "Yes."

"I beg your pardon, I did not catch that. Hearing is the second thing to go, I suppose."

"Yes, Hyvecuous, I've found... the chest" I croaked.

"You know my name. Why, that's very impressive, Lealight. I thought it was lost among people a long time ago. Such an affront to be called something as offensive as It for so long--like an animal of some kind. I'm glad something's finally being done about that. But anyway, my following question to that would be *where is it*?"

I, once again, said nothing.

"Do not think I would feel guilty about killing a child, you little twit! You will tell me where it is or I'll choke you--right here, right now."

I was thinking frantically for a way out, some way to escape Hyvecuous'ss grasp and from there I knew I could outrun him. But nothing I did would make him even flinch until a full and agonizing thirty seconds later when he suddenly gasped and dropped me as if I'd burned him. I wasted no time, scrambled to my feet, and ran as fast as I could around the corner only to stop when a bookcase fell directly on the spot where I would've been if I'd continued. I had all of two seconds to process what just happened and think about what I was going to do next when I was lurched off the floor and held about eight feet off the ground almost as if I was trapped inside an invisible fist.

"Well, it looks like you might turn out to be a problem after all" Hyvecuous sounded like he was mostly talking to himself as he examined his hand that he'd had around my throat a minute earlier. I saw, to my amazement, there was a long gash with a little golden glow emitting from within it across his palm. And realized shortly afterward that I was responsible for it. "But do not worry, I have ways to dispose of stubborn people like you who insist on trying to stop what is coming even though they know they'll never succeed."

Completely ignoring him, I continued trashing around and screaming before I was rocketed upward and smacked against the ceiling. Really, really *hard*. My head cracked up against it and I cried out in pain before I plummeted down from the twenty feet and hit the floor with just as much force. Blankness crept up on the corners of my vision. I pushed it down as much as I could, but my head throbbed to the point where the pain alone could've been enough to knock anyone unconscious. And it only took one more drop for it to do just that to me. The very last thing I saw was Hyvecuous coming in my direction. And the look on his face combined with his infamous past? Believe me, it doesn't exactly result in a peaceful slumber.

Chapter 32

The next thing I remember was waking up in a small, dark room on a stone floor and it taking every ounce of my strength to simply sit up and lean against the wall. I couldn't feel much immediately. But within two minutes, I came to notice I had a splitting headache that felt similar to having a little idiot inside my skull hammering merrily away with a pickaxe. My neck was about as effective at holding up my head as a toothpick was when trying to support a cinderblock. I stayed there for what seemed like hours before I remembered what had happened. And everything hit me full force--knocking all of my current exhaustion, pain, and fear down to priority number two.

I had been ambushed by Hyvecuous. And what's more? The entire freaking Universe could have fallen into shambles for all I knew. The others--oh my gosh, *the others*.

I pushed myself off the ground and found, much to my irritation, I couldn't stand without leaning heavily against the wall. But I wasn't too concerned about that at the moment. All I cared about was getting back to everyone else and finding out how long I was gone.

Unfortunately, there was simple logic to describe exactly how that worked out. The more I tried to move, the more my head throbbed. The more my head throbbed, the harder it was to move. Basically no matter which way you turned it, I just couldn't win.

Of course I stubbornly kept inching my way along the wall anyway until my left foot hit something. It was nearly pitch-black, so I obviously couldn't see that well, but I still slowly knelt down and picked up the object. Of all things, it was a book. You know, I was hoping for, oh I don't know, maybe some bizarre way to *get out of there*. But of course there was no such luck, and I stood back up clutching the thing closely. There was a little note attached to the cover, and my curiosity to read what it said eventually got the better of me. I shone a light from the palm of my hand directly on the slip of paper. It was ten times dimmer than it usually was and flickered several times before it became steady. I squinted to make out the words.

"*This belongs to the Grand Summits. It's time it was returned to you,*" was all that was written. As I expected, there was no signature.

Still holding the light, I leafed through the book not really paying attention to what was inside as I thought about what to do. But before long I didn't need it to see the pages. And that didn't register as something strange to me until a few minutes later. I finally figured out the reason why my light had long since gone out and I could still see. The contents of the book were glowing, especially the page where I had paused.

I stared blankly and watched in shock as a picture of the Library emerged. Frowning, I started to wonder how that was supposed to help me in any way. All of the books in my Library could show images. What made this one special? I watched the picture for several seconds before both of my questions were answered. The illustration began to contort into a completely new one. It was still of the Library, but it was almost as if the field of view had panned over to a specific spot on the floor directly on top of a rug. Then, the small carpet vanished, but instead of looking at plain floorboards, I was looking at a trapdoor. It was bolted down, locked, and obviously unused for quite some time considering the dust and rotting wood. First thought: that's what this thing's trying to tell me! *Where I am*. It's telling me I'm under the Library! Second thought: how could I have spent a good portion of nearly every day for three years in a place and not know about a secret trapdoor under a rug...

Anyway, I knew where I was. Check. Next issue--find some way to, once again, get the heck out of there. I closed the surprisingly thin book and held it under my arm as I felt across the room. I found what I guessed was the next best thing to finding the other side of the trapdoor itself--a ladder.

I sighed. My head still pounded relentlessly, and I couldn't stand up without being shaky. I couldn't climb a ladder--there was no way and I knew it. Ignoring all common sense and logical reasoning, I clutched it. Even though it was only seven feet tall at the most, it took me a good five minutes to reach the top and cautiously let go with one hand to feel the wood of the trapdoor. And now, I thought, to address the "bolted down" part. I gave it as hard a push as I could (not hard at that particular moment), stupidly hoping since the thing was so old it might just give way. But it held strong, and I knew the wood from which the trapdoor had been made was old as dirt. Even with Woodland, I couldn't do anything to get out. I was at another dead end.

But I then did what any normal person who was suddenly slammed with claustrophobia, starting to breathe rapidly, and needed to get out into the open right away for the sake of their own stretched-to-the-breaking-point *sanity*. I pressed my hand against the damp wood and found an alternate use for the Woodland Talent. Even though I couldn't see them, I could feel small vines growing and coiling around the hinges of the trapdoor--loosening the bolts and picking the lock until one shove later it flung open. Remember how I said "I'll let you know when I think of some" about the advantages of being a Woodland? Illydia, this would be Exhibit A.

So, there I was back in the Library again--sitting on the floor holding my head in my hands. But finally out of the tiny, dark room below that I had no idea existed. And I was frankly unnerved by the fact that Hyvecuous did. Quickly shaking the thought, I stood unsteadily, grabbing onto a bookcase, and painfully inched my way toward the table by the support of the many shelves. Once I reached it, I placed the thin book bound with red leather (strange) with very intricate swirl designs all around the edges (even more strange) on top. I decided I needed to find out more about this book that apparently belonged to me and could show clear, moving images and I definitely needed to try to get behind the fifth wall again to see what all the fuss with the chest was about. But not right then. The others came first and I needed to get to them. And as much as I didn't want to admit it, I really needed their help. There I said it. *Happy*?

Reaching the bottom of the stairs seemed to take me forever. Afterwards, there was the matter of climbing all the way up. Using the same amount of stubbornness as I did with the ladder, I managed to trudge all eight stories. I was so relieved to see the Citadel unharmed and everything outside look just like it had before I went into the Library... however long ago that was. I almost forgot about my need to hang onto something as I practically dove out into the hallway. Only after I was clutching the opposite wall, did I notice what was wrong.

The place was deserted.

I felt horror rising inside of me until I heard something coming from the great room.

"Are you absolutely *sure* about this?" Aaron said from around the corner.

"Of course I'm sure, Aaron," answered another familiar voice that I couldn't place right away. "Ten people is what she said. *Ten* people and he'll be here again soon. Who knows what he'll try and what measures he'll take to-"

"When? *Why*?" Katrina interrupted.

"You know perfectly well *why*. And it's been days."

Having enough of just standing there, I took a deep breath.

"Hello?" I tried to yell only for it to come out as more of a pathetic whimper. "*Hello?*"

"W-who's there?" Macalynn's voice echoed from around the corner.

"It's me" I began only to run into her as I turned into the great room.

"Macalynn, I'm so glad to see you're all okay," I told her as I noticed that everyone was there--Jarmony, Isetha, and all the other Summits.

But her eyes showed no sign of relief, and she didn't look delighted like I had expected. In fact, she shrieked bloody murder as the color drained from her face. She backed away from me slowly before running back to the others and into Aaron's arms. Nice to see you, too.

"Guys?" I asked as everyone stared at me terrified. "What's wrong?"

I stopped dead and cupped my hand over my mouth to keep from screaming--my headache suddenly the last thing I was thinking of as I figured out exactly what was wrong pretty quickly. Someone with long, dark, curly hair stepped out in front of the others protectively. She had deep blue eyes and fair skin with some freckles. The Grand Summit's cloak was resting on her shoulders.

I was looking at myself.

Chapter 33

Isetha immediately grabbed a protesting Jarmony, and the two of them took off down the stairs--leaving the others, me, and my apparent clone staring at each other.

"Okay--what's going on, Lealight?" Harmon asked, but to the other one.

"Exactly what I just told you all," she replied in *my* voice irritably.

"Well, would you mind letting me in on that because I have no clue what you're talking about," I interrupted while taking a few steps out into the open.

They all tensed just as the other me balled up her fist. Thick, brown vines suddenly shot up out of absolutely nowhere all around--grabbing me by my neck, wrists, ankles, and hair while trying to force me to the floor. I instinctively tapped on them and they shrank back, leaving me only three seconds to regain my balance before they came back to life twice as forceful and effective at knocking me over as before. Only this time, they were compliments of Illydia.

I tried to hit them again while gagging from the vine coiling tighter and tighter around my neck, only to be restrained by more shooting upward at me from all directions. I decided right then and there I wouldn't tolerate her droning on and on about how the Woodland Talent was useless anymore, either.

"What are you doing?!" I yelled at Illydia who continued to will the vines tighter.

Harmon stepped up beside her. "Don't think you're fooling anyone in that disguise, *Hyvecuous*! Lealight told us everything!" he shouted.

"*What*?! I'm... Lealight... that's... Hyvecuous!" I choked. The others snarled angrily, and I knew no one believed me.

Feeling as if I was about to be crushed, I finally found a way out by lighting on fire just as Amiselle had done down in my Library. I scrambled to my feet amongst the broken, burning vines and ash just as Katrina, who was now wearing a Summit's uniform instead of the Charge one, stepped in and drenched everything that was on fire--again. What joy she finds in leaving almost everything wet, I do not know. Amiselle's eyes flashed in the way we all knew too well, and I had just enough time to jump upward and flatten myself against the ceiling before a giant, roaring fire sprang up where I had just been. I was too focused on avoiding becoming a human torch to notice Macalynn coming up fast. She flew straight into me, roughly knocking me out the window.

Chapter 34

Isetha tore through the trees as fast as she could--oblivious to Jarmony's shouts telling her to stop running from far behind her. What no one else knew about the night her parents disappeared was that after Teller Hallsmen had sent them to the Citadel, she told Isetha something she didn't say to Asteria, Greo, or Tarron. She had said, "Isetha, listen to me. If anything strange ever happens there I need you to come let me know about it right away, alright?"

Being too upset about losing her parents then to answer, Isetha just nodded, caught up with the others, and thought nothing of it. That was until several days later when she saw two Lealights. Figuring that definitely counted as strange, Isetha took off down the stairs and across the yard with Jarmony. For she remembered Lealight saying she needed to stay close to her or one of the others.

Isetha actually ran into Litheney when she walked into the door of the school. The Teller looked increasingly panicked.

"There… were… two… Lealights." Isetha began--wheezing from running the two miles through the woods.

"I know," Litheney answered. "I think I know what to do. Come with me."

Jarmony then ran inside and asked, "Isetha, what were you thinking just running off like that? And why'd you drag me with you?"

"I was thinking that Teller Hallsmen told me I needed to come see her if anything weird ever happened, and Lealight said I can't go through the woods alone," the little girl answered hastily.

Jarmony looked at Litheney as if to say "*Why*?"

"That's all beside the point, Jeremy. We have to go right now--or who knows what might happen?" With that, she turned and strode out onto the yard motioning for the two to follow her.

"It's Jarmony for the thousandth time," Jarmony grumbled under his breath and rolled his eyes as they started after Teller Hallsmen.

Isetha smiled, but then left him behind as she ran to catch up with Litheney.

Chapter 35

I caught myself just a few feet above the ground and narrowly avoided a lightning bolt from Harmon. Before I had a chance to catch my breath and scold myself once more for shaking like I'd just been in a giant snowstorm, everyone poured out of the Citadel. Afterward, everything was a blur of me telling myself to deflect the fire, stop the ice ball that can easily take your head off, and for heaven's sake *get out of the freaking way*.

It slowly dawned on me that with every passing minute, I was getting closer to being overpowered. I mean, Aaron is just as good at Earth as I was, and Illydia is just as good at Woodland. So it was almost like I was being attacked by six of me, plus one more (Hyvecuous). And I'd spent a while locked in a small underground room after acquiring some sort of concussion, so I wasn't exactly at the top of my game. Let's not forget that the others weren't holding back at all while I, on the other hand, was only using defense. Not exactly a fair fight.

Even so, I was holding out okay until I was suddenly blown off the cliff.

Chapter 36

The three finally came to a stop in front of one of the nearly identical houses on one of the many identical streets that Isetha always got lost in. But the Teller, apparently, did not. Litheney knocked forcefully on the door and waited impatiently until it was opened by a girl with dark brown hair that was pulled neatly to the side and rested on her shoulder. She had freckles all across her nose and green eyes that were speckled with more brown.

"Teller Hallsmen? What are you doing here?" she asked.

"Avley, you must come with us at once. Grab a jacket or something and *let's go.*"

"Why? What's going on?"

Teller Hallsmen sighed and quickly answered, "Lealight is in danger, and she needs you."

Avley frowned. "Lealight is the Grand Summit now. I'm sure that she can handle whatever it is herself. And if it's that bad then the other Summits can help her."

She started to close the door, but Teller Hallsmen wedged her shoe in it before she could.

"That's not going to happen considering the other Summits might be attacking her as we speak. And I know you've been upset that she turned out to be who she is, but Lealight didn't choose to be the Grand Summit. Do you really want her to be killed when you know you could've stopped it?"

Avley threw the door back open.

"*Killed*? Why are they attacking her?!"

"We'll fill you in on the details along the way, so grab your coat and *be quick about it,*" Teller Hallsmen said sternly.

She left and came back within ten seconds flat. "I'm going out!" she yelled into the house before slamming the door shut. She addressed the group as she pulled a dark blue jacket over her tunic. "Don't just stand there, *hurry up!*"

Chapter 37

It happened so fast I didn't have a chance to react before I whacked against a tree and plummeted downward. The wind was knocked out of me when I landed flat on my back. I laid there struggling to breathe for all of five seconds before I was launched upward and pressed against the cliff just above the heads of the others. Pure hatred and rage possessed them to the point where they were unrecognizable. I knew there was no way I could convince them I was the real me. And the situation looked pretty similar to what Macalynn and I did to Merrhet before sending him to the fourth dimension. I had a horrible feeling in the pit of my stomach that that was what awaited me. My own fellow Summits were going to send me off to my death if they didn't just kill me right then. Which, of course, they could have. I was much too weak to fight back, anyway.

As horrible as it all sounds, that still wasn't the worst part. What bothered me the most was Hyvecuous'ss smug look. It was pretty clear he'd already accomplished whatever he'd come to do. He was just enjoying seeing me be attacked by the six people I considered my closest friends, my only family. It occurred to me that I was about twenty seconds away from never seeing them or my home again. My only hope was maybe Hyvecuous would have a change of heart and let me see them one last time before he blew us all to smithereens.

I was regarding everyone through half closed, half teary eyes. But I couldn't find my voice and just hung there helplessly before fire was sent in my direction. I threw my arms over my face and the flames bent around the shield of nothing but air that I'd surrounded myself with. Of course the fact that I was now pleading for them to stop and even crying didn't make them falter. The flames I was just keeping off of me were followed by lightning, and then a tugging at the air I had surrounding and shielding me. I kept it up as long as I could before the others succeeded in breaking it down. I felt the unbearable heat of the fire and lightning against me and screamed shrilly before a muffled shout came from below. Afterwards, everything halted.

"Stop it! *STOP IT THIS INSTANT*!"

The fire and lightning vanished simultaneously. Macalynn's focus apparently broke because I fell from the air and landed face down on the ground.

"Have you all completely lost your minds? Just what did you think you were *doing*?" Litheney's voice echoed as the sound of footsteps ran toward us. "You could've killed her!"

"Litheney, that's not Lealight. That's Hy-" Katrina began only to be cut off.

"If you six would open your eyes, you'd figure out the truth! Honestly, were you really that blinded that you didn't notice she was hurt the very second you saw her?!"

"Anyone can put on an act, Litheney," Aaron said coldly. "Including Hyvecuous."

"That may be true. But even so, did it ever occur to you that this *could* be Lealight? If you have two of them and no evidence as to which one is real and which one isn't then perhaps you should not have just picked one to attack because I have news for you-- you picked wrong! I saw what Hyvecuous did to her and I brought someone who could have proved who is who but I did not think he could have talked you all into taking it this far!"

Okay, it was embarrassing enough that Litheney was the only one in the way of the others finishing me off. I couldn't stand her saying that I was unable to prove I was myself even with someone else's help in front of not only them, but also *Hyvecuous*. And because I just had to be humiliated even further, someone then came over and pulled me up.

"You okay, Lealight?" A voice asked me. I immediately recognized it as Jarmony's. He was helping me regardless of the stare he was getting from Aaron.

I shook my head--once again holding it in both hands and seeing no point in lying. And I thought it was pretty clear I was anything but.

"Don't worry, we'll get this straightened out," he answered now with one arm around my shoulders and the other arm propping me up so I could face Hyvecuous and the others with at least a little dignity. I'd never been so thankful to him in all the three years he'd been with us.

Everyone just looked at me for a while before Litheney agreed, and I finally took notice of another person standing there. It was the same girl who I said I could've sworn I knew from somewhere when the kid met up with her after I'd asked him to spread the word about Katrina. And I felt horrible for not remembering the someone who was my only friend growing up.

"Avley?" I blinked several times to make sure I was seeing the right person and realized shortly afterwards, to my sheer annoyance, that Hyvecuous had said her name too.

"She is going to prove which one of you is the true Grand Summit because clearly the Talent ones will not simply take my word for it," Litheney continued--the concern in her voice now cancelled out by irritation. "Nevertheless, Hyvecuous looks and sounds exactly like Lealight, correct?"

Everyone besides me and Hyvecuous-in-me-form nodded.

"But he doesn't have her memories. And since Avley and Lealight practically grew up together, she's going to ask the both of them questions about things they did. Of course the goal is we will eventually get to something where only the real Lealight will be able to answer her."

The others were silent for a few moments before Aaron responded. "It's worth a try."

Everyone then stepped back and left Avley, Hyvecuous, Jarmony, and me some space.

"I'll keep this simple. What's my last name?" Avley began.

"Plenstion" we answered simultaneously.

She looked surprised and pretty freaked out by the fact that Hyvecuous would know that (yeah, I kind of would be too) before she continued. "When's my birthday?"

"The 243rd day of the 588th year," we responded in unison once again just as Macalynn groaned and sank onto the ground under the branches of a nearby tree.

"We're going to be here all day."

Chapter 38

Apparently Macalynn has psychic powers--because she was pretty close to being right. Some ten or fifteen questions later, everyone was staring off into space while Avley continued. At that point, my head throbbed to the point where it hurt just to keep my eyes open, but I didn't exactly have a choice. I had no idea what I would've done if it wasn't for Jarmony still being on my side.

By the time we'd hit the twenties, Avley seemed to be running out of questions. She looked at Litheney for what to do.

"This is getting ridiculous," she answered. "You are going on about things that are obvious. Is it that difficult to come up with something you think Hyvecuous won't know?"

Avley shrugged and looked at the Teller as if to say, "As you can see, *yeah it sort of is*."

Another silence set in before she, at the end of her rope, asked, "What's the last thing I said to you before you guys left on the 100th day of the 600th year?"

Neither of us responded immediately, and everyone looked up suddenly interested.

"This is it," Amiselle said under her breath.

Well, it might be if I knew the answer. All I remembered was a tearful good bye and the whole I'll-never-see-you-again-because-you-have-to-go-off-and-be-a-Summit-now ordeal.

"It was something along the lines of "I'll miss you and good luck", right?" Hyvecuous guessed lamely, but still in my voice.

Avley looked at him in a strange way before her expression went back to normal and everyone stared at me--waiting for an answer.

"No, that definitely had nothing to do with it," I began slowly, thinking aloud more than anything else. "I remember that when I walked over, some other kid from our class was being a jerk and told everyone standing there something like 'Well, we didn't see that coming. Who would've thought she'd turn out to be someone important' and you punched him for it. Then you said 'I want you to know that I'll never forget you and I'm always here if you need me.' After that, we didn't say anything else. The five minutes was nothing but a teary goodbye."

Everyone was on their feet and gathered around us as Avley and Litheney exchanged glances.

"The second answer is right. That one's Lealight," Avley finally said while nodding at me.

I sighed in relief while Hyvecuous, most likely just trying to annoy me, refused to drop the act and yelled, "That's not true! I'm-"

"You know what? *Enough*," I interrupted while storming in his direction and leaving Jarmony behind. "I know you're basically out to destroy everyone one day, and whether you actually accomplish that is something we'll all find out when it comes. But you *will not* waltz around pretending to be me while I'm alive!"

Jarmony and Avley rejoined the others. They'd basically formed a circle around the two of us---waiting to see whether or not to do something. Harmon looked like he was about to before everyone grew wide eyed and backed away quickly.

I had no idea what caused them to. At first, I thought it might be an appropriate late reaction to being told the notorious and very much feared It was standing right there, but scratched the idea because Litheney was among them. Hyvecuous was also taking a few steps backward with an expression that looked like a mixture of confusion and alarm. I finally figured out it was at me. What do you know? The shoe's on the other foot. After looking at the ground, which seemed to be where everyone was staring, I saw what was causing them to back away as if I were some contagious disease. A thick and vaguely familiar haze was rising all around me. Its golden color gave off much of the light visible under the Clouds, and I could only assume what it was.

The actual, pure Magic that Veronica said was the only thing I could use to kill Hyvecuous. I had no idea where it came from, or how I did it, but I was glad for once it was being useful.

I balled up my fists, and something that looked like a little lightning bolt with the golden haze around it whizzed past my head. It hit Hyvecuous'ss, or rather, my cloak and he immediately turned back into the man that had ambushed me down in the Library.

I'll let you use your imagination for what it looked like because it wasn't exactly a pleasant sight. And I'm leaving the full description out of this to keep it rated for general audiences.

Avley shrank back behind Litheney, Jarmony, and the other Summits.

Hyvecuous, a truly one-of-a-kind villain, cackled manically. "*Bravo*, Lealight. I must say I underestimated you. Not only did you escape, but you also seem to have a bit of that Magic in you after all. You see, I was expecting you to put up more of a fight back in your Library, and was pretty disappointed."

I stood there shaking: a little because I was still unstable but mostly in rage. The *nerve* of that guy.

"But I've just seen that I will be getting the memorable fight I was looking for. Until then, I must be going."

Hyvecuous then turned and faced the others.

"I have enjoyed getting to know you all. It'll be a shame that next time we meet will be the end of the Summits. It is unfortunate that they are realized so young. But you can thank all of the foolish, *foolish* Tellers for that."

Litheney looked like she was about to go knock his lights out, but was held back by Amiselle and Aaron, both their faces reading "*Don't.*"

Taking notice of Teller Hallsmen's glare that dared him to go on, he smiled in that horrible, twisted way before finally ending with, "Another thing I enjoyed was your parents' company, Isetha."

She went pale, and Katrina put a protective arm around her.

"It was truly an honor to work with them," Hyvecuous continued. "Unfortunately, all good things must come to an end and I regret to inform you that they were... laid off yesterday."

The color came back to Isetha's face. She was scarlet red with anger.

"You're lying," she said under her breath.

"What was that?" Hyvecuous persisted mockingly.

"You're lying!" the little girl's voice echoed through the trees. "I know you're lying!"

"Now, why would you think-"

"I suggest if you've decided against invading right this minute, you get out of here before the first Grand Summit to ever unlock the secrets of real Magic and the only remaining Charmer kill you where you stand," Litheney cut in icily.

"That little girl? Don't be ridiculous," he rolled his eyes in disbelief and annoyance--as if Teller Hallsmen was a bratty kid who'd just spoke out of turn. "And very well. Goodbye Teller, Summits, Charge, children."

With that, Hyvecuous vanished within an appropriate darkened haze that gave off the same repelling force as the field around the chest. Since it was my privilege to be standing right there, I was abruptly thrown backward at an increasingly fast speed like some ragdoll. I tumbled along the ground several times before I finally skidded to a halt and lay sprawled. Everyone gathered around me within fifteen seconds.

Leave it to Lealight to point out the obvious, but that was definitely not my day.

Chapter 39

Coughing several times because of all the dirt that had been knocked into the air from my trip backward, I gathered up my remaining will power and a single shred of dignity. I got onto my knees before Illydia and Amiselle came over and pulled me to my feet. Of course the second they let go, I stumbled forward and started shaking so violently that Amiselle had to wrap her arms around me in support like Jarmony had done. They sat back down with me in between them as the others joined us. Illydia took notice of me holding my head in my hands to ease the pain. She gently placed it on her shoulder and stroked my hair out of my face. I started crying again and there went that single shred of dignity I'd tried, but obviously failed, to hold on to.

"We're so sorry, Lealight," Macalynn choked when the dust finally thinned out. "We weren't thinking straight, and we thought Hyvecuous was you and since he said that you were him we-"

"It's okay," I croaked. "You guys didn't know."

"But we should've listened to what you had to say, but instead we attacked you even when you were obviously hurt. And now, you're much worse because of us," Katrina added--her voice cracking.

I looked around at the faces surrounding me. Macalynn and Katrina both had tears streaming down their cheeks; Aaron and Harmon looked pretty close to it. Jarmony, Isetha, and Avley were hanging back a little, but were still watching me with worried expressions. Teller Hallsmen looked just about as concerned as I'd ever seen her look before.

Well, that just about confirmed my suspicion that all I was good for was upsetting people.

"It's not... that bad, I'm-" I began only to be interrupted by an exasperated Litheney.

"Lealight, you are as pale as a ghost, shaking like you have just fallen into freezing water, and you cannot even stand up on your own. Don't even try it--you clearly are hurt."

I sighed and looked down.

"Tell us what happened," Aaron said after about a minute of silence.

I kept my gaze focused on the ground until someone took my hand in theirs and squeezed it.

"Please tell us, Lealight. We want to help you," Isetha added earnestly with the kind of look only a little kid can give that's impossible to shut out and ignore.

With a half-smile that quickly faded, I looked back toward the others and said "First off, I haven't seen any of you since I went into my Library after coming back with Isetha on the day I found the chest. How long has it been?"

Their comforting smiles vanished.

"Three days. Hyvecuous must have been impersonating you for three days," Harmon finally answered. "But where were you? How did he... keep you there for so long?"

"That rock in the chest turned out to be a... key. A key that unlocks a wall in the Library and behind it is supposed to be the information we need. But when I was about to open it, Hyvecuous showed up. He lifted me off the ground by my neck all the while trying to choke me."

"And you didn't do *anything* to get away?" Jarmony chimed in, though he quickly realized he shouldn't have.

"Of *course* I did," I snapped, "and not just anything. *Everything*. But none of it worked. I mean, it all went through him like he was nothing but a ghost. He basically said he was going to kill me, but he'd make it less painful if I answered his questions. So the entire time I was trying to think of a way out. Then he suddenly dropped me like I'd burned him, and I saw a gigantic cut across his hand."

"Wait, if the Talents didn't do anything... then how did you burn him?" Amiselle asked in the same tone as Harmon and Aaron had. I was already starting to get sick of them talking to me as if they thought I was going to completely break down.

"I think it was Magic. I didn't mean to do it... I just did. But it didn't matter. The second I started running, he jerked me off the ground and held me in midair for a while before he launched me upwards. I hit my head on the ceiling really hard and on the floor even harder. And then he did it again and... it just hurt so much that I, um... it knocked me out. I woke up locked in some dark and tiny room under the Library."

Illydia hugged me tighter, and I felt Amiselle lean me forward slightly so she could see the back of my head. After pushing my hair to the side to get a better look, she winced as if she was the one who'd been hit hard enough to be knocked unconscious after only two good strikes.

"It's swollen all through here," her finger gently traced around the edges of what I knew must have been a lump the size of an egg. "That's really bad, Lealight. It looks like a concussion."

"Of course it's a concussion," Litheney rolled her eyes. "She was completely out cold when I saw her yesterday."

My face burned with shame as Harmon asked what I'd been wondering about for a while. "What do you mean you saw her yesterday? She was under the Library."

"I'm sure Lealight knows how," she looked back at me and so did everyone else. To my complete humiliation, of course. I was still shivering in Illydia's arms.

"I... I can't remember right now," I answered slowly.

She didn't say anything except, "Try harder."

"Litheney, just tell us," Aaron sighed. "Lealight's been locked underground with a concussion for three days."

"The tunnels." I finally nailed down what I was trying to think of and everyone except Teller Hallsmen looked at me in confusion.

"Exactly," she nodded at me. "I decided it was time to return the book and planned to leave it in that room for you to eventually find. But when I got there, you were in it... and you were unconscious. I tried everything to get you up, but couldn't and realized after about five minutes that the reason was because you had been hit very hard in the back of your head. I thought about taking you back to the Village with me to get help, but I knew I couldn't do that... so I dropped the book off there like I had planned and ran back through the tunnels to the school. Once I reached it, I left immediately for the Citadel to see if you all knew she was missing. But Lealight was the one who opened the door--standing upright and completely unharmed. I knew immediately that I was looking at Hyvecuous. But I couldn't tell any of you that. You would not have believed me. So I did the only thing I could think to do and went back to the school. I stayed there all of yesterday thinking about what I was going to do. I couldn't let Hyvecuous go on impersonating you and leave you down in the tunnels, but I couldn't tell anyone, either. Of course Isetha then came to me and said there were two

Lealights, and I knew that you had escaped and you were not going to be welcomed back."

The others all stared at the ground.

"So I got Avley because, like I said before, I knew you all wouldn't just take my word for who was the real Lealight."

We just looked at her for several seconds before anyone said anything.

"Okay, so let me get this straight," Harmon began dubiously. "There are underground tunnels running all the way from the school to Lealight's Library and you and she are the only ones who knew about them? And you used them to deliver a book? Why didn't you just bring it to the front door like a *normal person*?"

"Remember the map in the scroll we found in Merrhet's room?" I spoke up. "That's the only reason I knew about them. And-"

"First, the tunnels connect many places. Not just the school and the Citadel," Litheney either didn't hear or paid no heed to what I had begun to say. "And it's not just a regular book. If it was, then yes, I would have just brought it to you normally. But I'm assuming Lealight told you all about the one I showed her that can let you see moving pictures and shows the next set of Summits when it is time?"

They nodded.

"Well, the book I left for her is the same one."

"That doesn't make sense," I said. "The one you had was thick and black and the one I found is red and much thinner."

"Because I had a cover over it in case Hyvecuous or his Shadows ever came looking and fake pages at the end to throw them off further."

I didn't respond right away. "And you're giving this to me why?"

"It has always belonged to you," she answered. "Did you not read the note I placed on the cover? It has always belonged to the Grand Summits. It was originally created to be handed down among them like every other book in your Library. However, Veronica Calodie gave it to the Teller of her time to hold on to until Hyvecuous returned. That is when the idea of the Test was created. So people would not know about the book's existence."

"Why would she do that in the first place knowing that she would be lying to the entire dimension for generations to come?" Macalynn spoke up.

"I do not believe Summit Calodie wanted to lie," Litheney shrugged. "She had no choice but to give this book up before Hyvecuous escaped the ice. If he knew it had been left with the Teller, then it would defeat the purpose of her hiding it to begin with. She knew Hyvecuous was not gone permanently. He wanted that book so he could know who the Summits are the moment they are born and kill them as infants. Instead of keeping it in the Library, where he could easily send Shadows to search without her knowledge, she gave it to the only person outside the Summits who she believed could be trusted with the secret of Hyvecuous'ss eventual return. It has been passed down for the last four hundred years from Teller to Teller until now that I have given it back to you."

I nodded, not really knowing what else I could say on the topic, just as Aaron spoke up again.

"Not to rudely change the subject, but Lealight, I'm sure we're all wondering what that thing was with you and the yellow fog… we've never seen you do that before."

I, once again, didn't say anything immediately. I was debating about whether or not to show the others the letter and risk getting another Litheney Hallsmen death glare. Somewhat creepily reading my mind, Litheney rubbed her temples like people do when they're telling themselves to remember that what doesn't kill them makes them stronger.

"Just show them. You've managed to get everyone involved now that you have put on a little show."

I rolled my eyes at her and answered, "I already told you I didn't mean to do that. As you probably guessed, I haven't read one thing behind the wall. It just happened, and I'm pretty glad it did. Otherwise I'd still be standing there trying to prove I was me."

She raised an eyebrow as if she didn't believe me, but I pulled Veronica's note from my pocket anyway and gave it to Amiselle. She read it aloud while I thought, *gee, if I wanted Avley, Jarmony, Litheney, and Isetha to know what it said I would have read it myself.*

"Okay," said Macalynn. I knew immediately that my five minutes of soothing talk because they felt guilty about attacking me were up. "Where did you get this?"

I looked back to the ground. I didn't want to admit that I'd kept something from them.

"Lealight, *where did you get this?*" She repeated vehemently.

"It was in the chest. Along with the rock," I finally answered.

"Why didn't you show it to us?" Katrina asked--hurt.

"I, uh..." I stammered before Teller Hallsmen oddly came to the rescue.

"She didn't show it to you because I told her she couldn't."

The others looked infuriated.

"*Why not?*" Aaron demanded--almost baring his teeth.

"Because it was meant to be read only by the Grand Summit during the time of Hyvecuous'ss return and it didn't concern any of you," Litheney defended herself. "*I* didn't even know what it said until Amiselle broadcasted it."

"You have absolutely *no right* to tell us what we can and cannot say to *each other*," Harmon practically spat. "Lealight doesn't have to keep anything from us. Especially something this important, and I really couldn't care less if she has your approval or not."

Litheney looked somewhat taken aback but shrugged it off. "Fine. Agreed. You all have every right to tell each other whatever. And as unbelievable as it may seem after these past three years, I want the seven of you know that I'm on your side. I also hope you are aware that the worst is yet to come, and all I'm trying to do is help you all get through this. Why do you think I sent that child into the woods to tell you the Citadel was burning? Why would I bother to send the letter about the chest?"

After I thought about it, I decided that in some way, shape, or form it could be perceived that Litheney meant well and actually cared about us as people. I guessed it was possible, but barely.

Chapter 40

Everyone sat or stood around in silence for a while before Isetha spoke up.

"I'm a *what*?" she asked Teller Hallsmen.

"What do you mean?"

"You called me a Charmer. What were you talking about?"

Litheney sighed. "I did not mean to say that. You weren't supposed to be told until you turned eighteen, Isetha." She paused as if to consider what to do next. "But these are not normal circumstances, so I'll tell you now. Please wait and listen to everything and then I will help you in any way that I can."

Well, that didn't sound too good. Obviously trying to control her anxiousness, Isetha looked back at me, and I squeezed her shoulder as reassuringly as I could manage.

"I don't even know where to start with this," she began uncertainly. "But-"

"Do spit it out" I interrupted, mimicking her voice.

The Teller shot me a particularly impressive evil eye and said something to herself that sounded along the lines of "I suppose I should have seen that coming. At least we know we have the right Lealight," under her breath before continuing.

"Well, Isetha, the reason Hyvecuous kidnapped the parents was because the Shadows reported that there was a Charmer in the

Village. He eventually narrowed it down the possibilities to your four houses. You all live very close to each other. And since you, Greo, Tarron, and Asteria weren't around at the time, you didn't get taken. Once he found he only needed your parents, he dropped everyone else off in the middle of the woods with no memory of what had happened. Apparently, he thinks your parents are the Charmers. But they are not. You are."

"Wait," I cut in. "You said you didn't know why they were taken yester--I mean, four days ago."

"That's true," she responded. "I didn't. But before I started through the tunnels to drop off the book, I found out from it."

"If you're going to call me a Charmer," Isetha chimed in. "Could you tell me what one is?"

Litheney nodded and continued. "You see, you'll always be a Woodland, Isetha. That never changes. But Charmers have a… a special touch of Magic. Now, it's nothing like what we just saw Lealight do. It can't be seen or used like that in any way. But, simply stated, you're the only person who has the ability to create actual Charms. I trust you have at the very least heard of them before… they are fairly simple ways to apply Magic to objects to make them behave differently than they would under normal conditions."

Litheney paused and looked at me as if waiting for my approval of her definition. I gave a slight nod and she continued. "The last Charmer lived over four hundred years ago. He made them as a service to help just regular people. But there was a small…um, accident, and that was banned very quickly. Afterward, no one knew what happened to him, and no other Charmer was ever discovered. Until you, Isetha."

"But how do you know it's me?" she asked.

"That book," everyone consecutively answered before she did.

Clearing her throat, Teller Hallsmen simply added, "Yes, exactly."

"Okay, so what am I supposed to be doing now?" Isetha continued--looking like she feared the answer.

"You need to learn everything there is to know about being a Charmer" the Teller began. "I promised I would help you with whatever I can, and I will, but Lealight will be of more use to you than anyone else."

"Why-" we both began at the same time only to be interrupted.

"Because, Lealight, you have dozens of books on everything there is to know on Charms in your Library. And you are the only *Magical* Talent, so that's bound to count for something when trying to teach someone things that have to do with Magic. Besides, you both now need to study similar things, and I figure you two can help each other. Of course I wouldn't advise you to try doing anything until you can recover some from this concussion. It seemed pretty bad the second I saw you, and now it only looks worse."

"I'm fine, Litheney," I refused to look at anyone--annoyed and embarrassed she had said that in front of them. "I don't need to recover from anything."

"Whatever you say," she answered doubtfully while motioning to Avley. She was still hanging back behind her. "Avley, I think we should leave them alone now."

She nodded slowly, and the two of them turned around. They headed through the trees without a backward glance.

"Wait," I called as I lifted my head off of Illydia's shoulder and promptly sucked in my breath as another wave of pain hit me. It felt like my skull was going to explode. Illydia reached to grab my arm, but I stood and walked off before any of the others could pin me down. Avley stopped at my call, but Litheney did not-- knowing who I wanted to speak with. The two of us stood there awkwardly until the others started back toward the bottom of the cliff.

"Thank you" I began. "You haven't seen me in over three years and the fact that you still came when I was in danger and that you didn't turn your back on me even when I had to turn mine on you means a lot to me."

She half-smiled, but quickly looked away uncomfortably. "You didn't choose this, Lealight. No one ever chooses to be a Summit... And I would never let anything that horrible happen to you if there was something I could do to help. Besides, seeing It... I mean, Hyvecuous's face when your Magic stuff came up was worth the trip. I'm just sorry he got away."

"Yeah, well his time is coming," I huffed and crossed my arms. "One would think somebody passed off to be so powerful would at least have the courage to face all seven of us instead of just randomly ambushing me alone. Like he's scared we could all take him. Some villain he turned out to be. We'll all show that coward a thing or two when he shows his sorry face around here again."

Avley smiled. "You really haven't changed, have you?"

"Nope," I said with a smirk. "And you see what good that's done me."

She laughed, but suddenly got very serious. "In case we never get to talk face to face again, there's one favor I'd like to ask of you."

"Avley, you just saved my life. I can manage a favor."

"When Hyvecuous does come back, please be safe and..."

"What?"

"For what he did to you, I hope you blow him into oblivion."

I grinned broadly. "I might be able to pencil that in."

Chapter 41

After saying a final goodbye to my childhood friend, I hobbled back to the cliff where the others waited. The second they saw me coming, Aaron and Harmon jumped up, ran to my sides, and supported me the rest of the way. Normally, I would've protested. I would've told them I was perfectly fine and could handle something as simple as walking. But the truth was, I probably would've collapsed if they hadn't. They were almost, but not quite, carrying me by the time we reached Illydia, Katrina, Macalynn, and Amiselle. The two eased me onto the ground, and I was promptly enveloped by everyone. And I couldn't help it--I immediately started crying. But it wasn't like before when it was just a couple silent tears until I managed to shame myself into stopping. This time, I was literally writhing with sobs.

"Shhh," Katrina said gently. "Don't cry, Lealight. Please don't cry, we really didn't mean to hurt *you*."

I kept on--now with guilt piled on top of everything like icing on the cake of my life. Let's just put it this way; I was thanking my lucky stars it was just the six of them there seeing me like that and Jarmony and Isetha had gone somewhere else for the time being.

"It's not that," I choked. "I'm so sorry, guys. I'm so, so *sorry*."

They looked confused.

"It's all my *fault*. I was such an *idiot*."

"Stop, just stop right there," Amiselle gripped my shoulders tightly and forced me to look at her. "You, Lealight, are *not* an idiot and don't you ever say that about yourself again. All this is not your fault. It could've happened to any of us. If that is what you're so upset about right now, then stop. It's over, we're here, and you're safe now. If there's something else... then tell us, okay? Just calm down, and tell us."

I took several deep breaths and wiped my face on my sleeve. "Sorry about that, guys... the headache's just getting to me some. But it's nothing. I-I'm fine."

They looked at me skeptically, but didn't press the issue any further. We sat there in silence for a while before I worked up the nerve to ask something that'd been weighing on my mind since I found out I was being impersonated by my Universe's arch-nemesis. I'd just been too afraid to mention it in front of everyone else.

"Um, what did Hyvecuous do as me? Anything I need to fix or clean up?"

The others looked at one another as if to ask "Where do we start?" I felt my stomach turn in knots.

"No," Amiselle finally said from beside me. "Nothing that would make people suspicious or doubtful of you, anyway. But... there is something you should know."

Harmon wrapped his arm around me and rubbed my shoulder.

"People have started disappearing," Amiselle continued. "Ten now. Ten people just vanished. And Asteria, Tarron, and Greo are included. We hoped they'd turn up soon like some of the others did... but it's been two days and nothing. If Hyvecuous was here impersonating you then I guess it makes sense. He wanted you out of the way, and then to keep us from looking for you."

"But that's not something we want you to worry about right now," Macalynn quickly added. "Before any of that, we need to get you inside. You're probably starving and some ice for that goose egg on your head wouldn't hurt, either."

The others all nodded at each other before gathering closely around me. I realized she planned on simply teleporting us back into the great room because they had apparently decided I couldn't handle the journey from the bottom of the cliff. Even though I knew they were probably right, I momentarily thought about refusing and telling them I just wanted to walk. But I had a feeling it'd be no use even if I did. So I kept my mouth shut for once as Harmon still on my left and Amiselle on my right wrapped their arms around me tightly so I couldn't get separated from them in the middle of the teleport. Because there are only three outcomes of that happening. One: you are sent back to your original spot. Two: you are sent to the fourth dimension. Or three, the most likely option and of course my personal favorite, you are torn into a million pieces. So yeah, that's why it's sort of important we hold hands--to make sure everyone's head is still on their shoulders afterwards.

On that lovely note, I closed my eyes so I could help Macalynn. She apparently saw my intention and gingerly touched my shoulder. "Just let me handle this one, okay? You're too tired."

Despite her gentle voice, I knew the translation was 'let me handle this one, you'll blow us all up'. But I still sighed and regretfully nodded without opening my eyes.

Macalynn then exhaled deeply and a small but still icy blast of wind blew straight into my face. When we appeared back in the great room, the feeling of needles up your skin that usually comes with being teleported without any effort toward it on your part didn't bother me as much as I had expected.

"Where are Jarmony and Isetha?" I asked after everyone had settled.

Katrina shrugged as she sat down next to me in the corner. She placed ice wrapped in a cloth that'd obviously been torn from a sheet or something on top of my head. "They probably went to bed. It's getting late and Jarmony said something to Isetha about letting us have some time alone."

I nodded, adjusted the ice, and tried to think of something else we could talk about that wouldn't involve our most recent abundance of problems. "Have you been to the third dimension while I was gone?"

They shook their heads.

"Good," I smiled. "That means I'm going to be there when you first see it tomorrow, Katrina."

"*If* you're well enough," Illydia told me sternly. "Then we'll consider going. But right now, the answer is no."

"Come on, Illydia. Katrina could use the space and the river. And she wouldn't have to worry about anyone besides us seeing her," Harmon nudged Amiselle with a sly smile.

We looked at him in confusion before we remembered what he was talking about. Everyone except Amiselle started snickering.

"That was not funny!" she finally exclaimed--realizing what we were laughing at. "That was just *embarrassing*."

About two years ago, Amiselle was out on the yard practicing when someone apparently came up behind her and we all heard from inside, "*Help*! Someone's *burning*!"

Watching from the window, we all saw her get extinguished by the owner of the voice. Drenched, she spun around and yelled, "I was not *burning*! I was on fire and wasn't reduced to ashes because I'm the *Fire Talent* Summit, you egghead!"

Her ticked off expression changed when she saw that the person standing there wasn't who she thought it was. She then nervously stammered for words at the now petrified little boy that just realized he'd put out Summit Amiselle. He immediately screamed, and sprinted back down the path.

"I thought it was Merrhet!" Amiselle defended herself. "And I went after the kid and told him that later. Didn't make him feel any better, but what can you do?"

"Um, maybe *not* light on fire in the middle of the yard?" Aaron answered and was promptly punched for it while she retorted, "Or maybe people should stay out of the woods around here unless something's wrong."

We huffed in agreement before I changed the subject once again. "So, right now it's the 107th day and around what time?"

Illydia shrugged. "Like Katrina said, it's pretty late. I guess maybe eleven or so."

"Really?" Harmon stared at her strangely. "It's only been a week since this whole mess started? It feels like it's been so much longer."

I smiled slightly. "It does. Even though I've only been here for four of the seven days. Guys, just something I was wondering… am I really so predictable that Hyvecuous impersonated me for that long and *none* of the six people who know me best noticed?"

Everyone shook their heads and said "No," simultaneously.

"Please, no sooner would you be predictable then Teller Hallsmen be patient," Macalynn began with a somewhat forced sarcastic smile. "Actually, we did notice you were acting like you were taking everything in for some reason and being unusually quiet. But we assumed it was just stress."

"Wow, were we wrong," Aaron sounded like he was talking to himself, but we all heard him. Everyone silenced.

Naturally, within a few seconds the quiet had turned awkward. I slowly started to retreat further into the corner of the room until I could rest my head against the wall. Cold, solid stone had never been so comfortable to me, and I let out a deep sigh. I was finally home with everyone else. It felt like it'd been weeks since I was last even though it'd only been three days... one day if you only count for how much of the time I was conscious. My eyelids then began to feel twice as heavy and I struggled to keep them open for all of the two seconds it took for the others to notice. Katrina whispered something to them I couldn't hear before turning back to me and saying, "Get some sleep, Lealight. We'll talk tomorrow, okay?"

I opened my mouth to say something but Illydia, correctly assuming I was going to refuse, told me in her strictest voice yet, "Don't even bother arguing. We're staying right here until you're asleep. You know you won't start to feel like yourself again until you rest."

I looked at them for a few seconds before gladly giving in-- though too tired to do much more than nod. They weakly smiled back at me, and I hoped Illydia was right about being better the next day. But as you've probably noticed I tend to be pretty unpredictable.

Chapter 42

"Lealight," I heard someone's voice followed by a violent shake of my arm. "Lealight, *wake up.*"

I opened my eyes and my gaze blearily focused on the stone ceiling.

"Lea-"

"I'm *awake,*" I interrupted and looked up to face Macalynn and Katrina. "What's going on?"

Macalynn dropped my arm as if it was a hot potato. "We just wanted to make sure you were okay."

"That, and it's well past morning," Katrina added.

Macalynn glared at her as if to say, *way to act concerned and be supportive.* She sat down next to me.

"How are you feeling?"

I pushed myself into a sitting position and at first thought that someone had draped a woolen blanket over me, but soon after realized that I wasn't in the great room anymore. I was in my bed. After I'd fallen asleep, the others must've moved me to my room. That and they were probably up with me half the night because the ice on my head had to have been replaced every hour or so before it melted. And of course the first thing I felt was embarrassment at the fact that someone, either Harmon or Aaron, actually had to pick me up and carry me to bed like some helpless little kid.

"Don't worry about it" Macalynn read my expression and figured what I was thinking of. "Did you think we were going to let you spend the night on a stone floor? Of course Aaron moved you. But really, it's okay. We don't want you freaking out about stupid stuff like that."

I gave a somewhat half-hearted nod and she repeated, "How are you feeling?"

After sliding the ice off of my head (quickly melting and evaporating it so nothing actually got wet) and pulling my sheets tighter around myself, I answered slowly. "Better, my head doesn't hurt as much. But where's everyone else?"

"Aaron, Illydia, Amiselle, and Harmon went to the Village," said Katrina. "Just to check up on things because we haven't been down there in a couple days. Well, technically I haven't been down there at all since I became a Summit, but it just feels like it's been this way the whole time for some reason. Wow, Harmon's right. It does feel like this past week's been several."

I nodded again, but quickly found a weak spot in the plan like the pessimist I tend to be. "Wait... If only the four of them go, then don't you think people are going to ask where we are and, more importantly, why we aren't there?"

"Harmon said they'd come up with something. We'll see whether or not it's something good when they get back, I guess," Macalynn shrugged.

"I hope there are decent liars among us," Katrina chuckled at her own joke.

I smiled back at her and said, "Mhmm, we couldn't convince someone with a lie if our lives depended on it, so this should be interesting. What about Jarmony and Isetha?"

"He's outside somewhere, and she went up onto the roof about ten minutes ago," Macalynn answered.

Well, "outside somewhere" was pretty vague, but I decided to let it go because it was the middle of the day. And I didn't think Hyvecuous would be back so soon after what happened less than twenty four hours before.

"Okay, do you think the others will be back from the Village any time soon?" I continued to ask.

"They left several hours ago, so they should be here any minute now."

I was suddenly alert. "*Hours* ago? What time is it?"

Katrina and Macalynn looked at each other. "Maybe two or three in the afternoon" Katrina finally answered.

"*In the afternoon*?!" I practically yelled as I forgot everything, threw back the blankets, and jumped to my feet. I immediately placed both hands on my head when another sharp pain hit me.

"Calm down, Lealight," Macalynn said sternly as she stood up next to me. She wrapped her arm around my shoulders, and barely gave me two seconds to shove my feet into my boots as the three of us walked out the door and into the openness of the great room. Once we were at the windows, she forced me to sit back down. "First, if you don't learn to sit still for a while and let us handle what else is going on, you'll only get worse. Second, and this is the last time I'm going to tell you this, you're not fine. You were locked up underground with a bad concussion for *three days*. No one expects you to jump right back into things. Because regardless of what you told Litheney, you do need some time to recover, and that's perfectly understandable. Okay? You've got to promise us you won't do anything dangerous until you know you can handle it."

I looked at the floor.

"*Lealight*?" Macalynn persisted.

"*Alright,*" I snapped--but quickly realized my tone and changed it. "I promise I won't do anything risky."

She was about to respond, but Katrina cut her off. "There they are" she pointed out the window to four figures coming from the woods. "Let's go meet them in the yard."

"No, Katrina. We can't go down all those stairs with her like this," Macalynn said squarely. "But we can take the faster and easier way."

"*No!*" we both shouted in unison, but either she didn't hear us or decided to pay no heed because she grabbed both our wrists. Five seconds later, we appeared against the Citadel as Aaron, Illydia, Amiselle, and Harmon came over to us from the middle of the yard. There came those needles again.

"*Macalynn,*" we both groaned as the others approached. She looked at us as if to say "What?", before a flicker of recognition crossed her face.

"Oh, right. The needles. Sorry." she held her hands up as we rolled our eyes.

"That was a dramatic entrance," Amiselle said once they'd reached us. It was obviously taking all of her strength not to laugh.

"Compliments of Macalynn, the Airhead Talent," Katrina replied while scratching up and down her arm to try to get rid of the prickling. Everyone nodded in understanding and suppressed a smile as Macalynn shot her a "say-that-again-and-you'll-be-visiting-Merrhet" glare. The focus then, unfortunately, switched to me.

"You feeling any better?" Aaron asked.

"Better than yesterday… though it'd be hard to be worse."

"You have some color back in your face and you're not trembling like you were, so that's a good sign," Illydia chimed in and I already felt my face turning red with humiliation--a now very familiar feeling to me. "What about your head? You looked like you were in a lot of pain earlier."

"It hurts some, but not like it did last night," I avoided their concerned gazes. Desperately trying to change the subject, I asked, "In the Village... is everything okay?"

They shrugged and Harmon answered, "Same old. Everyone wanted to know why it was just the four of us as opposed to all seven. So we came up with you and Macalynn taking Katrina to the third dimension for the first time and still being there."

Aaron, Illydia, and Amiselle suddenly burst out laughing.

"Please, you're making it sound like everything went smoothly," Illydia finally said.

"What happened?" I asked--trying to keep the dread out of my voice.

They exchanged glances before Aaron explained. "First, be glad that Harmon's the Light Talent Summit and not a teacher."

"Why? What'd he do?" Katrina persisted amongst the snickering.

"When asked where the three of you were, he meant to say "In the third dimension," but he accidentally said "In the *fourth* dimension" and everyone *freaked out*."

We just stared at him.

"You told everybody we were in the fourth dimension?" Macalynn finally began slowly, in disbelief. "What the heck were you thinking?!"

"Would you relax?" Harmon groaned, but his face was flushed red with embarrassment. "I told everyone I meant the third dimension, and it's fine now."

Amiselle started chuckling again and commented, "It was less of 'I meant the third, everyone. It's okay' and more of 'Uh, I meant the third! *The third*! Calm down, they're in the *third* dimension, not the fourth!' And his voice was at first drowned out by everyone else's. But apparently Litheney was standing close enough to hear him, and she stepped up next to us and yelled at them to be quiet. Everyone shut up in two seconds flat. *Then* Harmon said he meant the third and you guys were fine."

Katrina continued to stare before saying, "Very smooth, Harmon. We'll never live that one down."

"Give him a break, Katrina," I began with a smirk that already made the others look apprehensive. "There's obviously not much difference between a grassy field with the occasional tree and an endless labyrinth of darkness. The two are easily interchangeable."

He rolled his eyes. "I guess you're feeling better. You're back to your usual wisecracks and sarcasm. I'm not sure whether to be happy about that or not."

I glared at him. "If I didn't feel like my limbs were half made of jelly right now, I'd so punch you."

He just smiled.

"But it would be very impolite of me to deny you the right, so Amiselle, would you be kind enough to hit him instead?"

She promptly whacked him as hard as she could.

"Real mature, Lealight," Harmon grumbled under his breath as he rubbed his arm before turning back to Amiselle. "And that's so not fair, you heated your fist!" She grinned broadly and gave him a mocking bow. Everyone, everyone except Harmon that is, laughed.

"Couldn't have said it better myself," I continued. "And for the record, Harmon, maturity has nothing to do with it. I can guarantee you we'll still be punching you and Aaron when you're annoying us ten or fifteen years from now."

Illydia, Katrina, Macalynn, and Amiselle all smiled and Aaron opened his mouth to say something, but he was cut off by a scream. Not a scared or hurt yell for help, but one filled with rage.

"What was that?" Illydia asked with an edge of fear in her voice.

"Someone screaming," Aaron answered, looking around for an apparent source like everyone else.

A low sound came from Macalynn's throat as if she was holding her tongue. "Thank you, detective. We got that," she said through her teeth. "The question is, where did it come from?"

"What's going on?" Isetha's scared voice came from the doorway.

"We don't-" I began only to be cut off with more yelling.

"Don't you even think about it!"

"I don't want any trouble."

"Yeah, right! Not only do I not believe you, but after what you did, they won't either. Please, you'll be lucky if they don't kill you!"

"Look, I'm sorry! I got pulled into this thing and I know what I did was wrong. But I'm going to set it right and there's nothing you can do to stop me!"

At that moment, Dillon, pursued by Jarmony, burst through the trees.

Chapter 43

Dillon skidded to a halt in front of us. Jarmony, however, was not as lucky. He ran directly into him and they both fell to the ground.

"Let go of me!" Dillon yelled as he tried to shake him off. But Jarmony was not to be beaten, and he bent Dillon's arm back.

"Both of you knock it off!" Aaron shouted and, sure enough, they both froze. "Jarmony, what's going on here?"

Jarmony by then knew Aaron's tone of voice that meant he was serious. "I was in the woods when Dillon ran into me. He said he had to get to the Citadel. I wouldn't let him by and so he dove past me and ran. I chased him all the way here."

During his short explanation, I'd been sitting behind everyone completely out of sight--being held back by Katrina and Amiselle. Every time I moved in the slightest, they both gripped my shoulders tightly. I shot Amiselle a look reading "what are you doing?" As a response, she hissed under her breath, "You're in no condition for this. We just got you back, and we are not going to lose you again." So with great difficulty, I stayed there, perfectly still. We just stared at Dillon--who was held with his arm pinned behind him like a criminal by Jarmony. Eventually, Macalynn stepped forward and glared menacingly at Dillon, which seemed pretty strange because he towered over her by at least four or five inches.

"You have some nerve coming back here after what you did, Dillon," she said coldly. "And you also have five minutes to tell us why you're here before you join Merrhet, got it?"

He nodded vigorously, and a reluctant Jarmony released his grip on him.

"First off, what happened to the Lealight that came from the Library yesterday?"

"Anything that happens to the seven of us is none of your business anymore," Illydia hastily answered.

Dillon's expression changed from scared to hurt. Frowning, he replied, "This is my business, actually. I was with Hyvecuous when he ambushed her, and I was supposed to stay in the Library and tell him if she escaped. But instead I just watched her leave. I decided that I was not going to work for him regardless of his threats. I need to know what happened to that Lealight."

Everyone tensed up, and I could bear it no longer.

"*That* Lealight is standing right here," I cut in as I pushed my way to the front of the group so Dillon could see me. "And you have no idea how dangerously close *that* Lealight is to blowing you into next week after finding out that not only did you stand by when I was about to be electrocuted, but also hung around in my Library while your little mentor impersonated me for three days!"

Dillon's face flooded with relief and he continued with something I hadn't been expecting from someone who was okay with my murder a little over seven days ago.

"I'm so glad to see you're still alive."

"Yeah, just like you were last week," I replied icily. "And if you've come to regain our trust only to go report to Hyvecuous again, I suggest you leave either the same way you came or Macalynn and I will give you a lift. Choose now."

The look of anxiety returned to his face. "I know you must be furious after what I did, and I'm really sorry. I got sucked into this, and I thought that there was no way out of it. But there always was. I found that out the minute Hyvecuous slammed you against the floor the second time and you didn't move. I thought you'd died. And I tried to open the trapdoor several times, but I couldn't. Hyvecuous had it bolted down. Besides, I'm not asking for your trust back. I wouldn't expect you to trust me ever again, but I know can help you."

"Well, that's spectacular!" Aaron wrapped his arm around me and pulled me closer to him as if to protect me. "We're glad your personal insight occurred after Lealight was nearly murdered! Do you honestly think you can just come back apologize and make us believe a word you say? Just how *stupid* do you and Hyvecuous think we are?! There's no way we'd listen to any of your "*help*" after all of this. So you can just leave now, never return, and keep your life. Or you can stay loyal to the most horrible monster ever to exist in our Universe and die before he does!"

By that point, Dillon was almost trembling with fear. "I'm not working for Hyvecuous. I swear, I'm not. I honestly want to help you all defeat him. Do you think I willingly walked into this? I thought Merrhet really was the Water Talent Summit when I accepted to be his Charge. I didn't find out who he was until a year afterwards when I caught him sneaking out and he finally told me what he was planning to do. He also said he'd kill me if I told anyone, so *yeah*. I didn't. I never was working for Hyvecuous. He cut me off in the woods after I left the Citadel, and I told him Merrhet had been sucked into the fourth dimension. Hyvecuous forced me to go with him when he came to kill Lealight down in the Library. But she'd only been knocked out, and he knew that. After he locked her down there, he told me to wait and when she came around, I was to tell him. Which I didn't do."

"Oh, *really*?" Katrina scoffed. "Then how did he just *happen* to make up a lie the day before? He told us that Litheney said

Hyvecuous might try to impersonate Lealight with some disguise Charm!"

"I don't know why he made that up! Could have been anything from simple paranoia to a hunch to... wait, *you're* the Water Talent Summit?" Dillon's jaw dropped for a few seconds.

Katrina's face turned red and she yelled, "That's none of your concern! And I recommend you get back to how you think you can "*help*" us soon because you have only two of your five minutes remaining!"

Dillon still looked on the verge of a nervous breakdown as he took a deep breath and began, "First off, in order to defeat Hyvecuous Lealight has to-"

"learn Magic. I know," I finished his sentence. He looked surprised, but continued anyway. "The only way to do that is to-"

"Find the chest Merrhet demanded, take the rock from it, and then place it inside a hole in the fifth wall of the Library to find all the information," I interrupted again. "Check, check, and would have been check, if it wasn't for this little incident."

"Uh yeah..." his voice momentarily trailed off.

"So if that's it then how about you go get lost in the fourth dimension, traitor."

Clearly both upset and annoyed, he continued on--speaking faster. "That little girl over there in the doorway is a-"

"Charmer. Got it," I cut in once again, suppressing a smirk.

"She's the only one-"

"With a touch of Magic that enables her to create Charms."

"Would you cut it out?!" he finally lost his patience.

"No, Dillon. I will not cut it out because as you can see your help is not necessary. It's time for you to leave, *now*," I snarled.

He swallowed and then looked me straight in the eye.

"Fine. But just one more thing before I go. The fourth dimension is not what you think it is. The place is only a pitch black, endless labyrinth on the outside. The inside is basically Hyvecuous Headquarters. He's never left except to attack us in the six hundred and three years we've existed--the Clouds appear and disappear only when he decides for them to. If you want to rid this Universe of him once and for all, you have to not only drain him, but also destroy the fourth dimension itself. It's the only way to get rid of the Shadows and rescue the people he's holding there. In order to do so, you all will have to go there and attack him before he comes and invades us. So Lealight, you have... maybe a week at the most to master your Magic and sneak into the fourth dimension if you want to win this battle. Because if he comes here first, there's no hope for the Summits. And if there's no hope for the Summits, then there's no hope for the Universe at all."

On that pleasant note, Dillon turned around and ran away down the path.

Just to be clear, I'm going to repeat myself once again and say that the absolute last thing anyone would want me to feel in my position is pressure. *Obviously.*

Chapter 44

Everyone stood there for several minutes before I spoke up. "Guys, maybe I should-"

"No, you will *not*," Macalynn cut in irritably--already knowing what I was going to say. "You don't seem to get it, Lealight. We're not letting you do anything even remotely dangerous until you can handle it. Invading the fourth dimension included."

"Well, we don't exactly have two or three weeks for me to *recover* anymore. You heard Dillon. If we're going to win this battle, we've got to be ready to go fight for everything and everyone in less than seven days. Since we've already established losing isn't an option, I should go investigate this thing that's supposed to be behind the wall as soon as possible, don't you think?"

"What I think is that Dillon is a *lying twit* who *is* working for Hyvecuous and apparently believes we're stupid enough to teleport ourselves into the inescapable fourth dimension," Aaron answered for her.

"He's not lying," Isetha injected shyly, which sent all eyes in her direction.

"How can you be so sure?" Harmon asked as she walked over and joined our huddle.

"I just... know. I've always been able to tell when people lie. I think now it has something to do with this whole "Charmer" thing," she answered with a shrug as if it was normal. "And Dillon is definitely not lying."

Everyone was silent for a while before Illydia answered. "Isetha, we appreciate you trying to help, but we need more than just a hunch as proof before we will even consider teleporting ourselves into the fourth dimension."

"It's not a hunch. I'm positive he was telling the truth," she defended herself with some annoyance in her voice.

"I think she's right," I began hesitantly. "Charmers can do a lot of the existing Charms and of course all the ones they create themselves. I don't see why you couldn't have unknowingly made one that detects lies and that's how you've always been able to tell."

She nodded just as Amiselle said, "Well, let's test it out. We'll tell her things, and she'll say whether it's a lie or not."

Everyone exchanged glances and Harmon began with, "Macalynn has pushed Lealight off the roof."

We both glared at him as Isetha answered.

"True, and I don't think I want to know why."

"Lealight has pushed Macalynn off the roof," I continued with a smirk.

"Also true," she replied. "Is that like a game with you guys?"

"*No.* And see? It doesn't work. That never happened," Katrina said dismally.

"Yes it did," Macalynn and I both corrected her at the same time.

"When?" Amiselle asked.

"Right after the Clouds showed up, and we left the Citadel to go talk to everyone outside," I told them. "Long story short, Macalynn was in shock so I pushed her off the roof to snap her out of it."

"Cause we're all just a big happy family and are nice, supportive, and caring enough that we push one another off the top of eighty foot tall towers on a regular basis," Macalynn added--making all of us smile and nod in agreement.

"Anyway," Aaron chimed in. "I think we've just seen Isetha can tell when people are lying and since Dillon wasn't, that means..."

"That Hyvecuous's time is up," I finished his sentence--dead serious. "And everyone has one week to prepare, so obviously the third dimension is a go. But if you guys are alright with it, I want to go see this thing behind the wall first... just so I know what it is."

They looked hesitant and unsure about the whole "teleport-into-the-fourth-dimension-*on-purpose*" scenario, but no one dared to disagree with me after everything that had happened.

Because clearly rule number one around here is that I always know what I'm talking about.

Chapter 45

The others refused to let me go into my own Library by myself. They wouldn't say it, but they were obviously worried I'd manage to get myself in another... bad situation. Eventually we settled on Macalynn and Aaron going down there with me. Isetha tagged along too, and was obviously made very uncomfortable by it. But I figured that if this place had information on Magic, then it would definitely have something on Charms she could use.

Anyway, I bet by no stretch of your imagination you could picture what the four of us saw after I lit the pitch black room. It will seem completely and totally impossible that this next thing actually happened to us. But guess what, everyone? There was absolutely nothing left of what I could tell was probably another, smaller library behind the fifth wall. Hyvecuous, apparently, had beaten me to it and burned every last shelf to the floor. And recently, by the looks of it all--probably while I was locked underground. That explained why he didn't seem worried about the little haze that I'd accidentally created... because he knew I would never get the chance to learn anything more. But I'm not going to write down all the words I called him in my head right then. For as I stated earlier, *general audiences*.

 Macalynn sighed. "I'm sorry. I know how important this was to you."

"It wasn't just important to me, Macalynn," I couldn't keep the hopelessness out of my voice as I looked around the room, searching for anything that might be in any better condition than ash and the occasional hunk of charred wood. "Veronica's letter said the information in here was pretty much essential to getting out of this alive. How am I supposed to learn the stuff if there's literally no record of it? I don't know how to *make* Magic. The only things I know are that the Library's door opens when it senses it, and all of the books down here have some I guess because it seeped into them somehow. That's why they show the pictures. And now not only is everything that could have been remotely helpful gone, but Veronica said she teleported another note in here. We'll never find that either."

"Come on, Lealight," Aaron put his hand on my shoulder. "You're smart enough to figure out Magic without any of this. And we'll help you. We'll manage like we always do."

I must've looked pretty doubtful because Macalynn quickly added, "Think about it this way. Magic is the Talent you were born with so maybe it'll be just as natural to you as Air is to me, Woodland is to Isetha, and Earth is to Aaron. All this would've probably been a waste of the small amount of time we have left, anyway."

"What's that?" Isetha spoke up from behind us.

"What are you talking about..." my voice trailed off when I noticed what she was looking at.

A little slip of parchment poking casually out of the rubble.

I walked over and knelt down next to her just as she gently tugged at the corners of the paper to get it out. It came, but naturally half of it was burned.

"Oh," she sighed. "I guess there really is nothing left in here."

"Hold on," Aaron spoke up. "There's something written on it."

Isetha handed the paper to him, and he squinted to read the words. "Um, Lealight... I think this is Veronica's note. But it's written so that half of each line is burned off." I looked over his shoulder and saw that the legible words were indeed in her handwriting.

Dear The Finder Of

Assuming that you are the same person who
letter, I guess I should start with the few things I know about
yourself become overwhelmed by the many books. From
should not be like mastering Air, Earth, Fire, Light, Water,
no time to spare with Hyvecuous around once again, you should
Lastly, I found some strange, and quite frankly disturbing, information in
helpful to you. It was very unclear, but what I could
Hyvecuous has some sort of connection with the fourth dimension
whatever plan he has. ~~I really hope I didn't make a huge mistake that~~
find this in time.

I read this note out loud to Aaron, Macalynn, and Isetha. They too had no idea what to say about it. There wasn't much to be said.

You thought things couldn't get worse, didn't you? Well, first thanks for jinxing the problem and for future reference, things can always get worse in our lives. Point A, we were going to have to teleport ourselves into an inescapable, pitch black labyrinth--willingly. Oh, and let's not forget the reality that we very well may not have come out of it alive, and if we didn't, the Universe would fall.

I shook the thought and made a quick decision. Hoax or not, the fourth dimension wouldn't know what hit it if it was putting itself up against a seriously irritated set of teenage Summits who were sick and tired of dealing with so much baggage. And if there's one thing I hope you know by now, it's that when the seven of us are determined to do something, nothing can stop us. Whether or not that still remained a true statement, I thought, is something we'd all find out soon enough.

Chapter 46

"That was fast," Illydia said as Aaron, Macalynn, Isetha, and I rejoined everyone in the great room after deciding there was no point in hanging around down there. She obviously knew something had gone wrong, or in Litheney's terms, something *unexpected* happened.

"Yeah, bad news," I answered. "Hyvecuous beat us to it. The entire place has been burned down."

Their faces fell and I unsuccessfully tried to reassure them with a fake smile. "But I guess I'll figure it out. And it leaves us more time in the third dimension."

"Lealight," Macalynn wasn't the only one who looked wary. "Are you absolutely sure you can? I mean, you know how much focus it takes, and it hasn't even been a day since Hyvecuous. And your head is still messed up."

"Macalynn, my head isn't *messed up*," I tried to keep the embarrassment and exasperation out of my voice. "I'm fine. Really, I can handle teleporting again."

She looked at me apprehensively, but agreed and I took that as my cue to say something to Isetha and Jarmony.

"Do you guys think you can handle being alone for a while?" I asked. "We won't stay long. An hour or two max. We need to see what we're dealing with and start to make a plan of some sort."

The two exchanged glances before Jarmony answered, "I think we can manage that long. But guys... be careful, okay?"

We were silent for several moments before Aaron spoke up, "It's only the third dimension. We've been there hundreds of times."

"But you know what happened last time Hyvecuous attacked. The seven of them were alone in the third dimension and..." Jarmony's voice trailed off. "I just don't want that to happen to you guys."

We sighed simultaneously. He just *had* to remind us of that, didn't he?

"We'll be fine, Jarmony," Katrina finally said. "I don't think Hyvecuous would come back so soon after what happened yesterday. And sometimes... in situations like these... we just have to take our chances."

"And we know we have to go to the third dimension," Amiselle added. "For several reasons: Katrina needs the space, Lealight needs the practice, and we have to be able to come up with a plan of some sort. But like Lealight said, we won't be gone long and... we'll be careful, okay?"

Jarmony looked to the floor for a few seconds before he nodded and Macalynn asked, "Everyone ready?"

"Yep" we chorused.

Jarmony and Isetha took a few steps away from the seven of us. He somewhat awkwardly waved goodbye, and then looked out the window. He'd seen us teleport out multiple times. It no longer interested him. Which was fine by me. In case you haven't noticed or weren't paying attention, I'm not a huge fan of being gawked at like an extraterrestrial every time we did anything. And since the Charges were used to it, they generally left us alone. Isetha, on the other hand, was watching with a fascinated expression. Trying to ignore her, the seven of us formed the same circle we had been together in over one week ago--only this time, without Merrhet and with Katrina. Macalynn and I closed our eyes, and I pictured the third dimension. The last thing I heard before we left was Isetha saying, "Wow."

Chapter 47

"Geez, how long does it go on for?" Katrina asked after all of two seconds of getting there.

I shrugged. "No one's been stupid enough to try to go all the way to the end, so naturally, no one knows. Though it's been said that there is no end and the landscape just repeats itself over and over again."

"What?"

"She's joking, Katrina. It doesn't go on forever," Macalynn's eyes narrowed at me. "But it does cover at least a couple hundred miles so we can't be tracked while we're here. It'd be easy for Hyvecuous to locate us if it was just a small patch of land, but it's nearly impossible since we're never in the same place."

"Oh," was Katrina's simple response before she got straight to the point. "So, are we going to make a plan first?"

We sat in a semicircle on the ground as our answer.

"Where do we even start when planning to invade a place like the fourth dimension?" Harmon rubbed his forehead already in frustration. "It's not like we can just walk in there. We don't even know the way around, much less where Hyvecuous is in it."

Everyone stared at the ground for a while before I finally spoke, "Well, we do know when we get there, it'll be insanely dark. It's a safe bet we'll find some of those missing people there, and they might be walking around. The place is pretty much a giant maze, so we'll have to do everything we can to make sure we stay together. But aside from that, our top priority has to be keeping a low profile. *No one* can know we're there. If somebody hears that the Seven Summits showed up, then it will spread around until it eventually reaches Hyvecuous. Him knowing we're there kind of defeats the purpose of a surprise attack. So I don't think we can show up looking like this. Call me old fashioned, but we'll need... disguises of some sort."

The others just looked at me.

"What? Like a fake moustache?" Amiselle retorted. "It's not like we can go to a shop or something and ask someone for dark cloaks without rising suspicion. If you tell people what we're doing, then we're bound to be labeled completely insane."

Everyone nodded in agreement and another dead-end silence set in before I remembered something. "I think Avley's mom is a seamstress... and a good one at that. I bet she'd have some things in stock and be willing to help us."

They shrugged as if to consider the idea, but Illydia looked dubious.

"Lealight, are you sure you trust that family so much? What if she decides to tell people?"

I shook my head. "Ms. Plenstion would never do that. She was almost like a second mother to me whenever I went over with Avley and there's no way she'd betray our trust. And I think that's what we have to do. It's one of few options that won't end in disaster."

Everyone sighed, but nodded. We finally had the first part of our plan.

"So, are we all just going to... show up at their door in broad daylight?" Aaron asked.

"No, we're not" I quickly making one of my executive decisions that, as you know, always end so well. "Illydia, Katrina, and I are going. We'll leave later in the evening when no one's out, okay? We'll be fine."

Amiselle, along with everyone else, didn't say anything. But when she looked back up, she abruptly turned white faced and shrieked "*Oh my gosh, what the heck is that*?!"

After following her gaze, I nearly screamed myself and clamped my hand over Macalynn's mouth to keep her from doing so. Dense, black fog was quickly coming from the horizon and making its way toward the Clouded sky and us at the same time.

Apparently, Hyvecuous was running out of original ideas for what to send when foreshadowing one of his oh-so-pleasant plans and really wanted us to know when he made an entrance.

The seven of us scrambled to our feet and stood there like statues until the fog began to surround our little spot. It rose off the ground to about the height of our knees. Something about its dark color and ominous vibe said, "Touch me, and bad things will happen." The others were most likely getting the same feeling from it because the closer the fog came, the more we squished together to avoid it.

The dank clouds eventually came to a halt when it had all seven of us encased in a little circle with a diameter of no more than eight feet. The whole thing reminded me of how a pack of wolves surround their prey before attacking. Only in this situation, the fog was the predator and we were the deer about to be devoured.

Anyway, happy thoughts, *happy thoughts*.

"W-what is that?" Katrina repeated a lot more quietly.

"Probably something we should avoid," Aaron answered her as the fog began to rise higher and higher until it was twice Harmon's height. "Macalynn, Lealight, you guys going to teleport us out of here before this stuff gets any closer?"

I nodded, but froze when I heard someone coming from not too far away.

"Why are you even bothering with this place? There's nothing here. Believe me I came almost every day when I was stuck with those six."

"I know that," another slightly irritated voice answered. "But like you just said, the Summits come often--so I am going to finish them off here instead of having to deal with them later. It shall be much easier this way and I'm sure they will turn up within the next few hours or so."

"Well, then what's with this fog?"

"Just to distract them at first. While they wonder what's going on, we'll be pin pointing exactly where they are. And you already know that they won't be able to get away because once the fog finds and surrounds them, the six Talents they know are useless."

At the words "Talents they know are useless" the others all gasped in horror, realizing we were trapped. Unfortunately, the owners of the voices heard, and less than a second later the words "Wait here" came along with the clearing of a single, narrow path of the fog that revealed Hyvecuous standing there with a smug look on top of his usual twisted smile. I was fighting down the same cold that always came when he was nearby as he began with, "So nice of the seven of you to drop in. You're certainly saving me a lot of time." None of us responded. I took the time of silence to hiss under my breath the word "*Run*". Taking everyone else's looks that read "Into the fog? Are you out of your *mind*?" into consideration, I took a deep breath. I knew what I had to do, but of course I doubted the fact Magic would suddenly work for me.

"Any last words, children?" Hyvecuous asked---mocking us.

I shut my eyes tighter and thought harder to no avail. What had I done last time that I was missing then?

"I'll take your silence as a no," he took a few steps forward.

Then I realized what was wrong. Yesterday when I escaped from under the Library, I was so blinded with rage I didn't even realize I was doing Magic until after the fact. So, I thought, I've got to be... well, ticked off again.

But despite what anyone else tells you, it is not an easy task to force yourself into feeling a certain emotion. But I desperately kept recalling multiple images of being slammed against the ceiling and floor, impersonated, and attacked by my family. Finally, I had built up enough anger and hurt that I felt tears streaming down my face. It literally took all of my strength to use the Magic to get us out of there instead of just exploding at Hyvecuous. I grabbed Katrina's wrist and everyone must have caught on to what I was trying to do. We soon stood there grasping each other's hands like we did when teleporting by air. Hyvecuous must have figured out what I was doing too, because the fog began to quickly cave inward.

The next two things happened within one second of each other. The golden haze started to rise around us and, ducking to avoid the fog that I was now sure meant bad news, we disappeared to a yell of aggravation from Hyvecuous. It wasn't until then that I remembered I hadn't pictured any particular place. That pretty much meant we could appear *anywhere.* From the Citadel, to the Village, to a foot away from where we just were.

And that wouldn't be too good.

Chapter 48

I didn't have any longer than ten seconds to wonder where we'd end up before we were abruptly lurched forward and the seven of us lost our grip on each other. As an unexpected result, we were all blown apart as if an explosive had gone off in the center of our sloppy-looking circle. Fortunately, we weren't too high up because there wasn't any plummeting downward like I'd feared. Instead, I, like the others, was thrown back for at least ten yards at two feet above the ground before hitting it with a loud and pretty painful "*thud.*"

"What was that?" a distant voice began while I (and I assume everyone else) lay sprawled on the ground unmoving. A gasp of horror roused us.

"It's the Summits! All seven of them are... oh no, are they *dead*?!"

Shortly after the word "dead", I sat bolt upright but immediately grimaced as I put my hand to my head.

Apparently, the idiot with the pickaxe's break was over and he was back to work again.

"No, they're not dead" I heard someone else answer. "They're getting up... but wow, that looks like it really hurt."

I stood slowly with my hand still over my forehead and looked around. We were in the middle of the square. More and more people were flooding into it to see what was going on, surrounding us. "Oh great," I said under my breath as the others started making their way towards me.

"Everyone okay?" Harmon asked once we stood together in the center of the square--which was still filling rapidly. The others were all ghastly pale, and I knew I probably was too. Still, we all nodded in unison and turned to face the crowd just as it parted for Litheney Hallsmen.

"What's going on here?" She demanded. But once she saw us, she continued instead with, "What happened to you all?"

Once she'd joined us, Amiselle replied under her breath. "Hyvecuous happened."

The Teller looked shocked.

"*Already*? It hasn't even been one day since-"

"We are *not* going to talk about that in the middle of the square," I interrupted. "And what's happened is he's taken over the third dimension. We had the pleasure of being there at the time, and we were caught in his fog."

"Fog?" some guy apparently overheard.

"Do *shut up* and listen to what she's saying before you jump in with questions!" Teller Hallsmen snapped at him before turning her attention back to me and saying simply, "Continue." I figured it was no use trying to talk only to her and began addressing the crowd.

"His fog that we can assume is bad news because surrounded us completely into a small circle, and then rose to over twice our height. Also, when he was ranting the "any last words" speech, it began to cave inward. We couldn't use the six Talents during any of it."

"What do you mean you couldn't use Talents?" another person toward the front of the crowd asked, even under Litheney's glare. "They don't just stop working suddenly."

"It was the fog," Macalynn answered. "We tried, but nothing would happen. I felt the energy, but it just wouldn't come out. Our Talents were... gone inside of it."

A mixture of anxious murmurs and gasps came from the crowd of well over a hundred people. Even though the square is gigantic, houses surround it so our voices always echo. Meaning people even in the very back will almost always be able to hear you speak.

"So if this fog drained your Talents, then how did you get out?" someone else continued to ask.

The others all looked to me, and I stared at the ground. I didn't want to tell everyone I knew about Magic in fear of them asking further questions. I thought it might force us to bring up anything that'd happened over the past week that they didn't already know about. But as the minutes ticked by and the square got more and more crowded, the question didn't get dropped and I finally answered.

"I teleported us here with Magic."

Everyone stared at me as if I was on fire for several, seemingly endless seconds.

"There is no such thing," a too familiar voice broke the silence.

"Just because you have never seen it doesn't mean it is nonexistent," Litheney pointed out as my old teacher Miss Cyerson stepped out from the crowd.

"Please, Litheney, don't tell me you believe in such rubbish," she retorted and the crowd stared at her as if she'd lost it. "We are all very well aware of what the Seven Summits have been capable of throughout the centuries and Magic is nothing more than a legend. Lealight Roverdee, we are *not* going to tolerate someone in your position lying to us in times like these. Either you know what you are doing or you do not."

"Do not speak to the Grand Summit that way, Estrella," Litheney told her sternly. "You have no right to accuse her, or any of them for that matter, of anything after all they've done."

Anyone but me finding it ironic that Litheney Hallsmen was sticking up for and defending us by telling someone to not speak to me in a certain way that used to be the only tone she used?

"All they've done? I haven't seen them do *one thing*. And I can speak to her however I wish. If her misguided mother and father could see how she's lying to everyone with **It** in the Universe, they would be most disappointed."

She stared directly at me when she said that last part, and I snapped. Miss Cyerson was the only person who knew the whole story about how they had died since she was my teacher and the one in charge of keeping the orphans straight. Even the neighbors and Teller Hallsmen didn't know the exact details. They just knew something happened to our family. Besides, the story faded quickly. It was almost as if the fire never happened and I'd be really surprised if someone even remembered six years later. Miss Cyerson was a witch, but I couldn't believe she actually had the nerve to throw my parents' death in my face.

I marched over to my former teacher and started shouting, my voice shaking with rage. "Magic is no legend, Miss Cyerson. I believe I, *of all people*, would know that! And I *know* I misheard you because it sounded like you just said we *haven't done anything*. You have absolutely no idea what we've been through this past week to continue holding Hyvecuous, also known as **It**, off! What happened just now in the third dimension was not my first or second, but third encounter with him and nearly the twentieth time the seven of us have narrowly escaped being killed! And how *dare* you accuse me of being a liar! You may never address me as such, understand?! I am not a child who has the misfortune of being stuck in your class all day anymore, and if you value your job, you will never speak of my parents that way again. *Have I made myself clear*?"

Miss Cyerson was dumbstruck and to my delight as well as annoyance, some of my former classmates were clapping. I heard Avley shout "You tell her, Lealight!" However, it wasn't until after their cheering did I realize the same golden haze had started to surround me. Embarrassed, I quickly moved to rejoin the others as everyone in the square stared at me bug eyed. The white faced teacher left hastily.

"Well, you've really done it now," Illydia murmured under her breath once I'd reached them. "Can't say I wouldn't have done the same thing, though. How in this Universe you managed with a teacher like that for six years with your sanity is a miracle. And I just met her."

Chapter 49

The crowd dispersed not far behind Miss Cyerson and I knew it was going to take a while for me to live my little production down. "Don't you think that went a little too far, Lealight?" Litheney asked once the eight of us stood alone. I just shrugged and kept my gaze focused on the ground.

"But although some people may have thought it was uncalled for, I saw it coming the moment she addressed you by your first and last name as if you were disrupting her class. In my opinion, Estrella Cyerson got what she deserved. She had a lot of nerve to call you a liar and insult your parents in front of all those people when she knows you all haven't seen them in years."

What did I tell you? Litheney didn't even remember they weren't alive anymore. But I was not about to correct her and open that door, I simply nodded and changed the subject.

"Guys, Dillon was definitely right about us having to take Hyvecuous down before he attacks us first. And we have even less time than he made it out to be. We don't have days to plan and practice anymore. Hyvecuous is probably just waiting for the right time."

"So what exactly are you saying?" Harmon asked. "That we need to go earlier than a week... like, three days?"

I shook my head. "No, Hyvecuous won't wait even that long now that he knows we've found out about the fog. It obviously means bad news if it touches someone because even he was careful not to walk into it. And something tells me that's how he plans to get rid of us. We can't give him an opportunity to come first. We will leave early tomorrow morning... around four."

The others just stared at me.

"So you're actually serious about this?" Amiselle asked slowly in disbelief. "You don't think there's any risk that Dillon was lying and Hyvecuous showing up in the third dimension was just a coincidence?"

Sighing, I answered, "Of course I'm not sure. Guys, I know it's risky and I know you're scared. I am too. But this is the only way for all this mess to end. If we just wait for him to attack us first there's no way we'll get out alive. You know that just as well as I do."

Everyone nodded solemnly just as Litheney chimed in with, "Would you mind telling me what you're talking about?"

I kept my answer simplistic. "In a few hours, the seven of us are going to teleport ourselves into the fourth dimension and take down Hyvecuous within his own domain. We will return once he is gone. You all will know when that has happened because the Clouds will clear."

She looked at me in horror, but before she could say "*Have you completely lost your mind*?" or the like, I turned back to the others.

"Illydia, Katrina, we should go speak with Ms. Plenstion now. This is short notice as is and I don't think it's a good idea to wait much longer. And you guys can head back to the Citadel. Please make sure Isetha and Jarmony know what's going on. Be prepared to leave soon after we get back, okay?"

Everyone nodded and I, really hoping I remembered Avley's address after all those years, set off to the east side of the Village followed by Katrina and Illydia. Harmon, Amiselle, Macalynn, and Aaron went the opposite direction--heading toward the path that led to the Citadel. We left Litheney Hallsmen alone in the square with a blank expression on her face.

Chapter 50

After walking down the many narrow streets on the eastern side of the Village, I finally came to a stop at one of the houses that I hoped was the Plenstion's. I knocked somewhat cautiously on the door, and it was opened less than thirty seconds later by Avley's younger brother.

"Hi Lureo," I tried smiling. "Um... I was wondering if I could talk to your mother. Is she here?"

He just stared up at us for a while before running off screaming, "Mom! *Mom*!"

"What's wrong, dear?" a woman's voice came from the other side of the home.

"Someone's here! They want to talk to you!" he yelled back.

There was a loud *clang,* and Avley's mother appeared in the doorway. "*Lealight*?" she looked completely shocked. "Lealight... you look so different."

I rubbed my forehead--embarrassed. Illydia and Katrina started snickering. I glared at them and they shut up pretty quickly.

"Well it's been three years, Ms. Plenstion."

She nodded. "Yes, it has been that long, hasn't it? Oh... I'm sorry, what brings you three here tonight?"

I took a deep breath and said, "I have a huge favor to ask of you."

Ms. Plenstion looked surprised, but still opened the door for us and waved Illydia, Katrina, and me inside.

Being one of the older houses in the Village, the Plenstion's home was not very big. There was one room in the center (the one we had just walked into) that was lit by a wood-burning fireplace. It barely illuminated the tiny sitting area and a kitchen even smaller than ours nestled in a lonely corner. Off to the left was one door, and on the opposite wall there was an unstable-looking staircase that I remembered led to Avley and her younger brother's rooms.

"You have to forgive Lureo," Ms. Plenstion began as she closed the door. "He's been a bit frightened of the seven of you ever since he was walking through the woods and saw someone on fire at the edge of the Citadel's yard. I suppose he assumed they were in trouble, and so he smothered the flames only to realize it was actually Summit Amiselle. She yelled at him and he came home very upset that evening."

The three of us exchanged glances and stifled a laugh before Katrina spoke up. "Yes, Amiselle told us about that. She thought it was Merrhet who had put her out as a joke and that's why she snapped at the person standing behind her. Amiselle didn't know it was really a little boy. Otherwise she wouldn't have raised her voice, and we're all sorry she scared him."

Ms. Plenstion turned to her son, who was standing at the bottom of the stairs, and said, "See, Lureo? Amiselle *did* think she had been put out by another Summit and that's why she yelled at you. Doesn't that make you feel better?"

He just shrugged and headed upstairs just as Avley came down.

"Mom, what's with the noise?" she stopped abruptly when she saw the three of us. "Lealight? What are you guys doing here?"

"We've come because we need to ask your family for a big favor, Avley," I answered more nervously than I intended. "Please, this is very important and we don't have much time."

Avley looked very worried, but nodded just as Ms. Plenstion said, "Well, why don't we sit down and the three of you can tell us what's going on."

And so we did. Illydia, Katrina, and I squished onto a bench across from Avley and her mother in front of the fire. We sat there in silence for several minutes before Illydia nudged me with her elbow and mouthed the words, "You start."

Chapter 51

I sighed and began with, "First I'd like to say that three years ago I decided that you guys are the first people I'd trust enough to go to outside of the Summits if there was ever a problem I couldn't solve myself. Now, something did come up. You must know that what I'm about to tell you is a strict secret and even if you decide not to help us, you have to keep it as such. Knowing that, do you still want me to tell you what's going on?"

The two looked at each other and Ms. Plenstion answered, "We'll help the seven of you in any way we can."

I smiled with relief. "Thank you. Okay so, Ms. Plenstion, I'm going to assume Avley told you about... what happened yesterday."

She nodded.

"I was so sorry to hear about that. It looks like you are okay now, though."

"We pulled through as usual," I answered. "But back to why we're here, um... we're leaving soon. In less than eight hours actually and... where we're going... we can't be there looking like this. We were wondering if you'd be willing to give up some dark cloaks so no one will be able to recognize us."

They just stared. Well, whatever--it was a typical reaction to a lot of what I'd said recently.

"Where could you possibly go that you don't want people to know who the seven of you are?" Avley asked suspiciously.

I kept my gaze focused on my boots and said quietly, "The fourth dimension."

"*What*?" they practically yelled.

"Be *quiet*," Illydia said sternly. "You have a window open. Someone might hear us."

Ms. Plenstion immediately stood up, walked across the room, and slammed and locked the window shut. Once she'd rejoined us, she whispered, "The seven of you are teleporting *yourselves* into the fourth dimension? Why would you do that? You'll be trapped there, and then It will attack us because you won't be around to stop him!"

"Please, just hear us out," I tried to keep my voice firm so it wouldn't sound like I was pleading them. "Hyvecuous is in the fourth dimension. He's been there this entire time and we know for a fact the only way for us to defeat him is to invade before he attacks us. Since we know about this fog, that probably won't be in the distant future. But we can't just show up. This is supposed to be a surprise attack, and if someone sees us and word gets out that we're there, we're in trouble. Please don't try to talk us out of it... we have to do this. We're willing to take the risk that we may not return because it's now obvious to us that we won't stand a chance if we just wait to be attacked... with this fog and who knows what else. So the question is will you help us?"

The two looked at each other, at the floor, and then back to us.

"Are you absolutely sure?" Avley finally spoke up. "I mean, not to sound like Miss Cyerson, but you really do *know* what you're doing, right?"

"Yes," Katrina, Illydia, and I replied at the same time.

Ms. Plenstion nodded. "Then I will give you the cloaks if it means you will be safer."

She stood up and left the room. I turned to face Illydia and Katrina. They looked extremely nervous.

"Well, we got the cloaks so our identity will be safe for the time being," Katrina murmured.

"But do you actually have a plan as to how we're going to locate and defeat Hyvecuous?" asked Illydia.

I returned their shaky smiles and answered, "Some things you just have to learn about as you go along. The fourth dimension and Hyvecuous are definitely some of those things. Besides, my plans never work. But winging it might."

Chapter 52

About three hours later, I lay in bed staring at the ceiling. I'd been tossing and turning for what felt like an eternity trying to find a comfortable position so I could rest before we had to leave. But every time I closed my eyes, I saw darkness. When I saw darkness, I thought of the fourth dimension. Needlessly stated, I didn't keep them closed very long. But I eventually fell asleep. When I woke up, there were no little bits of sunlight shining in between the Clouds. Which was a good thing--that meant the sky itself was still pretty much black and it couldn't have been any later than four. I quickly sat up and buried my face in my hands. The few seconds I stayed there I spent trying to think optimistic. But I'm not very good at that. So I got out of bed and grabbed the dark cloak draped across the headboard before I could convince myself to not follow through. I fastened it over my usual red one, pulled on my boots, and drew my hair out of my face with a leather tie I found in its pocket.

I would never admit it, but I was thoroughly petrified. I had nothing but doubt in my ability to face Hyvecuous and win after what had happened in my Library. The only thing that convinced me to regard my own room for what I hoped wouldn't be the last time and leave was the fact that I knew I would never forgive myself if I waited there and did nothing until Hyvecuous came and killed us. If I was going down, I was going down fighting. And that was that.

Macalynn, Amiselle, and Harmon were waiting by the windows. They too were wearing their cloaks and didn't say anything or even look up after I joined them for at least two minutes.

"Lealight, I can still see red in your hood and down by your ankles," Harmon finally spoke up. "I think that'd be a pretty dead giveaway, don't you?"

I opened my mouth to answer, but a snarky response was put in for me by Amiselle.

"We're going to have the hoods over our heads, genius. And no one's going to see that little--the fourth dimension is in this thing called an unchanging state of darkness. We only have these because it really would be a dead giveaway if seven people all wearing the same thing and one with a bright red cloak were walking around. Even without much light, I'm sure that'd be noticeable."

Everybody nodded in agreement just as Illydia and Katrina came out of their rooms and Aaron walked in from the narrow hallway leading up to the roof. We stood around the window lost in our own thoughts before I finally asked the question we'd all been dreading.

"Everyone ready?"

"*No,*" was the unanimous answer.

"But I guess we don't have a choice," Katrina added. "Let's just hope we live to see this place again once we leave it."

And Miss Dejection strikes again.

But with everyone feeling empty of sarcasm at the moment, we started walking toward the roof. I halted our progress.

"We should say goodbye to Jarmony and Isetha. I know it's not exactly pleasant to think about, but we might never see them again. We can't just leave without saying anything."

The others all looked relieved we were going to be stalled as Illydia said, "I think so, too. But they disappeared after dinner... Maybe they're in the yard?"

"It's a safe bet," Aaron replied. "Let's just go and we can teleport out from there."

Everyone agreed, and we changed directions. After an awkward silence down the stairs, we saw the two sitting against the Citadel also staring off into space. They looked up when the door closed behind us, but their solemn expressions didn't change.

"We came down to say goodbye," Macalynn said with her gaze focused on the ground uncomfortably.

"You guys are actually going to do this?" Jarmony asked in disbelief. "I can't believe you guys are actually going to do this. You're risking your lives and basically this entire Universe because of something *Dillon* told you. This is a *suicide mission*, Aaron. You can't go through with this!"

Aaron sighed before calmly answering, "We don't have a choice, Jarmony. And we're not just going because of what Dillon said. You know just as well as we do from what we've seen so far that there's no way we'll be able to defeat Hyvecuous if we just stay here and wait to be attacked. At least this way we stand a chance. Please don't make us leave knowing you're angry with us."

Jarmony stood up but continued to look at the ground. "I'm not angry with you. I'm just worried I'll never see any of you again."

"Hey, you will," Amiselle chimed in with a slightly nervous smile. "We don't go down that easily."

At that moment, Isetha came over to me. "Are you sure you have to do this, Lealight? What if this is all a trap?"

I put my hand on her shoulder and squeezed it reassuringly. She kept her eyes fixed on the ground, and I could see the tears rolling down her cheeks. "Yes, we have to. But please don't worry about us, Isetha. We'll see you again soon and I remember my promise."

She stared at me with a confused look on her face and I clarified, "Getting your parents back."

Isetha smiled. "You still haven't forgotten about that?"

"Of course I haven't," I responded. There were a few seconds of silence before she abruptly threw her arms up around my neck and hugged me. I had to stoop down a little so she wasn't standing on the tips of her toes.

"Be safe, Lealight. All of you be safe and please come back home."

I hugged her back. "We will."

Chapter 53

Figuring we didn't have time for a long goodbye, within five minutes the seven of us were standing in a circle. Jarmony and Isetha were nearby watching. We were about to join hands and leave when Litheney Hallsmen strode through the trees yelling, "Wait!"

With many exasperated groans and Amiselle's "Oh *come on!*" our circle broke up and we turned to face the lecture that was sure to come. However once the Teller had joined us, she said, "So you really are going to do this? You seven know all the risks involved and you are still going through with it?"

We nodded in unison.

"I'm not going to try to stop you, if that's what you're thinking," she continued, noticing our expressions. "This is your choice and if you feel that this is the only way then who am I to interfere? But please don't get yourselves killed."

I rolled my eyes.

"Great advice. We'll try to remember that. Anything else?"

Her expression abruptly softened as she took my hand. She turned it palm-up, pulled the Magic-draining gem from her pocket, and gave it to me. Litheney closed my fist and released me. She looked like she was choking up. I'd never seen her that way. I had only seen evidence she had emotions at all a handful of times.

"You might... need this." She paused and I could've sworn she was going to cry. *Oh no* I thought. *If Litheney Hallsmen starts crying, then it really is hopeless.* But then she finally caught herself, blinked a couple times, and began speaking normally again. "I-I just thought it'd be fitting for me to see the seven of you off to the fourth dimension. Because the next time we meet Hyvecuous will be gone... or we won't ever meet again."

"Why would I need-" I began before I was interrupted by Harmon, who apparently hadn't seen her near tears a couple seconds earlier.

"Yep, we got that. Thanks for the added pressure, though. Okay so, take three, is everyone ready?"

I decided not to make a big deal about the gem or her random episode, and slid it into the pocket of my red cloak along with the map of the tunnels and Veronica's letter. I managed a half-smile.

"As ready as we're ever gonna be."

The seven of us formed the circle for the second time and I ended up standing between Macalynn and Illydia.

"I don't know if I can do it, Lealight," Macalynn suddenly burst out--also almost in tears. "I mean... I know we have to, but I just can't bring myself to focus on teleporting into the fourth dimension when that's what I've been avoiding my whole life."

She was practically trembling with anxiety when Harmon, who was standing on her other side, put a supportive arm around her.

"Come on, Macalynn. It's going to be okay," he said. His own voice was shaking a little, but he was obviously trying hard to cover it up for her sake. "We're all nervous about what's to come... but we'll be together and we'll pull through like we always have. But you and Lealight have got to get us there first. And we know you can both do it--just trust each other."

Macalynn and I exchanged glances as everyone joined hands. I held my eyes shut and tried to get an image of the fourth dimension, but wasn't very successful because none of us knew what it looked like. We had our presumptions, of course, but trying to teleport on a guess never works out. After about a minute we hadn't moved and were still standing in the Citadel's yard.

"You guys okay? You haven't left yet," Jarmony eventually spoke up.

"We *know*," Amiselle groaned irritably. "Macalynn, Lealight, what's the hold up?"

"Trying to picture a place you've never been and are quite frankly petrified of is relatively hard, Amiselle," Macalynn retorted as she and I momentarily gave up, opened our eyes, and dropped our hands from the others. "Any bright ideas, Lealight? I have nothing."

Yeah, join the club. I'd tried picturing everything I could think of that might relate to a giant, pitch black maze, but, as you can infer, none of them were very productive. Yet I knew there was something I was missing. Something that I'd seen, heard, or read somewhere that basically means you automatically go to the fourth dimension if you accidentally think of it while teleporting. So of course, it was my instinct to push it toward the back of my mind whenever we did, but if I could find out what it was then I could probably go from there. I knew it wasn't just darkness, or just a labyrinth, or a *dark labyrinth* for those of you who like to nit-pick everything.

"Why don't you try-" Aaron began only to be cut off by yours truly who had finally remembered.

"Shadows" I exclaimed, sending everyone's eyes in my direction.

"What do they have to do with anything?" Katrina, still the perky one, asked doubtfully.

"Of *course!*" said Macalynn. "Why didn't I think of that? Shadows supposedly come from the fourth dimension and we know some are there because we're the ones who sent them! *Duh.*"

I nodded and everyone's nervous smiles returned, knowing nothing would stop us this time. Reforming our joined circle, I thought of the Shadow from the dream I'd had over a week before. Yeah, they all look the same but this one just seemed special, alright?

And sure enough, no more than five seconds later, the air around us began to swirl and cave inward. I had to push down the panic welling up inside of me and struggle to keep my thoughts focused on an image of the Shadow running off with Veronica's chest as the seven of us disappeared from the first dimension.

Part 3--People Who Say Revenge Is Unhealthy Clearly Haven't Met The Seven Summits

Chapter 54

Our little trip was not like any teleportation we'd done before. There wasn't just a simple gust of wind and we were where we'd pictured like the many times we went back and forth between the first and third dimensions. In fact, it was quite the opposite considering it was almost as if we were being blown around inside a tornado. But no matter which way we were lurched, we didn't dare let go of each other.

"What's going on?!" Aaron shouted at Macalynn and me over the howl of the wind.

"How should we know?!" we both yelled back.

Another sudden lurch came and, even though I still had my eyes squeezed shut, I knew someone had been blown out of our circle because of two screams. The first was shrill, terrified, and definitely came from at least two of us. The one that followed shortly afterward was, "*Amiselle! Katrina!*"

My eyes snapped open, but I couldn't see them anywhere. Where was I looking from, you ask? Well, I had no clue because opening my eyes didn't shed any light on the situation. I mean that literally: it was nearly as dark with them open as it was when they were closed. So for all I knew we could be blowing above the fourth dimension and my practical little sisters could be falling to their deaths, or we could be in some sort of middle state in between dimensions and they could still be falling to their deaths. Either way, the options looked pretty grim for Amiselle and Katrina.

In my panic about the two of them, my focus wasn't pinpointed on our course and clutching Macalynn's and Illydia's hands for dear life. And when the next powerful gust came along, the name that was called was *"Lealight!"* as I also fell screaming into the darkness below.

Chapter 55

Having no idea how long I'd fall before hitting the ground and coming to a very painful end, I tried to gather some air to stop myself. But nothing happened, of course, and I tried several more times before accepting the fact it wasn't going to work. I also realized the frustrating truth that my focus on keeping us on course earlier was actually doing nothing because apparently the Talents were just as useless in the fourth dimension as they were when we were surrounded by that fog. That's when the panic set in all over again.

The good news was that, even though it was still extremely dark, my eyes adjusted some and the longer I fell the easier it became to see. I could tell we weren't in some in between state, but in the beloved fourth dimension. Of course the equivalent bad news is the exact same thing because I could faintly see the ground approaching and, well, the *fourth dimension* part.

My horror continued to grow the closer I got to inevitably going "*splat*" and as a last resort I threw my arms over my face and thought about halting. I didn't have much of a reason to think Magic would cooperate with me again, but I was pretty desperate and I'm very glad I did because I ended up doing exactly what I'd pictured no more than eight feet above the rocky soil.

Smiling with relief, I dropped my arms and landed almost gracefully somewhere in my favorite labyrinth of darkness. The first thing I remembered was keeping my presence a secret, and I pulled the hood of Ms. Plenstion's cloak over my head. The next thing I thought of was Amiselle and Katrina. And just considering the limited selection of what could've happened to them made tears prickle behind my eyes. But I knew I had no choice but to push the thought away for the time being and move forward… whichever direction forward may be in this place.

The walls of the labyrinth were shadowy, foreboding slabs of stone that towered high above me. A mixture of dark dirt and small rocks made up the ground that I was relieved to be on again in one piece. However, since Hyvecuous wasn't kind enough to set up arrows pointing the way to his place, I was stuck to choose between four different paths.

"Great," I mumbled to myself before I slipped my hand into the pocket of my red cloak and felt the gem. For some bizarre reason, it gave me a sense of reassurance to have something that came from my home in the first dimension with me. I started blindly down the second path from the right.

Chapter 56

Meanwhile, Amiselle and Katrina had a very rough landing. In fact, the only reason they survived it at all was they had abruptly and miraculously halted about fifteen feet above a small overhang, for Lealight had unknowingly stopped everyone when she had saved herself from falling. It was from there that they dropped a few seconds later. Although their meeting with the ground wasn't as horrific as the other Summits had thought, it was still a terrifying experience that neither of them would ever forget.

The two lay on the cliff unmoving and pallid for several minutes before Amiselle finally found her voice and asked, "Are you okay?"

Katrina, on the other hand, felt as if her ability to speak had been blown halfway across the Universe and it took so long for her to reply that Amiselle had worried she'd hit her head and been knocked out.

"Y-Yeah, are you?"

"Fine," Amiselle answered as she sat upright and tried to get her eyes to adjust to the darkness. "But we've got to find the others. They probably think we've been killed."

"The only reason we weren't is because we just... stopped above this thing," Katrina added--scanning the darkness for any sign of life with no results. "How do you think that happened? I didn't do that and I'm going to go ahead and assume you couldn't either."

"My guess is Lealight had something to do with it," Amiselle shrugged just as Katrina promptly started sobbing.

"Lealight, Macalynn, Harmon, Illydia, Aaron…how are we going to find them? They're probably on the other side of this thing by now! We'll never get to them from here!"

Amiselle sighed exasperatedly. She knew from the past three years that Katrina tended to overreact, and in that situation, it was to be expected from her. But she didn't have the patience or temper to watch her cry.

"Get a *grip*, Katrina," she said sternly. "Sitting around feeling sorry for yourself isn't going to solve anything. I know you're new at this, but you should know by now that we'll always find a way to do the impossible. Trust me, we'll find them."

Katrina looked up, taken aback after being scolded by Amiselle, but for some reason still comforted by what she was saying. If there was one thing Katrina had learned in the past week it was that the word "impossible" didn't exist for the Summits. And if that rule made almost all their problems, she didn't see why it couldn't create just one solution. So she ended up nodding somewhat uncertainly as Amiselle got to her feet and pulled her cloak's hood over her head. After Katrina had done the same, the two climbed down the overhang with as little slipping as possible and picked a random path to follow.

Chapter 57

Macalynn, Harmon, Aaron, and Illydia weren't having any better luck than the other three. Shortly after Lealight was blown away, they were also torn apart. Macalynn and Aaron spiraled downward (leaving Illydia and Harmon alone inside the raging vortex) but were saved from their falling in the same way as Katrina and Amiselle. Shortly after they were separated from the other two, Macalynn tried to stop herself and Aaron in the middle of their fast decent, only to find out just as Lealight did that the fourth dimension had the same effect on Talents as the fog they'd encountered only hours before. Once she'd realized this, Macalynn was overcome with panic and was sure their time was up until they slowed to a halt just above a tall crag nearly dead center in the dimension.

Shaken, but still okay, Aaron quickly got to his feet once they'd landed and didn't even notice he was with Macalynn until he saw her unmoving inside the cloak that was several sizes too big.

"Macalynn?" he asked four times to no response. "You alright?"

She didn't stir and Aaron was suddenly hit with the horrible thought that she may not have survived. Refusing to even consider the idea, he then reached down and shook her shoulder.

"*Macalynn.*"

She started coughing and blearily opened her eyes; only to quickly remember what was going on and sit bolt upright.

"I'm fine. It... it could have been a lot worse," Macalynn croaked as she buried her face in her hands. "What's with all the wind? It felt like we were being blown around inside a twister."

Aaron shrugged. "No idea. But I'm glad we stopped when we did... otherwise we would've splated."

Macalynn decided they had bigger things to worry about besides exactly how they'd just halted in mid air. She nodded in agreement as Aaron helped her stand up. It took several minutes for her eyes to adjust to the darkness, but she soon realized where they had landed. They were on top of one of the many crags in the middle of the fourth dimension, so in other words, on top of one of the many crags in the middle of nowhere.

"We've got to get off this thing," she said. "If there's any hope of finding the others, it'd be down there in the actual labyrinth. I guess we could climb down."

"Or I could make this rock sink into the ground," Aaron pointed out. "I am an Earth Talent, you know."

"Not here, you're not," Macalynn quickly answered. "This place drains Talents, Aaron, just like that fog. Do you think I'd be stupid enough to do nothing when we were free-falling to our deaths? I tried to make us stop, but I couldn't. And we can only hope the others were as lucky and survived being tossed from a thousand feet above the dimension."

Aaron stopped to think about what she said. He had many questions--the most prominent one being what happened to the others but a close second was if they were powerless, how were they supposed to defeat Hyvecuous? Something told him Macalynn didn't have the answers and saying this out loud would just upset her. So he kept these to himself and instead told her, "I'm sure they lived. In the words of Amiselle, we don't go down that easily. But the first thing we need to do is climb down off this thing and then we can worry about finding the others."

Macalynn dreaded having to search for their disguised fellow Summits in an endless, and almost totally black labyrinth. But she knew they didn't have any other options. She followed Aaron down the overhang. At the bottom, the two pulled their hoods over their heads and picked one path out of the available five.

Chapter 58

Illydia had always been known for keeping a cool head in all situations. But after five of her fellow Summits had disappeared screaming, she was so shocked and terrified she was practically frozen. Harmon, ten feet away, wasn't doing much better. However, he was determined to keep them alive. He fought his way over towards her and yelled to get her attention. Of course his voice was drowned out by the wind, but Illydia knew he was there. She buried her face into his shirt and continued screaming as she clung to him. Harmon wrapped his arms around her and screamed himself as they were nearly ripped apart by another powerful gust. He usually wasn't one to think pessimistically, but the odds for any of the others making it were slim. He was convinced that if he'd lost them, he wasn't going to lose Illydia. So he kept a tight grip on her as the two of them were thrown around. Although they didn't know it, Harmon and Illydia were both momentarily thinking the same thing.

After this, they would never complain about teleporting again.

Fortunately, they didn't get as rough a landing as the others. It was as if the vortex they were stuck in took pity on them. It took a well-aimed shot, and they were flung as fast as bullets nearly straight downward. But they too unexpectedly halted after about thirty seconds of horrifying descent and were dropped at only six feet above the ground.

The two were motionless for several minutes before they scrambled apart--simultaneously standing up and saying, "We've got to find out what happened to the others."

They stared at each other for a while before Illydia continued.

"I know they're still alive. They have to be alive. And we've got to find them... now."

"How are we supposed to do that?" Harmon asked solemnly. "Amiselle and Katrina must be miles away from Aaron and Macalynn. And Lealight's alone somewhere in the middle. For all we know, they could have been killed-"

"Don't think like that!" Illydia shouted at him and he abruptly stopped. "We *will* find them. But not by standing around here, I can guarantee you that. We should start by walking around and keeping our eyes open for something that points us in the right direction."

Harmon opened his mouth to protest, but Illydia had made up her mind, pulled her hood over her head, and was already striding purposefully away. Not wanting to be left to face the fourth dimension alone like his unfortunate friend, Harmon yanked his hood upward and called "Wait up!" as he trotted after her. Only after a few minutes of walking, Illydia began to laugh.

"What the heck?" he stared at her.

"You scream like a girl."

Chapter 59

Three lefts, four rights, and several winding, diagonal turns later, I finally accepted the fact that I was hopelessly lost. Well, I guess that's the point of a labyrinth. But it's still extremely creepy when it's not only in almost total darkness, but also drains Talents. So naturally, I was a lot more worried about the others (if they were still alive) than I was about myself.

Everywhere I turned there were the same dark, colossal, rock walls and black dirt as there'd been for the past twenty minutes, which felt more like an eternity. There were no landmarks for me to use, no change in scenery to tell me if I was going in circles, and not one sign of life. The only sound was the howling wind and my own tentative footsteps. I was sure I'd reach insanity before coming across anything that might give me some indication of where I was supposed to be going.

Deciding to take some time to plan out what I would do if, on the off chance, I did find where Hyvecuous was, I stopped at the edge of yet another slab of rock. What I was thinking was if Hyvecuous was presiding over the entire dimension, then he must have someone helping him do it. My first guess was Merrhet, and I'd been kicking myself during the past several minutes for being stupid enough to send him exactly where he needed to go. But I continued to believe that one sidekick wouldn't be enough for this giant plan he apparently had for the seven of us and the people of our Universe. Then there were Shadows... but as mentioned before, they're not exactly a threat and the only things I could see them doing for Hyvecuous were causing diversions and doing a small amount of his dirty work-- like kidnapping people. The longer I thought about the idea, the more confusing it got so I eventually replaced it with something else that had been weighing on my mind. The golden question, which was how was I supposed to defeat Hyvecuous with my limited knowledge and control of Magic. I'd only done it purposely twice in my life, so the pessimistic voice inside my head kept saying that there was absolutely no way I'd be able to fight a battle against Hyvecuous with nothing but.

For at least ten more minutes, I went over many ideas in my head. The first five or six plans turned out to be unproductive and were sure to end in disaster if executed. But I continued until my train of thought until it was abruptly derailed by the first voice I'd heard since we were being thrown around inside a twister probably at least a eight hundred feet above the ground.

"Darien, please stop," a scared woman's voice gave a slight echo from around the corner. "If we get caught again-"

"We will be fine, dear. I don't know what kind of fools he takes us for--thinking he can just hold us here and we'd tell him what we know. If we knew anything... one would think that after how many times we've told him we don't know what he's talking about, he would get it by now that we actually don't. No, he thinks we're lying so we are stuck here for now. But he'll eventually get what's coming to him and all of us will get out."

A small flame from a torch then came around the corner and I tried my best to blend into the shadows. But it was a relatively narrow passageway. Since the two people would hear me if I turned and ran the way I'd just came, there weren't many places I could go.

Sure enough, the seemingly hovering flame suddenly stopped dead and one of the people behind it yelled, "*Who's there*?"

I pressed myself harder against the wall and sank to the ground. I wanted to be anywhere in the entire forsaken fourth dimension than where I was.

"Who are you talking to?" the woman's voice spoke again.

"Someone's there, Serena. I can see the shape of a person right against that rock."

You know, everywhere else I'd been in the past half hour had at least three different and equally intimidating paths to chose from and of course I had to run into people in the only one where there was nowhere to run to. Typical.

"*Show yourself*!" the one who'd been called Darien continued vehemently.

I still said nothing.

The fire then started bobbing up and down in the air, and I hoped that meant this Darien person thought he was seeing things. That the two were going to walk right past me, and I could keep going.

But there was no such luck, of course.

The flame came to a stop once again, and I could faintly see the outlines of the two people. The one holding the torch was on my left, the one without was on my right. There was a solid stone wall directly in front. It takes a good amount of skill to get yourself cornered in an endless labyrinth, everyone. And yet I'd managed to do it.

"Are they dead?" the one who I assumed was Serena asked slowly.

"That's what they want us to think. But we'll see," was the other's nonchalant response, and he started to bring the flame closer to my face.

Chapter 60

I dug my nails into the palm of my hand and fought down panic. Darien apparently and unfortunately wasn't stupid. He knew I was alive and was going to bring the fire closer until I eventually had to move out of the way to avoid being burned. Now don't get me wrong, I would have loved to see the look on his face if he found out who I was. But I quickly decided it wasn't worth the risk of any information getting back to Hyvecuous.

So I chose to make a break for it and waited until exactly the right time to knock the torch out of his hand. Serena screamed and leapt backwards at the surprise of my sudden movement as the torch sputtered out and rolled along the ground. Taking that as my cue, I quickly stood up and planned to run down the way the two had just come from. But Darien saw it coming and stepped firmly on my cloaks.

"What's the matter with you?!" I hissed as I tried, to no avail, to pull myself free. "Let *go!*"

"Not until you tell us who you are and what you're doing here," he said squarely.

After giving another yank at my cloak, I figured it was no use and started running fake names I could give through my head.

"Well?" Darien demanded.

"Avley," was all I could come up with. "My name is Avley."

"How did you get here, Avley?" Serena stepped up and asked a little more gently than her partner. "And… how old are you?"

"I don't know how I got here," I answered lamely. "And I'm fifteen."

"Oh," Darien's harsh voice turned sympathetic as he released me. "I'm sorry if we frightened you. You never know who or what you will run into in this place... I did not know you were just a child."

Just a child? I stifled a laugh. Most people assumed by my red cloak that I was this invincible person who should always know what I'm doing and how to fix things. Which, of course, I'd been the exact opposite of recently. So naturally, being referred to as a child seemed pretty ironic to me.

But after disregarding the thought, I simply nodded and said, "That's okay. But I need to keep going."

I began to move past them when Serena stopped me.

"Where could you possibly be trying to get?" she said before sighing. Serena then put a hand on my shoulder and rubbed it kindly. "You won't find a way home anywhere in this place, honey. We've been trying to for the past week."

"Well, where are you two trying to go?" I asked--shrinking away from her touch. I knew she thought she was comforting some lost, scared kid, but that was too weird for me. "Have you already given up on the idea of finding a way out of here? Are you planning on just walking around in the labyrinth forever?"

There was a long, uncomfortable silence.

"The way we just came from is not the way you want to go, Avley." Serena finally spoke up again, ignoring my second question. "Hyvecuous and his Shadows have their... hideout back there and they are preparing to invade the first dimension tomorrow night. He is convinced that we're Charmers, and he's threatening to kill our daughter if we don't cooperate. No matter how many times we tell him we are not, he won't believe us. When he left earlier today, everyone snuck out."

"Don't tell her that!" Darien blasted out in a loud whisper.
"I really don't see any harm in her knowing what's going on," Serena protested.

I motioned with my hands as if to say stop--realizing what was oddly familiar about their story.

"Wait. You said you two were accused of being *Charmers*? And you have a daughter? What's her name?"

"Isetha," the two answered, obviously wondering why I cared. "Why?"

"Hyvecuous won't harm her as long as I can help it."

Having gotten used to looking around in almost total darkness, I could see them both sigh and smile weakly.

"We appreciate that, Avley," Darien began. "But the fact of the matter is we're trapped here and Isetha is probably stuck at the school by now far off in the first dimension."

"No, she's been staying with the Summits ever since you two disappeared. And she's the Charmer in your family that Hyvecuous is looking for, but he thinks you are so that's why you were taken. But trust me, she is perfectly safe and I'll get you both out of here and back to her."

Isetha's parents just stared at me.

"How would you know all this?" Darien's tone changed yet again from gentle to suspicious. "And what are you talking about? We are all powerless here. And even if we were not, no one knows how to get out."

I suddenly got the feeling we were being watched. Who knew? Maybe I was still paranoid even after all that'd happened during the past week, maybe not. I started walking down the way I'd come from and motioned for them to follow me. They didn't budge for several seconds, and I could hear them debating.

"She's a fifteen year old girl. I don't think she can hurt us. And she obviously has some very important information that might help us get back to Isetha."

"Serena, we don't know who that person is. For all we know, it could be a Shadow simply *saying* they're a fifteen year old and that they'll help us get home just to lure us into a trap."

"Shadows don't speak. Besides, if it means getting out of here and back to the first dimension where my daughter is, I'm willing to take the risk. Now hurry up before she changes her mind and takes off."

"I'm just saying be prepared to run."

Serena and Darien then hesitantly followed behind me until we reached a more open area with multiple paths leading from it.

Looking reassured that they had places they could escape to in case I turned out to be some Hyvecuous-loving whack job, Darien didn't waste any time when we had stopped and immediately said, "Out with it then, Avley"

"My name isn't Avley, Mr. and Mrs...."

"Napollon," they answered.

"Mr. and Mrs. Napollon. Avley is the name of my friend from when I was younger, and I lied because I agree with you. You never know who or what you'll run into in the fourth dimension and I didn't want my presence here getting back to Hyvecuous. But anyway, I truly can reunite you with your daughter."

The two had the apprehensive looks back on their faces. "Who are you, then?"

"I'm Le-"

Serena suddenly shrieked and Darien clutched her. I was about to ask what was wrong before I quickly figured it out for myself.

We were surrounded by at least twenty black figures that looked like nothing more than Hyvecuous's fog condensed into human-shaped molds.

We were trapped by Shadows.

Chapter 61

The three of us and the Shadows didn't move for well over a minute. I knew I couldn't do anything to escape because it'd be a pretty dead giveaway that I was there, and I refused to leave Isetha's parents behind. So for the first time since I'd mastered the six Talents and come across Magic, I was truly powerless. And I hated that feeling more than anything I'd ever despised before--Hyvecuous included in the list.

"This them?" one Shadow asked another in an unfeeling, indifferent voice.

The second it spoke, I knew they either weren't real Shadows or they were like none I'd ever seen or heard of. Normal Shadows, as mentioned before, are *mindless* beings (which is why they weren't supposed to be able to speak, see, or hear anything) that can only do simple tasks for Hyvecuous and were never really considered a danger. But these... not only did one ask a question, but they all assembled around us in the same way the fog had. In my opinion, no mindless beings could do that.

"Yes, them... plus one more, apparently," the one that seemed to be in charge answered as it stepped out of the Shadow's circle and toward us. "It was very naughty of you all to scare Master Hyvecuous by running off while he wasn't around *again*. But don't worry--we'll take you and your little friend back now."

"Leave her alone." Darien stepped in front of Serena and me. "She didn't do anything."

"And it's truly an all-time low for even Hyvecuous," a woman's voice spoke up. "Taking children and leaving them to wander the fourth dimension alone."

The Shadows looked back behind themselves and in the process parted slightly. I immediately saw where the voice was coming from. Surrounded by yet another group of fifteen or so more Shadows, were the rest of the kidnapped people. Or I assumed they were. There was the right number of them including Isetha's parents. And the woman who'd spoken had one arm around Asteria--holding her close to herself as if to protect her. I watched her get shoved so roughly she almost fell over, and by impulse clenched my fists.

"And on the contrary, Napollon," the Shadow continued as it walked over to me and tightly grabbed my arm. "She did do something that interested Master Hyvecuous otherwise she wouldn't have been... picked up along with you two and the others."

I didn't even try to break free of the thing's grasp--not in fear of being discovered, but because I thought I finally had a plan, or half of one at least, which was to cooperate and act like some pathetic, scared kid so those things would take us straight to Hyvecuous.

Now normally, people want to get away from others trying to kill them, but I knew our final confrontation was coming. I felt as if I had the advantage because Hyvecuous didn't know we were there. Maybe the surprise would be enough to throw him off for just one second--just long enough to give me the upper hand. The trick would be waiting until exactly the right time to reveal myself. I couldn't give Hyvecuous time to strike first, and I also couldn't be too late. And in the process, I had to protect Isetha's parents and the rest of these people so I could return them home. Plus, after I got rid of Hyvecuous but before I destroyed the fourth dimension, I'd have to find out what happened to the other Summits.

Wow, my life was a train wreck. But what else was new, right?

Chapter 62

Being marched through the fourth dimension by some creep of a Shadow constantly jabbing my back to make me walk faster without just turning around and blowing them into next week, is one of the hardest things I've ever done. When we started walking, I was practically tossed next to Asteria, Greo, and Tarron. Apparently, the Shadows couldn't have cared less about us because we were just kids. But nevertheless we were herded together and pushed along. I shook with anxiety the entire time, but still managed to keep my mouth shut. With my hood covering my face no one had any reason to suspect me of anything besides being another kidnapped person who'd strayed too far away from wherever Hyvecuous was keeping the people he'd taken. Well, I thought, we'll see how long my innocent girl act lasts.

After about five minutes of silent walking, we stopped in the middle of what looked like a random, hexagonal shaped area with a smaller (but still taller than I was) rock off to the side. The leader Shadow grabbed my arm again, paced forward, and along with several others pushed the rock over to the right to reveal a hole leading underground. The Shadow then motioned to another one, and it compliantly stepped into the hole and headed down what sounded like a stone staircase by the tapping sounds its footsteps made. I looked over to where Serena and Darien were standing and saw them watching me with worried looks on their faces. Stupidly forgetting my need to stay hidden, I decided I should say something to them. So I shook my arm loose and started to walk over only to be told "Stop!" by one of the other men.

"What-" I began shortly before being grabbed by my shirt and pressed against the stone. The Leader Shadow's face of nothingness was probably glaring at me in some form as it scoffed, "Trying to run off again, are you? I'm sure you don't want me to tell Master Hyvecuous you were being uncooperative."

"N-no" I didn't have to force myself to croak in a scared voice. "I w-wasn't trying to run away. I just-"

"Be quiet, you stupid child!" it came closer to my face and I ducked my head. Partially to prevent the thing from realizing who I was, but mostly because I couldn't bear to look at it. "No one cares what your intentions were!"

Then, of all things that could have happened next, the dead nothingness of the Shadow blew casually away. In its place, was by far the creepiest looking woman I'd ever seen in my life. Her hair and eyes were just as black as the darkness that had previously surrounded her, and she was indeed glowering at me. The woman then slammed me against the stone and I accidently cried out--more in fear than pain. Serena took a step in my direction but was of course held back.

"We imagined you might be surprised," she swung me around and forced me to look at the other Shadows, which had all become human. Of course in the process she was also forcing me to look at the other people from my Universe nearly cowering with fright and disbelief... and Tarron, Greo, and Asteria crying. "Did you really think we were mindless minions all this time? Honestly, we should be thrilled to know that we are ridding ourselves of a Universe full of idiotic people."

The other Shadows laughed coldly. I didn't react--my brain was still trying to comprehend the fact that Shadows were *human*. Actual human beings with free will that *chose* to serve Hyvecuous. And if they weren't from our Universe, where did they come from? The only other one? Hyvecuous was recruiting Shadows from our *neighboring Universe*?

I didn't have much longer than thirty seconds to take it all in before she shoved me in the direction of the hole.

"*Move*. And don't try anything else funny or there will be consequences. *Got it?*"

I nodded meekly and was pushed inside.

My confusion was quickly replaced by anger and it took all my strength to not to blow her into smithereens right then and there. I had to focus ironically on anything and everything not related to Magic as Mr. and Mrs. Napollon dropped down next to me followed by more of the Shadows, then more of us, then more of the Shadows. This kept going until we were all in a somewhat straight line walking further and further underground.

"You said you'll help us get home to our daughter but still haven't told us who you are," Serena began so quietly I could barely hear her once the Shadow in front and the ones behind us were out of earshot. She and Darien obviously had no idea that they were human either. They were pale with fear. "So are you a fifteen year old or were you just putting on an act?"

The three of us turned a corner, and I knew I'd have a good twenty seconds or so before anyone behind us turned around the same bend and could see me again. Unless Hyvecuous had watchtowers mounted on the wall, I thought it was pretty safe.

"Both those statements are true, actually," I answered just above a hoarse whisper. "I really am fifteen but what happened up there was also an act."

They stared at me strangely for a few seconds before I pulled the hood concealing my identity off. The two grew wide eyed.

"Summit Lealight... these people kidnapped *you* from the first dimension as well?" Darien asked with just as much confusion as shock.

I shook my head. "No, I teleported here with the others to defeat Hyvecuous, rescue the people he's been holding hostage, and destroy the fourth dimension itself. We came willingly."

Isetha's parents were silent for a while.

"With all due respect, but aren't you powerless here as well?" Darien eventually continued. "The fourth dimension drains all six Talents... even yours."

"That's true," I shrugged as I quickly pulled the hood back over my head in fear of the approaching Shadows. "But Magic isn't considered one of the six Talents, Mr. Napollon. Anyway, those... people are going to be able to hear us again soon, so as the last thing I'm going to tell you right now, please don't give away my position. In order to defeat Hyvecuous and get everyone out alive, I need to wait until exactly the right time to do anything. So please do whatever you can to direct any attention away from me."

Mr. and Mrs. Napollon exchanged glances.

"We will help you stay hidden for as long as possible," Darien finally replied under his breath.

"This is a very brave thing you are doing, Summit Lealight," Serena added as she somewhat hesitantly placed her hand on my shoulder again. I let her. "I think what people tend to forget about you and the others is that even as the Summits, you seven are still just children. The fact you had the nerve to come here says a lot about you as people."

I grinned slightly as light became visible from the bottom of the staircase.

"That's one word for it. Teller Hallsmen thinks I'm insane, Jarmony called it a suicide mission. I haven't heard brave yet."

The two returned nervous smiles.

"What you are doing is not a suicide mission, nor does it suggest in any way you are not in your right mind" Darien said even more faintly. "I actually find your plan pretty clever. And you seven will be fine. From what I've seen in the past three minutes, Hyvecuous will not know what hit him."

I nodded in thanks and wished I agreed as the Shadows caught up with us and we all stepped into a colossal, dimly lit corridor to face the last person besides Hyvecuous I wanted to deal with at the time.

Merrhet.

Chapter 63

"Well, that certainly took you all long enough," Merrhet snarled at the Shadows. "But at least you found the two Charmers and the rest of them... but who is that?"

Serena, Darien, and I said nothing as the Shadow/woman/thing answered simply, "Just some uncooperative girl that was with them. We figured she snuck out shortly after these two did."

I kept my head ducked, thinking Merrhet would ask more questions. But thankfully, he was uninterested in some Shadow's spot-on description of me as an "uncooperative girl", and for some reason not wary about my suspicious appearance.

"Fine. You can take them all back now. But Master Hyvecuous wants to have a word with the Charmers."

The people each looked at one another, and then they all moved toward us. One of them grabbed and quickly turned me in the direction of an open door that I could tell had another staircase behind it. Of course Greo had been right next to me at the time and must have seen red under Ms. Plenstion's cloak when they spun me around. And before we'd moved one step, he said quite loudly, "Wait, *that's the Grand-*"

Darien clamped a hand over his mouth before he could say the word "*Summit,*" but Greo had already gotten Merrhet's attention.

"The Grand *what*?" he demanded while looking me up and down with the evil eye. "Let him finish!"

Fortunately, Greo had got Mr. Napollon's message that I needed to stay hidden and after Isetha's father hesitantly removed his hand, he answered, "the grand... daughter of my mom's friend. She-she looks like the granddaughter of my mom's friend."

Merrhet looked annoyed and rolled his eyes. "Well it's a small Universe, isn't it? But no one cares, you little brat."

"Don't be rude to our guests, Merrhet," a familiar, icy voice cut through the air. The one and only Hyvecuous joined us from another hall to the left of where we were standing.

The Shadows let go of us and everyone started to shrink back against the wall. I decided I should be among them to blend in. Strangely being used to the frigid feeling that always came when around Hyvecuous, I tried to stand in the back so he wouldn't notice someone with a hood over their head who wasn't shivering like everyone else. That might've been a small hint.

"It's so nice of you two to rejoin us," Hyvecuous continued toward Serena and Darien as he gestured toward the Shadows. Four obediently took hold of them, and they were marched into the open. "I brought someone who's just dying to see you."

Merrhet then disappeared through the open door down the stairs and returned two minutes later dragging Isetha behind him with a firm grip on her forearm.

"Let go of me, you goon! I'll kick you into next month!" she snarled while digging her heels into the ground and trying to shake Merrhet off.

Despite the shock of realizing Hyvecuous had gone back to the first dimension to kidnap her too, I smiled--proud that Isetha was at least resisting (and there's nothing cuter than a little girl looking daggers and threatening a seventeen year old guy twice her size). Of course it was quickly replaced by a scowl when

Merrhet roughly pushed her into the middle of the floor in between our group and Hyvecuous.

"Isetha!" Mr. and Ms. Napollon both sighed in relief as they tried unsuccessfully to break free of their Shadow's grasp.

She looked up and at first smiled at the sight of her parents, but her face quickly flushed with anger. "Let them go!" she yelled menacingly at Hyvecuous with her fists balled up as if she would punch his nose in. "*Now!*"

That same disturbing smile spread across his face. "You have been spending too much time with that pathetic excuse for a Grand Summit if you think that you can sound threatening, child. And speaking of which, of course you and your parents shall have front row seats to watch the first dimension crumble and those seven pests go down with it."

"Oh please," she retorted. "They'll crush you like a puny, disgusting maggot! I don't know what Lealight's so worried about. She doesn't need any Magic to get rid of bigheaded *cowards* like you!"

Hyvecuous's face contorted with anger, and I silently chuckled to myself along with a few others in the back if the group.

"You think that's *funny*, do you?!" Hyvecuous shouted at us. "We'll see how amusing you find this!"

And with that, the dark fog seeped into the corridor we were standing in and surrounded Isetha, her parents, the rest of the group, and me.

Chapter 64

"We are *so lost*," Katrina bemoaned as she trailed behind the Fire Talent Summit throughout the twists and turns of the fourth dimension.

"Really? You *just noticed*?" Amiselle retorted as she turned around to look at her. She could see that Katrina looked on the verge of crying again even though her face was mostly concealed by the hood of her cloak.

Sighing, she put her hand on her former Charge's shoulder and said, "I'm sorry, Katrina. I guess the pressure is getting to me. But I shouldn't take it out on you. It's just that we've got to find the others in this endless maze or they might give up on us and move on to destroy the dimension. And we'd still be..."

What happened next was something Katrina had never seen before in the three years she'd spent with the Summits and never expected to.

Amiselle Nyete's voice trailed off shortly before she choked up and burst into tears. And naturally, Katrina had no idea what to do. To her, Amiselle had always seemed like this invulnerable person who would stand up to anything. And to see her breaking down didn't improve Katrina's already grim outlook on their situation.

"Come on, Amiselle" she tried to sound reassuring. "Don't be upset. We'll find a way out of this."

The uncertainty in Katrina's voice didn't make her feel any better, and Amiselle didn't look up. Running out of ideas, Katrina then reached out and hugged her until the silent tears stopped running down her cheeks.

"They're not going to move on without us," Katrina spoke the first confident thing she'd said since they'd been separated from the others. She let Amiselle go, but kept her hands on her shoulders. "Lealight said it herself. No one gets given up on, no matter the circumstances. We *will* find them. I promise."

Amiselle abruptly clamped a hand over her mouth and looked around nervously.

"Did you hear that?"

"Hear *what*?" Katrina asked equally as fearful.

"There it is again," Amiselle whispered sharply. "Someone's *coming*."

Before Katrina could say anything else, Amiselle grabbed her arm, paced over to a nearby looming stone, and the two tried to blend into the darkness.

"Do you have any idea where you're going?" a voice came from one of two dark figures that came to a stop directly in front of the same rock--only a few feet from Katrina.

"Nope. But Harmon, we've got to get somewhere. And standing in one place isn't going to help us. Don't you want to find the others?"

"Of *course* I do, Illydia. But do you honestly expect to just run into them in this place?"

"*Harmon*! *Illydia*!" Amiselle and Katrina cried in relief as they came out of their hiding spot and the hoods blew off of their heads.

"Guys?!" the other two exclaimed as they threw their arms around them. "You're *alive!*"

"Don't sound so surprised," Amiselle grumbled and the four started laughing.

"Wait, where are Macalynn, Aaron, and Lealight?" Katrina asked.

The Light and Woodland Talent Summits immediately pulled away and looked to the ground.

"We don't know," Harmon answered painfully. "Right after you guys fell, Lealight did. Then Aaron and Macalynn were blown out, too. We came next."

Katrina was at loss for words, and Amiselle looked at the two horrified.

"So Macalynn and Aaron are out there somewhere like we were... but Lealight's *alone*?" she asked slowly and probably louder than she should have. "That sounds like the moment Hyvecuous has been waiting for to try to kill her *again*, doesn't it?"

"Relax, Hyvecuous doesn't know we're here," Harmon pointed out, lowering his voice as if afraid of jinxing them simply by saying the fact aloud. "But we've still got to get to Aaron and Macalynn, and especially Lealight. She's probably terrified stuck in a place like this alone."

The four nodded in agreement, pulled their hoods back up to continue hiding their presence from any snooping Shadow that might be lurking in the darkness, and set off together.

Chapter 65

I told myself over and over again that Hyvecuous was bluffing. There was no way he'd randomly kill Isetha's parents and ten other unfortunate people who had probably done nothing except be at the wrong place at the wrong time. And as far as he knew, I made eleven. So there was no reason for him to get rid of us.... You know, unless it was for his own entertainment of watching living things suffer and die.

Anyway, on that pleasant note, Isetha, Greo, Asteria, and Tarron had silent, terrified tears rolling down their cheeks and most of the adults were white-faced and stood as if glued to the spot.

"What are we going to do, Summit Lealight?" Greo whispered nervously. "You do have a plan, right?"

I gave a half-hearted nod as my response and continued to try to think of one.

"Are you still refusing to admit it and cooperate?" Hyvecuous glared Mr. and Ms. Napollon menacingly.

Darien balled up his fists and practically shouted, "For the final time, Hyvecuous, there is nothing to admit because we *are not* Charmers and there is no way we would oblige even if we *were*."

After his answer, the fog lifted and everyone in the group let out a sigh of relief.

"Do you honestly expect me to believe what that Teller said?" Hyvecuous continued. "That little girl cannot be a Charmer, so it has to be the both of you!"

"My mom and dad are telling the truth!" Isetha cut in. "And why do you think it couldn't be me?"

Hyvecuous just stared at her before answering, "Because you are a seven year old!"

"I'm *nine* years old. And just for the record, the person who's going to destroy you is fifteen so I don't think it matters!"

Everyone was quiet until Asteria bravely, but stupidly, commented, "She has a point."

After another long silence, Hyvecuous, who was apparently getting desperate, said, "Fine. If she can prove it, I'll let her parents go."

Call me crazy, but I didn't trust Hyvecuous to keep his word for one second. In fact, I believed he had every intention of murdering the people he'd taken--Isetha and her parents included regardless of what she could "prove". So I ended up putting a hand on her shoulder and shaking my head before she could respond.

Isetha looked up at me with a confused expression before realizing who I was. "Lealight?" she mouthed, facing away from Hyvecuous and Merrhet so neither of them could see. "Is that you?"

I nodded and she reluctantly turned back towards the two.

"I don't have to prove anything to you people."

"You do if you ever want to see your parents alive again," Hyvecuous responded coldly.

Darien's eyes grew wide and he once again pulled Serena to him just before the two disappeared within a puff of black smoke. Isetha, much to the satisfaction of those total psychopaths, screamed and burst into frustrated tears.

No longer afraid of being discovered, I knelt down and hugged her, as did Asteria. "Don't worry, Isetha," I said soothingly. "I'll get them back. I promise."

"We'll find them after you get rid of Hyvecuous," she said in a steady voice that I wasn't expecting from a little girl who'd just seen her parents vanish in a black haze. "Just... get rid... of Hyvecuous."

Chapter 66

Illydia, Harmon, Amiselle, and Katrina had just stepped into a hexagonal shaped area with a six foot tall stone below the usual ones off to the right side. There, they stopped for a few minutes.

"Harmon, I swear we're just going in circles," Amiselle groaned as she joined Illydia and Katrina on the ground.

"I would agree with you if it weren't for this boulder," he began while pacing around the rock. "Do you guys remember it? Because I don't and if we haven't passed it yet, it might mean we're finally getting somewhere."

"Just because we're someplace that we weren't before doesn't mean we're any closer to Aaron and Macalynn or Lealight," Illydia pointed out. "For all we know, we could be walking in the opposite direction as them."

The four sighed and let the silence surround them before it was broken by the echoing sound of footsteps. Feeling a sliver of hope, Katrina, Amiselle, and Illydia stood up and joined Harmon-- waiting for somebody to walk in from one of the many paths. But after a minute passed, no one came.

"Do you think it was just leaves in the wind or something?" Illydia asked in a disappointed voice.

"We're in the fourth dimension, Illydia," Harmon answered. "As far as we've seen, there're only giant slabs of stone... no trees. And those were definitely footsteps."

A single cloaked figure then paced into the hexagon and abruptly stopped when they saw the four.

"Lealight?" Katrina asked hopefully.

"*What*? I mean, no," the person answered nervously.

Another form then ran into the first.

"Why'd you stop, Maca-"

"*Shut up*" Macalynn hissed nervously and Aaron was taken aback before he noticed the figures and realized why she'd said it.

Of course Katrina, Amiselle, Harmon, and Illydia had heard the second figure begin to say "Macalynn", and assumed who the two were.

"Okay, so our next guess is Aaron and Macalynn," Amiselle said with a hidden smile.

"*No!*" they responded much too hastily.

"You both are still terrible liars," Illydia laughed as she took the hood off of her head to reveal her cocked eyebrow. The other three did the same. "It's us, geniuses."

Broad smiles spread across Aaron's and Macalynn's faces and their hoods blew off as well.

The Talent Summits were reunited.

"I thought we'd lost you guys," Macalynn nearly cried with relief as Katrina, Amiselle, and Illydia enveloped her in a hug.

"We should have known it was you, though," Aaron added. "We just weren't expecting everyone to be together already."

The five exchanged solemn glances, and Harmon was the one to correct him.

"Not everyone, Aaron."

"What do you mean?" he said while looking around at his fellow Summits before realizing there were only five of them. "Where's Lealight?"

"We don't know. She's out here alone, and we have no clue where," Amiselle answered--her voice cracking.

"But" Katrina didn't allow another silence to set in and immediately followed up. "When we were in our groups of two we didn't know where anyone else was. Here we are after finding each other in an endless labyrinth. I'm sure we'll find Lealight, too."

Everyone half-smiled and took a grand total of about two steps before a terrified but muffled scream cut through the air. The scream of Isetha after her parents vanished from underground.

The six immediately halted and looked at each other for several seconds before Illydia spoke up. "You don't think that was Lealight, do you?"

Everyone shuddered at the thought.

"No, it didn't sound like her," Amiselle answered. "Is it me, or did it seem to come from... underground?"

 Katrina nodded. "That's what I was thinking. But how?"

"I'll tell you how," Aaron cut in from next to the boulder. "Look at this."

He and Harmon then gave the rock a powerful shove--causing it to topple back and forth before falling onto its side to reveal a hole in the ground.

Chapter 67

"Well?" Hyvecuous demanded.

Isetha looked up at me, and I squeezed her shoulder again.

"Like I said, I don't have to prove anything to you people," she half asserted, half grumbled.

"What? Did your little friend in the cloak tell you that? Because if so, she couldn't be more wrong."

He then abruptly reached out and grabbed both of our arms. My hood almost fell off at just the sudden movement, and I had to grab it with my free hand.

"She does not have any idea what she's talking about. You do not have a choice! You *will* tell me what you know right now if you ever want to see your parents again, understand?"

Isetha was obviously petrified, but she still stood her ground and said nothing.

After about thirty seconds of that, however, he tossed me aside like a broken toy and a when I hit the floor, my hood did fall back for no more than the three seconds it took me to put it back on. The good news: Hyvecuous and most of the group weren't looking and didn't see. The not-so-good-news: Tarron and Asteria were staring at me bug eyed and Merrhet was also gawking. So by the time I had stood up, he had already begun to announce my presence in the most eloquent way.

"Oh my gosh, that's *Lea-*"

Now, I had no clue what to expect after the day I'd had. But figuring I didn't have much to lose at that point, I tried to focus my mind back on Magic (like that's ever been helpful except for my couple lucky shots) and glared at Merrhet. He paused in the middle of saying my name and his expression changed from alarm to fear. I was enjoying every second of the look being on *his* face instead of mine after realizing I'd somehow temporarily taken away his ability to speak. However my feeling of triumph faded at the sight of Isetha being roughly thrown against the wall, her head making a loud "*crack*" when it hit the stone, and her crying out in pain. That was the absolute last straw for me.

I wouldn't be surprised if someone told me I had smoke pouring out of my ears as I stormed up behind Hyvecuous and said, "Excuse me."

He spun around and impatiently began with, "What *is* it, Merrhet?" But he then looked at me and said, "You again? For some kidnapped child, you've got a lot of nerve!"

"*I've* got a lot of nerve?" I asked shortly before I yanked the ties on the dark cloak and it fell off my shoulders to the gasps from the group of people and the expression of disbelief on Hyvecuous. "Because I clearly remember you calling me a "pathetic excuse for a Grand Summit" about three minutes ago. Thoughts?"

At that, I saw to my relief and delight that I was being surrounded by the familiar golden haze. Just as I had done two days before, I balled up my fist and the same lightning-shaped object was created. Only instead of being about the size of my hand, it was the length of my entire arm. And the look on Hyvecuous's face when I hit him with it is an image I will always cherish. He was shot through the air not unlike a rocket, and whacked against the wall on the opposite side of the rectangular room with a deafening "*thud*".

I immediately knelt next to Isetha and shook her arm. "Come on, Isetha. Don't black out on us now."

She blearily opened her eyes, and I noticed the blood running down her face from an open gash just above her left eyebrow. "I'm fine," she croaked while shivering.

I took Ms. Plenstion's cloak from the floor, wrapped it around her, and pulled Isetha to her feet. After walking her over to the group, I continued to say, "You all need to get out of here. Go out into the dimension, and get as far away as possible."

"So you think it's that easy?" Hyvecuous's voice rang out and everyone froze. "It's going to take a lot more than that to finish your predecessor's job."

I gently pushed Isetha into the group and stepped away from them--hoping that Hyvecuous would target me and they could sneak out. Taking my hint, Asteria put a protective arm around Isetha's shoulders and they all shrank back towards the staircase only to stop abruptly when Hyvecuous yelled at the Shadows.

"Don't just stand there! *Kill her!*"

***

Hyvecuous's words "*Kill her!*" echoed throughout the entire underground chamber--including up the stairs and into the ears of Macalynn, Amiselle, Aaron, Katrina, Harmon and Illydia. This momentarily halted their progress and the six, assuming automatically who "her" was, exchanged horrified glances before breaking into a sprint for the rest of their downward journey.

Chapter 68

Five of the Shadows immediately surrounded me in the middle of a circle and I started to wonder now that I was looking at them as people and not mindless masses of black. What were they capable of? Could they actually hurt me? My question was answered when I noticed each and every one of them had a long, crooked knife. Well, that's convenient enough.

So there I was. Standing in the center of the room enclosed by a bunch of people all pointing blades at me. And one can only remain so positive and confident in that situation.

"*No!*" Isetha cried as she tried to fight against the quickly retreating crowd. "Run, Lealight!"

"Isetha, quit drawing attention to us," I heard Asteria in a loud whisper. "Summit Lealight is going to be *fine*. She's distracting them to give us a chance to escape. So hurry up before one of those *things* try to slice her head off!"

"I'm not leaving without Lealight," she said stubbornly just as six hooded figures burst through the doorway.

"*Guys*?!" I accidently exclaimed before I could stop myself.

"Lealight!" they returned while pulling the hoods off of their heads.

"Well, isn't this just *priceless*?" Hyvecuous cackled in that way only *really* tough evil villains can. "The six *powerless* Talent Summits coming to the rescue? How very touching and sweet. But of course, you're too late."

The fog then sprang up around them and a shrill scream escaped Katrina.

"I told you to kill her!" Hyvecuous continued menacingly at the Shadows, who immediately turned back into their friendly dark nothingness and raised their knives up to my neck. The other Summits stared at them awestruck for several seconds. Not until the Shadows advanced upon me more did they squeeze their eyes shut and look away painfully--tears running down most of their cheeks.

I too closed my eyes, but instead of waiting for a wave of agony and total stillness, I was focusing hard on doing something, anything, I could protect myself. I cautiously opened one eye after hearing several muffled laughs and saw that I had created what looked like no more than a hazy sheet of Magic around myself. Truth be told, it was even more embarrassing than it was disappointing. I mean, the stuff looked like golden freaking *fairy dust*.

But it turned out that *my* fairy dust was a lot more perilous than the kind in little girl's storybooks. And wrongly assuming it was harmless, the Shadows one by one walked into it. None of them ever got the chance to take a swing at me because they disintegrated from head to toe on contact as if they were nothing more than dust in the wind. The knives fell to the floor with an echoing "*clank.*"

My film disappeared just as the swords rose from the ground on their own. Assuming Hyvecuous was going to point them at me, I readied myself to do another before realizing what he planned to do.

"You may be able to protect yourself," he grumbled as the knives arranged themselves around the fog that encased the others. "But they can't."

Chapter 69

The six of them tensed up, the color drained from their faces. Amiselle grabbed Illydia's wrist as she tended to do when she was nervous and Harmon put a protective arm around Katrina's and Macalynn's shoulders. Meanwhile, Aaron looked at me as if to say "*Do something!*"

Even though I was practically blinded by rage, I tried to focus on making sense of Hyvecuous's and the knives every movement. Finally, I figured out how he was controlling them by the way the handles of the swords were higher than the blades. Traces of the Shadows, I thought, must've remained on the ends of the weapons and he was using that to lift and have power over them. After deciding quickly what I was going to do, I momentarily appreciated how satisfying the turn of events was going to be after the course of that day.

I locked my gaze on one of the hovering knives. Because of the well-known Deadly Weapon See, Deadly Weapon Do Effect, all of them halted and gradually began to turn in the opposite direction of the others. Unfortunately, Hyvecuous noticed before they'd even pointed straight upward and he quickly set them back on the course he'd determined.

I took a step forward and tried to focus harder. Soon, I'd managed to halfway overpower him and we were locked in a stalemate for at least three agonizing, exhausting minutes as the swords wobbled unsteadily from slightly tilted in one direction to the other. At some point the very last trace of Shadows had been shaken off, and the weapons were under my control. See, what came next was supposed to be the fun part.

But, of course, it wasn't. Instead of getting to enjoy watching Hyvecuous run from a bunch of Magical knives on his heels, I heard the others nervously yelling, "Uh, *Lealight*."

I looked over to where they were standing and saw them squishing together just as all seven of us had done in the third dimension to avoid the fog around them that was caving in.

After immediately dropping the knives, I desperately tried to lift it to no avail until I felt tears welling up behind my eyes for the second time that day. I guess the added pressure and stakes made my Magic decide to be more efficient, because I ended up clearing the lethal fog when it rested no more than a foot away from a very pale Macalynn. The others all sighed in relief, and I turned to face Hyvecuous once again only to find no one there except all eleven people.

"What happened to Hyvecuous?" I asked the group.

"He disappeared" the same woman who'd spoken up aboveground responded. "When you were trying to clear the fog, you did... something and he and Merrhet practically leaped backward in surprise and the two of them vanished."

The seven of us didn't say anything.

"Do you think they're dead?" Isetha asked after many seconds of silence.

I shook my head. "What I did probably had nothing to do with them disappearing. I mean, they might have left because of it, but I didn't actually do anything to them. And I don't think someone as powerful as Hyvecuous could be killed off so easily, anyway. He and Merrhet just retreated for the time being. We'll run into them again."

Everyone looked disappointed, but knew it was true. I decided on our next step. "How many people are trapped here? Is it just you ten or are there more?"

"It's just us as far as we know," Greo answered with a shrug.

"Okay," I began while trying to work something out. "Guys, if you take the group and I-"

"Not going to happen," Amiselle interrupted squarely, but still with a grin as she and the others gathered around me. "Do you honestly think we're going to let you fight this battle alone, Lealight? After everything we've gone through?"

I smiled and was about to agree before I snapped myself back into reality--remembering that I had to get the group out somehow and, of course, the others were powerless. So my next decision was one of the hardest I've ever made. But knowing there were no other options, I hugged everyone closely.

"Calling the seven of us best friends is a major understatement. You guys are my brothers and sisters and there's nothing I want more than for you to be there with me when all this goes down. But you can't stay. You need to take everyone and get as far away from here as possible. I'll come find you after Hyvecuous is gone."

"Don't be ridiculous, Lealight. There's no way we'd just leave you here to face him alone," Aaron responded.

"I wish you didn't have to. I'm so sorry guys, but the fact of the matter is you're powerless here and Hyvecuous will take advantage of that. He'll kill you the second he has an opportunity and even if I survived, I'd never forgive myself for putting you in that kind of danger with no way to defend yourselves. Please take the group and escape before something else happens."

The others all exchanged glances before turning their attention back to me.

"Well, we'd never forgive ourselves if you got hurt and we weren't there to help you," Illydia protested earnestly.

I sighed--knowing that my next statement may or may not be true. "I'll be okay. And don't worry... I'll see you guys again soon."

They looked at me apprehensively and I could tell they didn't believe one word of my last two sentences.

"Are you sure?" Katrina finally asked after over a minute of silence.

I nodded and was about to say something else before Macalynn found her voice after being so close to Hyvecuous's fog.

"If we take these people and leave you here, you've got to swear you'll make it home. Remember your own words and never stop fighting, okay?"

I tried a reassuring smile, but failed because tears came first. The others pretended not to notice and gave me one final squeeze before pulling away and motioning for the group to go with them. Everyone went by without as much as a smile in my direction until the four children that'd turned up on our doorstep less than a week ago came.

Asteria and Greo both passed with a small half-smile, and Isetha hugged me for a few seconds before trotting after the others.

Tarron, however, said the first words I'd ever heard from him. "Good luck."

I grinned. "So you do talk."

"Yep. So... does this Magic stuff really exist?"

"Apparently."

He paused for several seconds before continuing to say, "I know you'll win."

And with that, he took off up the stairs and I stood alone in Hyvecuous's hideout underneath the ground of the fourth dimension.

Chapter 70

The others hadn't been gone for more than five minutes before I started to regret not going with them. I mean, for all I knew Hyvecuous had already moved on to attack the first dimension, or was taking another four hundred year long holiday. Now, I'd done a lot to try to defeat him so the people of my Universe would be safe again. I could handle coming to the fourth dimension, being purposely captured by a bunch of Shadows, and nearly getting decapitated by them. But I was *not* going to hang around for the rest of my life waiting for him to show up again. That was his imaginary girlfriend's job.

So there I was walking through the seemingly endless hallways and corridors of Hyvecuous's underground headquarters that, if you ask me, was just as confusing as the fourth dimension's surface when I started to hear footsteps behind me. I froze and listened to nothing but silence for several seconds before figuring I was hearing things and continuing onward. Less than a minute later, they started again. I didn't waste any time.

With my arm extended just in case I needed to destroy a sixth living being in one day (prime evil or not, Shadows were apparently still people and I was truly living up to that "Biggest Goody Two Shoes" title by feeling guilty about them being disintegrated), I spun around and my victim rose halfway up the twelve foot ceiling. His arms flailed around in the air as he groaned loudly in frustration.

"Put me *down*, Lealight!"

"*You!*"I snarled as I did what I was told for once and dropped Dillon so he face-planted from six feet high. "What are *you* doing here?!"

"Where else would I be?" he replied irritably as he got back to his feet and rubbed the side of his head that'd hit the stone floor. "And what were you *thinking*? Hyvecuous isn't going to come back! He's going to attack the first dimension now because there's no one there to protect it! How could you possibly believe that staying behind was the right decision?!"

"Don't you dare talk to me about *right decisions*, Dillon. And for the record, I was thinking that the group of people your little friend kidnapped needed to get out of here and me accompanying them would do nothing except put everyone in danger considering I'm Hyvecuous's number one target. And I figured I'd find out where he and Merrhet went after I thought they'd gotten far enough away."

Dillon just stared at me.

"Well, that's fine until you get to the fact that you have no idea where they went. Lealight, you do realize they could be *anywhere*, right? Hyvecuous could have left already or he and Merrhet..."

Dillon's voice then trailed off. He looked like he was coming up with something.

Concurrently, I kept telling myself that this was the same person who'd stood by when I was about to be killed *twice* and that I couldn't trust anything he said. But over thirty seconds later, my curiosity got the better of me.

"What?"

"I think I know where they went," he answered slowly as if he himself didn't believe it. "Never mind that, I know exactly where Hyvecuous and Merrhet are."

Chapter 71

"I'm going to warn you in advance," I began sternly as the two of us paced up the stairs back toward the surface of the dimension. "If this is some sort of trap, hoax, or anything else that will hurt the others, the people in the Village, or the Universe itself, you'll regret it."

Dillon sighed before we reached the top and he began to feel along the earth. "Lealight, I don't know what else I can do besides say I'm sorry and hope you accept my apology."

"This has nothing to do with me not forgiving you, Dillon," I answered as he continued to search. "You can forgive someone, but that doesn't mean you'll forget what happened. Especially when you were nearly killed. But while what you did was wrong, I've recently started to see why you did it and it's pretty obvious you're not completely to blame. Like you said, you didn't willingly walk into this and the fact that you're trying to set things right now certainly means something. But honestly, you shouldn't be surprised at our hesitance to trust you again."

"I'm not. In fact, I'm amazed that you guys didn't disregard what I said yesterday entirely. But it's a good thing you did come... otherwise, we would be completely screwed."

"Don't sigh in relief yet. Our Universe is still hanging by a thread until all this blows over."

We were silent for at least another ten seconds.

"So how do you plan on moving that gigantic rock out of the hole? There's no way you can just push it aside."

"We're not going up," he said while taking what looked like a very old, rusted key from a hidden hook driven into the rock. "Please, we'd be discovered within five minutes if we did. But nothing's guarding this way because no one's used it in almost six hundred years."

It wasn't until then that I noticed an equally ancient and corroded door of solid, dark metal just beyond the hole we'd come through earlier. I followed behind Dillon towards it, and he slid the key into a large padlock on the door's handle. After it clanked heavily to the ground, he pushed the door open and the smell of mold hit us.

"Well, I guess that's why this passage hasn't been used in so long," Dillon complained. "The last person to go through must've choked and died because of that stench."

I nodded in agreement but said nothing as he continued with, "This is the farthest I can go. The rest is up to you."

"What do you mean this is the farthest you can go?" I asked. "It's not like Hyvecuous is at the end... is he?"

"No, he's not. But he and Merrhet are very close and you can't be worried about me while you're there. Please, just go."

"Do you expect me to be able to come back for you after Hyvecuous is gone and the fourth dimension itself is in the process of complete destruction? It's already a long shot that I've got to find the others afterwards. I'll be lucky if I can get them out... much less come underground again to get you."

"I'll find my own way out. Seriously Lealight, *go*. We don't have time to argue about this."

I looked at him uncertainly, but his anxious expression eventually convinced me that by then, seconds counted for the survival of my Universe. So I stepped inside the tunnel.

"Lealight, one thing," Dillon nervously persisted and I turned back around to face him. "At the top of the stairs at the end of this passageway, there'll be what looks like a stone wall and you'll have to push it out. Once you do and you're on the surface again, please be careful. Fog is *everywhere* up there. Keep to your right the entire time and you should get there within a few minutes. Hurry and good luck."

With that, he slammed the door shut, and I could hear the padlock being snapped back onto its handle.

"Thanks for the tip," I said under my breath while rolling my eyes. Suddenly beginning to worry I'd been tricked, I cautiously continuing onward down the dank, dark tunnel until I reached a staircase identical to the one in front of the hole.

Chapter 72

One nerve-wracking climb later, I stood completely boxed in on three sides. Behind me were the stairs I'd just climbed. To the left and right were blocks of densely packed, rocky dirt. And directly in front was a giant slab of the familiar dark stone that I was pretty sure lead into the dimension and, according to Dillon, into the deadly fog. Let's put it this way, I'd definitely been more excited in my life.

But lacking other options, I dropped my cloak that I'd been holding over my nose to avoid the reek of mold and tried to thrust the rock out of the way. To my surprise, the thing gave no resistance whatsoever, fell over with a powerful "*thud*", and I stumbled out into the middle of a relatively narrow pathway made by the same stone as the rest of the labyrinth.

I hadn't been standing there for more than five seconds before an immense, murky cloud shot by just a foot above my head. Swallowing a scream, I ducked low to the ground and was as still as a statue until it passed. Once I'd regained some composure, I stood up and tried unsuccessfully to prepare myself for confronting Hyvecuous while taking the first right turn. At least eight corners and several close-calls with the fog later, I heard his voice coming from just around the next bend.

"I cannot believe that ignorant child actually knows what she's doing. She has to have gotten in touch with Veronica in order to be able to lift that fog!"

"Master, Summit Veronica Calodie died three hundred and twenty-six years ago. She never knew any Magic, and Lealight couldn't have had any idea what she was doing either. All the information on it was burned."

"Well, if she did something like that by accident then imagine what she's capable of *on purpose,*" Mr. Napollon chimed in mockingly.

"*Quiet!*" Hyvecuous's enraged voice bounced off the stone walls. "The only reason you and your wife aren't dead right now is that these incompetent Shadows haven't located your daughter yet."

"How exactly do you expect your little henchmen to find anything in this endless labyrinth?"

"I said *quiet!* You two are standing on incredibly thin ice and your little one is on even thinner. If it turns out she's the Charmer then you two are as good as gone!"

There was a long silence, and I took the time to creep around the corner to stand in the shadows in full-view of the situation.

Hyvecuous was pacing back and forth along the edge of a stone square that rose about two feet off the usual rocky dirt. Believe it or not, there was actually some light emitted from four torches that rested on each corner of the platform. All together, the flames made it just visible that fog hovered above their heads in a "just in case" fashion.

Wow, I thought. *Someone's not as confident as they used to be.*

"Merrhet, go see what's keeping the Shadows," Hyvecuous demanded impatiently. "We can't leave until we have the Charmer, and if that little girl is it then so be it. She'll be easier to manipulate, anyway."

I chuckled to myself at the fact that Hyvecuous honestly thought he could get Isetha to do anything as Merrhet stepped off the square. He headed toward one of the four paths that led away from it. I was about to move in closer before abruptly freezing when he stopped and looked straight in my direction. I didn't so much as breathe deeply for several seconds as Merrhet glared at me, hoping that I was blending in with the shadows and if I was still enough, he would think he was seeing things and walk away.

Anyone but me noticing the similarities between that problem I'd managed to get myself into and the one earlier in the same day when I was cornered by Serena and Darien? Apparently, I was a natural at blowing my own cover.

Almost positive Merrhet was going to broadcast my presence again, I was struggling to not run away by the time he shrugged and ambled off. I let out a sigh of relief, and quickly decided that it was time for me to quit acting like a little kid eavesdropping on their parents' conversation and confront Hyvecuous for the final time. However, facing an extremely powerful monster who's nearly killed you twice and is still trying is a lot easier said than done. I spent three minutes ignoring what was happening less than twenty feet away so I could persuade myself to get closer. But before I'd taken five steps forward, I was harshly grabbed and pressed against a nearby stone.

Chapter 73

"Well, look who decided to show up," Merrhet snarled as he twisted my right arm painfully behind my back. "Did you honestly think I couldn't see you? In that obnoxiously bright red cloak? You don't blend into the darkness very well wearing that, oh powerful Grand Summit. I guess the person who came up with it didn't think everything through, now did they?"

My head throbbing where I'd hit the solid rock, I tried (and failed miserably) to make my voice sound threatening as I responded. "Let go of me, Merrhet. Let go of me, and maybe I won't completely destroy you along with Hyvecuous."

"*You*?" he laughed. "Destroy *Hyvecuous*? Do you really believe that just because you could clear that fog on... what, your twelfth try, you're even half a match for him?"

"You have no idea what I'm capable of," I hissed--thinking ironically that *I* had no idea what I was capable of, either. "And if you don't-"

"*Shut up!*" Merrhet barked as he once again slammed me against the stone so hard I saw stars. "You don't give the orders anymore, Lealight. In fact, if you plan on living to see the next hour or so, I suggest you cooperate with me. I won't think twice before breaking your arm if you don't. And of course Hyvecuous won't hesitate to snap your neck."

The next thing I said was a complete surprise to the both of us. I just blurted it out without thinking, and it was definitely one of those times when you say something but immediately afterward wish you hadn't.

"Why are you doing this, Merrhet? This Universe is your home just as much as it is mine, and you're helping to *destroy it*. Hundreds of innocent, defenseless people will be massacred if this happens. You'll be partly responsible for their deaths!"

His grip momentarily loosened and I thought for all of ten seconds I could get through to him.

"If for some reason you hate me--then fine, hate me. I really couldn't care less! But you can't just wipe out an entire Universe of people! Or you *won't* while I'm alive, I can guarantee you that!"

Merrhet was about to answer before Hyvecuous's irritated voice cut in. "Merrhet, is that you over there? I thought I told you to go find the Shadows!"

I craned my neck around to see his expression. Merrhet looked like he was at war with himself---his eyes darting in all directions and his grasp indecisively going from half-hearted to a death grip.

"You did, and I was going to," he responded slowly and I felt a sliver of hope that was quickly annihilated by what he followed up with. "Before... before I found *someone* snooping around nearby."

Merrhet then swung me around and, despite my resistance, managed to keep a hold of arm and marched me forward in the direction of the platform. Serena and Darien were both standing closer to us. The two of them saw me first and gasped as I was pushed roughly onto the square.

"Hello Lealight," Hyvecuous began scornfully once he too saw me. I could've sworn I saw the fog above us churn excitedly upon hearing it had a victim. "How very thoughtful of you to join us for this historic occasion. You're alone, I presume? Well, it is unfortunate that your little friends won't get to watch you fall for the final time, but we'll manage without them."

I briefly cradled my arm that Merrhet had twisted in my other before dropping it back to my side and scowling. "You're right. It *is* a shame the others aren't here. That means they're going to miss out on seeing you blown into oblivion."

He formed his usual, twisted smile before getting straight to the point. "Don't make me laugh. Now, are there any last words you'd like me to deliver to the people of the first dimension after I tell them you've been killed?"

"How about Hyvecuous is a *raving lunatic* who really needs to chill with the black? Seriously, you've got your get-up, the Clouds, the entire fourth dimension in a state of total darkness, and now this fog? Doesn't it ever get old to see what you have inside of you all around every day? I know it'd get on my nerves after a while."

His face contorted with anger just as Serena added, "I agree. This place could stand some lighting aside from scattered, hand-held torches. Oh, I know! Before your little rain clouds tumbled in, we had this colossal light bulb in the first dimension that lit up the entire sky during the day and magically turned off at night. It was very nice. I believe it's called *the sun.* You should look into it."

To Hyvecuous's further irritation, I snickered loud enough to make sure he heard me.

"On that note, it'd only be fair for me to ask you for any last words as well, Hyvecuous."

He just stared at me with an amused expression. "Do you honestly believe I view you as a threat? Please, you're more like an annoying insect than a feared nemesis."

"Didn't sound like it from what I heard," I retorted as my beloved golden haze enveloped me---twice as bright and dense as ever before. "I mean, 'She has to have gotten in touch with Veronica'? Yes Hyvecuous, I ran into her in the Village and she handed me a pamphlet. Give me a *break*."

There was a minute long silence before Hyvecuous decided to eliminate a pre-battle rant about his evil master plan and finished simply with, "If that is all, let's get this over with, shall we?"

My heart was pounding, I felt like I was going to jump out of my skin, but my voice sounded calm as I replied.

"Ladies first."

Chapter 74

Illydia stopped in her tracks and did the second head count she'd done since she, the other Talent Summits, and the group surfaced from Hyvecuous's underground chamber. Murmuring to herself, she added as everyone trotted past her.

"Two, four, six, eight, ten, eleven--okay. One, two, four, five---alright we have everybody."

"No we don't," Amiselle said dismally and a wave of panic shot through her.

"*What*? But I counted sixteen total, plus me, that's all seventeen!"

"Thank you, great mathematician, but I'm talking about *Lealight*. You know, the one we just left there to face Hyvecuous alone. I know she told us to go on and that she'd be fine... but how could we have done that after everything that's happened?"

Amiselle then slowed to a regular walk and Illydia stayed behind with her.

"We didn't have a choice, Amiselle. Lealight is the only one of us who isn't completely powerless here so she at least stands a chance against Hyvecuous while we'd be killed in an instant. And all these people would too if they were around when he showed up again. They can't just walk through the fourth dimension alone. That's why we're here with them."

"Well, just because she isn't powerless doesn't mean the odds are in her favor. In fact, I'd say it's the exact opposite! Even though we're not Talented here, it's not right for us to just abandon her!"

"Amiselle, we're no use to anybody dead," Illydia said strictly. "We'll just have to keep going and hope, okay? Now, come on. We're falling behind and you don't want to be separated from everybody again, do you?"

Amiselle shook her head but was still unsure, not unlike every other person in the group, and the two ran to catch up with the others.

Chapter 75

On that note, the entire body of fog swooped downward and, instead of coming directly on top of me like I thought, gathered itself at the opposite side of the square. I didn't have any longer than ten seconds to wonder what Hyvecuous was doing before it instantaneously charged at me. It expanded outward as well as inward which, looking back now, was probably only for intimidation purposes. Well, whatever its intentions, it definitely freaked me out.

My reflexes kicked in and I threw my arms over my face-- squeezing my eyes shut. Hyvecuous at first laughed at how small and afraid I looked before he abruptly stopped and I heard him snarl, "Oh, look at *that*. You've picked up a new *trick*, haven't you?"

I cautiously looked through a slit in one eye. I saw a brightly glowing, seven foot tall, golden screen in front of me which scattered the fog that was still plowing into it to no avail. The whole thing reminded me of how a knight uses his nifty fireproof shield when attacked and ruthlessly sneezed on by dragons. But anyway, yeah, "trick". I totally meant to do that.

"Well, you'll need a *lot* more than a flimsy little force field to save your Universe!" Hyvecuous continued to yell as the receding fog sprang back to life, looped around my temporary wall of protection, and launched itself at me from behind.

I quickly brought one of my hands over, aimed it toward the approaching cloud, and smiled as my "little force field" stretched itself and encased me inside a messy, but still functional, cylinder without a lid. Just in case Hyvecuous got any ideas, I quickly added a top to it and enjoyed his expression of disbelief before beginning to focus on pushing the shield out around the entire platform. Within five seconds of my attention, it spread like wildfire and Hyvecuous, Isetha's parents, and I were soon standing inside a gargantuan dome with Merrhet trapped on the outside and the fog beating against it, but with absolutely no hope of getting in.

Before Hyvecuous had a chance to react, I flicked my wrist in his direction and what looked like three thin, but sharp and fast, waves shot toward him. He dodged the first and second, but the last one hit him square in the chest. This time *he* was tossed like a ragdoll across the dome until finally coming into contact with it, and falling flat on his face from at least eight feet up.

"Not so strong without your fog, are you Hyvecuous?" Darien mocked him from the sidelines behind me. Probably not the best idea.

Seeming to have momentarily forgotten the two were there, Hyvecuous looked caught off guard as he stood quickly and snapped, "You stay out of this, Napollon! The end of your Universe has already begun and nothing will stop it now, so wipe that smirk off your face before I do it for you!"

More dark clouds rose from the ground around me--not taking the form of fog, but of Shadows. There were eight of them, each wielding a knife, just like the ones I'd wiped out underground.

As they approached me, I heard Serena say to him, "Great, now look what you did! You just *had* to chime in, didn't you?"

He didn't respond.

Chapter 76

Nearly halfway across the labyrinth, the group of six Summits and eleven people walked in silence before someone asked the question no one had the answer to.

"How are we supposed to know what's happened to Summit Lealight? I mean, whether she is alive or not after Hyvecuous comes back. And if she does defeat him, then how are we supposed to find her?"

"*When* Lealight defeats him," Harmon corrected them. "She'll probably come find us. She can't destroy the fourth dimension without making sure everyone's out of it first. It wouldn't make sense..."

Harmon's voice trailed off and he suddenly wore a confused expression. Everyone followed his gaze. The people in the group just stared when they saw the same, but the Summits and Isetha smiled broadly. A blinding source of light was coming from the top of what looked like a large dome off in the distance. The glow was enough to dimly illuminate most of the dimension, including the part where the group now stood. Everyone froze in their tracks.

"What is that? Who's doing it?" Greo asked. He was quickly followed by a typical response from Amiselle.

"I'll give you a hint. Who's the only person we know that-"

"It's *Lealight*!" Isetha interrupted excitedly. "She's found Hyvecuous!"

At that, she and the other Summits set off quickly in the dome's direction--Katrina hanging slightly behind telling the others "*Come on!*"

But the group, for ten, was apprehensive about going towards the danger instead of away from it as they were told to do. They didn't see anything good that could come out of them being there and, after their prior experiences with Hyvecuous, wanted to get as far away as possible from all things related to the fourth dimension.

"Look everyone," Katrina began in exasperation after they hadn't moved in several seconds. "I know you don't think it's a good idea for us to head in the direction of the battle, but Lealight's part of our *family*. We would never forgive ourselves if something happened to her and we weren't there to help. Do any of you know what I mean? What if it was a member of your family out there alone? Wouldn't you go to them... no matter the costs?"

The group looked uncomfortably at the dirt beneath their feet as if considering the scenario before Greo, Asteria, and Tarron bravely stepped forward.

"I don't know about you all," Greo turned back as the other two kicked dust into the air in their haste to catch up with the Summits and Isetha. "But if it was *my* sister out there, I'd risk anything to save her."

With that, he turned and continued running to catch up. The group uncertainly followed behind. It wasn't that they didn't care what happened to Lealight; if was more fear of what they might find once they reached her. No one knew what to expect from Hyvecuous. He'd do anything to get what he wanted and no method of obtaining it was below him--killing off a child included. As they saw it, the fact of the matter was that there was no stopping the Talent Summits from going and, powerless or not, they were still the Summits. Unless you were Litheney Hallsmen, you didn't argue with them. Besides, only Lealight could get them home. And only if she survived.

So with that in mind, the group of seventeen had stretched itself from its original shape of a closely-packed blob to a snake winding swiftly through the fourth dimension's pathways towards the dome. In front, were Macalynn, Aaron, Amiselle, Harmon, Illydia, and Isetha--practically sprinting along. Tarron, Greo, and Asteria followed a short distance behind them and some thirty or forty feet afterwards came the rest of the people. Katrina stayed at the rear to make sure everyone kept together.

And as if she thought Lealight could hear her, Katrina whispered reassuring words under her breath--hoping that someway, somehow, she could.

"We're coming, Lealight, and we're going to help you whether you like it or not. Just hang in there a little longer. We'll be there soon."

Chapter 77

"Hello again, sweetie," one of them snarled. I automatically assumed it was that creepy woman again. "I'm very sorry we weren't properly introduced. If I'd known who you were, then I would have killed you much sooner."

A Shadow lunged at me from behind. I easily moved out of the way and blew it to smithereens using a thin, but powerful, almost sonic-looking, wave similar to the one I'd used to attack Hyvecuous. When I turned around, the Shadow-form of the woman was gone. I immediately heard something to my left and sent another blast in that direction. There were two of them, and they both dodged it. I barely blew them away before they swung at me with their knives. The one good thing about fighting Shadows in their *Shadow* form was no blood and gore because there's pretty much nothing inside of them. This made fighting easier because you don't consider that behind the churning blackness lies a real, breathing person. The idea that I'd fought and "killed" Shadows before and never gave them a second thought was currently bothering me. I fought these feelings, pushing them down deep. I didn't care what the things were. They were trying to kill me. And, mindless or human, they all had major anger issues when it came to the wielding of knives.

I'd blindly gone through seven of the eight Shadows and at first didn't notice the last one stalking up behind me. When I spun around to face it, the thing was close enough and I ducked just in time to get a long gash across my cheek instead of down my throat like they were probably planning. I cupped my hand over the left side of my face and stumbled backward to the sound of Hyvecuous's laughter.

"Oh, did that nasty Shadow give you a little paper cut?" he taunted.

"*Look out!*" Darien's voice reached me before I did anything else. I dove out of the way just as a knife was brought down through the empty air that would have been my head if I'd stayed put for one more second. Flat on the ground, I glared into the Shadow as it ran in my direction until it imploded and vanished less than five feet away from me. I was alone in the middle of the square, and Hyvecuous just stared, dumbfounded. I quickly got to my feet in time for him to thrust his arm skyward. This promptly sent me flying both backward and upward until I smashed into the unquestionably strange feeling of my own Magic.

"It was completely foolish of you to come here!" he yelled as I fell to the ground, but still managed to stick a decent landing. "What you have seen in the past few hours is only the beginning, child. The beginning of something even you can't stand up to. All you've done by infiltrating the fourth dimension is make this more painful for yourself and the people of your Universe!"

"You've already made it clear that you intend to *obliterate* us, so I think that's as painful as you can go!" I snapped back at him. "What could you possibly hope to gain from destroying the Universes?! You reduced one to absolutely nothing over six hundred years ago, left four so weak they had to join together to survive, and now you've come back to finish the job? If all the Universes are gone, where will *you* go? There will be nothing left, Hyvecuous. Then even you will die!"

He just stared at me as if annoyed.

"Don't be melodramatic. I'm not going to stand here and tell you what I plan on doing just because-"

"You're that predictable?" I interrupted mockingly.

Hyvecuous's face twisted with anger. "This ends here."

Wow, and he'd called me melodramatic.

"Yeah, it does," I responded icily. Hyvecuous then balled his fist and more fog appeared.

I rolled my eyes and thought *"Really? Again?"* but quickly realized where this cloud was going. It wasn't coming toward me, it was flying in the direction of Isetha's parents.

Chapter 78

Aaron and Harmon had long since taken the lead and were sprinting down the same, but currently fog-free, passageway Lealight had entered from. However, they abruptly halted before turning around the second to last corner and began backing away slowly. Of course it was too late for them to go unnoticed. Merrhet was standing right there, no more than eight feet away.

"Well, look who it is *this* time," he snarled.

"Get out of the way," Harmon demanded menacingly.

"Can't do that," Merrhet retorted. "We don't want you going down there causing trouble, do we?"

Harmon and Aaron scowled and walked up to him. "If you know what's good for you, you'll *move,* Merrhet," Aaron threatened. "Or we'll-"

"You'll what? In case you forgot, you're *powerless* here," Merrhet cut in--intentionally taunting them.

Infuriated, the two ganged up further. "We don't need Talents to drive you into the ground if you don't get out of our way in the next five seconds."

"That's a *great* idea," said Merrhet and the two momentarily exchanged hesitant glances. But before they could react, Merrhet made a fist, and punched Aaron as hard as he could in the face. The blow nailed him just to the right of his nose, which promptly started gushing blood. Gasping in pain, he stumbled backwards. Merrhet saw the opportunity, stuck his foot out in time to trip him, and Aaron hit the dirt with an echoing "*thud.*"

"*Aaron!*" Illydia's voice echoed as she, Macalynn, Amiselle, and Isetha rounded the corner.

"You're going to pay for that," Harmon was nearly shaking with rage as Illydia and Isetha knelt beside Aaron and Macalynn and Amiselle stepped up beside him.

Merrhet regarded them just as much amusement as disgust. "Oh please, what are you going to do? Have the thirteen year old-"

"Don't underestimate us, Merrhet," Macalynn threatened.

He laughed coldly, making the three more livid than they already were. "Hate to break it to you, but we're already in the fourth dimension so that's not exactly a threat anymore."

"I'm warning you," Amiselle cut in. "Move or face the consequences that really should have gone your way nine days ago."

Merrhet stifled another chuckle. He was about to land another blow in Harmon's direction before Macalynn stomped hard on his foot and punched him even harder in the stomach. Even though she was four years younger and a good eight inches shorter, she knocked the wind right out of him. Merrhet promptly fell over.

"She warned you," Macalynn said with a shrug as Harmon snickered and Amiselle patted her shoulder approvingly.

When they turned to face the others, they saw Aaron standing upright, though leaning against a stone, as if he'd never fallen. He was pressing part of his cloak against his face to stop his nose from bleeding.

"You okay?" Harmon asked.

"Just splendid," was his answer as he dropped the fabric and rubbed the right side of his face. Though Aaron quickly shook it off and continued to say, "We need to move."

"Oh my gosh, is that Merrhet?" Katrina asked as she and the rest of the people came around the same bend. "What's he--what happened to *you*, Aaron?"

She joined the other five as Isetha went back to Asteria, Tarron, Greo, and the rest of the group.

"Merrhet sucker-punched him," Harmon looked disdainfully at his crumpled form on the ground. "Such a nice guy. It's comforting to know his true colors after three years. But we've got to keep going."

"I wouldn't count on... finding her there," Merrhet huffed as he laboriously stood and glared angrily at the Talent Summits, particularly Macalynn.

The color drained from the girls' faces as Harmon and Aaron paced over, grabbed Merrhet by his shirt, and flattened him against the rock wall.

"Then where... is... Lealight?" Aaron demanded vehemently.

Merrhet was silent, looking at the two with a smug expression.

"Where is she?! What did you *do* to her?!" Harmon shook him violently until he cracked.

"Last I saw, she took a knife in the face and stood in shock for several seconds before collapsing. Then she narrowly avoided getting the same knife in the back of her head and after that, I assumed like anyone else would that it's over for her and left to go figure out what was taking the Shadows so long to locate *you all*."

The entire group had gathered around him, Aaron, and Harmon--staring mortified.

"A *knife*?!" Illydia broke the silence.

"Don't just stand there!" Isetha yelled impatiently. "*Run!*"

Harmon and Aaron dropped Merrhet and left him coughing on the ground before all seventeen of them continued in the direction of dome in a sprint.

Chapter 79

Serena screamed shrilly, and Darien wrapped his arms around her for at least the third time as the fog shot through the air. I darted in their direction and, once I'd reached them, threw my hands outward to create an even more flimsy-looking sheet of gold in between us and the fog. In this process, my dome disappeared and I was hit with the horrifying realization that I was starting to fade. It hadn't even been one day and I was already running out of the energy and focus to keep it up for much longer. Then again, I'd gone from not having the faintest idea what I was doing with Magic to suddenly having to fight for my life (and everyone else's for that matter) with it. It was a miracle I could do what I'd done so far. However, that happy little thought didn't make me feel any better, believe it or not, and panicking wasn't doing me any good either. But it's kind of natural to freak out in situations like that, you know?

So after my giant, sturdy film surrounding the entire platform vanished, the original fog came rushing in. I quickly extended the delicate piece of field I'd just made so it completely encased the three of us in a smaller dome. From the inside, the thing looked like it was ready to give out on its own any second. As you would expect, I had my doubts about its ability to hold fog at bay and kept my eyes squeezed shut after that. But I figured that having some protection was better than just standing there doing nothing, so I held it for what seemed like forever before I dared to look at the situation.

Lo and behold, when something seems bad, remember, it can always get worse.

The fog's pressure was so great it made our only protection tremble violently. And to make matters worse, out of the corner of my eye and a slit in the fog, I could have sworn I saw the others followed by the group rushing in. I blinked several times to get rid of what I could only hope was nothing but a figment of my imagination, but the shapes remained not only there, but also in motion. And unfortunately, Hyvecuous saw them, too.

"Coming to the rescue again, are we?" he laughed coldly "When will you six learn that you're completely powerless here?"

"Where is she, Hyvecuous?" Macalynn demanded, apparently not seeing me or Isetha's parents within the fog.

"I'm afraid I do not know the 'she' you are speaking of" he taunted.

"You know very well who we're *speaking of*!" Aaron yelled back. "Where is Lealight?!"

"Yes, *her,*" Hyvecuous continued smugly. "If my memory serves, I believe it had something to do with a knife."

The rest of the group gasped in horror, but the others, Isetha, and the three children stepped forward.

"We don't buy that for one second, Hyvecuous," Illydia began stubbornly. "Tell us where she is! *Now*!"

From inside the fog, I'd been trying to think of a non-risky way to get Serena, Darien, and myself out with very few results. I could push the fog outward by making the dome expand like I did before. But if it started to deplete the little Magic I had the first time, then a second time probably wouldn't be a good idea. Or maybe I could've flipped the sheet inside out so it would encapsulate the fog instead of us? Or maybe not because if even one section was left outside the dome, we'd be as good as dead.

"I just told you your little friend isn't... with us anymore," Hyvecuous responded--a tone of annoyance starting to replace his confidence. "So let's move forward, shall we?"

I didn't need to see any more than their outlines to assume what that meant and do yet another involuntarily, day-saving (or maybe minute-saving in my case), Magic-related... thing. You're probably not going to know what to think when I tell you what it looked like, but if you want to question my sanity, grab a ticket and get in line. Simply stated, I made a giant explosive out of my dome.

At first, the thing shrank and I thought that meant the fog was just getting closer to overpowering it. But I figured out pretty quickly I was wrong when it suddenly... well, *exploded* in all directions--sending the fog back and away by what looked like at least a hundred feet. That's just how large and powerful this outburst was, yet it barely reached the edges of the platform.

Now don't get the impression that I walked over to greet the others in triumph just because I'd blown Hyvecuous clean off his feet, out of the square, and against a surrounding stone. In fact, it was quite the opposite. I was breathing heavily as if I'd just broken the water's surface after holding my breath for two minutes, and stood slightly hunched over in exhaustion as the sound of many footsteps echoed through the air. Most of them stopped close to the edge, but seven still rushed onward.

"Mom! Dad!" Isetha cried as she ran past me and into their outstretched arms.

I smiled as I watched them--reminded of my family before the fire. But less than a second later, I was pulled erect by Katrina and Harmon before being enveloped in yet another hug by all the others. Aren't we just the cheesiest bunch you've ever seen?

"Thank goodness you're okay," Aaron breathed a sigh in relief. "Merrhet made it sound like you'd already been killed."

"You were talking to Merrhet?" I asked skeptically before remembering he'd been trapped outside of my original dome.

"We stopped and politely asked for directions," Macalynn smiled and the others started chuckling.

"Translation, she punched him in the gut shortly after stamping his foot in," Amiselle clarified with a fond smile at the memory. "The look on his face was absolutely priceless."

"*Nice,*" I smiled broadly and Macalynn blushed bright red. "I can't tell you how many times I wished I could've done that to the jerk in the past week."

Everyone laughed as all three Napollon's came over to us. The others hadn't moved to stand beside me in a semi-circle to face them for more than two seconds before Isetha threw her arms around me. It was obvious she was holding back more tears.

"I'm so glad you're alright," she began. "We thought you were gone."

I squeezed her back. "I'd never leave like that. Hyvecuous can't do anything to hurt me as long as I've got you guys to remember and keep fighting for," I paused--debating whether or not this was the right time. Seeing the three together convinced me it was. "And speaking of which Isetha, I want you to know I would've never had the courage to come here if it wasn't for you, I would've never even found the chest to begin with. You're very special, and I'm not just talking about you being a Charmer. I know you'll do great things one day and make a huge difference in people's lives just like you have in mine."

She pulled away and beamed up at me. I was trying to pay attention to this mushy moment while also keeping a look out for Hyvecuous. This wasn't the end of the game, this was a dragging half-time show.

"You've done a lot in my life too, Lealight. You didn't know me, Tarron, Asteria, or Greo and you still took us in. Then you stood up for me to those jerks in the woods, and you were willing to help me be a Charmer. And on top of it all, you *did* keep your promise to get my parents back. I'll never forget all you did for me. Thank you so much."

I pushed a strand of her hair that was dangling down in her face behind her ear.

"Absolutely."

Isetha's smile abruptly vanished and her face flushed with concern.

"What?" I asked, quickly switching the focus of my gaze to the edge of the square looking for any sign of Hyvecuous. "Do you see him?"

"No," she said while shaking her head. "You have a... um..."

The other Summits then came around to see what Isetha was talking about. Once they'd apparently seen whatever it was, they obtained similar expressions.

"What is it?" I repeated nervously.

"You really did take a knife in the face," Katrina said. "Merrhet said you did just before you blacked out, but we didn't believe it once we saw the gigantic cloud of fog next to Hyvecuous."

Well, I'd completely forgotten about that. I guess adrenaline kept me from feeling the pain. But since someone just had to remind me, I became aware of the blood practically gushing out of the cut and a pounding ache from beneath the skin.

"I didn't *black out*," I scowled--infuriated by yet another one of Merrhet's attempts to make me look weak and feeble in front of the others. "Yeah, I got caught with one of the Shadow's knives, but I jumped out of the way of the second strike. I was not *unconscious*."

"Okay, okay," Harmon tried to calm me down. "We didn't say you were. That's just what we heard. But whether or not you were out really isn't important. What matters is that you're alright."

Katrina took the hood of my cloak and began to press it to the cut. She quickly dropped it at Tarron's cry.

"*Look out!*" his voice rang in the air. It was shortly followed by everyone in the group asking "You talk?"

"Of course I talk!" he retorted before repeating "*Watch behind you!*"

I spun around and saw Hyvecuous trudging across the square.

Chapter 80

"Guys," I whispered. "Take the group and get them somewhere safe. Hurry, I'll distract him."

"There is absolutely, positively *no way* we're going to leave you again, Lealight," Illydia replied sternly, but also under her breath.

"Illydia please, just get them out," I insisted--unable to keep the desperation out of my voice. "I can't protect them all and Hyvecuous will take advantage of that. He'll *kill* them. If you refuse to leave, then okay. But you've got to get the others out of here."

I watched the approaching Hyvecuous with a horrible sense of dread while also trying unsuccessfully to listen in on the other's hushed, uncertain voices. I was worried they wouldn't agree on a decision before Hyvecuous reached us. Finally, out of the corner of my eye, I saw Katrina and Macalynn walk tentatively in the direction of a path leading away from where we were while motioning for the group to go with them. Darien and Serena followed behind with Isetha practically glued to their side once everyone else had disappeared down the trail--leaving Macalynn and Katrina standing in front of it telling them with silent gesticulations to pick up the pace. However, once they'd done just that, Hyvecuous noticed them, all *three* of them, and stopped in his furious tracks nearly fifteen feet away.

"Finding the Charmer is becoming more of a hassle than I believe it is worth," he began icily in their direction. Shortly afterward, Isetha, Darien, and Serena froze. "So let's resolve that issue first."

Expecting either fog or Shadows to spring up, I started pacing over to them only to be restrained by Aaron and Harmon grabbing both of my arms.

"Don't," they told me simultaneously.

"What are you talking about?" I hissed as I tried to shake them off to no avail.

"Just wait a second, Lealight," Harmon said strictly. "See what happens. If that fog does show up again, then you can do something. Otherwise, you looking like you're about to will only provoke him to create it in the first place."

I knew they were right, but still had to fight down my instinct to try to stop disasters before they happened and keep still. But even after I'd nodded in agreement, Aaron and Harmon wouldn't release their grip as if they expected me to crack any second.

"So to keep this brief, Isetha, you're going to tell me who in your family is a Charmer *right now*, understand?"

"What makes you think I'll tell you anything?" she crossed her arms just before she lifted off and hovered six feet above the ground.

At first, I thought there was a lot more to the whole "Charmer" thing than I'd expected. But Isetha's look of alarm and Hyvecuous's haughty expression quickly made me scratch the theory and replace it with this guy was really at his wit's end, so he had resorted to threatening a little girl to get information.

"I'm going to give you one last chance, Isetha," Hyvecuous snarled. "Speak up now or suffer the consequences!"

Isetha was obviously petrified (once again) and there was nothing I could do to help her (also *once again*), but she still refused.

"So that's how it's going to be?" he snarled. "If you won't admit it, I'll-"

Unfortunately, we never got to find out what he'd do because Isetha snapped her fingers and for a grand total of maybe half a second, Hyvecuous's black clothes were tinted a light shade of lavender before he hastily changed them back. Well, I, for one, thought that a Charm on changing the color of things was one of the most worthless things I'd ever seen. But Isetha had apparently managed to find a use for it, and if we both got out of the fourth dimension alive I would definitely have to give her a lecture about the appropriate times and places to joke around with her Charms. And of course which people to mess with… because if Hyvecuous had many things, a sense of humor was not one of them.

"You think that's funny, don't you?"

Considering Isetha was cracking up, I'd say a little.

"Well, you've just proven that you *are* the Charmer and that means you'll be meeting a similar fate as the one your little friend possesses."

The horrible look of excitement on Hyvecuous's face was a pretty big clue that he was about to kill someone, so naturally, I thought that it was a *very* appropriate time for me to intervene. Not even bothering to give another yank at my arm to try, and most likely fail, to free myself, I glared at Hyvecuous hoping for something that would force him to drop Isetha.

My expectations were met in an unexpected and unplanned way as usual. I literally watched a dark outline of whatever Hyvecuous had Isetha trapped in flip over and he became the one that was encased. You know, momentarily. But I did take advantage of the five seconds I was in control of the dark-lined orb and oh-so-carefully flung it to the center of the square away from us.

Aaron and Harmon immediately let go of me as if worried I'd "accidentally" do something to them without moving next and I rolled my eyes.

Yes, be afraid of the person who obviously has *absolute control* over their abilities to randomly throw the enemy around and buy an equivalent of about thirty seconds to try and fail to work problems out little by little... by little.

Chapter 81

"*Run!*" I screamed at Isetha once she hit the ground close to Macalynn and Katrina. She'd been sent backward by the impact of the orb switching sides. "Get out of here! Catch up with the others!"

Her eyes darted from me, to her parents, to the exiting passage shortly behind her that everyone else had taken several seconds before. Macalynn and Katrina said something to her I couldn't hear from back on the platform. Though I could see her eyes well up with tears and her head nod in understanding before she took off sprinting down the path.

Darien and Serena began to follow before Hyvecuous's hand shot out and every slab of rock next to an exit began to topple and fall.

"*Watch out!*" Katrina shouted as she grabbed Macalynn by a fistful of her cloak. They dove out from the shadow of a stone balancing on one point to the right of them.

The two stumbled away just in time to narrowly avoid being flattened and tore across the dirt. "You guys okay?" Illydia asked them once they'd rejoined us breathing heavily. "You're as white as sheets."

Katrina nodded and Macalynn simply stared at the ground before the focus of attention shifted to Isetha's parents and Hyvecuous, but more importantly, how the heck we were supposed to keep him from killing them.

And it begins, I thought, *anew*.

Of course I had less than ten seconds to try unsuccessfully to come up with something. Hyvecuous had apparently decided two can play at my game of making explosives out of our little powers, and the second he simply glared in my direction was the moment a similar, dark-colored orb sprang up in between me and the others. It expanded quickly, growing from whichever point on the ground it had started on to the height of the school within five seconds. Simply stated, it felt like I'd run straight into a brick wall when it hit me head on. As a result, the others went one way and I went the other--flying backwards until I skidded once or twice across the square and came to a halt.

"Well, it seems as if the little Charmer has gotten away," Hyvecuous sighed as I got to my feet and locked eyes with him as menacingly as I could manage. "But no matter, she can be caught later. A more pressing issue is what is to be done about *you*."

I was about to give a snarky response before noticing that a field had reappeared around the square. Only it wasn't mine of Magic, it was Hyvecuous's of the deadly fog. And what's more? I could hear the other's voices and footsteps from the other side and realized they were trapped out with no way to get back in without first touching the clouds. And since we'd pretty much established that was a *horrible* idea, I was on my own... which after I thought about it was probably for the best because I wouldn't have to worry about Hyvecuous going after them. But still, the whole idea of that long-dreaded confrontation continued to intimidate me and I found it very difficult to keep eye contact as the seconds ticked by.

But the time where I usually retorted was filled up with Hyvecuous doing yet another one of his wrist flicks skyward, and I'm pretty sure you've picked up by this point that always meant something bad was about to happen. That time was no exception.

Instead of tossing me to the side so I could just get up again and come back, Hyvecuous decided to be original and it felt almost if I'd been launched from an everyday cannon straight upward. Yes everyone, that *does* mean I was heading for the fog.

I shot my hands out in front of me--praying to do the same thing that I'd done to save myself from free falling eight hundred feet above the dimension.

Well, it worked... sort of.

I abruptly halted in mid-air less than a foot away from the fog. Assuming that if I remained in the spot any longer it would come down and kill me by simply licking against my face just because it could, I tried to begin a descent. This is where the "sort of" part comes in considering I didn't exactly bring myself down. Gravity did, and it also took no mercy on me. I hit the ground hard. But I was alive, so I wasn't complaining.

It took me a total of two seconds to scramble upright before realizing something that I probably should've already known, but completely forgot about. Directly on the opposite side of the square, were Darien and Serena.

Chapter 82

Now normally, it wouldn't matter to someone on a mission to save their Universe and everyone in it if there were two extra people standing around. But it mattered to me *a lot*. I had the feeling Hyvecuous was going to use them to force me to put myself in a worse predicament because of my need to protect them. In other words, he was going to kill three birds with one cloud of fog/Shadow/dark orb thing or who really knew what else he had up his sleeve he could use to get rid of us?

But anyway, on that delightful note, it turned out I was right. That is *exactly* what Hyvecuous did. He would either send something in my direction or send me in the direction of something before doing the same towards Isetha's parents. They were by no means letting the fact that they were defenseless render them useless, and they busied themselves trying to find a slight weak spot in Hyvecuous's approaches, occasionally yelling advice (ninety percent of the time it was the words "watch out" or the like) in my direction. But nevertheless, they couldn't do anything to defend themselves from whatever he tried to do, so that part was still up to me. The focus I spent on protecting them for a split second was more often than not just long enough for Hyvecuous to do something else to me. Every now and then however, I'd manage to counter--attack him. If he didn't dodge whatever I threw completely, then the most it made him do was flinch.

It was a horrible, vicious cycle. However I actually managed to keep Darien and Serena alive and the two of us in a pretty solid stalemate. At some point I sent Hyvecuous stumbling backward with the whole "miniature explosive" technique I mentioned earlier and had since taken a particular liking to. But although he was temporarily down, it didn't last long. What made this time different was our way of taking turns when it came to trying to murder each other abruptly came to an end. But, as you've probably guessed, a shift came, and it definitely was not in my favor.

At first, everything was the same as it'd been the entire time. Hyvecuous overpowered my maneuver and stood up without so much as a scratch to his dignity. Instead of launching me like a rocket toward the fog, he launched the fog like a rocket toward me. But that was nothing new; he'd only done it a million times in just the past hour or two. So I just brought up the old hazy shield that should have stopped it in its tracks. And hey, I thought that maybe while I was at it, I'd use his own power against him and return the entire package back to sender. But neither of these things happened. The fog looped around it completely and encased my Magic inside to the point where you could barely see it glowing. Figuring it was a lost cause, I quickly dropped it and did it again. Closer to me, and a whole lot bigger. Same result and at that point I swore under my breath. Less than five feet behind me was the rest of the fog that still surrounded the platform. Literally out of options, I gave one final effort and this time held a shield behind me as well... in case he got any wise ideas. Sure enough, he did. But it wasn't quite what I thought it was going it be. It was much, much worse.

The fog panned out around the base of my Magic and I stood there on the inside watching his silhouette move toward me. I wondered what he was doing before I saw it. It being a very faint but still visible dark-orb-thing. To be honest, the stuff almost looked like Magic, but no duh it was black and was a smidge more foreboding than fairy dust. It came down hard--every square inch of gold was covered except for the side facing the fog. For some strange reason, Hyvecuous didn't try harder when it failed at breaking it down completely. He didn't seem upset or angered in the slightest that I was still unharmed on the inside. It took me a while, but I eventually realized why. And I can't believe

I was so stupid to not have noticed it before that point. I had just allowed him to trap me. I couldn't push my Magic out because of his little dome. I couldn't take it down because then all the fog would be waiting there. Hyvecuous had made me a prisoner of my own defenses. And to top it all off, I then noticed where he'd expertly placed me. In the full view of Isetha's parents. I knew automatically what he was planning. And that son of a shrew was also going to make me watch helplessly with no way to stop it.

Well, as you might imagine, that did not sit very well with me, and I struggled hard against the thing. If I could break it down, then I could get out of that situation. But I got absolutely nowhere until I heard Serena scream. After that, I decided not to even bother destroying Hyvecuous's entire trap. I just needed to get out of it. Maybe I could... ram through one section in time to get Isetha's parents away from the danger. Besides, Hyvecuous wasn't even paying attention to me. He was talking to them as if he *knew* I wasn't going to get out. Deciding to make him pay for thinking that little of my ability and then making it apparent in front of two other people, I surrounded myself from head to toe in the golden haze. One hundred percent sure I looked like some deranged fairy of death, I backed up as far as I could go until I could feel the airy yet almost silk-like texture of my Magic against me. Taking a deep breath, I dropped my original shield and ran as fast as I could into the fog.

I was immediately pressured to the point where I thought I would be stripped of my protection, but I somehow broke through alive. And in time to see Isetha's parents in the opposite corner as Hyvecuous continued what I assumed was one of his master-villain, cliché, "I-am-going-to-kill-you-when-I-finish-monologuing" speeches.

Assuming he was too into himself to notice me, I stalked up behind him and was about to end his lecture before he spun around. I was immediately hurled upward again.

"Did you honestly think I didn't see you there, you little twit?" he called me that name for the second time. I threw my arms out in front of me and instead of hitting the fog, I hit a rather hard section of gold. "How stupid do you think I am?"

Despite smacking my face, I managed to land on both my feet and stand firm for several seconds.

"*Very.*" Mr. and Mrs. Napollon didn't need to be told that I was trying to distract Hyvecuous so they could get out. The two of them quickly moved away. "For starters, you thought you could keep me in a corner while you killed people and then you-"

Hyvecuous decided not to let me complete my list and shot his arm out as if he was backhanding someone. The same stuff I'd just broken through sprang up and then blew straight into me. It knocked me off my feet and back farther and farther away from him and Isetha's parents until I had to stop myself. Of course the only way to do that was to make another one of my shields to collide with. But figuring it was better than greeting the fog, I did it anyway.

And that was a big mistake.

I don't even think words can describe how much it hurts to be sandwiched by the two opposing forces. So I'm going to paint a nice little image for you about what it felt like. First, picture being shrunk down and stuck on the nose of a bullet. Next, imagine that bullet hitting a building composed entirely of concrete at a hundred miles an hour. And, well you get the idea. Simply stated--it could definitely shatter a bone or two if you crash into it at the wrong angle. Fortunately, that wasn't the case as far as I could tell. On the flip side, just because I hadn't completely snapped in two didn't mean I was perfectly fine. In fact, there was an echoing "*thud*" when I made impact, fell flat on my face, and lay in an exhausted heap on the ground.

Chapter 83

For the first time, I didn't scramble upright after being knocked over. Instead, I was fighting the familiar horror of unconsciousness that was creeping up on me from hitting the back of my head (that was still pretty bruised from the concussion) with the most force. Hyvecuous took advantage of the time, and I could hear his footsteps heading in my direction. Panic welled up inside of me until it by far surpassed the pain. I succeeded only in getting onto my side when I tried to stand to face him. And that moment right there is one of the many things I'm most ashamed of.

"Well, just look at the Universe's only hope *now,*" he loomed over me and scorned. "Nearly dead on the ground of the fourth dimension. Truly disappointing and *pathetic*, is it not? Although I must say that I am impressed with your significantly increased ability in so little time, it clearly just wasn't enough in the end. I will be sure to tell everyone what a valiant effort you put forth for them. But before we get into that, let's see what there is in store for the two parents of the little Charmer."

The mere idea that I wasn't able to help Darien and Serena caused me to forget all determination, the promise I'd made to Macalynn and the others to remember my own words, and I couldn't look in their direction. But the second I heard one of them scream "*Run!*" I snapped back into reality and saw another, larger section of fog speeding along after the two--waiting until just the right time to knock them into the mass that sat in the same still silence around the platform.

Hyvecuous apparently saw my movement and as a result, I took a sharp kick in my ribcage. "Going to come to the rescue now, Lealight? Isn't it a bit late for that?"

"It's never... too late," I huffed as I curled my fingers into a fist and found an alternative use for the glow Magic gave off--which was shining a blinding light directly into Hyvecuous's face. Sure it was amateurish and underhanded, but it allowed me the few seconds I needed to get back to my feet.

I left him stooped over, covering his eyes and swearing at me, and chased after the dark haze. When I knew I couldn't get much closer without practically yelling at Hyvecuous, "Look, I'm running right alongside death. Hit me instead!," I tried to do something to knock it off course to no avail.

"Noble effort," Hyvecuous finally regained his composure and took several steps in our direction. "But no matter what you *think* you can do, no form of Magic can affect this."

Ignoring him, I desperately continued until I saw to my horror he was right. Nothing I did could completely get rid of the fog that was now cutting quickly through the air and was just about to corner Darien and Serena. I wasn't about to let them be killed after I promised Isetha I'd get them back. Since she'd already seen them and knew they were alive, me not bringing them home would be even more traumatic for her. So I stupidly did the only thing I could think of at the time under that kind of pressure. I jumped in front of it and set up the usual wall to protect myself and hopefully Isetha's parents.

"You honestly think that little strip of film," Hyvecuous chuckled in amused disbelief, "can stop this? You *are* getting desperate, aren't you?"

I scowled at him just as the fog paraded right through my field, obliterating it completely this time, and knocked me with the most force yet up over the heads of Serena and Darien. And because my good luck streak was becoming too long, I ended up doing *the wrong thing* in a panic over Isetha's parents. I was hurtled across the square at an increasingly fast speed because my most trusted tactic backfired on me. Instead of catching myself in mid-air like I'd planned, I was flying away from the very people I had to protect. There was practically no chance of getting back to Mr. and Mrs. Napollon. After hitting the ground some twenty feet away, the wind was knocked right out of me and I struggled to breathe while on my hands and knees. I immediately thought that Hyvecuous was going to take advantage of my current weakness, but I still stood up a whole thirty seconds later alive. I wondered what possessed him to play fair for once when I saw the reason he didn't attack me while I was on the ground. And it was by far the worst horror I'd ever had the misfortune of watching.

"*No!*" I cried even though I could plainly see I was much too late. I hadn't even heard them coming. I had no reason, or a very small and easily deniable reason, to think that Serena and Darien would do what they did. But they still did it. And I still feel a horrible sense of guilt whenever I remember. The small part of the scene I saw through my own teary eyes was them taking the final step together out in front of the dark haze that was supposed to be Hyvecuous's death blow--intended to kill *me*. And even though I was technically fighting for everyone, and if I died that'd be the end of us, I could tell from the last glances they shot in my direction that they were mostly doing what they were doing for me as a person and not just a Summit. I watched in absolute terror as the two were engulfed by the dank, deadly fog. Shortly afterwards, I heard a scream and watched helplessly as the clouds lifted, but they were nowhere to be found within.

Now, take the horrendous scene you're currently viewing and multiply it times ten. That would be what I saw, everyone. And very few things haunt me more than the memory of those two sacrificing their own lives just so I would have another chance to try, and probably fail, to rid the Universe of Hyvecuous. But that moment, right after the fog recoiled, I was occupied by only one thought.

How was I going to tell Isetha that not only could I not save her parents, but they'd given themselves up to save me?

Chapter 84

Down the path in the opposite direction of the one Merrhet was left in, the only sound to be heard was the unsteady breathing rhythm of seventeen people. It took much convincing, but the six Talent Summits finally gave up on being able to get to Lealight behind the fog. They went after the group (for the stones set themselves upright again after the fog appeared) and stayed with them. But they kept less than a quarter mile away from where Lealight, their sister, was fighting either to save the Universe and everyone in it, or was facing her own death. And as they'd been shown in the past week, death was the most likely option.

The group had found a small, almost circular area just large enough for everyone to fit. Macalynn, Aaron, Amiselle, Harmon, Katrina, and Illydia were all keeping completely silent, lost in their own similar thoughts. The Seven Summits were supposed to make their stand against Hyvecuous *together*. They were supposed to be there for one another, watch each other's backs, and keep everyone safe so that they could return home *together*. And most importantly, in the words Lealight had spoken without knowing the true affect it had on the others, they were never to give up on each other--no matter the circumstances. That short sentence was currently pounding away at the six and had been since they took the first steps away from the fog-covered platform.

"What are we gonna do now?" Asteria's voice broke the stillness. "We can't just sit around and wait to see what happens."

Harmon and Aaron acted as though they didn't hear her and refused to look up from the spot of dirt they had been keeping their eyes fixed on the entire time. Katrina, Macalynn, Illydia, and Amiselle remained on the ground huddled together with distant and solemn expressions. Every so often, a few tears would manage to find their way out of one of their eyes and halfway down their face before they were wiped away in hope that nobody had noticed. But the group was not blind and could plainly see the six silently breaking down under the immense pressure and fear of never seeing their seventh member again. Although no one expected any of them to step up and act like the leaders they were supposed to be right then and there, it was still strange to them to see the Talent Summits so distraught. For Darien and Serena Napollon were right, most people stopped viewing the seven as children the second their names were read off of Teller Hallsmen's list.

"What *can* we do?" Macalynn finally answered with a question of her own--desperation shaking her voice. "I know we're supposed to help... but we're just as powerless as anyone else here. We'd only get in the way, and Hyvecuous would use us against Lealight. You know, to force her to put herself in more danger to protect us. We can't get past the fog surrounding the square, anyway. We're useless, Asteria. We can't do anything."

"You see, that's where your weakness lies," a voice came from around another path leading further into the labyrinth that the six couldn't place immediately. "You think you need your Talents to be of any use? That's absolutely ridiculous. Really, you guys, I thought I knew you better than what I'm seeing right now."

Thinking for a moment that it could be Merrhet, the six quickly stood and surrounded the group in the middle of a sloppy oval, wanting to make sure that whoever the person was would have to go through them first to hurt any of the others.

"*Who's there?*" Amiselle demanded in a trembling voice. "Come out so we can see you, *now!*"

"Okay, okay," it replied, and the six watched as Dillon took several steps forward in their direction.

"*You!*" they yelled simultaneously. "What are *you* doing here?!"

"Funny. That's exactly what Lealight said when I ran into her down in that-"

"You ran into Lealight?" Harmon interrupted suspiciously. "When?"

"Right after you all left the underground. I told her where Hyvecuous and Merrhet were."

"Well, how did you know?"

"Because I remembered that spot in the labyrinth specifically from when he kidnapped all you people. Didn't you recognize it? That square is where you appeared after the Shadows took you from the first dimension. Well, except for Isetha, but that's not important. What is would be the question why are you hanging around here doing *nothing*?"

The six sighed, and their gazes averted back to the ground until Harmon answered for them.

"We can't do anything to help her, Dillon. None of us have any power here."

"And that's where you're wrong. Guys, look at yourselves. You're acting like you've already given up--as if the Universe is already gone and there's nothing left to fight for. But that's not true, and you know it. Come on, where are the people I spent years with who never gave up? The ones who always acted fearless and strong and would do just about anything for each other? Aside from the whole Water Talent Summit mix-up, you're still the same people and you've got to step up and act like it."

The six just stared at him for several seconds before Amiselle spoke up.

"Dillon, we get the point. We've hit rock bottom, but thanks for the reminder. And I'm sure I speak for all of us when I say the question isn't whether or not we want to help Lealight. The problem is how we're supposed to do it. Like Macalynn said, we'd do more harm than good even if we could get to her through that fog."

"Well, Macalynn's right. Lealight would have to put herself in more danger to protect everyone if you went back. But who said anything about that? You don't necessarily need to be there to help her."

"Just tell us where you're going with this, Dillon," Aaron cut in irritably. "We're not in the mood to solve your riddles."

Dillon paused for a second. "Simply stated, the fourth dimension's not going to destroy itself and Lealight seems to be... tied up at the moment."

"Are you actually suggesting we go ahead and obliterate the dimension while she's fighting Hyvecuous?" Illydia asked in disbelief. "I think being stuck here has done something to your head."

"Of course not!" Dillon practically shouted. "How stupid do you guys think I am? Lealight would freak out just like anybody else would if she thought the sky was crashing down and she wasn't anywhere near everyone to get them out."

The group was silent.

"Then spit it out," Amiselle broke the stillness. "What do you mean?"

Dillon took a deep breath, and began to explain his plan to the group.

Chapter 85

It was my fault. Isetha's parents had been killed, and it was completely my fault. Not like that should surprise all you people who've seen quite a few of my most famous screw ups, but just picturing the horrendous scene of the two doing what they did simply because they knew I couldn't win if I constantly needed to protect someone, simply because they wanted me to live, made me feel both guilt-ridden and nauseated at the same time. I couldn't push the thought out of my head. It replayed over and over again like a broken record. It wasn't playing a happy tune, either--saying that I'd basically caused the murder of Isetha's mother and father. And I'd have to tell her that. Oh, and not to mention the whole thing reminded me of my own parents' death. I could barely see straight through the tears I kept blinking back.

But anyway, you're probably thinking "yeah, yeah--guilt, anguish, whatever. Get back to what's *happening*. The *action*." Well, I'm sorry to report that there's not much to tell as far as that goes. Hyvecuous was prevailing, and I was starting to run on fumes as well as from them. Everything I could come up with--he had a response and counter attack for. And that counter attack, whatever it was, would always be twice as powerful and effective as whatever I'd done.

We'd been going at it for the past hour--me taking the majority of the damage. I'd been sent tumbling along the ground more times than I could count, opening the gash already on my cheek even wider. As for the very few times I did collect enough of my remaining energy and launch something in his direction... let's put it this way. If I made him stumble, he drove me into the ground. Yeah, the ground was in fact solid stone. So naturally, defense was a more pressing issue on my mind considering offense just caused me more pain.

"Already giving out, I see," Hyvecuous scorned from the other side of the square for, according to my calculations, the forty-fourth time. "I never expected you to allow yourself to be killed off so *easily*, Lealight."

I snarled angrily and began to gather enough focus for one of my rare offenses. But Hyvecuous apparently saw it coming and stopped me--originally, of course, with fog. Only it wasn't trying to surround or hover over me. This time, it sprang up just to my left and lunged. Now obviously I wasn't hit head-on, or I probably wouldn't be writing this now. But it did manage to brush against me before I could get completely out of the way. And, well, it felt like my arm had been drenched in corrosive acid before being lit on fire. Then add an extremely intense version of the "needles" you get after being teleported alone and you have about what I was feeling for several seconds before it went totally numb. I actually worried whether or not my arm was still there. I know it must sound pretty stupid to you... but trust me, you didn't live it. Even though the pain only existed for moments, it was still enough to make me scream. But as usual, I tried to shake it off and refocus on the current situation. Which I'm very glad I did because the fog looped around in a tight circle and shot back at me. Knowing that it was spanning out too wide this time to even consider jumping out of the way, I did the only thing I could think of to avoid it. I ducked low to the ground and surrounded myself with what I hoped was a field but couldn't be sure because I kept my eyes closed tightly.

Survey said I'd done it--but barely. When I finally opened one eye, I saw the fog had cleared. A thin and shaking golden screen was the only thing separating me from Hyvecuous, who was standing directly in front. He said something I couldn't hear from inside before my film disintegrated and I was lurched out into the center of the square. But what he said next, however, I heard every word of.

"Surely if you'd known who you were six years ago you would have put up a similar fight for your own parents as you did those of the Charmer. Of course, if *I'd* known who you were, I would not have decided to let you live after I killed them. It sure would have my life easier if the Grand Summit was dead before she even knew who she was."

I tensed up and stood quickly--keeping an eye out for any form of attack he might be creating while that little conversation distracted me from it. "You're lying," was all I could manage. "They were killed in a house fire."

"You truly are as naïve as they come, aren't you?" he rolled his eyes and sighed in what sounded like exasperation "How do you think it started? Surely you didn't believe all these years *they* did it and simply let it grow until it engulfed the entire home? I sent the Shadows to first kill them and then set the fire to make it look like that was what happened."

I was at a complete loss for words for several seconds before stammering, "What motive could you possibly have to just randomly pick a family to murder?!"

"Dear Lealight, I did not pick your family unsystematically. Six years ago, I believed I would be taking care of two people I suspected to be Charmers. Recently that I figured out that wasn't the case when Merrhet reported back to me and said there was definitely another one somewhere. I eventually narrowed it down to those four children's households."

Talking to myself more than anything else, I cut into his little death-time story.

"So when you figured that the other three families were of no use to you, you dropped them off back in the woods with no memory of being taken from the Village so Jarmony would find them. And you figured Darien and Serena were the Charmers so that's why you didn't bother to come back to take Isetha. Because you thought it couldn't be some little kid."

"Precisely," he continued--interjecting my rambling. "That was also the same case with you. Once I'd figured out that you were not killed as well, I assumed you were no one of importance to me and decided to let you live. But here you are six years later the Grand Summit. It's a small Universe, is it not? But anyway-"

So, *you* killed my parents," I interrupted--my brain still trying to absorb that fact.

"You sound surprised," he taunted as more fog began to gather itself to my right. "Well, don't be. Wherever they are, you're about to join them."

The fog lunged, but instead of screaming or trying to jump out of the way like Hyvecuous probably thought I would, I looked at it almost nonchalantly before bringing my good arm out and holding it there just like a crossing guard does to traffic. The clouds abruptly came to a halt, and I could tell Hyvecuous was working to set them back on their course to no avail. You see, I would've enjoyed that moment if my blood wasn't boiling as it ran through my veins and my thoughts weren't being clouded by various flashbacks. The last morning I saw my parents before the fire. Walking home later that day only to find smoke rising from the remaining ashes, burned wood, and fallen stones in its place. All the neighbors gathering around completely pallid as the previous Fire, Water, and Grand Summits came from around the back of the wreckage shaking their heads solemnly. How I ran, and ran, and ran deep into the woods shortly after everyone noticed me standing there and hid for several hours before Avley and her mom found me.

"*You* killed them," I repeated loudly. "You killed my parents! *You're* the reason I was stuck in that school *and* the reason I could never bear to look at fire for two years afterwards *and* the reason I've always had to keep my past from the others!"

I balled up my fist that was facing the fog, and it shot backward until it blended in with the dome surrounding us. I took several steps in his direction. I didn't need to do any planning to send Hyvecuous straight up into the air and bring him down from at least ten feet just as hard as he'd done to me many times in the past twelve hours.

"And you know what? You're going to pay for what you've done to me, Macalynn, Aaron, Amiselle, Harmon, Katrina, Illydia, *every single* other Summit before us, my parents, Isetha, Darien, Serena, and then basically everyone who has ever been born into this Universe!"

He started to say something, probably something along the lines of how I couldn't hit the wide side of a barn with a chuckle, but I interrupted with a sonic wave I smacked across his face that plowed him backwards. He narrowly stopped before running straight into the fog. I didn't waste any time thinking about what to do next as I'd done the few times I'd managed to put distance between myself and him, and immediately took off in the direction he'd gone in. Because suddenly, my mission had another purpose besides to save our Universe.

I was going to get revenge on the man who killed my parents.

Chapter 86

"You guys, I'm serious," Dillon persisted for the third time. "This is important. Does Lealight have the other one with her?"

"So let me get this straight," Harmon continued to dodge the question. "If that tiny rock is shattered, it's going to cause a major earthquake? And you're just going to randomly pick a time to crush it. Then, once the ground splits, we have to jump into the crevices and that will take us back to the first dimension?"

"This is absolutely ridiculous, Dillon," Illydia blurted out. "For starters, it sounds just a little too convenient for us, don't you think? And even if it was true, there's no way we're just going to leave Lealight in the process of the fourth dimension's destruction. We all know she won't teleport herself out if she still thinks we're still here."

The others nodded in agreement with their eyes still fixated on the ground as Dillon responded. "As farfetched as all this may sound, it really is true. And you're not going to leave her here. She'll figure out what's going on."

"And what if she doesn't?" Macalynn pointed out. "I know I wouldn't exactly be calm and collected if the ground started giving way and I had to first kill Hyvecuous, find seventeen other people who were wandering somewhere in an endless maze, and teleport them out all before the dimension was reduced to rubble."

"For the last time, this is not going to destroy the dimension. In order for that to happen, you'd need to shatter both of them.

Which brings me back to the question of does she have it with her or not?"

The six were silent.

"Don't you get it?" Dillon finally snapped. "I'm not and never was working for Hyvecuous and I'm not trying to trick you, or trap you, or whatever else you think I'm trying to pull, okay? This is the only way for everyone to get out alive and be sure Hyvecuous is actually gone and can never come back. Don't you recognize this thing, anyway? This is the counterpart of the gem Merrhet used to drain Lealight's Magic."

"Wait, that's the other one of the only two that exist? Why do you have it?" Aaron demanded accusingly.

Ignoring his second question, Dillon continued with, "These things don't just drain. They're extremely powerful and if I shatter it, yes it will cause something like a small earthquake. But it'll be only enough for us to get out of here and that's not what we want. We've got to completely destroy this place. Otherwise there will always be a chance for Hyvecuous to escape and come back no matter what Lealight does to him. But if we break both gems at the same time, the impact should be enough."

"Well, how will Lealight know we got out?" Katrina spoke up. "Like we said, she won't teleport herself out of here if she thinks we're still here!"

"We're going to tell her so she knows to meet us back in the first dimension," Dillon responded in a tone that suggested that was the obvious answer.

Everyone, including the rest of the group who had moved to the other side of the tightly packed circle to give the seven some space, simply stared.

"Yes, because that's a great idea," Amiselle finally retorted. "Let's just go back and scream from the other side of the fog 'Hey Lealight, we're going to split open the ground and jump through the cracks and fall, not into boiling magma, but into the first dimension, okay? Meet us at home after you kill this Hyvecuous guy who's probably standing right there!' That's *bound* to end well."

Dillon groaned exasperatedly. "Look, I could stand here for half an hour trying to explain this in great detail and you still wouldn't get it, alright? As hard as it may be, you're just going to have to trust me. Because the bottom line is Lealight has a pretty small chance of making it out of this alive and even if she turns Hyvecuous into dust, Merrhet and all these Shadows would still be out here. Trust me, they'll find a way to restore him if we give them the opportunity. I'm sure you can make the connection and figure that is what will not end well."

The six exchanged glances before Aaron hesitantly answered the question.

"Before we left, Litheney came by and gave the other gem to Lealight. She said that maybe she'd need it. Lealight stuck the thing in her pocket so I'm assuming she still has it. But how do you plan on making sure she knows she needs to shatter it? And not only that, but at the exact same time as you smash that one?"

Dillon smiled--making them even more apprehensive than they already were. "The fact that she has it is all we need to know to get going. I'll explain the rest on the way."

"And why should we believe you?" Illydia raised her eyebrows with crossed arms. "Why should we believe anything you say? Just because you came and told us about needing to come to the fourth dimension doesn't mean we just forgot about what happened."

Dillon's patience with them continued to wear thin as he responded. "Please, we don't have any more time to waste. We've got to get there now so we can see what's going on. For all we know we might be waiting there for five minutes or five days. Though I really doubt Lealight would last that long-"

"Not helping," Amiselle said hastily.

Dillon's face flushed with embarrassment. "Sorry. That, um... came out wrong. We'd better get going."

"Where exactly are you talking about?" Macalynn asked. "Back towards the actual battle?"

"No, if the two impacts of these things are going to reach all edges of the dimension," Dillon thought aloud. "Then they've got to be far enough away from each other. But we've still got to be able to see Hyvecuous's fog because it lifting is our cue. In order for Lealight to know what's going on, someone has to be there to tell her after she kills Hyvecuous that she needs to shatter that gem, too."

"We'll do it," Macalynn, Aaron, Amiselle, Harmon, Katrina, and Illydia said at the same time and Dillon shook his head as a response.

"I know you guys want to be there for her after all this, but you can't. Like it or not, you're Summits and if no one else we've got to make sure you get out because the Universe is dependent on you. No one else can take your places."

They opened their mouths to argue, but were cut off by Isetha. "Then I'll do it. My parents are with her, after all."

"No Isetha, you're the only living Charmer," said Katrina. "We need to make sure you get out, too."

Everyone in the group looked around uncomfortably under the stares of Dillon, Isetha, and the six Talent Summits for several seconds before Asteria finally spoke up.

"Whoever's there to tell her needs to be someone she knows. So if the other Summits or Isetha can't, then that leaves me, Tarron, and Greo. We don't know Summit Lealight all that well, but she'll at least recognize us."

Everyone looked at each other for a couple seconds before agreeing that the three should be the ones to go. Asteria, Greo, and Tarron got very little instructions of what they should be doing and were quite frankly terrified of what they would find when they reached the square again. Still, they separated from the group and took off down the opposite path as the rest of the people (quickly), Isetha (somewhat reluctantly), and the six Talent Summits (extremely reluctantly) went in the other direction with Dillon leading the way.

Chapter 87

Hyvecuous probably would've won if he hadn't made the fatal mistake of telling me he was the one who killed my parents. If he'd kept that little piece of information to himself, I would have given out right about then as far as time goes. But instead, my exhaustion was replaced by rage and my objective was made clear in my head--to get Hyvecuous down long enough and then I'd figure out how to kill him. It was getting to that point that was difficult. Even so, it was a lot easier to focus on offense without fear now that I felt a burning need for revenge. I found myself thinking of him as not only my Universe's nemesis, but my own. I didn't feel like a checker on a game board who'd just been put in this position anymore. He'd just made it personal.

It was almost as if the tables had completely turned. Now I was the one who had a response to his every move and it was me who was pulling the puppet strings. But at the time, I was completely oblivious to that and pretty much everything else except tracking Hyvecuous's every movement and finding the best way to mess him up. For the first time, I was succeeding at it.

But don't get the impression that just because I was finally fighting back that Hyvecuous was fading at all. He, in fact, seemed to be growing more and more powerful as well, which only added to the frustrating truth that neither one of us could quite overcome the other.

Anyway, so there we were. I didn't know how long we'd been there, and I didn't know how much longer we'd be. I just knew I had to bring him down, find the others, destroy the entire dimension, and then get everyone out. Which is a lot easier said than done, but I was going one step at a time... even though the purpose of that is kind of defeated if step one is to get rid of Hyvecuous. And let's not forget that he acted like he didn't know any better than to continue his usual scorn even when I was finally becoming a match for him as opposed to that "pesky insect" as he'd referred to me as earlier.

"Well, look at how *far* you've come, Lealight," he said in the same mocking voice while marching across the square in my direction. I had once again blown him backward with as much force as I could manage. "Surely your dead parents would be so proud to see their *little girl-*"

My eyebrows rose, and my jaw dropped open in disbelief that Hyvecuous had that kind of nerve. I didn't allow him to finish his sentence. Instead, I shot a gleaming light just inches from his eyes that shifted into a rock solid, orb-shape. It filled out quickly and smacked him across his pinched face so hard I could have sworn I heard the "*crack*" of a nose being broken.

"Don't you dare," I snarled as he stumbled slightly. I took the opportunity to trip him up with a flick of the only wrist I had control over (his nice little fog cloud had rendered my other arm completely useless), and he fell over his own two feet. "By the end of this, you'll be screaming like one."

Hyvecuous was up in two seconds flat. The usual twisted smile appeared on his face as I took several steps back. But before I'd even stooped moving, a blast came up behind me. I blew forward in his direction--stumbling over no more than six feet away from the tips of his boots. And as you probably guessed, the events of the past week or so continued to repeat themselves. Even though I was quick, he was faster and hauled me off the ground by a fistful of my cloak. In this process, however, is when he made his second fatal mistake that ultimately resulted in his own downfall. Which was indeed very smooth on his part. The second my cloak lurched backwards, the inside pocket ripped. The gem I gave to Litheney who then turned around, had a nervous breakdown, and gave it back to me before we left clanked to the ground.

My eyes were locked on it, but Hyvecuous was apparently oblivious. He was yelling something I was completely tuning out. Because I was getting an idea.

A bad one? Maybe. But an idea nevertheless.

"I can't believe you thought by coming here you'd be able to save your Universe!" Hyvecuous's voice cut its way into my spinning thoughts.

I tried to put on a scared-looking face to distract him while I slowly moved my hand directly over the gem. It compliantly flew up into my palm, and I clutched it for dear life--worrying he'd noticed. But Hyvecuous *was* too into himself this time to see what I was planning. So of course he didn't perceive me bringing it between us. I was just waiting for the right time. And it was then I heard the three-word question I'd officially been asked for the fourth time in nine days.

"Any last words?"

I let a smirk spread across my face and Hyvecuous's triumphant as well as disturbing smile faltered for a moment.

"Yeah. *Goodbye.*"

At that, I quickly brought the gem upward and held it above our heads, my fist glowing so brightly it just looked like a ball of light was attached to the end of my arm. He looked up at it and then at me as if to say "Really? That's the best you can do in your last stand?" for no more than a couple seconds before his expression changed into disbelief. And Hyvecuous dematerialized slowly from head to toe. He disappeared into the gem and the fog lifted slowly, revealing the same scene I'd walked into only hours before.

Chapter 88

During this time, not too far away from where they just were, Dillon, Macalynn, Aaron, Amiselle, Harmon, Katrina, and Illydia were standing on top of a rickety crag that looked as if it was ready to collapse under its own weight. It loomed about fifteen feet over the rest of the dimension.

"Dillon, is it absolutely necessary for us to-" Amiselle began nervously before he cut her off with a simple and stern-sounding,

"Yes, it is."

"But why are we standing here?"

"I told you, we've got to watch the fog from a safe distance so we know when to crush this thing and get out of here.

"But what if-"

Dillon groaned exasperatedly, again. "Look, we've got to be able to see what's going on there because we sent those other kids to tell Lealight to send up a... signal to let us know she's alive, Hyvecuous is gone, and that they're about to smash theirs. You do want to see her again, don't you?"

"I can't believe you'd even ask that stupid of a question," Harmon said crossly. "And I think what Amiselle's trying to say is why are we standing up here as opposed to, oh I don't know, someplace that doesn't look ready to give out?"

"This is as far away as we can get from that place without completely losing sight of it. And you know we only get one shot at this. That means, no matter how long it may be, we cannot miss Lealight's signal if it comes at all."

Everyone was silent for a while with their eyes fixed hopelessly on the churning fog not too far away from where they assumed Lealight was facing Hyvecuous alone. Their thoughts were interrupted by the soft "*clank*" of falling rocks echoing up from the bottom. The seven tensed and readied themselves for something catastrophic to happen only to see a small face poke over the edge. Sighing in relief, Macalynn was the first to speak up.

"You scared us, Isetha. Why aren't you with the others?"

She shrugged while walking over to them.

"They're still standing at the bottom." Isetha paused for a moment. "And I wanted to see what's going on with that fog you guys were talking about... you said that when it disappears, we know Lealight's still alive and she's gotten rid of Hyvecuous. I'm really worried about her right now and the grownups are acting like they just don't care. It gets annoying after a while."

Illydia gave a half-hearted smile. "We're afraid for her too, Isetha. I'm sure I speak for all of us when I say the fact that we can't be there right now is..." Her voice trailed off and Aaron quickly changed the subject.

"It's probably not that the adults don't care, they just don't know what to do or say. I guess it's kind of weird for them to see us like this. They think that because we're... us, we should be all... I don't know, collected and making plans and, well, leading. That's kind of our job."

"I don't know what they expect," Harmon muttered. "It's not like they'd handle the situation any better if they were us. They just stand there and gawk like we came over from another Universe all the time."

"Harmon, please," the desperation in Amiselle's voice returned as she quietly sagged to the ground and buried her face in her hands. "Just stop."

Stillness then lingered eerily in the air as the fog remained in the exact same position it'd been in for the past several hours. The others had all joined Amiselle on the ground and didn't look up at all in the next few minutes. That was until Katrina lifted her head so the wind would blow in her face. It dried the nervous sweat lingering on her brow and she averted her eyes back to the ground. But Katrina realized something shortly afterward. She hadn't seen the fog. Thinking that her eyes must've been playing tricks on her, Katrina looked up again. She smiled broadly. For she was right, it wasn't there.

"Guys" she nudged Macalynn with her elbow--barely able to keep her relief and excitement under control. "Look."

Chapter 89

I dropped to the ground on my knees and simply stared at the gem I had clutched in my good fist almost in disbelief myself. I'd done it. I'd rid my Universe of Hyvecuous. Well, for the time being. I still needed to find a way to make sure no one could ever find the gem that trapped him. But on a more pleasant note, I was there and he wasn't. And that would be what I called *progress* after everything that'd happened.

The pebble-sized stone turned from its murky gray to a glowing bright red. I first thought that if a gem had the ability to turn only two shades, black and white, which told whether it was full or empty of Magic suddenly glowed red--that must say something about Hyvecuous's personality. And the thing wouldn't contain him for twenty more minutes, much less forever, and I'd have to think of something fast because it was already starting to vibrate. But before I had even run the first idea through my head, a shout came from not that far away.

"There she is!" I could have sworn I heard Asteria and glanced up in the direction of the sound.

But as she, Tarron, and Greo approached, they apparently took the fact that I was on the ground and assumed I was badly hurt. I figured that out after hearing her next few sentences.

"Are you okay, Summit Lealight? Can you stand up? Can you walk?"

"Asteria, calm down," I answered as I pushed myself off the ground--irritated by how shaky and pathetic my voice sounded.

"I'm fine. But where is everyone else? Why are you three *alone*? What's going on here?"

They looked at each other for the answers, but none of them spoke up.

"Lots of good questions there," Tarron finally muttered. "But we don't actually know what's going on. We were hoping you did."

"*Tarron,*" Asteria scolded him. "What he means is everyone else is fine. We're here alone because this guy named Dillon showed up and-"

"*Dillon*?" I interrupted--completely forgetting about him being there. "What did he want?"

"From what we heard it sounds like he's planning to crush some rock that he says will destroy half the dimension. And you're supposed to have another just like it and you have to smash that one, too," Greo responded vaguely.

Reading my expression, Asteria clarified. "It wasn't a rock. I saw it. It's more like a... gem. We heard one of the other Summits say something about that one and the one you're supposed to have being the only two of the kind in existence. And he said you have to smash yours because both of them shattered at the same time will have a big enough impact to destroy this place."

I just stared at the three for several seconds.

"But in this master plan of his did he mention anything about how I'm supposed to find them *wherever they are* and get everyone out while the sky is practically falling?!"

"That's the part I don't get," Tarron obtained an expression that looked both confused and afraid. "He said that basically these two tiny things will cause earthquakes when they break and then when the ground splits open it will just... take us back to the first dimension."

"*What*?!" I blurted out before I could stop myself. "Last time I checked earthquakes cause *volcanic eruptions* because there's *magma* under the ground! And he's saying that the fourth dimension doesn't and will just know to teleport us back home? That's the biggest and most obvious *lie* I've ever heard of! How could the others possibly fall for that? Oh my gosh, I've got to stop them before they get themselves and everyone else vaporized!"

"He wasn't lying," Tarron looked up at me earnestly. "It didn't look like he was."

I sighed while rubbing my temples with the fingertips of my still tightened fist.

"It doesn't matter whether it looked like he was lying or not. Anyone can put on an act, Tarron. Merrhet pretended to be the Water Talent Summit for three years. We believed and trusted him completely before I went to my Library and caught him there... with all my Magic drained into this thing."

I hesitantly showed the three the gem that was now pulsating energy and was still glowing bright red.

"That's the one!" Asteria exclaimed excitedly. "Only it's red and... why is it vibrating?"

"Long story," I grumbled. "But the bottom line is I can't exactly shatter it and get us out of here okay. In fact, it'd cause a whole new problem considering Hyvecuous is inside."

The three stared wide eyed at me and then at the stone in my hand.

"You put Hyvecuous... in that tiny thing?" Greo asked slowly. I nodded and he in turn gave a long, low whistle.

"He won't escape the very second I crush it," I told them despite the protesting of the little voice inside my head I had a habit of ignoring named *Common Sense*. "But it would only be a matter of time before he did if I just leave it here. It would be child's play for someone to collect the pieces and reassemble the gem. If they did, then he would definitely escape. It might take a couple weeks after we leave here or it might take another four hundred years. I don't know who else Hyvecuous might have working for him or how efficient they are. And I don't really care. The whole idea is to permanently get rid of him. Not to pass the Universe's apocalypse threat down to the next set of Summits and for them to do the same until he eventually succeeds in eradicating us."

There was a long silence before Greo changed the subject back. "Well, Isetha's the one who said Dillon wasn't lying, and she seemed pretty sure. Speaking of him, he also said we needed to tell you to send up a signal of some kind to let them know that you're alive and about to smash that gem-thing."

"Greo, she just said she couldn't because Hyvecuous is in it," Asteria thumped him on the side of his head. "Well, I'm confused now as to how we're supposed to get out of here. I mean, if you shatter the gem, we get out, but you can pretty much guarantee Hyvecuous's return. If you send the signal up but don't smash it, then the others will leave and the fourth dimension won't be destroyed like it needs to be. If we don't do anything they are going to assume you've been killed because they've probably already noticed that fog isn't there anymore. They're waiting for you to-"

She didn't get the chance to finish her sentence before a hand shot out of the gloom and held one of the Shadow's abandoned knives to her throat.

Chapter 90

Her shrill scream echoed through the air as I stuck my arm out in front of Tarron and Greo and took several steps back. Both of them protested, but I ignored them and squinted to make out the hand's owner. When I saw who it was, I no longer needed to put forth effort to keep a scowl on my face.

"Drop the knife, Merrhet," I said slowly. "Drop the knife, and I won't have to hurt you."

His grip tightened around the dagger and, still keeping it pressed against Asteria's neck, he marched her forward in our direction. "Well, well, well. It looks like you *did* have it in you after all. But unfortunately, none of you will be leaving this place. You'll be too busy going down with it."

"You're delusional," I snapped. "And don't make me tell you again to drop that *now*."

His dead-serious expression didn't falter, and I knew he wouldn't give a second thought about killing Asteria. So, I did something to stop him. However, the idea of whether or not it was smart is still debatable.

"I've tried to give you second chances" I shook my head in disappointment. "In the name of who we thought you were for three years. I thought maybe this wasn't something you wanted to do but you were somehow forced into it. But it's clear to me now that you've made your choice. And the only thing I'm sorry for at this point is that I didn't realize all this and stop it sooner."

A flicker of suspicion crossed his smirk that was insanely similar to Hyvecuous's before I did the only thing I could come up with at the time. But before I get into that, let me just warn you in advance that this is by far the riskiest and stupidest thing I've done so far with outcomes that ranged the entire spectrum and I'm kindly asking you to refrain from shouting "*What the heck did she do that for*?!" in the crowded room you might be reading this in.

I raised my hand that still contained the gem skyward. A small stream of golden light shot from my fingertips and rocketed high above our heads. It slowly billowed outward and lingered in the air for several seconds like a miniature firework set in slow motion before it fizzled out and the sky went dark once again. Merrhet's look of confusion was replaced by amusement.

"And the purpose of that was? Are you trying to intimidate me or something into letting this little twerp go? Because that's…"

He stopped himself and simply stared as I not-so-dramatically moved the same fist up and threw the gem toward the ground. It split into four pieces on contact--all of them still glowing red and trembling violently. Of course the five of us only saw them that way for half a second before an invisible impact rippled outward. I had to keep my feet planted firmly on the ground and a tight grip on Greo, who in turn kept a grasp on Tarron, to keep them from being blown clean off the platform. But just as my expectations started to nose-dive, the sound of crushing rocks chorused and I grew wide eyed at the colossal cracks slicing their way effortlessly through the earth. Everything began moving in all directions. And it just so happened that one crevice had begun to separate me, Greo, and Tarron from Merrhet and Asteria. We were rising upward while they sank into the ground.

Merrhet had let the dagger clank to the rapidly shifting stone almost silently because of the earsplitting sound of the massive earthquake. Asteria reacted quickly--running out in our direction and away from him before he had a chance to grab her again. Since we were already standing on what was becoming a cliff over seven feet tall, I knelt down and extended my arm toward her. Asteria had to jump to reach my hand before I laboriously hauled her over the side just as Merrhet realized she was gone. We were both standing by the time she'd come over and the second her feet touched the ground next to us she burst into tears. I hugged her and stroked the hair that had fallen from its braid out of her face as she cried--all the while peering over the side of the overhang. I could've sworn that two of the four pieces had already found each other and were connected as a half while the others were bouncing around like corn kernels over a fire. You see, I'd planned to take one piece of the shattered stone with me so that it could never be whole and Hyvecuous could never come out. Easy, right? Mhmm, *wrong*.

First off, feeling was slowly starting to leech back into my arm that'd been grazed by Hyvecuous's fog. And that feeling was pain, so yeah, that left me with one useable limb to catch a tiny piece of gem rolling around nearly seven feet below. Since that was literally impossible, I was left with two other options. One was to jump down to collect it; the second was to try to make it fly up into my hand just as I'd done previously when it was whole. I decided to go with option number two, but it wouldn't work. Something told me it was because Hyvecuous was inside, but I wasn't given time to ponder the subject before Tarron took Asteria by the hand and Greo grabbed the wrist of my bad arm (after which, I had to swallow a scream of pain) and the two began to drag us behind them away from the scene.

Even though I was fully capable of wrenching myself free of an eleven year old's grip, I decided against it and followed along with them--knowing all the while what I had to do. I was going to teleport them out of there and then go back for the gem fragment so Hyvecuous could never escape. But that was, I thought grimly, if Merrhet didn't find it first.

Chapter 91

Twenty minutes earlier, back in the first dimension, Litheney Hallsmen was pacing around the main room of her stout home. The wooden floorboards groaned as she stepped mercilessly on them over and over again--the echoing of her footsteps reverberating up the stone walls all the way to the thatched ceiling that sat slightly crooked on top. People, in fact, often joked about this saying that a giant had torn through many years ago, lifted the roof off, peered inside, and carelessly dropped it back. The angle it had landed on was exactly how it stayed. There was a door that led to the bedroom on the left side and one larger but still cramped room where not much more than a hearth, chair and table, shelf, and counter lay. It wasn't a very nice or spacious house, but Litheney kept what she had well maintained and spent most of her time at the school anyway--- rarely going home until well after everyone else had ended their day late at night. It was all she needed for just herself, she told the occasional nosy neighbor if she wasn't particularly crabby that day, otherwise she'd most likely answer with "Now, is where *I* choose to live any of *your* business?"

Litheney strode over to a window, unlatched the lock, and gave the shutters a powerful shove. To her disheartenment, but not surprise, the sky was still overrun by Hyvecuous's Clouds. The Teller told herself she was being ridiculous, but she couldn't help but think they were darker, and were churning even more violently, than usual. After quickly shaking the thought, she sat down at her desk and buried her face in her hands.

How could you have let them do this?! She waged a war within her own mind. *You knew they wouldn't make it back, you knew they'd get themselves killed, and yet you did absolutely nothing to stop them!*

But this was the only way! Litheney began to fight against the voice. *We all would have been killed if they hadn't done anything. And Lealight can handle herself and the others just fine.*

Please, the Talent Summits have seen, you have seen, and practically the entire Village has seen that the child has no control over her own abilities. She's no match for someone who's had hundreds of years to plan this! Hyvecuous probably had a trap set up just for the seven of them the second they appeared!

The whole point of them going in the first place was so he would not know they were there. And what happened yesterday was simply triggered by emotion. Anyone would have been furious after openly being called a liar in front of everyone.

Well, if that little episode was because of anger then that just proves how little practice she has!

Her mind in turmoil, Litheney stayed at the table for several more minutes before hearing a small and somewhat nervous-sounding knock from the other side of the door. Teller Hallsmen then started to do something she almost never did. She began to panic. If someone knew what had happened, where the Summits had gone, then everything would be complete chaos.

"What are you doing here?" Litheney almost sighed in relief after creaking the door open and seeing the street look just as it had for the past eight days--nearly empty with the very few people out not paying any attention to what was going on around them.

"Hello to you, too," Jarmony grumbled--still breathing heavily from running all the way from the Citadel, through the Village, to her home near the outskirts on the northeastern side. "Teller Hallsmen, something horrible has happened."

The features of her face narrowed as if to respond, "Really? You don't say?" But of course, Litheney was also rarely sarcastic, so she didn't comment any further than, "Well, I figured as much. Come inside, this isn't something to discuss in the middle of the street."

She moved aside for him, and he shuffled past her. The light emitting from the few candles mounted on the walls and hearth allowed Litheney to take in the look of horror in Jarmony's eyes. She jumped to the most apparent and grim conclusion in her mind. After closing the window quietly so not to be overheard, she said, "What has happened to them? Have they been captured? *Killed*?"

"Now how am I supposed to know that? They can't exactly send a letter saying whether they've gotten there safely or not."

The Teller was surprised by the tone of frustration in Jarmony's voice."I suppose I just... assumed by how aghast you look that you knew something."

The two stood in silence for a while before Litheney noticed something she probably should have realized the second she saw him standing at her door. "Where is the Charmer? Did you leave her *alone*?"

Jarmony's eyes filled with pain again but he maintained an irritated glare. "Isetha. Do you honestly not know our names? And speaking of her, that's why I came here."

"For goodness sake, Jarmony. What happened to your shoulder?" Litheney looked at him accusingly. "There are blood stains all over your shirt!"

"I'm *getting* to that," he snapped. "Litheney, Isetha's been kidnapped. There were these Shadows that suddenly sprung up out of nowhere with Merrhet. I tried to stop them, but there were so many... I got slammed against the side of the Citadel. And then they took her."

An even longer silence hung in the air before Teller Hallsmen responded. "Did this happen just now?"

"Um, no. They came right after you left."

"That was nearly *yesterday!*" Litheney's face turned scarlet red. "Why did you not come sooner?"

"I... I didn't really know who I was supposed to go to. I mean, if I told anyone in the Village what happened, then they'd want to know what the Summits were doing about it. And... well, I couldn't let what's really going on spread around. People would *freak out*. So then I figured I should tell you. But I went to the school and you weren't there. I didn't know where you lived, so I asked around until I found someone who did and came here."

"And that took you *fourteen and a half hours?*" Litheney demanded impatiently.

"That's not important right now!" Jarmony changed the subject. "What is would be the fact that the Summits are gone, Isetha's gone, and I'm not exactly sure at this point they're coming back!"

She was about to respond before a shout came from outside. Annoyed, Litheney threw open the window again only to grow wide eyed when she realized what was going on. "Jarmony," she said slowly. "You should come see this!"

Reluctant and afraid of what he'd find, Jarmony walked over next to Litheney. At first, he nearly choked because of what he saw. For the first time in what seemed like years, the people of the first dimension could at last see the sun as it set.

There were no longer Clouds in their skies.

Chapter 92

"The fog's gone!" Macalynn exclaimed excitedly as she, along with the others, stood quickly.

"That means one of two things," Dillon's voice alone crushed their enthusiasm. "We need to wait and see if Lealight's signal goes up."

"But-"

"Don't even think about it. You know just as well as I do this is the only way to be sure... and we'd never make it in time, anyway."

Macalynn scowled, crossed her arms, and grumbled to herself, "I swear if we weren't powerless here I'd blow you halfway across the freaking dimension."

"What was that?" asked Dillon.

"I didn't say anything."

A long, unnerving silence set in as the eight waited for something with which to prove Lealight was alive and she was leaving just as they were. But one minute passed and nothing happened. The minute then grew into two, then three, and four. By the time they'd passed the fifth minute since the fog lifted, the six Talent Summits were complete nervous wrecks. Harmon paced around the unstable crag, Katrina twiddled her thumbs, and everyone else was going mad with apprehension. Their despair increased rapidly for what seemed like hours. Still, they stuck it out until they saw what they'd been waiting for.

A long stream of light shot upward shortly before ballooning out and momentarily lighting up the sky. The signal reminded Katrina of a puffy, golden cloud while Amiselle thought it bore more of a resemblance to a firecracker. The eight stood there simply watching before Dillon got straight to the point.

"We need to get off this thing and tell everyone. Then we smash the gem and go from there. Let's just hope the two together are enough to start the earthquake."

"Wait a second," Aaron motioned *stop* with his hands. "What do mean 'let's just hope'? You said it would be enough! That's the whole reason we went with this plan. Because you said the gems had to be placed far away from each other! If you were always unsure, then why didn't we just go back for Lealight *ourselves*?!"

Much to Dillon's relief, his answer was delayed by violent rumbling that made the cliff sway from side to side as if it was nothing more than a tree's leaves blowing in the wind.

"She's smashed the first gem!" Dillon called over the earsplitting crashing sounds and confused yells of the people below.

"*What*?" the seven shouted in unison.

"*Lealight has smashed the first gem!*"

Macalynn, Aaron, Amiselle, Harmon, Katrina, Illydia, and Isetha only heard "*Lealight... smash... gem*", but they could assume what that meant and didn't need to be told in the first place to figure it out for themselves. So the eight joined the rest of the group at the bottom of the trembling cliff and, holding their arms over their heads to protect themselves from falling rocks, told everyone what they'd seen. They were very skeptical, but didn't speak up. Without further ado and absolutely no warning to anyone, Dillon placed the ebony jewel on the dirt and stepped on it as hard as he could.

That was probably the second worst decision that he'd made in the past nine days--for this gem too emitted an invisible impact that hit him directly. Dillon was blown up and backwards to the snickering of the six Talent Summits once they'd realized what happened.

"Wow, even Isetha stood her ground pretty well on that one" Amiselle laughed just as the full effects of both gems being destroyed began to unfold. The ground began to go from shifting slightly every few seconds to everything changing so quickly it left giant crevices in the ground.

"You can't be serious, Dillon," Illydia began once she and the others had managed to stay put against the constant movement of the rock beneath them for a few seconds. "It's pitch-black down there.

"Just wait for it," he said calmly. "The combined power of the gems should be enough to unlock the..."

Before Dillon had finished his sentence, everyone was shielding their eyes from a light that was familiar and almost normal to them as it poured out of the fissure. Its golden color was blinding and all eighteen members of the group couldn't look at it directly.

"*How-*" Amiselle yelled over the sound of crushing rocks just as Dillon shouted, "There it is! I can't believe that actually *worked!*"

"How the heck is that going to take us back to the first dimension?!" Amiselle finished her sentence. "It looks more like it'll blow everyone to smithereens!"

"The gems are Magical, Amiselle. We shattered both of them on the ground and so the *Magic* is going through it! This will take us back, I swear! But it'll die down soon--so hurry! We're all right behind you!"

"If you're so sure, then why don't you go first?!" Harmon shouted.

"Because I'm not an idiot! I know if I do you won't follow! You guys, come on, we don't have time to argue! The fact of the matter, *once again*, is that this is the only way to get out of here now---there's no turning back! And no one is leaving before you do, so either go now, we'll follow, and you'll meet Lealight back home, or we'll all be crushed!"

The six looked from the shaking ground, to the crevice, to each other for well over a minute despite Dillon's urgent calling. Just as Aaron was about to respond, he felt someone's hand grab his. Katrina then took the hand of the person standing on the other side of her, which happened to be Macalynn's, and gave them both a reassuring squeeze. After several seconds of trying to think clearly amongst the panic, Macalynn took Amiselle's hand and Aaron had grabbed Illydia's. Before long, Macalynn, Aaron, Amiselle, Harmon, Katrina, and Illydia had all stepped up in front of the shining gap hand in hand. Everyone watched nervously as the six, praying they weren't about to make a huge and fatal mistake, took a deep breath and finally allowed themselves to fall over the edge.

Chapter 93

Shortly after the four of us started running in the other direction, there was an earsplitting "*crash*" and the ground beneath us began to shift ten times more violently than it had before. Which, I thought, most likely meant the others and Dillon had smashed their gem and were leaving as we jumped, ducked, and weaved our way through the narrow passageways. So naturally, I thought it was a good idea to get Tarron, Greo, and Asteria out as soon as possible. Now I just needed to think of a way to tell them I was staying behind as the ground was giving way and the sky was literally falling. So I didn't say anything and instead stopped running. The three turned back and kept yelling for me to hurry up, but I shook my head as I struggled to catch my breath.

"Come on, we've got to find a gap in the ground big enough for us!" Greo insisted as he continued to pull on my arm that by then I had full control over even though it still hurt pretty badly.

"No, we're not going to find a crevice in these paths. They're too narrow," I answered. "But it doesn't matter, I'm teleporting you guys out."

Tarron and Greo smiled in relief but Asteria looked wary.

"What do you mean teleporting 'you guys'? What about you? You're coming, right?"

I sighed and kept my response as short as I could. "I've got to go back and stop Merrhet from getting all those pieces of the gem together again. So no, I'm not going. But I'll be right behind everyone. I promise."

"You *can't*." Greo protested. "What if something bad happens? What if you can't make it out in time? The fourth dimension is crumbling on top of us! You can't stay!"

"I can't just let Merrhet get all the pieces, either. I've told you guys, if the entire gem is reassembled, then Hyvecuous escapes. No question about it. So I'm sorry, but I have to go back. Now give me a second to think. The last time I teleported with Magic, I was with the others and I honestly had no idea what I was doing."

The three looked at each other uncomfortably. I thought momentarily that pointing out I was completely clueless on that crucial topic didn't exactly ease their minds. I shook the thought and focused hard on the first dimension. See? I remembered to picture a place this time. Sure enough, a haze slowly enveloped them, and only them to my relief, and the last thing I said from over my shoulder after turning in the other direction was, "Tell the others I'll be there as soon as I can!"

Greo and Asteria's eyes were filled with wonder and they weren't really paying attention. Tarron gave a half-hearted wave before his expression abruptly went from apprehension to terror. At first, I thought it had something to do with them being teleported, and I panicked for a split second that I'd done something wrong. But I quickly understood that wasn't the case when Tarron once again cried, "Watch out!"

The other two snapped back into reality, obtained similar looks, and shouted the same thing as I realized a colossal boulder was quickly maneuvering its way along the tops of the crumbling stones that used to make up the walls of the labyrinth. It was less than five feet away from falling on top of my head. I cut it very close when the thing obeyed that pesky rule of gravity and crashed to the ground on the exact spot where I had been standing.

Landing on the opposite side of where the three were, I heard them all cry "*No! Lea-*" before their voices were simultaneously cut off. I assumed that was because the Magic had picked the most appropriate time to take effect and teleport them out after they'd seen me nearly get crushed and probably thought I had been. But knowing there wasn't much I could do about that, I pushed the thought away and set off back toward the square (that didn't really look like it was or had ever been a platform anymore) to hopefully find a piece of the gem still lying on the ground. Of course I was thinking all the while that nothing was ever that easy for me and I'd most likely have to battle it out with Merrhet first. But as ticked off as I was right then? Trust me, it wouldn't have been much of a match if the jerk had a hundred lightning bolts.

Chapter 94

After making sure everyone in the group had gone, Dillon took one last look at the crumbling fourth dimension, and prayed he was right about the Magic from the two gems being enough to destroy the place and take them home. He followed behind everyone just like he had spent the last several minutes trying to convince Isetha and the rest of the group he would. Dillon was just in time too, for the second he disappeared beneath the glow was the same moment it died out and the massive earthquakes ripping through the entire dimension slowed to a halt.

Dillon, like everyone else, felt as if he would fall forever. He counted an agonizing sixty seconds since he'd jumped before he lost track and an overwhelming panic shot through him. He'd been wrong--he just knew it. The Magic wouldn't be enough and they were going to die. But worst of all, it would be his fault.

In total despair, Dillon continued to fall for several more seconds before another blinding light shone just below him. Before he noticed it was there, he hit solid ground, but not with the force he would have if he'd fallen at a hundred miles an hour for an entire minute. It was as if he had done nothing more than trip over a root in the middle of the woods.

"I can't believe we actually made it!" Amiselle's voice echoed throughout the field.

Dillon dared to open his eyes, and saw that she was right. All six Talent Summits, Isetha, the rest of the group, and him were there, in the middle of the field southwest of the Village. Everyone else was already standing--Katrina, Illydia, Macalynn,

Amiselle, and Isetha were all hugging each other while the group that'd just been liberated from the fourth dimension set off in the direction of a rapidly growing crowd without saying much more than a "thank you" because of all the excitement. Nearly all nine hundred and seventy-five people of the Village had seen the most blinding light beam yet shoot up from the place that had been almost completely abandoned because no one felt it necessary to practice Talents with Hyvecuous in their Universe, and they most certainly did not allow their children to go out alone anymore. If they weren't already in the field to marvel over the now Cloudless sky, they were on their way to see what the commotion was about. Of course they were sure it had something to do with the Summits, however none of them expected to see them standing there hugging each other and smiling at everything and everyone as if they thought they'd never see the place again. Only after every last person had formed a circle around the field, the ones toward the back being informed of what was happening by those closer to the front for they couldn't see over the gargantuan sea of people, did it register with them that the seven probably thought they wouldn't. After all, they'd just come back from doing something that had managed to expel Hyvecuous if the Clouds were no longer there.

"Hey, you okay?" Harmon extended his arm toward Dillon and helped him up.

"Yeah, fine."

"Listen," Aaron began. "We were wrong about you. Just because Merrhet turned out to be some two-faced liar doesn't mean you're like that, too. We shouldn't have threatened you like we did when you came by the other day. All you were trying to do was help and... well, without you we would never have gone and everyone would've been done for. I guess what I'm trying to say is-"

"Save it," Dillon interrupted with a half-smile. "Are you joking? I would've done the exact same thing you guys did if not worse after what happened. But the important thing is that we got back and everyone's okay."

"So, we're good?" Harmon once again extended his hand and held it out for Dillon to shake.

Having expected them to give him the cold shoulder from then on out, Dillon was a little surprised by Harmon's peace offering and stared at him for several seconds before he took it. "We're good."

At that moment, Litheney and Jarmony (having fought their way through the nearly quarter mile thick circle of people) came from everyone's left. For once, the six Talent Summits were happy to see the Teller as they moved to join them in the center.

"You guys did it!" Jarmony exclaimed as he ran up to them. "I can't believe you actually did it!"

"Yes, what was that you were saying about a suicide mission?" Aaron slugged him on the shoulder with a smile on his face before seeing his Charge wince in pain and noticing the deep red stains.

"Geez Jarmony, what happened?"

"Long story. Tell you later. But thank goodness you found Isetha. I was worried sick about you!"

"I'm okay," Isetha answered indifferently. "But, has anyone else noticed that-"

She was cut off by yet another entrance. This one started when someone in the crowd noticed a thin, golden film rising very slowly from seemingly nowhere. Everyone watched it--some with looks of terror, others with fascination. But for the most part, it was uncertainty.

Ten seconds later, Asteria, Tarron, and Greo appeared right in the middle of the haze that promptly disappeared and everyone's expressions, including the Summits, converted to confusion. The three were immediately overwhelmed by the mass of people staring at them and shrank together, going pink in the face. Feeling sorry for them, Teller Hallsmen motioned in their general direction for them to come over. Shuffling across the field, the three never met the eyes of the Talent Summits.

"Where's Lealight?" Macalynn was the first to ask, after which, the loud buzz of nine hundred people talking to one another excitedly died out and all eyes were once again upon the three.

Asteria began to silently cry once again, and the six Talent Summits each felt balloons of horror swell in their hearts. The continuous silence became torture for them as the three still refused to meet their gazes. The seconds seemed to tick by twice as slow.

"Where is Lealight?" Katrina croaked. "What happened?"

Tarron finally decided to explain, his voice shaky with nervousness of how the six were going to take it.

"Summit Lealight was... really brave," he tried to stall. "She got rid of Hyvecuous first of all, and then saved Asteria from Merrhet when he almost cut her head off. She was going to risk her life again to make sure he could never come back when..." He paused for several seconds. "She was... k-killed. The fourth dimension was falling on top of us and Lealight was crushed while she was teleporting us out."

The six, Jarmony, Dillon, Isetha, and Litheney said absolutely nothing while the horrible news spread through the crowd like wildfire. Only the first few rows of the circle heard Tarron's small voice, but they soon told the people behind them, who in turn told everyone around until it reached the very back of the circle. Even after hearing part of the shocking truth that the Summits had been in the fourth dimension, no one from the crowd dared to speak up.

"No," Illydia said in an even shakier voice. "No, I will never believe Lealight is dead unless I see her lifeless body, okay? *Ever*. And anything could've happened. The place is nearly pitch-black, she probably jumped out of the way and you didn't see it."

The three didn't respond and Dillon, wishing he didn't need to point out what he was about to, told the six very slowly, "You guys, if the boulder didn't kill her then something else must have because the fourth dimension was in the process of being completely obliterated. It's gone by now, and Lealight isn't here. I'm so sorry."

Isetha, who assumed her parents were crushed with Lealight, already had tears spilling over her eyelids. She slowly lowered herself onto the ground, hugged her knees, and cried into them as the other Summits and Jarmony fit the puzzle pieces together. Litheney wore a blank expression and shook her head solemnly. After about two minutes of dead silence from both the crowd and those standing in the middle, Katrina sat next to Isetha, wrapped one arm around her shoulders, and tried to comfort her before she burst into tears as well. No more than a couple moments later, Amiselle had both her arms wrapped around a weeping Macalynn right next to Katrina on the dirt of the field.

"After all we went through, after all she did," Macalynn choked between sobs. "She just dies. That easily. Lealight just gets killed by some stupid falling rock. It doesn't seem right, it doesn't even seem *possible*."

Amiselle also had tears streaming down her face, but she still kept trying to reassure Macalynn of something, anything, that would make her feel better. But she found nothing that could make up for the loss of one of their family members, and with no warning, she broke down too.

Aaron knelt on the other side of Katrina with his hand on her shoulder. But grief eventually got the better of him as well and he got onto his knees shortly before burying his face in his hands. Meanwhile, Harmon did the exact same thing after giving up on consoling Amiselle and Illydia sat in complete shock squeezed in between both groups. Jarmony kept his gaze fixed on the ground--not knowing what he should do. He'd spent so much time with the Summits and so he of all people knew there would be nothing he could say to offset Lealight's death. So, he did what he thought was best. Nothing.

Litheney stood off to the side with her hand cupped over her mouth and the same blank, solemn expression she'd had for the past minute plastered on her face. She knew she shouldn't be surprised and that this was the risk Lealight took when she and the others left. But the fact that it had actually happened, that she truly was dead, was still a horrible shock to her. The few tears that threatened too flow at the Citadel the day before did.

As for Dillon, Asteria, Greo, and Tarron, they joined the rest of the crowd sheepishly and kept their heads ducked and mouths shut along with everyone else. Some people were silent simply in respect for the Grand Summit who'd died to protect her Universe while others were in complete shock or even dismay at the fact. But one thing among them all was mutual. For once, they weren't viewing Macalynn, Aaron, Amiselle, Harmon, Katrina, and Illydia as Summits. But as people, and children at that, who'd just lost someone they considered to be their sister to Hyvecuous and the fourth dimension. Occasionally, someone would start to say something or the most sympathetic ones would make a move toward the middle, but they were either told by those around them not to or couldn't maneuver their way through the tightly packed crowd.

That was how everyone in the first dimension stayed. The six Talent Summits and Isetha--each wrapped in their dark cloak and each crying, Jarmony, and Litheney completely surrounded by the thick ring of people. No one moving, and no one speaking. The rustle of leaves and the seven sniffling were the only sounds to be heard as everyone solemnly took in what they thought had happened, and even though they weren't familiar with all the details, they knew one thing.

Summit Lealight Roverdee was never coming back.

Chapter 95

As I got closer to what had once been the square platform in the fourth dimension, the constant tremors, falling stones, and rippling crevices that kept throwing me off balance and blocking certain paths slowed to a halt. At first, this struck me in the form of horror because I thought that either something had gone wrong and the others didn't make it out, or Merrhet had already found all the gem pieces and Hyvecuous was released. Either of those options sucked. Of course, I knew I'd never know unless I reached the spot where I'd shattered the gem. So I pushed the thought from my mind as I'd recently learned to do and continued onward a little more tentatively until I recognized an open space with four sputtered out torches that were now rolling along the ground. If you could call it "ground" anymore--the entire area was a complete wreck. There were colossal overhangs mixed in with seven foot deep canyons as far as I could see in the darkness. And let's not forget the one giant fissure running straight through the chaos. Yep, that'd be pretty hard to miss. Oh, and then there was Merrhet. Can't forget that detail, either.

"Well, look-"

"Who decided to show up again," I finished his sentence in a high, mocking voice. "Yeah, I've been hearing you and Hyvecuous say that all day. It's starting to get old. You know why I'm here, so let's skip the speech and make this snappy, shall we?"

His face contorted with anger, and I couldn't help a triumphant smile spreading across my face in place of the one I never allowed myself when I'd trapped Hyvecuous inside of the gem.

"Agreed," Merrhet answered simply after a small moment of silence. "This *will* be quick."

At that, he pulled something out from behind him that glistened when it turned toward me---and I didn't think the long, metal object was a kitchen ladle. I glared deeply at the dagger just as he was about to lunge at me with it and the thing began to wobble unsteadily in his grasp. He at first stared at it with a confused expression and that gave me the two seconds I needed to begin forcing the knife in his direction as opposed to mine. Merrhet's eyes grew wide and he unclenched his grip on the weapon, which stayed under my control floating instead of clanking to the ground as he'd probably expected.

I stabbed the air just barely to the right of his face, and he leaped back in surprise. "Oh, is this nasty little thing going to give you a *paper cut*?" I snarled as I brought the dagger, which now looked more like a recoiling python preparing to strike, backwards and held it for a few seconds before sending it flying to purposefully just miss him again. "Don't worry. The pain will go away *real fast* if you don't tell me where those gem pieces are in the next ten seconds!"

Still startled from my whole "floating knife" trick, he didn't respond and I continued to stab the air around him until I'd forced Merrhet into a corner against one of the newly created overhangs and settled the knife about six inches from his heart.

"I'm done playing around--ten seconds are up. Last chance, Merrhet. Gem pieces, *now* or I promise I'll bring this thing *straight back* and *straight forward* again at sixty miles an hour until it hits the rock behind you."

His eyes widened as if he'd just then realized I meant business. "I don't know where they are!" Merrhet finally cracked. "Considering all the earthquakes that came through, I'd say they probably fell into that gigantic gap over there."

"You're *lying*" I momentarily flipped the knife around and jabbed him hard in the gut with the hilt. "I... know... you're... lying!"

"Okay, okay," he croaked. "One of them toppled over that way somewhere. But I don't know where the other ones went, I swear!"

I eyeballed him suspiciously before I flicked the knife into the crevice. "Don't even think about it," I said coldly--noticing where his gaze was focused.

He glowered at me before I set off with several backward glances in the direction he'd pointed me in. No, everyone. I had not lost my mind. I knew for a fact he was sending me on a goose chase to give himself time to escape or even counterattack, but I needed some time to just look around for the pieces myself. I realized I'd never be able to do that with Merrhet lurking around. So I'd reverted back to my old ways--buying little fragments of time to try to sort things out with miniscule attacks, or in this case threats, while the opposing side got stronger. But hey, sometimes it's one of very few options. And old habits die hard.

Anyway, after passing behind another overhang so Merrhet was out of sight, I turned a different way and started looking for a tiny fragment of red light. But the original gem was so small, and it splitting into fourths and being scattered across a pretty decent-sized area with extremely varying heights proved to be a problem.

I searched high and low, literally, for well over three minutes before I started feeling nervous about what Merrhet was doing. I decided to peer around the corner. On my way over there, however, I almost tripped over a random stone about the size of a head that I hadn't seen there several seconds earlier. Only this one wasn't like the other ones for some reason. It was paler, and had strange angles to it. I knelt down and twisted the rock to get a better view.

I really wish I hadn't.

A high-pitched scream escaped me and I fell backward--beginning to inch my way away from the stone on my hands and knees. I was shivering to the bone and breathing heavily with my arm pressed against my side. I thought I was going to be sick. For there was indeed a logical explanation as to why this rock was the size of a human head.

It was. The one of Merrhet Drotter, to be precise.

Chapter 96

Now don't get me wrong, I hate the guy. A *lot*. And I think I have a pretty good reason to. I mean, he tried to kill me for crying out loud. But while I may have wanted to slap, electrocute, or drive him into the ground, it really caught me off guard to see his disembodied head lying there. And what's more? *I touched it*. The realization of the cold and slime of what I thought was just a rock actually belonging to Merrhet's detached head made my stomach curdle horribly. I stayed there on the ground with my eyes squeezed shut while trying to regulate my breathing. I couldn't stop thinking about how much I wanted the others to be there with me right then. What I would've given to hear them telling me it'd be okay because I sure wasn't convincing myself.

Eventually, I sat up with my hands covering my eyes. I gradually worked up to peering through a slit in my fingers. The head was no longer there.

Officially *freaked out*, I just sat there staring mortified at where the thing used to be through that same slit. The question was already haunting me. Was Merrhet actually decapitated within the four minutes I wasn't standing right there, or had I imagined the whole thing?

Unable to bear picturing the gruesome image any longer, I turned around, got to my feet, and tried to shift my focus back to finding a gem fragment. But no matter how much distance I put in between me and where I'd seen it, my mind kept drifting back to the horrific picture. I shook my head as if expecting the thought to simply fall out of my ear.

"Calm down, Lealight. *Calm down*. It was just a head--it can't hurt you."

And there you have it, folks. I was talking to myself. I believe that is literally the definition used in dictionaries for insane.

Anyway, as I scanned at least half the area for a tiny, red glow, I found nothing except the same dark dirt and stones that'd been there the entire time--no matter where I went. I paused to reconsider the possibility of finding something in this dark wasteland, and wondered if it would be possible to use Magic to search for the pieces. This, however, also turned out to be unproductive. I figured that was the kind of stuff I'd be finding behind the fifth wall that'd conveniently been reduced to rubble before I got the chance to look around. Once again, typical. Then I thought that the gem may have stopped glowing or something. But I quickly decided against it because I knew if that was the case I'd *never* find it.

In frustration, I picked up a rock, making sure that it was indeed a rock first, and chucked it as hard as I could at a sloped cliff. I then leaned against it and continued to think of possible plans. That's when something hard and sharp hit me on top of my head and clanked to the ground. Now even more annoyed, I picked up the small object and glared at it, but quickly realized something. My major hint was its faint red color and smooth surface. I was holding a piece of the gem that contained Hyvecuous. Or I guess part of him. But that's a story I'd rather not venture into.

Since my pocket had ripped, I held it tightly and took maybe a grand total of six steps away from where I just was before being grabbed from behind. Someone's left hand clamped over my mouth, and their right arm was around my stomach trying to force me to the ground and pry the gem from my fist. Of course, this also wasn't something that sat very well with me and I squirmed around in whoever's grasp, stomped on their feet, and tried to punch them before my arms were pinned behind me. I was about to simply blow them off when I finally saw who it was, and I probably would've screamed if it wasn't for the hand that functioned as a gag across my mouth.

"*Merrhet*?!" I tried to shout only for it to come out too muffled to comprehend.

"Surprised? I thought you might be. Thank you so much for bringing the last piece of the gem, Lealight. You see, I knew you wouldn't focus on finding it since you thought I was around. So I decided it'd be best if you thought I wasn't. And lo and behold, you can do anything when you put your mind to it can't you?"

"But, your head was disembodied! And it disappeared!" I continued--my voice still sounding like nothing more than humming because of his hand.

But Merrhet, apparently, could assume what I was talking about. "Did you honestly believe that was me? Wow, you're easy to trick."

At that, a small puff of black smoke billowed out directly in front of us. The head with jaundiced skin appeared within. The rolled-back eyes nicely complemented the open mouth--which made it look as if it had been hacked off in the middle of a scream. My nausea instantly returned.

"It's *fake*, genius. And you probably would've found that out if you looked closer--so I didn't give you the chance. I decided to make you think you were losing it. The look on your face was priceless, by the way."

Just as quickly as it had arrived, the head vanished again.

"Did you think you could take Hyvecuous out of the picture and I'd just surrender or something? He taught me a thing or two about manipulating fog, you know."

Taking Merrhet by surprise, I quickly wrestled one of my hands free of his iron grip and socked him across his face as hard as humanly possible.

He let go of me for a second before regaining his composure and moving to grab me again. But he ended up clenching his fists in the empty air because I was already gone--standing a good fifteen feet away. Unfortunately, he had taken the gem piece and was holding it in his right hand. And even more unfortunately, he held the three other pieces already connected in his left.

"I'd watch out," he mocked as he brought the two closer together. "Hyvecuous might be a smidge upset with you. Wouldn't want to be in your shoes right now."

I took several steps forward, and as I did so the usual golden haze rose between us--eventually moving forward and colliding straight into Merrhet. It sent him flying backward and he narrowly skidded to a halt before falling into the fissure.

I knelt down and picked up both pieces that he'd dropped within an inch of each other. I knew that'd been way too close. I needed to destroy the dimension and get out of there before it could happen again. And even though I didn't want to admit it, I also knew I was running out of energy and didn't have enough in me to do much more than one final blow.

I just hoped I wouldn't completely mess it up again.

Chapter 97

Merrhet didn't stay down long. Before I could even send a blow through the ground large enough to split the entire dimension in two, I knew I'd have to set up some way to defend myself. But, as mentioned earlier, I didn't have much energy left and the little I did possess I was gathering and saving for one final strike to finish the place, Merrhet, and all of his little Shadow friends off. So I'm not going to bore you with details. You can probably guess where I was five minutes later. And if you can't, then where have *you* been for the past ninety seven chapters?

So there we were--me lying flat on my back after falling from an increasingly tall overhang that Merrhet had forced me off of backwards, and him looming over me with another Shadow's dagger in hand. I'd completely forgotten that there was more than one Shadow and Merrhet probably had a wide selection of other knives to choose from as well. The gash on my cheek had reopened again and blood was running out of it and down my face. My head was pounding like it'd never done before because of how often and hard I'd hit it throughout that day. I was too afraid to put a hand on my skull in fear of it crumpling. Let me just sum the rest up for you, there probably wasn't one part of me that didn't hurt in some way, shape, or form. And I just wanted the whole ordeal to be over--to be done with forever. But of course, the only thing that was keeping me from giving out was the thought of the others and my will to not give Merrhet the satisfaction. So yes, it was going to end. But it was going to end *my way*.

"And you thought you were done after you defeated Hyvecuous, didn't you? You thought you could just walk out of here and it would all be okay? Have you learned *nothing*?" Merrhet taunted.

I was regarding him with as much fury as I could muster under the circumstance. Quietly, I slid the gem piece that he hadn't taken back (the smallest shard, of course) under me. He, thankfully, seemed too wrapped up in making sure I felt horrible before meeting my demise at his hands. So he took no notice when I slowly ran my fingers along the ground and tried to assess how deep and powerful I'd have to make this thing.

Trying to tune him out, I sent a very small and almost undetectable wave down through the dirt and waited to hear a vibration of some kind to signal it'd reached as far as it could go, because that was exactly how big my last strike needed to be. An entire thirty seconds later, I felt it and sighed. The gems had only breached the surface of the fourth dimension--it barely did anything to its core. So this "final blow" of mine was going to have to be bigger, deeper, and more powerful than twice of what I could fathom. Ah well, more work for me.

I dug my fingers into the ground and became completely oblivious to Merrhet standing right there with his dagger. I was focused solely on what I was doing. After a deep breath, I tried my first one. Two words can describe it. They would be "miserable" and "fail". The thing made a slight tremor for all of five seconds before stopping. Fortunately, this escaped Merrhet's attention, and he continued his monologue that I had so politely asked to skip earlier. Of course now, I was glad for it. It gave me time to think and even plan--which was a new word in my vocabulary.

I sighed again. This wasn't going to be as easy as I'd hoped, not that I pictured it being simple or anything in the first place. But it wasn't impossible, either. So, I did what I thought would be best for the current moment in time. Because I couldn't exactly function well enough to destroy a dimension with a knife in my throat.

Deciding I could spare just a little energy to get Merrhet away from me, I balled up one of my fists. He was promptly smacked across his face once more with a good, old-fashioned, classic wave of pure Magic, which sent him sailing far to my right. Even so, I knew this was my last chance. It wouldn't take long for Merrhet to stand up and walk back over. I embedded my fingers as deep as they could go, planted my feet firmly, and basically stiffened my entire body to make sure the gem wouldn't slip away when everything started shifting again. And I wouldn't, either.

Starting to hear the dreaded sound of his footsteps heading in my direction, I wasted no time. I locked my gaze upward and ignored Merrhet the best I could before gathering up every last ounce of Magic I felt I had left and just releasing it into the earth.

That might have been a little overkill. Everything happened at once. The ground completely split in front of me (the inside of the crevice glowing) the canyons deepened, and all the crags were shaking overhead. And get this, my little light show was even ripping across the sky, revealing something I thought I might never see again.

The sun.

Wishful thinking, but no, Merrhet did not collapse on the ground screaming "I'm *melting*!" But I could finally see well enough to notice his eyes bulging as if they might pop out of their sockets. I could also see that he was making his way towards me fast, the look on his face disturbingly reading "If it's over for me, it's over for you too."

Of course he didn't get very far before being punched hard by upcoming rocks, and that was the last I saw of him for one day. But there was one thing I knew I was forgetting in the chaos of mass destruction. Something very, very important. Oh yes, how the *heck* I was going to get myself out of here? Upon examination, maybe using everything I had left to destroy the place wasn't such a great idea. While there was no doubt in my mind the fourth dimension was as good as gone, I didn't exactly want to be gone with it... and things were looking that way. No matter how many times I tried to teleport out, I was stuck. I stayed right there on the ground. But that was until luck actually decided it was going to be on my side for a change. Shocking, I know, but it happened.

A loud "*crack*" split through the air, and I began falling into the biggest fissure yet that'd opened up a few feet away from me. This caused the ground I was laying on to slope into it. My initial thought was to freak out because, you know, falling into a deep and glowing crevice usually triggers that reaction. But I then remembered what Tarron had said about the others jumping into one and being teleported back to the first dimension. I was extremely skeptical about that still, however I realized I was falling in it anyway. And even if I could get out, I'd be crushed on the surface not too much later. So I didn't really have many choices. I decided not to fight it, and I simply grabbed hold of the gem under me. I kept it clenched in my fist as I slipped over the edge and plunged downward into the brightness.

Chapter 98

I'm not going to lie to you people. I thought for every passing second of free fall I was getting closer to either being blown to smithereens or splatting on some form of ground. And how could I not after plummeting downward for at least a minute with no sign of stopping? Don't tell me you'd think differently because you wouldn't have, trust me on that.

Anyway, I'd been tumbling down farther and farther for what felt like an eternity. The wind whistling by was too fast for me to scream, and I had my eyes squeezed shut the entire time. I was trying to think about something else besides where I was and what was going on. But when such a plan failed, I instead worked on fighting panic. I didn't do so hot with that, either.

Just when I thought I was going to go insane with apprehension, I hit the ground. But for some strange reason, I wasn't flattened. It actually didn't hurt much at all, it was as if I'd done nothing but catch some of Katrina's klutziness and trip.

The liberation of the whole thing being over and the added bonus of me being alive at the end of it washed over me for a few minutes as I lay unmoving on the ground before I sat up and saw where I was. Somewhere in the woods, and pretty close to the Village considering I could see some houses not too far off in the distance.

I allowed a smile to spread across my face. I had defeated Hyvecuous, destroyed the fourth dimension, and managed to make it back with my life. I'd say it was a good day's work despite the details about how I'd gotten to that point. So I just sat there hugging my knees and letting the wind blow straight into my face for a few minutes before I noticed a colossal crowd through the trees gathered right next to the field.

Assuming what that meant, I stood, eager to see the others, but quickly found out I wasn't as stable as I thought I was going to be. I began to press my arm against a thick tree trunk for support before a sharp pain shot up it, and I hastily recoiled. That was the same arm that Hyvecuous had caught with his fog. I'd pretty much forgotten about it while I was tracking down a piece of the gem....

The piece of the gem. Where did it go?

I felt dismay surge through me. Had I really done all that to simply lose the gem piece at the last second? And with my luck, for it to beat the odds and eventually find its counterpart? I took one step forward before I froze and sighed in relief. It was resting at my feet. As if afraid of it vanishing, I snatched it up and twisted it around in my fingers. The gem was nearly its ebony color again. The only sign that Hyvecuous was still imprisoned inside was a now very faint, flickering red deep in its center. Well, the fact that my Magic could affect him since the gem was on the ground and Magic was constantly ripping through it had totally slipped my mind. But I wasn't protesting against my arch nemesis not only being put away, but also drastically weakened.

Forgetting for a second it had ripped, I held my cloak pocket open and realized the note from Veronica and the map of the tunnels were still inside--not small enough to fit through the tear. So I arranged them to be in front of the tiny hole and placed the gem safely behind--confident that it wouldn't fall out again. My mind then shifted focus back to the crowd. I took several deep breaths, not even wanting to know what a wreck I must've looked like, and set off limping in their direction.

When I stepped through the trees, no one looked up. They were all staring at the ground--wearing blank and solemn expressions.

I had a feeling about what they thought had happened to me. After wondering what I should say for a few seconds, I recognized a couple faces in the last row of the circle, the only two who were actually crying. Avley and her mother.

I smiled and laboriously walked over to them unnoticed. "What's going on?" I whispered, suppressing a laugh. "Why is everyone so upset?"

"Lea-Summit Lealight died." Avley choked before burying her face in her mother's shirt without looking my way and Ms. Plenstion stroked her hair without so much as an upward glance. "She was killed."

"Well, I'm sure she'd be saddened to hear you say that," I placed my hand on her shoulder. "You were her best friend, after all. If anybody besides the other Summits would refuse to believe she's been killed--it'd be you, Avley."

She looked up with a confused look upon hearing who she thought was a total stranger call her by her name--and that expression quickly wiped away when she saw me smiling at her.

"But..." she began in disbelief before cutting herself off and saying instead "Is that really you?"

Ms. Plenstion then looked up to see who Avley was talking to and her eyes locked on me in surprise as I answered.

"Yeah, and I can't believe you, of all people, could think I would just die that easily. Don't you remember how much Miss Cyerson would yell at me about never giving up when I probably should've? That hasn't changed in the slightest."

Avley and Ms. Plenstion chuckled and several people standing in front turned around to glare at them for being able to joke after I'd apparently been killed. They too simply stared as Avley reached out and hugged me.

"I knew you couldn't die like that" she said in a regular voice volume and more people looked over in our direction, bewildered.

I lightly patted her back, mostly because I knew people were staring, and felt Ms. Plenstion put her hand on my shoulder.

"We're so glad to see you alive again, Lealight," she smiled as I drew back from Avley. When she saw the gash across my cheek, it quickly faded into a concerned frown. "You're hurt."

"I'm okay," I shrugged, trying to stand up a little straighter so my limp would be less obvious. "It's not that big a deal. It could've been a lot worse, believe me."

She looked unconvinced, but thankfully didn't press the issue any further. Instead, what looked like a forced grin appeared on her face again and she changed the subject. "You might want to see the other Summits. They are a bit upset right now."

I nodded, even though I was happy to see them, I wanted to get to the others more and was glad to have an excuse to end the conversation. "Center?" I asked.

"Center," Avley answered. "Can you promise me it's not going to have to be another three years or Universe-wide doomsday for us to see each other again?"

The truth was I couldn't. Not about to tell her that, I nodded again and the two took my hint and saw me off.

Chapter 99

Since everyone nearby had already seen I was standing there and were still staring, they moved aside before I'd even said anything. Thankful, I smiled at them to fill the awkward silence that set in. After I'd reached what I thought was maybe one-fourth of the way into the circle, people didn't know I'd suddenly shown up again and I found myself saying "Excuse me" to countless bemused faces. It seemed like I had to repeat it every couple of seconds and it took a while for me to reach the middle of the circle. Of course then everyone on all sides could see me, and murmurs rippled through the entire crowd. But the other Summits, Jarmony, Isetha, and Litheney seemed oblivious.

I continued in their direction until I stood no less than ten feet away from them. Still, they paid no attention. Katrina had her arm around Isetha, Amiselle was hugging Macalynn, Aaron and Harmon had their faces buried in their hands, Illydia had her eyes squeezed shut hugging her knees in the middle, and Jarmony stood slightly off to the side. All of them were crying freely. Litheney looked like she had been and was about to. But instead, she stared blankly at the ground. Unable to bear it any longer, I spoke up.

"Hey guys, why the long faces?"

None of them glanced upward--much less moved.

"*Hey guys*, why the long faces?!" I repeated louder. Still nothing.

"Hello? *First dimension* to Talent Summits?!" I practically yelled and some people in the crowd laughed.

Litheney finally looked up. She seemed ready to bite someone's head off. The second she saw it was me, she actually smiled. "Everyone," she said in the others' direction. "Somebody has come to see you."

This time, Jarmony and Isetha glanced upward toward her as if to say "What do you *want*?" Her eyes narrowed, and she motioned impatiently towards me. The two, like everyone else, seemed confused at first but they soon wore broad smiles. But the others still wouldn't stop crying and look up. I mean, I was touched to know they really missed me that much in the few hours we'd been separated and were that devastated when they thought I hadn't made it... but come *on*.

And so in a final effort to get their attention, I decided to get all "Estrella Cyerson" on them.

"Macalynn Admiere, Aaron Cinnery, Amiselle Nyete, Harmon Ligg, Katrina Denisal, and Illydia Byline--I can't believe you all could actually think I'd die off that easily. I thought you knew me better than that!"

Isetha started laughing as all six of them looked up with furious expressions after hearing the tone, but my guess is not the words, of someone yelling at them. Their faces quickly flushed, and they simply stared at me for several seconds.

"Lealight?" Katrina croaked with her eyes squinted as if she expected me to be a hallucination and disappear.

"You *think*?" I barely kept myself from laughing. "You scared me for a second there. I thought you'd all gone deaf."

The others all had shaky smiles on their faces as they stood up, and Illydia looked like she was about to say something before Litheney's expression changed. She went from smiling to a genuine scowl as fast as if someone had flicked a switch. "Prove it then."

"Prove what?" I asked her.

"You say that you are Lealight. And you look like her, too. But I, for one, clearly remember when Hyvecuous came through and ambushed her when she was alone. He took on Lealight's appearance and impersonated her for three days until she escaped and made her way back. So how are we to know that you are not Hyvecuous once again? If you are the real Lealight, then prove it."

I rubbed my temples in exasperation as the crowd began to whisper again. Thank you so very much for telling them that, Litheney.

"Fine, here's what happened. It'd been hours and I knew I couldn't keep going like I was with Hyvecuous. So I drained him into the gem you gave back to me and shattered it--taking a piece with me which happens to be this one right here."

I pulled out the fragment and held it up in their direction. The entire crowd was watching with even more scrutiny than before. I felt like I was going to melt under their gaze if someone didn't say something soon.

"She's telling the truth," Isetha finally spoke up so softly I could barely hear her. "So that has to be Lealight."

Harmon abruptly laughed, and everyone looked at him. "Well, we have Charmer Isetha's approval, and I don't care who Hyvecuous is. No one can duplicate that glare she just gave Litheney."

"*Lealight!*" Macalynn tore from the group and nearly tackled me. "We thought we'd lost you..."

I hugged her back as Illydia, Katrina, and Amiselle came over, and I was soon enveloped by the four of them--all of us crying in relief. We stood completely oblivious to the crowd for a few seconds before I saw Aaron and Harmon standing there. "Don't think I didn't see you crying, too," I said with a sly grin.

They rolled their eyes but smiled before they each wrapped their arms around the five of us so that we stood in a complete group hug. We were all crying and continued to stand unmindful of everyone else until I heard a clapping sound. We all opened our eyes without letting go of each other and looked over at Teller Hallsmen. She was the one clapping. And then the first ring of people around us followed her example. And then the next ring. And then the next ring. The seven of us stood there in just as much disbelief as delight. We'd never been applauded before. I mean, people had thanked us when we helped them specifically, and if it was a large group sometimes we'd get a smile or whatever. But this felt *good*. There's no big, extravagant word to describe it. It just felt *good* to know that our Universe had some sort of feeling for us as people. And then to make it better, the clapping turned into cheering. The cheering turned into rejoicing.

"We're free!" somebody somewhere in the crowd shouted. "We're free!"

In the excitement of it all, I almost forgot about Jarmony until I noticed him standing there awkwardly as if he felt he was intruding. I'm pretty sure I changed his mind (and took him by surprise) when I pulled him into our hug.

"Thank you for what you did the other day."

"What are you talking about?" he asked. "All I did was help you up."

"Yeah, but you also stood by me the entire time even though you thought you'd be in trouble for it."

He paused. "Did you think I'd just leave you there on the ground hurt and unable to stand? Litheney told us what she'd seen on our way back through the woods. No one would be that heartless, Lealight."

I smiled as I pulled away, but then the happiness overwhelming me turned stale. Isetha was next to him. And picking the absolute perfect time, the others finally let me go so she could hug me, too. My feeling of guilt quickly doubled, and I knew it was just a matter of time before she asked me all innocently where her parents were. I'd have to tell her what happened in front of everyone.

Noticing and misinterpreting my abruptly solemn expression, she hugged me tighter and said quietly enough that only I could hear her, "It's gonna be okay, Lealight. You're home now."

At that, I did start crying again, and Isetha seemed confused before a flicker of recognition crossed her face. She pulled away and looked up at me with an expression of dread.

"Where are my mom and dad?"

The crowd, apparently seeing my sudden grimness, slowly fell silent as I knelt down on my knees and took both her hands in mine. But I could find no words to say to her.

"I... I'm so, so *sorry*, Isetha. I couldn't... save them."

Her face went pale, and she backed away from me slowly.

"Isetha," I began as I put my hand on her shoulder. "Please understand... I-I did everything I could."

She shook me off and started running in the other direction.

"*Isetha*!" I called after her. "Wait!"

"*Go away*! Leave me alone!" she shouted shortly before disappearing into the crowd in the direction of the woods, leaving me on my knees out in the open of that circle.

Everyone was watching me and I stayed there for several seconds before Illydia walked over, grabbed my arm, and pulled me up. She hugged me again and rubbed my back.

"I'm sure you did everything you could, Lealight. You're not invincible. You can't do it all. It's a miracle you got out alive and it wasn't fair for us to expect you to be able to protect yourself plus two other people from someone like Hyvecuous. I'm sure Isetha sees that and isn't angry with you--just at the fact that she's lost her parents. But she'll turn up."

"I'm not going to wait for her to *turn up*," I choked. "I'm going to go find her right now."

On that note, I tore from the others and limped to the edge of the circle. People started parting to let me by. The tears I kept trying to wipe away stung the gash across my face as I headed through the crowd and towards the woods. Aside from the humiliation of the entire freaking *Universe* seeing me like that, the worst part was what I heard as I went by.

"Wait... isn't she the same child whose parents died in that fire... maybe six years ago?"

"No, she can't be."

"How many other Lealight Roverdee's have you heard of? That has to be her."

"But that... you're right. That is the same kid."

At that, I reached the end of the crowd and tuned everyone out as best I could, not wanting to hear the outcome of whoever's conversation that was. I continued onward into the woods despite the sound of the others coming after me.

Chapter 100

Weaving my way through the trees, shrubs, and rocks---I left the others behind and was completely unaware and uncaring of the fact I was in the woods at night. I truly had no idea where I was going until I recognized a particularly tall tree with some familiar markings where it looked like branches had been. Still feeling completely drained of anything Talent-related, I had no choice but to climb all the way up the same tree I'd found Isetha in less than a week ago. Of course, as I mentioned earlier, the first branch towered nearly three feet over me and it took a while for me to jump up and get a grip on it. And then I was delayed further because of my bad leg and my worse arm, so at least ten minutes later, I saw her resting in the same branch. Isetha heard me coming, looked down, and frowned.

"What are *you* doing up here?" she still had tears streaming freely down her cheeks.

"Can I join you?"

"I guess you can do whatever you want, Summit Lealight."

Even though people had been calling me that for the past three years, to hear Isetha say it while sounding so angry and hurt felt pretty much like someone walking up to me and punching me in the face... by a boxing glove... with spikes on the knuckles... that was on *fire*.

"Why did you call me that?"

"That's who you are, isn't it?"

"Well, yeah… but…"

I sighed and lowered myself into the branch next to hers. We were silent for at least another minute before she finally spoke up--though it sounded like she was mostly talking to herself.

"I can't believe I actually thought of you as my *friend*. This entire time, you were just doing your job."

"That's not true, Isetha. Not even close to being true and it's not fair for you to assume that."

"Of course it's true!" she snapped. "You only did all this because you felt obligated to help me!"

"No, I didn't. I don't help people because I feel like I have to, Isetha. I do it because I want to. If I didn't want to help you, if you didn't mean something to me, I wouldn't have let you stay in the Citadel past a day. I wouldn't have come up and talked to you when your parents were the only ones we didn't find in the woods or stood beside you when we ran into those jerks through here a couple days ago. I wouldn't have let you in my Library or come to say goodbye to you before we left for the fourth dimension or screamed at you to run while you still could when Hyvecuous finally found out you were the Charmer."

She didn't respond.

"I also wouldn't have kept fighting for your mom and dad. I didn't spend that much time with them… but I know they were good people, Isetha."

"What happened? How did Hyvecuous… you know?" she asked slightly less bitterly.

I looked at my dangling boots for several seconds. "If I tell you, will you be angry with me?"

Isetha looked like she was thinking about it. "I want to know what happened to them. I think I deserve to know."

I knew that basically meant "No guarantees", but I still nodded and began to tell her what I thought was going to make the kid hate me forever.

"Hyvecuous was using your parents against me, Isetha. He would send an attack of some kind in their direction just so I'd have to put myself out there to protect them. Then he'd launch something at me while I did that. And your parents knew what was going on. They knew I was going to lose if that continued... that Hyvecuous would kill me soon."

I paused for a second--dreading the next part of the explanation.

"I-I didn't know what was going to happen. Otherwise I wouldn't have let them do it. They, your parents... well, I was standing in front of them with a shield. But by then I was getting weaker, and it didn't hold. Hyvecuous blew me up and over their heads. I panicked and accidently made myself land far away from them. The fall knocked the breath out of me, and I couldn't move for several seconds. By the time I could stand and see what was happening, it was too late. They'd already stepped in front of a colossal cloud of Hyvecuous's fog. Then it engulfed them. I'm so sorry, Isetha. It's entirely my fault. I should've been able to protect them, but... I'm just one person."

I expected Isetha to yell at me. I expected her to clamber down the tree and run away again. But she didn't. She just looked at me.

"I should be mad at you," she finally spoke up and I looked down. "I should hate you right now and never want to speak to you again. But I just... don't for some reason."

Another silence set in before I, without thinking, said, "I really do know how you feel right now."

Isetha shook her head. "I know you guys haven't seen your families in a long time, but you don't know what it's like to know they're dead. To know that someone killed them."

Now, if I was smart I would've nodded and that could've been the end of that. But I wasn't thinking about anything except making her feel better, and I didn't. "No Isetha, I actually do know. My par-" I realized what I was saying and shut up. But she was already looking at me confused, and I knew there was no dropping the subject then. I would have to tell her.

"I was almost nine, so about your age, and walking home from school. I saw the smoke above the houses, but I didn't think much of it. I was still a No-Talent then and I didn't know Fires never did anything around buildings or things that easily burn... I thought it was just someone practicing. But when I turned the corner, my house was nothing more than this giant pile of smoking stone and debris. All the neighbors were gathered around and none of them would look at me as I walked up. I was about to ask where my mom and dad were when the previous Fire, Water, and Grand Summits came from around back. They were really old by then, maybe seventy or seventy five and I'd never seen them up close before. They shook their heads at all the people standing around and then Amiselle's predecessor noticed me. He knelt down on one knee to my eye level and I started backing away from everyone. I had this horrible feeling I knew what had happened. But I still stayed there and he told me exactly "Your parents were inside when the fire started and could not get out. By the time we got here, they had already died. We are all so sorry." Then I ran and hid for hours until my friend came and found me. I spent the next three years living at the school with all the other orphans who had no other family they could stay with until... well, this happened. I always thought up until now the fire was an accident, but I never understood how my mom and dad let it happen. And today, I found out Hyvecuous was responsible... for everything. He sent Shadows meant to kill everyone in my family but since I wasn't home, they only got to my parents. Then, they set the fire to make it look like that was what happened. Hyvecuous said he "believed he was ridding himself of people he suspected to be Charmers" and didn't really care when he found out I had lived because he thought, just like with you, that a kid couldn't be it. But that doesn't matter to me. He killed my parents like he did yours, Isetha. So yeah, I actually do know how you feel."

She was quiet and I, once again, wouldn't look at anything but the branches below us. After a few moments of silence, I worried that she had climbed down while I was spilling my depressing back story. I glanced upward to make sure she was still there, and I saw her crawling over from her branch to mine. The foot deep limb easily supported the two of us as she sat back down next to me.

"You are just one person, Lealight," she took my hand in hers. "You couldn't have done anything to stop them... it's not all your fault. I'm sorry I yelled at you."

"It's okay. I would've yelled at me, too" I shrugged. "At the very least."

"I didn't know your mom and dad were dead," she continued.

"Well, I've never told anybody. Not even the other Summits know."

"Why not?"

I paused, not really knowing the answer. "I guess it's because the last time any of us ever brought up our families it was almost three years ago--before Katrina, Jarmony, or Dillon came, maybe a week or so after we were realized. And, I don't know, I guess I didn't want them feeling sorry for me. I didn't want their sympathy. I just wanted to forget it ever happened."

Isetha leaned against me. "You'll never just forget about your own parents, Lealight."

"I know. You won't either."

"I hope not."

Isetha then started crying again, and I put my arm around her. I, for one, felt like I'd cried enough in the past week for the rest of my life. So I just sat there with her for another ten minutes before we finally decided to go find the others.

Chapter 101

But the others had already found us.

I climbed down the tree first and a couple feet above me Isetha was still coming. I hit the ground only to turn and find the other Summits, Jarmony, and Litheney standing there waiting for us. Isetha hadn't jumped off and moved to stand beside me for two seconds before Harmon stepped out put his arm around my shoulders.

"What's wrong?"

He said nothing and instead led me toward everyone else. Illydia, Katrina, Amiselle, and Macalynn were crying. Teller Hallsmen and Jarmony took a few steps away from us.

"Guys, what's wrong?" I repeated.

Katrina then reached out and hugged me. She was followed one by one by the others until I was completely enfolded by everyone.

"Why didn't you ever tell us?" Macalynn asked.

"Tell you about what?"

"After we lost you, I flew up and looked around. I finally saw you and Isetha. I was about to speak up when I heard you say, 'I know how you feel', and I was hovering right behind you when you talked. I went and found everyone, told them, and we all came back here. I'm so sorry, Lealight."

I sighed. "I didn't think it mattered all that much. I mean, the only time we ever talked about our families was forever ago, and no one ever brought it up again."

"There's a huge difference between you not seeing your parents for a while, which is what you told us, and them being killed in a fire when you were eight," Aaron pointed out. "Of course, you said you found out today that Hyvecuous... was responsible."

"Yeah, I guess so."

"Well, he sucks," Amiselle expertly concluded simply to make us laugh.

"Keen observation, Amiselle," Illydia rolled her eyes with a smile. "But we got that."

"Sorry to interrupt," Litheney chimed in. I guessed her five minutes of acting like a normal human being were up. "But isn't there some planning to be done? As in, what will you do with the fragment of the original gem imprisoning Hyvecuous? You have to make sure it can never be found, Lealight."

Smiling as the others separated from me (though Harmon kept his arm around my shoulders), I answered, "I know just the place."

She nodded. Okay yeah, I was lying about knowing where to put the gem piece, but I didn't feel like listening to a lecture, especially one of Litheney's lectures, right then.

"Good. Now, the seven of you have had a long day. You should get some rest. And Isetha... do you, um, want to get some things from your house to take with you?"

"Take with me where?" she asked.

"The school. I'm sorry, but you know what happens now that your mother and father are... not coming back."

Isetha's face fell lower than it already was.

"Oh," she said quietly, and I couldn't bear the thought of her, that sweet, selfless kid, stuck in the school for nearly ten years. With *Miss Cyerson*, no less. Beware; objects in the mirror are ten thousand times nastier and more irritable than they appear.

And with that being said, I'm sure you understand why I did what I did next. Any other person with a heart would've done it, too. "Right. But first, I'd like to ask Isetha something." I knelt down to her eye level once again and she looked at me as if to say, 'What are you talking about? There's nothing you can do about this'.

Ignoring her look and the expression that clearly read, 'What kind of scheme are you planning?' on Litheney, I continued.

"Isetha, we've seen great things from you. I think your skill to create Charms will be wasted if you continue on at the school. No one there will be able to help you with your unique abilities."

"Just tell us where you're going with this, Lealight," Litheney spoke up again--still staring at me with a look that approached the evil eye, but wasn't quite there yet.

"I'm asking you, Isetha, if you would like to become my Charge."

She just stared at me for a few seconds before a small smile spread across her face. Of course at that exact moment, Teller Hallsmen the Supreme Crusher of Small Children's Dreams said, "Don't be ridiculous. No Grand Summit had ever taken on a Charge. And seven years old is much too young in the first place."

"I'm *nine*."

"And there's a first time for everything, Litheney" I added. "I believe I can help Isetha reach her full potential. Besides, you said it yourself that I am the only *Magical* Talent so it must count for something considering Charms are a part of Magic."

She looked at the ground as if considering what I'd just said.

"It is her choice," Litheney finally answered.

Isetha stayed silent for a while, and I smiled earnestly at her.

"It's a big decision, Isetha. I don't want you to feel pressured into accepting if this isn't what you want to do. Do you need time to think about it?"

"No," she smiled. "I accept. I would like very much to be your Charge."

Epilogue--All's Bad That Ends... Well? Is That Even *Possible*? It Is For Me, Apparently.

Chapter 102

When I was back in my room about thirty minutes later, I didn't even bother to kick off my boots before collapsing into bed. I felt so drained and exhausted I couldn't have cared less and for once, I slept the rest of the night and a good part of the next morning. But I, as you probably inferred, was still not woken up by chirping birds. One minute I was asleep and then the next I was screaming bloody murder as I sat bolt upright. Illydia and Amiselle were sitting on either side of my bed. They had both gotten four inches away from my ears and shouted "*WAKE UP!*" as loud as freaking humanly possible. I chewed them out for that all the way downstairs as they laughed hysterically. When we walked into the kitchen, everybody was smiling--waiting for me. We very rarely made big meals. In fact, I'd venture to say we'd never done it before. But that's what the others did. Everyone had sweetened oatmeal, milk, bread, and an apple. Yes, Illydia grew the apple tree. And we all sat there long after everyone was finished as I explained in great detail what happened each time we were separated. Katrina, Macalynn, and my new Charge screamed when I told everyone about Merrhet's disembodied head--though Aaron crossed his arms and said "*good*" only to be disappointed after I quickly clarified that it was a fake. Of course it took me forever to convince everyone that I was okay as far as physical injuries went. Especially after I told them about my arm being grazed with Hyvecuous's fog, even though I was moving it again with no difficulty and almost no pain. Bonus, my limp was already gone.

Though it took two full days for my Magic to start returning, and by that point I was worried that it never would. Every few hours I would do something small like grow flowers or create a flame in my hands. By the third evening I could teleport all over the Citadel with ease. And then we switched focus to the gem piece, the key to Hyvecuous's return that could never be found. We eventually settled on hiding it in the Library. I think he thought he was joking, but Harmon said that we should transform it into something small and stick it in one of the "quadrillion" (I didn't know that number existed either) books. That's what we did. Isetha and I went into the Library and set the gem piece on the table. We stared at it for the longest time until the thing turned into exactly what we were planning. A tiny, crimson leaf. I pressed it into the red, leather-bound book that Litheney had left, and then we stuck fastening strips I peeled off of multiple envelopes along the edges of the page it was on and the back of the page before it. Isetha and I pushed the two together and the seal ended up being so tight that the leaf couldn't fall out no matter which way you turned it. You couldn't even tell that two pages were glued together--anyone who didn't know it was there would have just turned them as one. And as we left, I stuck the book on a shelf. I'll tell you exactly what I told Harmon. Yeah, I'm going to use the book again but the pages are sealed together and the thing's a *leaf* now. Did you think we randomly came up with that? No, we chose the most insignificant thing we could think of.

And that everybody, is how I decided to make sure the gem was never found and pretty much covers everything that's happened up until... well, right now. I'm sitting with this previously empty book in my lap in the great room as everyone reads over my shoulders and asks for the thousandth time why I'm writing this in the first place. But I still don't know what I'm trying to accomplish. If we're lucky, this *is* for your entertainment, will always be for your entertainment, and you'll never have to go through any of this like we have. If we're lucky, Hyvecuous will never mean anything more to you than a villain in some random storybook.

But then again, I'm not exactly what most people would call "*lucky*" so we'll just have to wait and see what happens next, won't we?

ABOUT THE AUTHOR

Sidney McPhail is a ninth grader in the Mathematics and Science program at Clover Hill High. A major reason she began writing a novel is because she was bothered with the lack of choice teenagers were given when it came to books. She wanted to give people of her age group something new, something meaningful, to read. She began writing <u>Seven Summits: The Magical Talent</u> in the end of January 2011, when she was in eighth grade.

Sidney spends a lot of time each day writing, and then the remainder doing homework. She often Skype's with one of her best friends, Jennifer, and plays piano. Recently, she wrote a new composition for it. Like anybody else, Sidney loves the weekends because she has some rare free time to watch movies like "the Help" and "the Sorcerer's Apprentice" and spend some time with her dog, Phoebe Louise. On Saturdays, she looks forward to visiting her beloved grandparents in Cartersville.

Sidney lives with her mom and dog in Midlothian, Virginia, which is where she has lived all her life.

Seven Summits: The Magical Talent is the first book in the series. The next installment is underway. The first draft of ***<u>Seven Summits: The Second Dimension</u>*** is expected to be published in 2012.

Upcoming Books and Information

Interested in learning more about author Sidney McPhail and her novels?   Visit the Deep Sea Publishing website:

www.deepseapublishing.com.

The website provides more information about the author, book signing events, upcoming book releases, and character profiles. You can also leave messages for the author and others on the blog.

There is a **TEACHER'S GUIDE** available for ***Seven Summits***, which includes the plot overview, character list, analysis of major characters, themes, summary of the chapters, key facts, suggestions for further reading, study questions, and a quiz.

Deep Sea Publishing (DSP) is a Florida-based company that sells fictional novels, children's books, teen books, and reference guides.   The website has details on all DSP publications and the expected release dates on new material.

Deep Sea Publishing books may be purchased in electronic or paper formats. Check the DSP online store to buy this book or to find our list of resellers.

www.ingramcontent.com/pod-product-compliance
Lightning Source LLC
Chambersburg PA
CBHW070344260626
47161CB00001B/3